ANTONINA

or

THE FALL OF ROME

ANTONINA

or

THE FALL OF ROME

Wilkie Collins

ANTONINA OR, THE FALL OF ROME

Published in the United States by IndyPublish.com
McLean, Virginia

ISBN 1-58827-598-1 (hardcover)
ISBN 1-58827-599-X (paperback)

PREFACE

In preparing to compose a fiction founded on history, the writer of these pages thought it no necessary requisite of such a work that the principal characters appearing in it should be drawn from the historical personages of the period. On the contrary, he felt that some very weighty objections attached to this plan of composition. He knew well that it obliged a writer to add largely from invention to what was actually known--to fill in with the colouring of romantic fancy the bare outline of historic fact--and thus to place the novelist's fiction in what he could not but consider most unfavourable contrast to the historian's truth. He was further by no means convinced that any story in which historical characters supplied the main agents, could be preserved in its fit unity of design and restrained within its due limits of development, without some falsification or confusion of historical dates--a species of poetical licence of which he felt no disposition to avail himself, as it was his main anxiety to make his plot invariably arise and proceed out of the great events of the era exactly in the order in which they occurred.

Influenced, therefore, by these considerations, he thought that by forming all his principal characters from imagination, he should be able to mould them as he pleased to the main necessities of the story; to display them, without any impropriety, as influenced in whatever manner appeared most strikingly interesting by its minor incidents; and further, to make them, on all occasions, without trammel or hindrance, the practical exponents of the spirit of the age, of all the various historical illustrations of the period, which the Author's researches among conflicting but equally important authorities had enabled him to garner up, while, at the same time, the appearance of verisimilitude necessary to an historical romance might, he imagined, be successfully preserved by the occasional introduction of the living characters of the era, in those portions of the plot comprising events with which they had been remarkably connected.

On this plan the recent work has been produced.

To the fictitious characters alone is committed the task of representing the spirit of the age. The Roman emperor, Honorius, and the Gothic king, Alaric, mix but little personally in the business of the story--only appearing in such events, and acting under such circumstances, as the records of history strictly authorise; but exact truth in respect to time, place, and circumstance is observed in every historical event introduced in the plot, from the period of the march of the Gothic invaders over the Alps to the close of the first barbarian blockade of Rome.

CONTENTS

Chapter 1

GOISVINTHA

The mountains forming the range of Alps which border on the north- eastern confines of Italy, were, in the autumn of the year 408, already furrowed in numerous directions by the tracks of the invading forces of those northern nations generally comprised under the appellation of Goths.

In some places these tracks were denoted on either side by fallen trees, and occasionally assumed, when half obliterated by the ravages of storms, the appearance of desolate and irregular marshes. In other places they were less palpable. Here, the temporary path was entirely hidden by the incursions of a swollen torrent; there, it was faintly perceptible in occasional patches of soft ground, or partly traceable by fragments of abandoned armour, skeletons of horses and men, and remnants of the rude bridges which had once served for passage across a river or transit over a precipice.

Among the rocks of the topmost of the range of mountains immediately overhanging the plains of Italy, and presenting the last barrier to the exertions of a traveller or the march of an invader, there lay, at the beginning of the fifth century, a little lake. Bounded on three sides by precipices, its narrow banks barren of verdure or habitations, and its dark and stagnant waters brightened but rarely by the presence of the lively sunlight, this solitary spot--at all times mournful--presented, on the autumn of the day when our story commences, an aspect of desolation at once dismal to the eye and oppressive to the heart.

It was near noon; but no sun appeared in the heaven. The dull clouds, monotonous in colour and form, hid all beauty in the firmament, and shed heavy darkness on the earth. Dense, stagnant vapours clung to the mountain summits; from the drooping trees dead leaves and rotten branches sunk, at intervals, on the oozy soil, or whirled over the gloomy precipice; and a small steady rain fell, slow and unintermitting, upon the deserts around. Standing upon the path which armies had once trodden, and which armies were still destined to tread, and looking towards the solitary lake, you heard, at first, no sound but the regular dripping of the rain-drops from rock to rock; you saw no prospect but the motionless waters at your feet, and the dusky crags which shadowed them from above. When, however, impressed by the mysterious loneliness of the place, the eye grew more penetrating and the ear more attentive, a cavern became apparent in the precipices round the lake; and, in the intervals of the heavy rain-drops, were faintly perceptible the sounds of a human voice.

The mouth of the cavern was partly concealed by a large stone, on which were piled some masses of rotten brushwood, as if for the purpose of protecting any inhabitant it might contain from the coldness of the atmosphere without. Placed at the eastward boundary of the lake, this strange place of refuge commanded a view not only of the rugged path immediately below it, but of a large plot of level ground at a short distance to the west, which overhung a second and lower range of rocks. From this spot might be seen far beneath, on days when the atmosphere was clear, the olive grounds that clothed the mountain's base, and beyond, stretching away to the distant horizon, the plains of fated Italy, whose destiny of defeat and shame was now hastening to its dark and fearful accomplishment.

The cavern, within, was low and irregular in form. From its rugged walls the damp oozed forth upon its floor of decayed moss. Lizards and noisome animals had tenanted its comfortless recesses undisturbed, until the period we have just described, when their miserable rights were infringed on for the first time by human intruders.

A woman crouched near the entrance of the place. More within, on the driest part of the ground, lay a child asleep. Between them were scattered some withered branches and decayed leaves, which were arranged as if to form a fire. In many parts this scanty collection of fuel was slightly blackened; but, wetted as it was by the rain, all efforts to light it permanently had evidently been fruitless.

The woman's head was bent forwards, and her face, hid in her hands, rested on her knees. At intervals she muttered to herself in a hoarse, moaning voice. A portion of her scanty clothing had been removed to cover the child. What remained on her was composed, partly of skins of animals, partly of coarse cotton cloth. In many places this miserable dress was marked with blood, and her long, flaxen hair bore upon its dishevelled locks the same ominous and repulsive stain.

The child seemed scarcely four years of age, and showed on his pale, thin face all the peculiarities of his Gothic origin. His features seemed to have been once beautiful, both in expression and form; but a deep wound, extending the whole length of his cheek, had now deformed him for ever. He shivered and trembled in his sleep, and every now and then mechanically stretched forth his little arms towards the dead cold branches that were scattered before him.

Suddenly a large stone became detached from the rock in a distant part of the cavern, and fell noisily to the ground. At this sound he woke with a scream--raised himself--endeavoured to advance towards the woman, and staggered backward against the side of the cave. A second wound in the leg had wreaked that destruction on his vigour which the first had effected on his beauty. He was a cripple.

At the instant of his awakening the woman had started up. She now raised him from the ground, and taking some herbs from her bosom, applied them to his wounded cheek. By this action her dress became discomposed: it was stiff at the top with coagulated blood, which had evidently flowed from a cut in her neck.

All her attempts to compose the child were in vain; he moaned and wept piteously, muttering at intervals his disjointed exclamations of impatience at the coldness of the place and the agony of his recent wounds. Speechless and tearless the wretched woman looked vacantly down on his face. There was little difficulty in discerning from that fixed, distracted gaze the nature of the tie that bound the mourning woman to the suffering boy. The expression of rigid and awful despair that lowered in her fixed, gloomy eyes, the livid paleness that discoloured her compressed lips, the spasms that shook her firm, commanding form, mutely expressing in the divine eloquence of human emotion that between the solitary pair there existed the most intimate of earth's relationships--the connection of mother and child.

For some time no change occurred in the woman's demeanour. At last, as if struck by some sudden suspicion, she rose, and clasping the child in one arm, displaced with the other the brushwood at the entrance of her place of refuge, cautiously looking forth on all that the mists left visible of the western landscape. After a short survey she drew back as if reassured by the unbroken solitude of the place, and turning towards the lake, looked down upon the black waters at her feet.

'Night has succeeded to night,' she muttered gloomily, 'and has brought no succour to my body, and no hope to my heart! Mile on mile have I journeyed, and
danger is still behind, and loneliness for ever before. The shadow of death deep-
ens over the boy; the burden of anguish grows weightier than I can bear. For me,
friends are murdered, defenders are distant, possessions are lost. The God of the
Christian priests has abandoned us to danger and deserted us in woe. It is for me
to end the struggle for us both. Our last refuge has been in this place--our sepulchre shall be here as well!'

With one last look at the cold and comfortless sky, she advanced to the very edge
of the lake's precipitous bank. Already the child was raised in her arms, and her
body bent to accomplish successfully the fatal spring, when a sound in the east--
faint, distant, and fugitive--caught her ear. In an instant her eye brightened, her
chest heaved, her cheek flushed. She exerted the last relics of her wasted strength
to gain a prominent position upon a ledge of the rocks behind her, and waited in
an agony of expectation for a repetition of that magic sound.

In a moment more she heard it again--for the child, stupefied with terror at the
action that had accompanied her determination to plunge with him into the lake,
now kept silence, and she could listen undisturbed. To unpractised ears the sound
that so entranced her would have been scarcely audible. Even the experienced
traveller would have thought it nothing more than the echo of a fallen stone
among the rocks in the eastward distance. But to her it was no unimportant
sound, for it gave the welcome signal of deliverance and delight.

As the hour wore on, it came nearer and nearer, tossed about by the sportive
echoes, and now clearly betraying that its origin was, as she had at first divined,
the note of the Gothic trumpet. Soon the distant music ceased, and was succeeded by another sound, low and rumbling, as of an earthquake afar off or a rising
thunderstorm, and changing, ere long, to a harsh confused noise, like the rustling
of a mighty wind through whole forests of brushwood.

At this instant the woman lost all command over herself; her former patience and
caution deserted her; reckless of danger, she placed the child upon the ledge on
which she had been standing; and, though trembling in every limb, succeeded in
mounting so much higher on the crag as to gain a fissure near the top of the rock,
which commanded an uninterrupted view of the vast tracts of uneven ground
leading in an easterly direction to the next range of precipices and ravines.

One after another the long minutes glided on, and, though much was still audible, nothing was yet to be seen. At length the shrill sound of the trumpet again

rang through the dull, misty air, and the next instant the advance guard of an army of Goths emerged from the distant woods.

Then, after an interval, the multitudes of the main body thronged through every outlet in the trees, and spread in dusky masses over the desert ground that lay between the woods and the rocks about the borders of the lake. The front ranks halted, as if to communicate with the crowds of the rearguard and the stragglers among the baggage waggons, who still poured forth, apparently in interminable hosts, from the concealment of the distant trees. The advanced troops, evidently with the intention of examining the roads, still marched rapidly on, until they gained the foot of the ascent leading to the crags to which the woman still clung, and from which, with eager attention, she still watched their movements.

Placed in a situation of the extremest peril, her strength was her only preservative against the danger of slipping from her high and narrow elevation. Hitherto the moral excitement of expectation had given her the physical power necessary to maintain her position; but just as the leaders of the guard arrived at the cavern, her over-wrought energies suddenly deserted her; her hands relaxed their grasp; she tottered, and would have sunk backwards to instant destruction, had not the skins wrapped about her bosom and waist become entangled with a point of one of the jagged rocks immediately around her. Fortunately--for she could utter no cry--the troops halted at this instant to enable their horses to gain breath. Two among them at once perceived her position and detected her nation. They mounted the rocks; and, while one possessed himself of the child, the other succeeded in rescuing the mother and bearing her safely to the ground.

The snorting of horses, the clashing of weapons, the confusion of loud, rough voices, which now startled the native silence of the solitary lake, and which would have bewildered and overwhelmed most persons in the woman's exhausted condition, seemed, on the contrary, to reassure her feelings and reanimate her powers. She disengaged herself from her preserver's support, and taking her child in her arms, advanced towards a man of gigantic stature, whose rich armour sufficiently announced that his position in the army was one of command.

'I am Goisvintha,' said she, in a firm, calm voice--'sister to Hermanric. I have escaped from the massacre of the hostages of Aquileia with one child. Is my brother with the army of the king?'

This declaration produced a marked change in the bystanders. The looks of indifference or curiosity which they had at first cast on the fugitive, changed to the liveliest expression of wonder and respect. The chieftain whom she had addressed raised the visor of his helmet so as to uncover his face, answered her question in

the affirmative, and ordered two soldiers to conduct her to the temporary
encampment of the main army in the rear. As she turned to depart, an old man
advanced, leaning on his long, heavy sword, and accosted her thus--

'I am Withimer, whose daughter was left hostage with the Romans in Aquileia. Is
she of the slain or of the escaped?'

'Her bones rot under the city walls,' was the answer. 'The Romans made of her
a feast for the dogs.'

No word or tear escaped the old warrior. He turned in the direction of Italy; but,
as he looked downwards towards the plains, his brow lowered, and his hands
tightened mechanically round the hilt of his enormous weapon.

The same gloomy question was propounded to Goisvintha by the two men who
guided her to the army that had been asked by their aged comrade. It received
the same terrible answer, which was borne with the same stern composure, and
followed by the same ominous glance in the direction of Italy, as in the instance
of the veteran Withimer.

Leading the horse that carried the exhausted woman with the utmost care, and
yet with wonderful rapidity, down the paths which they had so recently ascended, the men in a short space of time reached the place where the army had halted, and displayed to Goisvintha, in all the majesty of numbers and repose, the vast
martial assemblage of the warriors of the North.

No brightness gleamed from their armour; no banners waved over their heads; no
music sounded among their ranks. Backed by the dreary woods, which still disgorged unceasing additions to the warlike multitude already encamped; surrounded by the desolate crags which showed dim, wild, and majestic through the
darkness of the mist; covered with the dusky clouds which hovered motionless
over the barren mountain tops, and poured their stormy waters on the uncultivated plains--all that the appearance of the Goths had of solemnity in itself was
in awful harmony with the cold and mournful aspect that the face of Nature had
assumed. Silent--menacing--dark,--the army looked the fit embodiment of its
leader's tremendous purpose--the subjugation of Rome.

Conducting Goisvintha quickly through the front files of warriors, her guides,
pausing at a spot of ground which shelved upwards at right angles with the main
road from the woods, desired her to dismount; and pointing to the group that
occupied the place, said, 'Yonder is Alaric the king, and with him is Hermanric
thy brother.'

At whatever point of view it could have been regarded, the assemblage of persons thus indicated to Goisvintha must have arrested inattention itself. Near a confused mass of weapons, scattered on the ground, reclined a group of warriors apparently listening to the low, muttered conversation of three men of great age, who rose above them, seated on pieces of rock, and whose long white hair, rough skin dresses, and lean tottering forms appeared in strong contrast with the iron-clad and gigantic figures of their auditors beneath. Above the old men, on the highroad, was one of Alaric's waggons; and on the heaps of baggage piled against its clumsy wheels had been chosen resting-place of the future conqueror of Rome. The top of the vehicle seemed absolutely teeming with a living burden. Perched in every available nook and corner were women and children of all ages, and weapons and live stock of all varieties. Now, a child--lively, mischievous, inquisi-tive--peered forth over the head of a battering-ram. Now, a lean, hungry sheep advanced his inquiring nostrils sadly to the open air, and displayed by the move-ment the head of a withered old woman pillowed on his woolly flanks. Here, appeared a young girl struggling, half entombed in shields. There, gasped an emaciated camp-follower, nearly suffocated in heaps of furs. The whole scene, with its background of great woods, drenched in a vapour of misty rain, with its striking contrasts at one point and its solemn harmonies at another, presented a vast combination of objects that either startled or awed--a gloomy conjunction of the menacing and the sublime.

Bidding Goisvintha wait near the waggon, one of her conductors approached and motioned aside a young man standing near the king. As the warrior rose to obey the demand, he displayed, with all the physical advantages of his race, and ease and elasticity of movement unusual among the men of his nation. At the instant when he joined the soldier who had accosted him, his face was partially concealed by an immense helmet, crowned with a boar's head, the mouth of which, forced open at death, gaped wide, as if still raging for prey. But the man had scarcely stated his errand, when he started violently, removed the grim appendage of war, and hastened bare-headed to the side of the waggon where Goisvintha awaited his approach.

The instant he was beheld by the woman, she hastened to meet him; placed the wounded child in his arms, and greeted him with these words:--

'Your brother served in the armies of Rome when our people were at peace with the Empire. Of his household and his possessions this is all that the Romans have left!'

She ceased, and for an instant the brother and sister regarded each other in touching and expressive silence. Though, in addition to the general characteristics of country, the countenances of the two naturally bore the more particular evidences of community of blood, all resemblance between them at this instant--so wonderful is the power of expression over feature--had utterly vanished. The face and manner of the young man (he had numbered only twenty years) expressed a deep sorrow, manly in its stern tranquility, sincere in its perfect innocence of display. As he looked on the child, his blue eyes--bright, piercing, and lively--softened like a woman's; his lips, hardly hidden by his short beard, closed and quivered; and his chest heaved under the armour that lay upon its noble proportions. There was in this simple, speechless, tearless melancholy--this exquisite consideration of triumphant strength for suffering weakness--something almost sublime; opposed as it was to the emotions of malignity and despair that appeared in Goisvintha's features. The ferocity that gleamed from her dilated, glaring eyes, the sinister markings that appeared round her pale and parted lips, the swelling of the large veins, drawn to their extremest point of tension on her lofty forehead, so distorted her countenance, that the brother and sister, as they stood together, seemed in expression to have changed sexes for the moment. From the warrior came pity for the sufferer; from the mother, indignation for the offence.

Arousing himself from his melancholy contemplation of the child, and as yet answering not a word to Goisvintha, Hermanric mounted the waggon, and placing the last of his sister's offspring in the arms of a decrepid old woman, who sat brooding over some bundles of herbs spread out upon her lap, addressed her thus:--

'These wounds are from the Romans. Revive the child, and you shall be rewarded from the spoils of Rome.'

'Ha! ha! ha!' chuckled the crone; 'Hermanric is an illustrious warrior, and shall be obeyed. Hermanric is great, for his arm can slay; but Brunechild is greater than he, for her cunning can cure!'

As if anxious to verify this boast before the warrior's eyes, the old woman immediately began the preparation of the necessary dressings from her store of herbs; but Hermanric waited not to be a witness of her skill. With one final look at the pale, exhausted child, he slowly descended from the waggon, and approaching Goisvintha, drew her towards a sheltered position near the ponderous vehicle. Here he seated himself by her side, prepared to listen with the deepest attention to her recital of the scenes of terror and suffering through which she had so recently passed.

'You,' she began, 'born while our nation was at peace; transported from the field of war to those distant provinces where tranquility still prevailed; preserved throughout your childhood from the chances of battle; advanced to the army in your youth, only when its toils are past and its triumphs are already at hand--you alone have escaped the miseries of our people, to partake in the glory of their approaching revenge.

'Hardly had a year passed since you had been removed from the settlements of the Goths when I wedded Priulf. The race of triflers to whom he was then allied, spite of their Roman haughtiness, deferred to him in their councils, and confessed among their legions that he was brave. I saw myself with joy the wife of a warrior of renown; I believed, in my pride, that I was destined to be the mother of a race of heroes; when suddenly there came news to us that the Emperor Theodosius was dead. Then followed anarchy among the people of the soil, and outrages on the liberties of their allies, the Goths. Ere long the call to arms arose among our nation. Soon our waggons of war were rolled across the frozen Danube; our soldiers quitted the Roman camp; our husbandmen took their weapons from their cottage walls; we that were women prepared with our children to follow our husbands to the field; and Alaric, the king, came forth as the leader of our hosts.

'We marched upon the territories of the Greeks. But how shall I tell you of the events of those years of war that followed our invasion; of the glory of our victories; of the hardships of our defences; of the miseries of our retreats; of the hunger that we vanquished; of the diseases that we endured; of the shameful peace that was finally ratified, against the wishes of our king! How shall I tell of all this, when my thoughts are on the massacre from which I have just escaped--when these first evils, though once remembered in anguish, are, even now, forgotten in the superior horrors that ensued!

'The truce was made. Alaric departed with the remnant of his army, and encamped at AEmona, on the confines of that land which he had already invaded, and which he is no prepared to conquer. Between our king and Stilicho, the general of the Romans, passed many messages, for the leaders disputed on the terms of the peace that should be finally ordained. Meanwhile, as an earnest of the Gothic faith, bands of our warriors, and among them Priulf, were despatched into Italy to be allies once more of the legions of Rome, and with them they took their wives and their children, to be detained as hostages in the cities throughout the land.

'I and my children were conducted to Aquileia. In a dwelling within the city we were lodged with our possessions. It was night when I took leave of Priulf, my husband, at the gates. I watched him as he departed with the army, and, when the darkness hid him from my eyes, I re-entered the town; from which I am the only woman of our nation who has escaped alive.'

As she pronounced these last words, Goisvintha's manner, which had hitherto been calm and collected, began to change: she paused abruptly in her narrative, her head sunk upon her breast, her frame quivered as if convulsed with violent agony. When she turned towards Hermanric after an interval of silence to address him again, the same malignant expression lowered over her countenance that had appeared on it when she presented to him her wounded child; her voice became broken, hoarse, and unfeminine; and pressing closely to the young man's side, she laid her trembling fingers on his arm, as if to bespeak his most undivided attention.

'Time grew on,' she continued, 'and still there came no tidings that the peace was finally secured. We, that were hostages, lived separate from the people of the town; for we felt enmity towards each other even then. In my captivity there was no employment for me but patience--no pursuit but hope. Alone with my children, I was wont to look forth over the sea towards the camp of our king; but day succeeded to day, and his warriors appeared not on the plains; nor did Priulf return with the legions to encamp before the gates of the town. So I mourned in my loneliness; for my heart yearned towards the homes of my people; I longed once more to look upon my husband's face, and to behold again the ranks of our warriors, and the majesty of their battle array.

'But already, when the great day of despair was quickly drawing near, a bitter outrage was preparing for me alone. The men who had hitherto watched us were changed, and of the number of the new guards was one who cast on me the eyes of lust. Night after night he poured his entreaties into my unwilling ear; for, in his vanity and shamelessness, he believed that I, who was Gothic and the wife of a Goth, might be won by him whose parentage was but Roman! Soon from prayers he rose to threats; and one night, appearing before me with smiles, he cried out that Stilicho, whose desire was to make peace with the Goths, had suffered, for his devotion to our people, the penalty of death; that a time of ruin was approaching for us all, and that he alone--whom I despised--could preserve me from the anger of Rome. As he ceased he approached me; but I, who had been in many battle-fields, felt no dread at the prospect of war, and I spurned him with laughter from my presence.

'Then, for a few nights more, my enemy approached me not again. Until one evening, as I sat on the terrace before the house, with the child that you have beheld, a helmet-crest suddenly fell at my feet, and a voice cried to me from the garden beneath: 'Priulf thy husband has been slain in a quarrel by the soldiers of Rome! Already the legions with whom he served are on their way to the town; for a massacre of the hostages is ordained. Speak but the word, and I can save thee even yet!'

'I looked on the crest. It was bloody, and it was his! For an instant my heart writhed within me as I thought on my warrior whom I had loved! Then, as I heard the messenger of death retire, cursing, from his lurking-place in the garden, I recollected that now my children had none but their mother to defend them, and that peril was preparing for them from the enemies of their race. Besides the little one in my arms, I had two that were sleeping in the house. As I looked round, bewildered and in despair, to see if a chance were left us to escape, there rang through the evening stillness the sound of a trumpet, and the tramp of armed men was audible in the street beneath. Then, from all quarters of the town rose, as one sudden sound, the shrieks of women and the yells of men. Already, as I rushed towards my children's beds, the fiends of Rome had mounted the stairs, and waved in bloody triumph their reeking swords! I gained the steps; and, as I looked up, they flung down at me the body of my youngest child. O Hermanric! Hermanric! it was the most beautiful and the most beloved! What the priests say that God should be to us, that, the fairest one of my offspring, was to me! As I saw it mutilated and dead--I, who but an hour before had hushed it on my bosom to rest!--my courage forsook me, and when the murderers advanced on me I staggered and fell. I felt the sword-point enter my neck; I saw the dagger gleam over the child in my arms; I heard the death-shriek of the last victim above; and then my senses failed me, and I could listen and move no more!

'Long must I have lain motionless at the foot of those fatal stairs; for when I awoke from my trance the noises in the city were hushed, and from her place in the firmament the moon shone softly into the deserted house. I listened, to be certain that I was alone with my murdered children. No sound was in the dwelling; the assassins had departed, believing that their labour of blood was ended when I fell beneath their swords; and I was able to crawl forth in security, and to look my last upon my offspring that the Romans had slain. The child that I held to my breast still breathed. I stanched with some fragments of my garment the wounds that he had received, and laying him gently by the stairs--in the moonlight, so that I might see him when he moved--I groped in the shadow of the wall for my first murdered and my last born; for that youngest and fairest one of my offspring whom they had slaughtered before my eyes! When I touched the corpse, it was wet with blood; I felt its face, and it was cold beneath my hands; I raised its body in my arms, and its limbs already were rigid in death! Then I thought of the eldest child, who lay dead in the chamber above. But my strength was failing me fast. I had an infant who might yet be preserved; and I knew that if morning dawned on me in the house, all chances of escape were lost for ever. So, though my heart was cold within me at leaving my child's corpse to the mercy of the Romans, I took up the dead and the wounded one in my arms, and went forth into the garden, and thence towards the seaward quarter of the town.

'I passed through the forsaken streets. Sometimes I stumbled against the body of a child--sometimes the moonlight showed me the death-pale face of some woman of my nation whom I had loved, stretched upward to the sky; but I still advanced until I gained the wall of the town, and heard on the other side the waters of the river running onward to the Port of Aquileia and the sea.

'I looked around. The gates I knew were guarded and closed. By the wall was the only prospect of escape; but its top was high and its sides were smooth when I felt them with my hands. Despairing and wearied, I laid my burdens down where they were hidden by the shade, and walked forward a few paces, for to remain still was a torment that I could not endure. At a short distance I saw a soldier sleeping against the wall of a house. By his side was a ladder placed against the window. As I looked up I beheld the head of a corpse resting on its top. The victim must have been lately slain, for her blood still dripped slowly down into an empty wine-pot that stood within the soldier's reach. When I saw the ladder, hope revived within me. I removed it to the wall--I mounted, and laid my dead child on the great stones at its top--I returned, and placed my wounded boy by the corpse. Slowly, and with many efforts, I dragged the ladder upwards, until from its own weight one end fell to the ground on the other side. As I had risen so I descended. In the sand of the river-bank I scraped a hole, and buried there the corpse of the infant; for I could carry the weight of two no longer. Then with my wounded child I reached some caverns that lay onward near the seashore. There throughout the next day I lay hidden--alone with my sufferings of body and my affliction of heart--until the night came on, when I set forth on my journey to the mountains; for I knew that at Aemona, in the camp of the warriors of my people, lay the only refuge that was left to me on earth. Feebly and slowly, hiding by day an d travelling by night, I kept on my way until I gained that lake among the rocks, where the guards of the army came forward and rescued me from death.'

She ceased. Throughout the latter portion of her narrative her demeanour had been calm and sad; and as she dwelt, with the painful industry of grief, over each minute circumstance connected with the bereavements she had sustained, her voice softened to those accents of quiet mournfulness, which make impressive the most simple words, and render musical the most unsteady tones. It seemed as if those tenderer and kinder emotions, which the attractions of her offspring had once generated in her character, had at the bidding of memory become revivified in her manner while she lingered over the recital of their deaths. For a brief space of time she looked fixedly and anxiously upon the countenance of Hermanric, which was half averted from her, and expressed a fierce and revengeful gloom that sat unnaturally on it noble lineaments. Then turning from him, she buried her face in her hands, and made no effort more to attract him to attention or incite him to reply.

This solemn silence kept by the bereaved woman and the brooding man had lasted but a few minutes, when a harsh, trembling voice was heard from the top of the waggon, calling at intervals, 'Hermanric! Hermanric!'

At first the young man remained unmoved by those discordant and repulsive tones. They repeated his name, however, so often and so perseveringly, that he noticed them ere long; and rising suddenly, as if impatient of the interruption, advanced towards the side of the waggon from which the mysterious summons appeared to come.

As he looked up towards the vehicle the voice ceased, and he saw that the old woman to whom he had confided the child was the person who had called him so hurriedly but a few moments before. Her tottering body, clothed in bear-skins, was bent forward over a large triangular shield of polished brass, on which she leant her lank, shrivelled arms. Her head shook with a tremulous, palsied action; a leer, half smile, half grimace, distended her withered lips and lightened her sunken eyes. Sinister, cringing, repulsive; her face livid with the reflection from the weapon that was her support, and her figure scarcely human in the rugged garments that encompassed its gaunt proportions, she seemed a deformity set up by evil spirits to mock the majesty of the human form--an embodied satire on all that is most deplorable in infirmity and most disgusting in age.

The instant she discerned Hermanric, she stretched her body out still farther over the shield; and pointing to the interior of the waggon, muttered softly that one fearful and expressive word--dead!

Without waiting for any further explanation, the young Goth mounted the vehicle, and gaining the old woman's side, saw stretched on her collection of herbs-- beautiful in the sublime and melancholy stillness of death--the corpse of Goisvintha's last child.

'Is Hermanric wroth?' whined the hag, quailing before the steady, rebuking glance of the young man. 'When I said that Brunechild was greater than Hermanric, I lied. It is Hermanric that is most powerful! See, the dressings were placed on the wounds; and, though the child has died, shall not the treasures that were promised me be mine? I have done what I could, but my cunning begins to desert me, for I am old--old--old! I have seen my generation pass away! Aha! I am old, Hermanric, I am old!'

When the young warrior looked on the child, he saw that the hag had spoken truth, and that the victim had died from no fault of hers. Pale and serene, the countenance of the boy showed how tranquil had been his death. The dressings had been skilfully composed and carefully applied to his wounds, but suffering and privation had annihilated the feebleness of human resistance in their march toward the last dread goal, and the treachery of Imperial Rome had once more triumphed as was its wont, and triumphed over a child!

As Hermanric descended with the corpse Goisvintha was the first object that met his eyes when he alighted on the ground. The mother received from him the lifeless burden without an exclamation or a tear. That emanation from her former and kinder self which had been produced by the closing recital of her sufferings was henceforth, at the signal of her last child's death, extinguished in her for ever!

'His wounds had crippled him,' said the young man gloomily. 'He could never have fought with the warriors! Our ancestors slew themselves when they were no longer vigorous for the fight. It is better that he has died!'

'Vengeance!' gasped Goisvintha, pressing up closely to his side. 'We will have vengeance for the massacre of Aquileia! When blood is streaming in the palaces of Rome, remember my murdered children, and hasten not to sheathe thy sword!'

At this instant, as if to rouse still further the fierce determination that appeared already in the face of the young Goth, the voice of Alaric was heard commanding the army to advance. Hermanric started, and drew the panting woman after him to the resting-place of the king. There, armed at all points, and rising, by his superior stature, high above the throng around him, stood the dreaded captain of the Gothic hosts. His helmet was raised so as to display his clear blue eyes gleaming over the multitude around him; he pointed with his sword in the direction of Italy; and as rank by rank the men started to their arms, and prepared exultingly for the march, his lips parted with a smile of triumph, and ere he moved to accompany them he spoke thus:--

'Warriors of the Goths, our halt is a short one among the mountains; but let not the weary repine, for the glorious resting-place that awaits our labours is the city of Rome! The curse of Odin, when in the infancy of our nation he retire before the myriads of the Empire, it is our privilege to fulfil! That future destruction which he denounced against Rome, it is ours to effect! Remember your hostages that the Romans have slain; your possessions that the Romans have seized; your trust that the Romans have betrayed! Remember that I, your king, have within me that supernatural impulse which never deceives, and which calls to me in a voice of encouragement--Advance, and the Empire is thine! Assemble the warriors, and the City of the World shall be delivered to the conquering Goths! Let us onward without delay! Our prey awaits us! Our triumph is near! Our vengeance is at hand!'

He paused; and at that moment the trumpet gave signal for the march.

'Up! up!' cried Hermanric, seizing Goisvintha by the arm, and pointing to the waggon which had already begun to move; 'make ready for the journey! I will charge myself with the burial of the child. Yet a few days and our encampment may be before Aquileia. Be patient, and I will avenge thee in the palaces of Rome!'

The mighty mass moved. The multitude stretched forth over the barren ground; and even now the warriors in front of the army might be seen by those in the rear mounting the last range of passes that lay between the plains of Italy and the Goths.

Chapter 2

THE COURT

The traveller who so far departs from the ordinary track of tourists in modern Italy as to visit the city of Ravenna, remembers with astonishment, as he treads its silent and melancholy streets, and beholds vineyards and marshes spread over an extent of four miles between the Adriatic and the town, that this place, now half deserted, was once the most populous of Roman fortresses; and that where fields and woods now present themselves to his eyes the fleets of the Empire once rode securely at anchor, and the merchant of Rome disembarked his precious cargoes at his warehouse door.

As the power of Rome declined, the Adriatic, by a strange fatality, began to desert the fortress whose defence it had hitherto secured. Coeval with the gradual degeneracy of the people was the gradual withdrawal of the ocean from the city walls; until, at the beginning of the sixth century, a grove of pines already appeared where the port of Augustus once existed.

At the period of our story--though the sea had even then receded perceptibly--the ditches round the walls were yet filled, and the canals still ran through the city in much the same manner as they intersect Venice at the present time.

On the morning that we are about to describe, the autumn had advanced some days since the events mentioned in the preceding chapter. Although the sun was now high in the eastern horizon, the restlessness produced by the heat emboldened a few idlers of Ravenna to brave the sultriness of the atmosphere, in the vain hope of being greeted by a breeze from the Adriatic as they mounted the seaward ramparts of the town. On attaining their destined elevation, these sanguine citizens turned their faces with fruitless and despairing industry towards every point of the compass, but no breath of air came to reward their perseverance. Nothing could be more thoroughly suggestive of the undiminished universality of the heat than the view, in every direction, from the position they then occupied. The stone houses of the city behind them glowed with a vivid brightness overpowering to the strongest eyes. The light curtains hung motionless over the lonely windows. No shadows varied the brilliant monotony of the walls, or softened the lively glitter on the waters of the fountains beneath. Not a ripple stirred the surface of the broad channel, that now replaced the ancient harbour. Not a breath of wind unfolded the scorching sails of the deserted vessels at the quay. Over the marshes in the distance hung a hot, quivering mist; and in the vineyards, near the town, not a leaf waved upon its slender stem. On the seaward side lay, vast and level, the prospect of the burning sand; and beyond it the main ocean--waveless, torpid, and suffused in a flood of fierce brightness--stretched out to the cloudless horizon that closed the sunbright view.

Within the town, in those streets where the tall houses cast a deep shadow on the flagstones of the road, the figures of a few slaves might here and there be seen sleeping against the walls, or gossiping languidly on the faults of their respective lords. Sometimes an old beggar might be observed hunting on the well-stocked preserves of his own body the lively vermin of the South. Sometimes a restless child crawled from a doorstep to paddle in the stagnant waters of a kennel; but, with the exception of these doubtful evidences of human industry, the prevailing characteristic of the few groups of the lowest orders of the people which appeared in the streets was the most listless and utter indolence. All that gave splendour to the city at other hours of the day was at this period hidden from the eye. The elegant courtiers reclined in their lofty chambers; the guards on duty ensconced themselves in angles of walls and recesses of porticoes; the graceful ladies slumbered on perfumed couches in darkened rooms; the gilded chariots were shut into the carriage-houses; the prancing horses were confined in the stables; and even the wares in the market-places were removed from exposure to the sun. It was clear that the luxurious inhabitants of Ravenna recognised no duties of sufficient importance, and no pleasures of sufficient attraction, to necessitate the exposure of their susceptible bodies to the noontide heat.

To give the reader some idea of the manner in which the indolent patricians of the Court loitered away their noon, and to satisfy, at the same time, the exigencies attaching to the conduct of this story, it is requisite to quit the lounging-places of the plebeians in the streets for the couches of the nobles in the Emperor's palace.

Passing through the massive entrance gates, crossing the vast hall of the Imperial abode, with its statues, its marbles, and its guards in attendance, and thence ascending the noble staircase, the first object that might on this occasion have attracted the observer, when he gained the approaches to the private apartments, was a door at an extremity of the corridor, richly carved and standing half open. At this spot were grouped some fifteen or twenty individuals, who conversed by signs, and maintained in all their movements the most decorous and complete silence. Sometimes one of the party stole on tiptoe to the door, and looked cautiously through, returning almost instantaneously, and expressing to his next neighbour, by various grimaces, his immense interest in the sight he had just beheld. Occasionally there came from this mysterious chamber sounds resembling the cackling of poultry, varied now and then by a noise like the falling of a shower of small, light substances upon a hard floor. Whenever these sounds were audible, the members of the party outside the door looked round upon each other and smiled--some sarcastically, some triumphantly. A few among these patient expectants grasped rolls of vellum in their hands; the rest held nosegays of rare flowers, or supported in their arms small statues and pictures in mosaic. Of their number, some were painters and poets, some orators and philosophers, and some statuaries and musicians. Among such a motley assemblage of professions, remarkable in all ages of the world for fostering in their votaries the vice of irritability, it may seem strange that so quiet and orderly a behaviour should exist as that just described. But it is to be observed that in attending at the palace, these men of genius made sure at least of outward unanimity among their ranks, by coming equally prepared with one accomplishment, and equally animated by one hope: they waited to employ a common agent--flattery; to attain a common end--gain.

The chamber thus sacred, even from the intrusion of intellectual inspiration, although richly ornamented, was of no remarkable extent. At other times the eye might have wandered with delight on the exquisite plants and flowers, scattered profusely over a noble terrace, to which a second door in the apartment conducted; but, at the present moment, the employment of the occupant of the room was of so extraordinary a nature, that the most attentive observation must have missed all the inferior characteristics of the place, to settle immediately on its inhabitant alone.

In the midst of a large flock of poultry, which seemed strangely misplaced on a floor of marble and under a gilded roof, stood a pale, thin, debilitated youth, magnificently clothed, and holding in his hand a silver vase filled with grain, which he ever and anon distributed to the cackling multitude at his feet. Nothing could be more pitiably effeminate than the appearance of this young man. His eyes were heavy and vacant, his forehead low and retiring, his cheeks sallow, and his form curved as if with a premature old age. An unmeaning smile dilated his thin, colourless lips; and as he looked down on his strange favourites, he occasionally whispered to them a few broken expressions of endearment, almost infantine in their simplicity. His whole soul seemed to be engrossed by the labour of distributing his grain, and he followed the different movements of the poultry with an earnestness of attention which seemed almost idiotic in its ridiculous intensity. If it be asked, why a person so contemptible as this solitary youth has been introduced with so much care, and described with so much minuteness, it must be answered, that, though destined to form no important figure in this work, he played, from his position, a remarkable part in the great drama on which it is founded--for this feeder of chickens was no less a person than Honorius, Emperor of Rome.

It is the very imbecility of this man, at such a time as that we now write on, which invests his character with a fearful interest in the eye of posterity. In himself the impersonation of the meanest vices inherent in the vicious civilisation of his period, to his feebleness was accorded the terrible responsibility of liberating the long-prisoned storm whose elements we have attempted to describe in the preceding chapter. With just intellect enough to be capricious, and just determination enough to be mischievous, he was an instrument fitted for the uses of every ambitious villain who could succeed in gaining his ear. To flatter his puerile tyranny, the infatuated intriguers of the Court rewarded the heroic Stilicho for the rescue of his country with the penalty of death, and defrauded Alaric of the moderate concessions that they had solemnly pledged themselves to perform. To gratify his vanity, he was paraded in triumph through the streets of Rome for a victory that others had gained. To pander to his arrogance, by an exhibition of the vilest privilege of that power which had been intrusted to him for good, the massacre of the helpless hostages, confided by Gothic honour to Roman treachery, was unhesitatingly ordained; and, finally, to soothe the turbulence of his unmanly fears, the last act of his unscrupulous councillors, ere the Empire fell, was to authorise his abandoning his people in the hour of peril, careless who suffered in defenceless Rome, while he was secure in fortified Ravenna. Such was the man under whom the mightiest of the world's structures was doomed to totter to its fall! Such was the figure destined to close a scene which Time and Glory had united to hallow and adorn! Raised and supported by a superhuman daring, that invested the nauseous horrors of incessant bloodshed with a rude and appalling magnificence, the mistress of nations was now fated to sink by the most ignoble of defeats, under the most abject of tremblers. For this had the rough old kingdom shaken off its enemies by swarms from its vigorous arms! For this had the doubtful virtues of the Republic, and the perilous magnificence of the Empire, perplexed and astonished the world! In such a conclusion as Honorius ended the dignified barbarities of a Brutus, the polished splendours of an Augustus, the unearthly atrocities of a Nero, and the immortal virtues of a Trajan! Vainly, through the toiling ages, over the ruin of her noblest hearts, and the prostitution of her grandest intellects, had Rome striven pitilessly onward, grasping at the shadow--Glory; the fiat had now gone forth that doomed her to possess herself finally of the substance--Shame!

When the imperial trifler had exhausted his store of grain, and satisfied the cravings of his voracious favourites, he was relieved of his silver vase by two attendants. The flock of poultry was then ushered out at one door, while the flock of geniuses was ushered in at the other.

Leaving the emperor to cast his languid eyes over objects of art for which he had no admiration, and to open his unwilling ears to panegyrical orations for which he had no comprehension, we proceed to introduce the reader to an apartment on the opposite side of the palace, in which are congregated all the beauty and elegance of his Court.

Imagine a room two hundred feet long and proportionably broad. Its floor is mosaic, wrought into the loveliest patterns. Its sides are decorated with immense pillars of variegated marble, the recesses formed by which are occupied by statues, all arranged in exquisite variety of attitude, so as to appear to be offering to whoever approaches them the rare flowers which it is the duty of the attendants to place in their hands. The ceiling is painted in fresco, in patterns and colours harmonising with those on the mosaic floor. The cornices are of silver, and decorated with mottoes from the amatory poets of the day, the letters of which are formed by precious stones. In the middle of the room is a fountain throwing up streams of perfumed water, and surrounded by golden aviaries containing birds of all sizes and nations. Three large windows, placed at the eastern extremity of the apartment, look out upon the Adriatic, but are covered at this hour, from the outside, with silk curtains of a delicate green shade, which cast a soft, luxurious light over every object, but are so thinly woven and so skilfully arranged that the slightest breath of air which moves without finds its way immediately to the languid occupants of the Court waiting- room. The number of these individuals amounts to about fifty or sixty persons. By far the larger half of the assemblage are women. Their black hair tastefully braided into various forms, and adorned with flowers or precious stones, contrasts elegantly with the brilliant whiteness of the robes in which they are for the most part clothed. Some of them are occupied in listlessly watching the movements of the birds in the aviaries; others hold a languid and whispered conversation with such of the courtiers as happen to be placed near them. The men exhibit in their dresses a greater variety of colour, and in their occupations a greater fertility of resource, than the women. Their garments, of the lightest rose, violet, or yellow tints, diversify fantastically the monotonous white robes of their gentle companions. Of their employments, the most conspicuous are playing on the lute, gaming with dice, teasing their lapdogs, and insulting their parasites. Whatever their occupation, it is performed with little attention, and less enthusiasm. Some recline on their couches with closed eyes, as if the heat made the labour of using their organs of vision too much for them; others, in the midst of a conversation, suddenly leave a sentence unfinished, apparently incapacitated by lassitude from giving expression to the simplest ideas. Every sight in the apartment that attracts the eye, every sound that gains the ear, expresses a luxurious repose. No brilliant light mars the pervading softness of the atmosphere; no violent colour materialises the light, ethereal hues of the dresses; no sudden noises interrupt the fitful and plaintive notes of the lute, jar with the soft twittering of the birds in the aviaries, or drown the still, regular melody of the ladies' voices. All objects, animate and inanimate, are in harmony with each other. It is a scene of spiritualised indolence--a picture of dreamy beatitude in the inmost sanctuary of unruffled repose.

Amid this assemblage of beauty and nobility, the members of which were rather to be generally noticed than particularly observed, there was, however, one individual who, both by the solitary occupation he had chosen and his accidental position in the room, was personally remarkable among the listless patricians around him.

His couch was placed nearer the window than that of any other occupant of the chamber. Some of his indolent neighbours--especially those of the gentler sex-- occasionally regarded him with mingled looks of admiration and curiosity; but no one approached him, or attempted to engage him in conversation. A piece of vellum lay by his side, on which, from time to time, he traced a few words, and then resumed his reclining position, apparently absorbed in reflection, and utterly regardless of all the occupants, male and female, of the imperial apartment. Judging from his general appearance, he could scarcely be twenty-five years of age. The conformation of the upper part of his face was thoroughly intellectual--the forehead high, broad, and upright; the eyes clear, penetrating, and thoughtful;-- but the lower part was, on the other hand, undeniably sensual. The lips, full and thick, formed a disagreeable contrast to the delicate chiselling of the straight Grecian nose; while the fleshiness of the chin, and the jovial redundancy of the cheeks, were, in their turn, utterly at variance with the character of the pale, noble forehead, and the expression of the quick, intelligent eyes. In stature he was barely of the middle size; but every part of his body was so perfectly proportioned that he appeared, in any position, taller than he really was. The upper part of his dress, thrown open from the heat, partly disclosed the fine statuesque formation of his neck and chest. His ears, hands, and feet were of that smallness and delicacy which is held to denote the aristocracy of birth; and there was in his manner that indescribable combination of unobtrusive dignity and unaffected elegance, which in all ages and countries, and through all changes of manners and customs, has rendered the demeanour of its few favoured possessors the instantaneous interpreter of their social rank.

While the patrician was still occupied over his vellum, the following conversation took place in whispers between two ladies placed near the situation he occupied. 'Tell me, Camilla,' said the eldest and stateliest of the two, 'who is the courtier so occupied in composition? I have endeavoured, I know not how often, to catch his eye; but the man will look at nothing but his roll of vellum or the corners of the room.'

'What, are you so great a stranger in Italy as not to know him!' replied the other, a lively girl of small delicate form, who fidgeted with persevering restlessness on her couch, and seemed incapable of giving an instant's steady attention to any of the objects around her. 'By all the saints, martyrs, and relics of my uncle the bishop!'

'Hush! You should not swear!'

'Not swear! Why, I am making a new collection of oaths, intended solely for ladies' use! I intend to set the fashion of swearing by them myself!'

'But answer my question, I beseech you! Will you never learn to talk on one subject at a time?'

'Your question--ah, your question! It was about the Goths?'

'No, no! It was about that man who is incessantly writing, and will look at nobody. He is almost as provoking as Camilla herself!'

'Don't frown so! That man, as you call him, is the senator Vetranio.'

The lady started. It was evident that Vetranio had a reputation.

'Yes!' continued the lively Camilla, 'that is the accomplished Vetranio; but he will be no favourite of yours, for he sometimes swears--swears by the ancient gods, too, which is forbidden!'

'He is handsome.'

'Handsome! he is beautiful! Not a woman in Italy but is languishing for him!'

'I have heard that he is clever.'

'Who has not? He is the author of some of the most celebrated sauces of the age. Cooks of all nations worship him as an oracle. Then he writes poetry, and composes music, and paints pictures! And as for philosophy--he talks it better than my uncle the bishop!'

'Is he rich?'

'Ah! my uncle the bishop!--I must tell you how I helped Vetranio to make a satire on him! When I was staying with him at Rome, I used often to see a woman in a veil taken across the garden to his study; so, to perplex him, I asked him who she was. And he frowned and stammered, and said at first that I was disrespectful; but he told me afterwards that she was an Arian whom he was labouring to convert. So I thought I should like to see how this conversion went on, and I hid myself behind a bookcase. But it is a profound secret; I tell it you in confidence.'

'I don't care to know it. Tell me about Vetranio.'

'How ill-natured you are! Oh! I shall never forget how we laughed when I told Vetranio what I had seen. He took up his writing materials, and made the satire immediately. The next day all Rome heard of it. My uncle was speechless with rage! I believe he suspected me; but he gave up converting the Arian lady, and--'

'I ask you again--Is Vetranio rich?'

'Half Sicily is his. He has immense estates in Africa, olive-grounds in Syria, and corn-fields in Gaul. I was present at an entertainment he gave at his villa in Sicily. He fitted up one of his vessels from the descriptions of the furnishing of Cleopatra's galley, and made his slaves swim after us as attendant Tritons. Oh! it was magnificent!'

'I should like to know him.'

'You should see his cats! He has a perfect legion of them at his villa. Twelve slaves are employed to attend on them. He is mad about cats, and declares that the old Egyptians were right to worship them. He told me yesterday, that when his largest cat is dead he will canonise her, in spite of the Christians! And then he is so kind to his slaves! They are never whipped or punished, except when they neglect or disfigure themselves; for Vetranio will allow nothing that is ugly or dirty to come near him. You must visit his banqueting-hall in Rome. It is perfection!'

'But why is he here?'

'He has come to Ravenna, charged with some secret message from the Senate, and has presented a rare breed of chickens to that foolish--'

'Hush! you may be overheard!'

'Well!--to that wise emperor of ours! Ah! the palace has been so pleasant since he has been here!'

At this instant the above dialogue--from the frivolity of which the universally-learned readers of modern times will, we fear, recoil with contempt--was interrupted by a movement on the part of its hero which showed that his occupation was at an end. With the elaborate deliberation of a man who disdains to exhibit himself as liable to be hurried by any mortal affair, Vetranio slowly folded up the vellum he had now filled with writing, and depositing it in his bosom, made a sign to a slave who happened to be then passing near him with a dish of fruit.

Having received his message, the slave retired to the entrance of the apartment, and beckoning to a man who stood outside the door, motioned him to approach Vetranio's couch.

This individual immediately hurried across the room to the window where the elegant Roman awaited him. Not the slightest description of him is needed; for he belonged to a class with which moderns are as well acquainted as ancients--a class which has survived all changes of nations and manners--a class which came in with the first rich man in the world, and will only go out with the last. In a word, he was a parasite.

He enjoyed, however, one great superiority over his modern successors: in his day flattery was a profession--in ours it has sunk to a pursuit.

'I shall leave Ravenna this evening,' said Vetranio.

The parasite made three low bows and smiled ecstatically.

'You will order my travelling equipage to be at the palace gates an hour before sunset.'

The parasite declared he should never forget the honour of the commission, and left the room.

The sprightly Camilla, who had overheard Vetranio's command, jumped off her couch, as soon as the parasite's back was turned, and running up to the senator, began to reproach him for the determination he had just formed.

'Have you no compunction at leaving me to the dulness of this horrible palace, to satisfy your idle fancy for going to Rome,' said she, pouting her pretty lip, and playing with a lock of the dark brown hair that clustered over Vetranio's brow.

'Has the senator Vetranio so little regard for his friends as to leave them to the mercy of the Goths?' said another lady, advancing with a winning smile to Camilla's side.

'Ah, those Goths!' exclaimed Vetranio, turning to the last speaker. 'Tell me, Julia, is it not reported that the barbarians are really marching into Italy?'

'Everybody has heard of it. The emperor is so discomposed by the rumour, that he has forbidden the very name of the Goths to be mentioned in his presence again.'

'For my part,' continued Vetranio, drawing Camilla towards him, and playfully tapping her little dimpled hand, 'I am in anxious expectation of the Goths, for I have designed a statue of Minerva, for which I can find no model so fit as a woman of that troublesome nation. I am informed upon good authority, that their limbs are colossal, and their sense of propriety most obediently pliable under the discipline of the purse.'

'If the Goths supply you with a model for anything,' said a courtier who had joined the group while Vetranio was speaking, 'it will be with a representation of the burning of your palace at Rome, which they will enable you to paint from the inexhaustible reservoir of your own wounds.'

The individual who uttered this last observation was remarkable among the brilliant circle around him by his excessive ugliness. Urged by his personal disadvantages, and the loss of all his property at the gaming- table, he had latterly personated a character, the accomplishments attached to which rescued him, by their disagreeable originality in that frivolous age, from oblivion or contempt. He was a Cynic philosopher.

His remark, however, produced no other effect on his hearers' serenity than to excite their merriment. Vetranio laughed, Camilla laughed, Julia laughed. The idea of a troop of barbarians ever being able to burn a palace at Rome was too wildly ridiculous for any one's gravity; and as the speech was repeated in other parts of the room, in spite of their dulness and lassitude the whole Court laughed.

'I know not why I should be amused by that man's nonsense,' said Camilla, suddenly becoming grave at the very crisis of a most attractive smile, 'when I am so melancholy at the thought of Vetranio's departure. What will become of me when he is gone? Alas! who will be left in the palace to compose songs to my beauty and music for my lute? Who will paint me as Venus, and tell me stories about the ancient Egyptians and their cats? Who at the banquet will direct what dishes I am to choose, and what I am to reject? Who?'--and poor little Camilla stopped suddenly in her enumeration of the pleasures she was about to lose, and seemed on the point of weeping as piteously as she had been laughing rapturously but the instant before.

Vetranio was touched--not by the compliment to his more intellectual powers, but by the admission of his convivial supremacy as a guide to the banquet, contained in the latter part of Camilla's remonstrance. The sex were then, as now, culpably deficient in gastronomic enthusiasm. It was, therefore, a perfect triumph to have made a convert to the science of the youngest and loveliest of the ladies of the Court.

'If she can gain leave of absence,' said the gratified senator, 'Camilla shall accompany me to Rome, and shall be present at the first celebration of my recent discovery of a Nightingale Sauce.'

Camilla was in ecstasies. She seized Vetranio's cheeks between her rosy little fingers, kissed him as enthusiastically as a child kisses a new toy, and darted gaily off to prepare for her departure.

'Vetranio would be better employed,' sneered the Cynic, 'in inventing new salves for future wounds than new sauces for future nightingales! His carcase will be carved by Gothic swords as a feast for the worms before his birds are spitted with Roman skewers as a feast for his guests! Is this a time for cutting statues and concocting sauces? Fie on the senators who abandon themselves to such pursuits as Vetranio's!'

'I have other designs,' replied the object of all this moral indignation, looking with insulting indifference on the Cynic's repulsive countenance, 'which, from their immense importance to the world, must meet with universal approval. The labour that I have just achieved forms one of a series of three projects which I have for some time held in contemplation. The first is an analysis of the new priesthood; the second, a true personification, both by painting and sculpture, of Venus; the third, a discovery of what has been hitherto uninvented--a nightingale sauce. By the inscrutable wisdom of Fate, it has been so willed that the last of the objects I proposed to myself has been the first attained. The sauce is composed, and I have just concluded on this vellum the ode that is to introduce it at my table. The analysation will be my next labour. It will take the form of a treatise, in which, making the experience of past years the groundwork of prophecy for the future, I shall show the precise number of additional dissensions, controversies, and quarrels that will be require to enable the new priesthood to be themselves the destroyers of their own worship. I shall ascertain by an exact computation the year in which this destruction will be consummated; and I have by me as the materials for my work an historical summary of Christian schisms and disputes in Rome for the last hundred years. As for my second design, the personification of Venus, it is of appalling difficulty. It demands an investigation of the women of every nation under the sun; a comparison of the relative excellences and peculiarities of their several charms; and a combination of all that is loveliest in the infinite variety of their most prominent attractions, under one form. To forward the execution of this arduous project, my tenants at home and my slave-merchants abroad have orders to send to my villa in Sicily all women who are born most beautiful in the Empire, or can be brought most beautiful from the nations around. I will have them displayed before me, of every shade in complexion and of every peculiarity in form! At the fitting period I shall commence my investigations, undismayed by difficulty, and determined on success. Never yet has the true Venus been personified! Should I accomplish the task, how exquisite will be my triumph! My work will be the altar at which thousands will offer up the softest emotions of the heart. It will free the prisoned imagination of youth, and freshen the fading recollections on the memory of age!'

Vetranio paused. The Cynic was struck dumb with indignation. A solitary zealot for the Church, who happened to be by, frowned at the analysation. The ladies tittered at the personification. The gastronomists chuckled at the nightingale sauce; but for the first few minutes no one spoke. During this temporary embarrassment, Vetranio whispered a few words in Julia's ear; and--just as the Cynic was sufficiently recovered to retort--accompanied by the lady, he quitted the room.

Never was popularity more unalloyed than Vetranio's. Gifted with a disposition the pliability of which adapted itself to all emergencies, his generosity disarmed enemies, while his affability made friends. Munificent without assumption, successful without pride, he obliged with grace and shone with safety. People enjoyed his hospitality, for they knew that it was disinterested; and admired his acquirements, for they felt that they were unobtrusive. Sometimes (as in his dialogue with the Cynic) the whim of the moment, or the sting of a sarcasm, drew from him a hint at his station, or a display of his eccentricities; but, as he was always the first soon afterwards to lead the laugh at his own outbreak, his credit as a noble suffered nothing by his infirmity as a man. Gaily and attractively he moved in all grades of the society of his age, winning his social laurels in every rank, without making a rival to dispute their possession, or an enemy to detract from their value.

On quitting the Court waiting-room, Vetranio and Julia descended the palace stairs and passed into the emperor's garden. Used generally as an evening lounge, this place was now untenanted, save by the few attendants engaged in cultivating the flower-beds and watering the smooth, shady lawns. Entering one of the most retired of the numerous summer-houses among the trees, Vetranio motioned his companion to take a seat, and then abruptly addressed her in the following words:--

'I have heard that you are about to depart for Rome--is it true?'

He asked this question in a low voice, and with a manner in its earnestness strangely at variance with the volatile gaiety which had characterised him, but a few moments before, among the nobles of the Court. As Julia answered him in the affirmative, his countenance expressed a lively satisfaction; and seating himself by her side, he continued the conversation thus:--

'If I thought that you intended to stay for any length of time in the city, I should venture upon a fresh extortion from your friendship by asking you to lend me your little villa at Aricia!'

'You shall take with you to Rome an order on my steward to place everything there at your entire disposal.'

'My generous Julia! You are of the gifted few who really know how to confer a favour! Another woman would have asked me why I wanted the villa--you give it unreservedly. So delicate an unwillingness to intrude on a secret reminds me that the secret should now be yours!'

To explain the easy confidence that existed between Vetranio and Julia, it is necessary to inform the reader that the lady--although still attractive in appearance--was of an age to muse on her past, rather than to meditate on her future conquests. She had known her eccentric companion from his boyhood, had been once flattered in his verses, and was sensible enough--now that her charms were on the wane--to be as content with the friendship of the senator as she had formerly been enraptured with the adoration of the youth.

'You are too penetrating,' resumed Vetranio, after a short pause, 'not to have already suspected that I only require your villa to assist me in the concealment of an intrigue. So peculiar is my adventure in its different circumstances, that to make use of my palace as the scene of its development would be to risk a discovery which might produce the immediate subversion of all my designs. But I fear the length of my confession will exceed the duration of your patience!'

'You have aroused my curiosity. I could listen to you for ever!'

'A short time before I took my departure from Rome for this place,' continued Vetranio, 'I encountered an adventure of the most extraordinary nature, which has haunted me with the most extraordinary perseverance, and which will have, I feel assured, the most extraordinary results. I was sitting one evening in the garden of my palace on the Pincian Mount, occupied in trying a new composition on my lute. In one of the pauses of the melody, which was tender and plaintive, I heard sounds that resembled the sobbing of some one in distress among the trees behind me. I looked cautiously round, and discerned, half-hidden by the verdure, the figure of a young girl, who appeared to be listening to the music with the most entranced attention. Flattered by such a testimony to my skill, and anxious to gain a nearer view of my mysterious visitant, I advanced towards her hiding-place, forgetting in my haste to continue playing on the lute. The instant the music ceased, she discerned me and disappeared. Determined to behold her, I again struck the chords, and in a few minutes I saw her white robe once more among the trees. I redoubled my efforts. I played with the utmost expression the most pathetic parts of the melody. As if under the influence of a charm, she began to advance towards me, now hesitating, now moving back a few steps, now approaching, half- reluctantly, half willingly, until utterly vanquished by the long trembling close of the last cadence of the air, she ran suddenly up to me, and falling at my feet, raised her hands as if to implore my pardon.'

'Truly this was no common tribute to your skill! Did she speak to you?'

'She uttered not a word,' continued Vetranio. 'Her large soft eyes, bright with tears, looked piteously up in my face; her delicate lips trembled, as if she wished to speak, but dared not; her smooth round arms were the very perfection of beauty. Child as she seemed in years and emotions, she looked a woman in loveliness and form. For the moment I was too much astonished by the suddenness of her supplicating action to move or speak. As soon as I recovered myself I attempted to fondle and console her, but she shrunk from my embrace, and seemed inclined to escape from me again; until I touched once more the strings of the lute, and then she uttered a subdued exclamation of delight, nestled close up to me, and looked into my face with such a strange expression of mingled adoration and rapture, that I declare to you, Julia, I felt as bashful before her as a boy.'

'You bashful! The Senator Vetranio bashful!' exclaimed Julia, looking up with an expression of the most unfeigned incredulity and astonishment.

'The lute,' pursued Vetranio gravely, without heeding the interruption, 'was my sole means of procuring any communication with her. If I ceased playing, we were as strangers; if I resumed, we were as friends. So, subduing the notes of the instrument while she spoke to me in a soft tremulous musical voice, I still continued to play. By this plan I discovered at our first interview that she was the daughter of one Numerian, that she was on the point of completing her fourteenth year, and that she was called Antonina. I had only succeeded in gaining this mere outline of her story, when, as if struck by some sudden apprehension, she tore herself from me with a look of the utmost terror, and entreating me not to follow her if I ever desired to see her again, she disappeared rapidly among the trees.'

'More and more wonderful! And, in your new character of a bashful man, you doubtless obeyed her injunctions?'

'I did,' replied the senator; 'but the next evening I revisited the garden grove, and, as soon as I struck the chords, as if by magic, she again approached. At this second interview I learned the reason of her mysterious appearances and departures. Her father, she told me, was one of a new sect, who imagine--with what reason it is impossible to comprehend--that they recommend themselves to their Deity by making their lives one perpetual round of bodily suffering and mental anguish. Not content with distorting all his own feelings and faculties, this tyrant perpetrated his insane austerities upon the poor child as well. He forbade her to enter a theatre, to look on sculpture, to read poetry, to listen to music. He made her learn long prayers, and attend to interminable sermons. He allowed her no companions of her own age--not even girls like herself. The only recreation that she could obtain was the permission--granted with much reluctance and many rebukes--to cultivate a little garden which belonged to the house they lived in, and joined at one point the groves round my palace. There, while she was engaged over her flowers, she first heard the sound of my lute. for many months before I had discovered her, she had been in the habit of climbing the enclosure that bounded her garden, and hiding herself among the trees to listen to the music, whenever her father's concerns took him abroad. She had been discovered in this occupation by an old man appointed to watch her in his master's absence. The attendant, however, on hearing her confession, not only promised to keep her secret, but permitted her to continue her visits to my grove whenever I chanced to be playing there on the lute. Now the most mysterious part of this matter is, that the girl seemed--in spite of his severity towards her--to have a great affection for her surly; for, when I offered to deliver her from his custody, she declared that nothing could induce her to desert him--not even the attraction of living among fine pictures and hearing beautiful music every hour in the day. But I see I weary you; and, indeed, it is evident from the length of the shadows that the hour of my departure is at hand. Let me then pass from my introductory interviews with Antonina, to the consequences that had resulted from them when I set forth on my journey to Ravenna.'

'I think I can imagine the consequences already!' said Julia, smiling maliciously.

'Begin then,' retorted Vetranio, 'by imagining that the strangeness of this girl's situation, and the originality of her ideas, invested her with an attraction for me, which the charms of her person and age contributed immensely to heighten. She delighted my faculties as a poet, as much as she fired my feelings as a man; and I determined to lure her from the tyrannical protection of her father by the employment of every artifice that my ingenuity could suggest. I began by teaching her to exercise for herself the talent which had so attracted her in another. By the familiarity engendered on both sides by such an occupation, I hoped to gain as much in affection from her as she acquired in skill from me; but to my astonishment, I still found her as indifferent towards the master, and as tender towards the music, as she had appeared at our first interview. If she had repelled my advances, if they had overwhelmed her with confusion, I could have adapted myself to her humour, I should have felt the encouragement of hope; but the coldness, the carelessness, the unnatural, incomprehensible ease with which she received even my caresses, utterly disconcerted me. It seemed as if she could only regard me as a moving statue, as a mere impersonation, immaterial as the science I was teaching her. If I spoke, she hardly looked on me; if I moved, she scarcely noticed the action. I could not consider it dislike; she seemed to gentle to nourish such a feeling for any creature on earth. I could not believe it coldness; she was all life, all agitation, if she heard only a few notes of music. When she touched the chords of the instrument, her whole frame trembled. Her eyes, mild, serious, and thoughtful when she looked on me, now brightened with delight, now softened with tears, when she listened to the lute. As day by day her skill in music increased, so her manner towards me grew more inexplicably indifferent. At length, weary of the constant disappointments that I experienced, and determined to make a last effort to touch her heart by awakening her gratitude, I presented her with the very lute which she had at first heard, and on which she had now learned to play. Never have I seen any human being so rapturously delighted as this incomprehensible girl when she received the instrument from my hands. She alternately wept and laughed over it, she kissed it, fondled it, spoke to it, as if it had been a living thing. But when I approached to suppress the expressions of thankfulness that she poured on me for the gift, she suddenly hid the lute in her robe, as if afraid that I should deprive her of it, and hurried rapidly from my sight. The next day I waited for her at our accustomed meeting-place, but she never appeared. I sent a slave to her father's house, but she would hold no communication with him. It was evident that, now she had gained her end, she cared no more to behold me. In my first moments of irritation, I determined to make her feel my power, if she despised my kindness; but reflection convinced me, from my acquaintance with her character, that in such a matter force was impolitic, that I should risk my popularity in Rome, and engage myself in an unworthy quarrel to no purpose. Dissatisfied with myself, and disappointed in the girl, I obeyed the first dictates of my impatience, and seizing the opportunity afforded by my duties in the senate of escaping from the scene of defeated hopes, I departed angrily for Ravenna.'

'Departed for Ravenna!' cried Julia, laughing outright. 'Oh, what a conclusion to the adventure! I confess it, Vetranio, such consequences as these are beyond all imagination!'

'You laugh, Julia,' returned the senator, a little piqued; 'but hear me to the end, and you will find that I have not yet resigned myself to defeat. For the few days that I have remained here, Antonina's image has incessantly troubled my thoughts. I perceive that my inclination, as well as my reputation, is concerned in subduing her ungrateful aversion. I suspect that my anxiety to gain her will, if unremoved, so far influence my character, that from Vetranio the Serene, I shall be changed into Vetranio the Sardonic. Pride, honour, curiosity, and love all urge me to her conquest. To prepare for my banquet is an excuse to the Court for my sudden departure from this place; the real object of my journey is Antonina alone.'

'Ah, now I recognise my friend again in his own character,' remarked the lady approvingly.

'You will ask me how I purpose to obtain another interview with her?' continued Vetranio. 'I answer, that the girl's attendant has voluntarily offered himself as an instrument for the prosecution of my plans. The very day before I departed from Rome, he suddenly presented himself to my in my garden, and proposed to intro- duce me into Numerian's house--having first demanded, with the air more of an equal than an inferior, whether the report that I was still a secret adherent of the old religion, of the worship of the gods, was true. Suspicious of the fellow's motives (for he abjured all recompense as the reward of his treachery), and irri- tated by the girl's recent ingratitude, I treated his offer with contempt. Now, however, that my dissatisfaction is calmed and my anxiety aroused, I am deter- mined, at all hazards, to trust myself to this man, be his motives for aiding me what they may. If my efforts at my expected interview--and I will not spare them- -are rewarded with success, it will be necessary to obtain some refuge for Antonina that will neither be suspected nor searched. For such a hiding-place, nothing can be more admirably adapted than your Arician villa. Do you--now that you know for what use it is intended--repent of your generous disposal of it in aid of my design?'

'I am delighted to have had it to bestow on you,' replied the liberal Julia, pressing Vetranio's hand. 'Your adventure is indeed uncommon--I burn with impatience to hear how it will end. Whatever happens, you may depend on my secrecy and count on my assistance. But see, the sun is already verging towards the west; and yonder comes one of your slaves to inform you, I doubt not, that your equipage is prepared. Return with me to the palace, and I will supply you with the letter necessary to introduce you as master to my country abode.'

*****

The worthy citizens of Ravenna assembled in the square before the palace to behold the senator's departure, had entirely exhausted such innocent materials for amusement as consisted in staring at the guards, catching the clouds of gnats that hovered about their ears, and quarrelling with each other; and were now reduced to a state of very noisy and unanimous impatience, when their discontent was suddenly and most effectually appeased by the appearance of the travelling equipage with Vetranio and Camilla outside the palace gates.

Uproarious shouts greeted the appearance of the senator and his magnificent retinue; but they were increased a hundred-fold when the chief slaves, by their master's command, each scattered a handful of small coin among the poorer classes of the spectators. Every man among that heterogeneous assemblage of rogues, fools, and idlers roared his loudest and capered his highest, in honour of the generous patrician. Gradually and carefully the illustrious travellers moved through the crowd around them to the city gate; and thence, amid incessant shouts of applause, raised with imposing unanimity of lung, and wrought up to the most distracting discordancy of noise, Vetranio and his lively companion departed in triumph for Rome.

*****

A few days after this event the citizens were again assembled at the same place and hour--probably to witness another patrician departure--when their ears were assailed by the unexpected sound produced by the call to arms, which was followed immediately by the closing of the city gates. They had scarcely asked each other the meaning of these unusual occurrences, when a peasant, half frantic with terror, rushed into the square, shouting out the terrible intelligence that the Goths were in sight!

The courtiers heard the news, and starting from a luxurious repast, hurried to the palace windows to behold the portentous spectacle. For the remainder of the evening the banqueting tables were unapproached by the guests.

The wretched emperor was surprised among his poultry by that dreaded intelligence. He, too, hastened to the windows, and looking forth, saw the army of avengers passing in contempt his solitary fortress, and moving swiftly onward towards defenceless Rome. Long after the darkness had hidden the masses of that mighty multitude from his eyes, did he remain staring helplessly upon the fading landscape, in a stupor of astonishment and dread; and, for the first time since he had possessed them, his flocks of fowls were left for that night unattended by their master's hand.

Chapter 3

ROME

The perusal of the title to this chapter will, we fear, excite emotions of apprehension, rather than of curiosity, in the breasts of experienced readers. They will doubtless imagine that it is portentous of long rhapsodies on those wonders of antiquity, the description of which has long become absolutely nauseous to them by incessant iteration. They will foresee wailings over the Palace of the Caesars, and meditations among the arches of the Colosseum, loading a long series of weary paragraphs to the very chapter's end; and, considerately anxious to spare their attention a task from which it recoils, they will unanimously hurry past the dreaded desert of conventional reflection, to alight on the first oasis that may present itself, whether it be formed by a new division of the story, or suddenly indicated by the appearance of a dialogue. Animated, therefore, by apprehensions such as these, we hasten to assure them that in no instance will the localities of our story trench upon the limits of the well-worn Forum, or mount the arches of the exhausted Colosseum. It is with the beings, and not the buildings of old Rome, that their attention is to be occupied. We desire to present them with a picture of the inmost emotions of the times--of the living, breathing actions and passions of the people of the doomed Empire. Antiquarian topography and classical architecture we leave to abler pens, and resign to other readers.

It is, however, necessary that the sphere in which the personages of our story are about to act should be in some measure indicated, in order to facilitate the comprehension of their respective movements. That portion of the extinct city which we design to revive has left few traces of its existence in the modern town. Its sites are traditionary--its buildings are dust. The church rises where the temple once stood, and the wine-shop now lures the passing idler where the bath invited his ancestor of old.

The walls of Rome are in extent, at the present day, the same as they were at the period of which we now write. But here all analogy between the ancient and modern city ends. The houses that those walls were once scarcely wide enough to enclose have long since vanished, and their modern successors occupy but a third of the space once allotted to the capital of the Empire.

Beyond the walls immense suburbs stretched forth in the days of old. Gorgeous villas, luxurious groves, temples, theatres, baths--interspersed by colonies of dwellings belonging to the lower orders of the people--surrounded the mighty city. Of these innumerable abodes hardly a trace remains. The modern traveller, as he looks forth over the site of the famous suburbs, beholds, here and there, a ruined aqueduct, or a crumbling tomb, tottering on the surface of a pestilential marsh.

The present entrance to Rome by the Porta del Popolo occupies the same site as the ancient Flaminian Gate. Three great streets now lead from it towards the southern extremity of the city, and form with their tributaries the principal portion of modern Rome. On one side they are bounded by the Pincian Hill, on the other by the Tiber. Of these streets, those nearest the river occupy the position of the famous Campus Martius; those on the other side, the ancient approaches to the gardens of Sallust and Lucullus, on the Pincian Mount.

On the opposite bank of the Tiber (gained by the Ponte St. Angelo, formerly the Pons Elius), two streets pierced through an irregular and populous neighbourhood, conduct to the modern Church of St. Peter. At the period of our story this part of the city was of much greater consequence, both in size and appearance, than it is at present, and led directly to the ancient Basilica of St. Peter, which stood on the same site as that now occupied by the modern edifice.

The events about to be narrated occur entirely in the parts of the city just described. From the Pincian Hill, across the Campus Martius, over the Pons Elius, and on to the Basilica of St. Peter, the reader may be often invited to accompany us, but he will be spared all necessity of penetrating familiar ruins, or mourning over the sepulchres of departed patriots.

Ere, however, we revert to former actors or proceed to new characters, it will be requisite to people the streets that we here attempt to rebuild. By this process it is hoped that the reader will gain that familiarity with the manners and customs of the Romans of the fifth century on which the influence of this story mainly depends, and which we despair of being able to instil by a philosophical disquisition on the features of the age. A few pages of illustration will serve our purpose better, perhaps, than volumes of historical description. There is no more unerring index to the character of a people than the streets of their cities.

It is near evening. In the widest part of the Campus Martius crowds of people are assembled before the gates of a palace. They are congregated to receive several baskets of provisions, distributed with ostentatious charity by the owner of the mansion. The incessant clamour and agitation of the impatient multitude form a strange contrast to the stately serenity of the natural and artificial objects by which they are enclosed on all sides.

The space they occupy is oblong in shape and of great extent in size. Part of it is formed by a turf walk shaded with trees, part by the paved approaches to the palace and the public baths which stand in its immediate neighbourhood. These two edifices are remarkable by their magnificent outward adornments of statues, and the elegance and number of the flights of steps by which they are respectively entered. With the inferior buildings, the market-places and the gardens attached to them, they are sufficiently extensive to form the boundary of one side of the immediate view. The appearance of monotony which might at other times be remarked in the vastness and regularity of their white fronts, is at this moment agreeably broken by several gaily-coloured awnings stretched over their doors and balconies. The sun is now shining on them with overpowering brightness; the metallic ornaments on their windows glitter like gems of fire; even the trees which form their groves partake of the universal flow of light, and fail, like the objects around them, to offer to the weary eye either refreshment or repose.

Towards the north, the Mausoleum of Augustus, towering proudly up into the brilliant sky, at once attracts the attention. From its position, parts of this noble building are already in shade. Not a human being is visible on any part of its mighty galleries--it stands solitary and sublime, an impressive embodiment of the emotions which it was raised to represent.

On the side opposite the palace and the baths is the turf walk already mentioned. Trees, thickly planted and interlaced by vines, cast a luxurious shade over this spot. In their interstices, viewed from a distance, appear glimpses of gay dresses, groups of figures in repose, stands loaded with fruit and flowers, and innumerable white marble statues of fauns and wood-nymphs. From this delicious retreat the rippling of fountains is to be heard, occasionally interrupted by the rustling of leaves, or the plaintive cadences of the Roman flute.

Southward two pagan temples stand in lonely grandeur among a host of monuments and trophies. The symmetry of their first construction still remains unimpaired, their white marble pillars shine in the sunlight brightly as of old, yet they now present to the eye an aspect of strange desolation, of unnatural mysterious gloom. Although the laws forbid the worship for which they were built, the hand of reform has as yet not ventured to doom them to ruin or adapt them to Christian purposes. None venture to tread their once-crowded colonnades. No priest appears to give the oracles from their doors; no sacrifices reek upon their naked altars. Under their roofs, visited only by the light that steals through their narrow entrances, stand unnoticed, unworshipped, unmoved, the mighty idols of old Rome. Human emotion, which made them Omnipotence once, has left them but stone now. The 'Star in the East' has already dimmed the fearful halo which the devotion of bloodshed once wreathed round their forms. Forsaken and alone, they stand but as the gloomy monuments of the greatest delusion ever organised by the ingenuity of man.

We have now, so to express it, exhibited the frame surrounding the moving picture, which we shall next attempt to present to the reader by mixing with the multitude before the palace gates.

This assembly resolved itself into three divisions: that collected before the palace steps, that loitering about the public baths, and that reposing in the shade of the groves. The first was of the most consequence in numbers, and of the greatest variety in appearance. Composed of rogues of the worst order from every quarter of the world, it might be said to present, in its general aspect of numerical importance, the very sublime of degradation. Confident in their rude union of common avidity, these worthy citizens vented their insolence on all objects, and in every direction, with a careless impartiality which would have shamed the most victorious efforts of modern mobs. The hubbub of voices was perfectly fearful. The coarse execrations of drunken Gauls, the licentious witticisms of effeminate Greeks, the noisy satisfaction of native Romans, the clamorous indignation of irritable Jews--all sounded together in one incessant chorus of discordant noises. Nor were the senses of sight and smell more agreeably assailed than the faculty of hearing, by this anomalous congregation. Immodest youth and irreverent age; woman savage, man cowardly; the swarthy Ethiopian beslabbered with stinking oil; the stolid Briton begrimed with dirt--these, and a hundred other varying combinations, to be imagined rather than expressed, met the attention in every direction. To describe the odours exhaled by the heat from this seething mixture of many pollutions, would be to force the reader to close the book; we prefer to return to the distribution which was the cause of this degrading tumult, and which consisted of small baskets of roasted meat packed with common fruits and vegetables, and handed, or rather flung down, to the mob by the servants of the nobleman who gave the feast. The people revelled in the abundance thus presented to them. They threw themselves upon it like wild beasts; they devoured it like hogs, or bore it off like plunderers; while, secure in the eminence on which they were placed, the purveyors of this public banquet expressed their contempt for its noisy recipients, by holding their noses, stopping their ears, turning their backs, and other pantomimic demonstrations of lofty and excessive disgust. These actions did not escape the attention of those members of the assembly who, having eaten their fill, were at leisure to make use of their tongues, and who showered an incessant storm of abuse on the heads of their benefactor's retainers.

'See those fellows!' cried one; 'they are the waiters at our feast, and they mock us to our faces! Down with the filthy kitchen thieves!'

'Excellently well said, Davus!--but who is to approach them? They stink at this distance!'

'The rotten-bodied knaves have the noses of dogs and the carcases of goats.'

Then came a chorus of voices--'Down with them! Down with them!' In the midst of which an indignant freedman advanced to rebuke the mob, receiving, as the reward of his temerity, a shower of missiles and a volley of curses; after which he was thus addressed by a huge, greasy butcher, hoisted on his companions' shoulders:--

'By the soul of the emperor, could I get near you, you rogue, I would quarter you with my fingers alone!--A grinning scoundrel that jeers at others! A filthy flatterer that dirts the very ground he walks on! By the blood of the martyrs, should I fling the sweepings of the slaughter- house at him, he knows not where to get himself dried!'

'Thou rag of a man,' roared a neighbour of the indignant butcher's, 'dost thou frown upon the guests of thy master, the very scrapings of whose skin are worth more than thy whole carcase! It is easier to make a drinking-vessel of the skull of a flea than to make an honest man of such a villainous night-walker as thou art!'

'Health and prosperity to our noble entertainer!' shouted one section of the grateful crowd as the last speaker paused for breath.

'Death to all knaves of parasites!' chimed in another.

'Honour to the citizens of Rome!' roared a third party with modest enthusiasm.

'Give that freedman our bones to pick!' screamed an urchin from the outskirts of the crowd.

This ingenious piece of advice was immediately followed; and the populace gave vent to a shout of triumph as the unfortunate freedman, scared by a new volley of missiles, retreated with ignominious expedition to the shelter of his patron's halls.

In the slight and purified specimen of the 'table talk' of a Roman mob which we have here ventured to exhibit, the reader will perceive that extraordinary mixture of servility and insolence which characterised not only the conversation but the actions of the lower orders of society at the period of which we write. Oppressed and degraded, on the one hand, to a point of misery scarcely conceivable to the public of the present day, the poorer classes in Rome were, on the other, invested with such a degree of moral license, and permitted such an extent of political priv-ilege, as flattered their vanity into blinding their sense of indignation. Slaves in their season of servitude, masters in their hours of recreation, they presented, as a class, one of the most amazing social anomalies ever existing in any nation; and formed, in their dangerous and artificial position, one of the most important of the internal causes of the downfall of Rome.

The steps of the public baths were almost as crowded as the space before the neighbouring building. Incessant streams of people, either entering or departing, poured over the broad flagstones of its marble colonnades. This concourse, although composed in some parts of the same class of people as that assembled before the palace, presented a certain appearance of respectability. Here and there--chequering the dusky monotony of masses of dirty tunics--might be dis-cerned the refreshing vision of a clean robe, or the grateful indication of a hand-some person. Little groups, removed as far as possible from the neighbourhood of the noisy plebeians, were scattered about, either engaged in animated conversa-tion, or listlessly succumbing to the lassitude induced by a recent bath. An instant's attention to the subject of discourse among the more active of these indi-viduals will aid us in pursuing our social revelations.

The loudest voice among the speakers at this particular moment proceeded from a tall, thin, sinister-looking man, who was haranguing a little group of listeners with great vehemence and fluency.

'I tell you, Socius,' said he, turning suddenly upon one of his companions, 'that, unless new slave-laws are made, my calling is at an end. My patron's estate requires incessant supplies of these wretches. I do my best to satisfy the demand, and the only result of my labour is, that the miscreants either endanger my life, or fly with impunity to join the gangs of robbers infesting our woods.'

'Truly I am sorry for you; but what alteration would you have made in the slave-laws?'

'I would empower bailiffs to slay upon the spot all slaves whom they thought disorderly, as an example to the rest!'

'What would such a permission avail you? These creatures are necessary, and such a law would exterminate them in a few months. Can you not break their spirit with labour, bind their strength with chains, and vanquish their obstinacy with dungeons?'

'All this I have done, but they die under the discipline, or escape from their prisons. I have now three hundred slaves on my patron's estates. Against those born on our lands I have little to urge. Many of them, it is true, begin the day with weeping and end it with death; but for the most part, thanks to their diurnal allowance of stripes, they are tolerably submissive. It is with the wretches that I have been obliged to purchase from prisoners of war and the people of revolted towns that I am so dissatisfied. Punishments have no effect on them, they are incessantly indolent, sulky, desperate. It was but the other day that ten of them poisoned themselves while at work in the fields, and fifty more, after setting fire to a farm-house while my back was turned, escaped to join a gang of their companions, who are now robbers in the woods. These fellows, however, are the last of the troop who will perpetrate such offences. With the concurrence of my patron, I have adopted a plan that will henceforth tame them efficiently!'

'Are you at liberty to communicate it?'

'By the keys of St. Peter, I wish I could see it practised on every estate in the land! It is this:--Near a sulphur lake at some distance from my farm-house is a tract of marshy ground, overspread here and there by the ruins of an ancient slaughter-house. I propose to dig in this place several subterranean caverns, each of which shall be capable of holding twenty men. Here my mutinous slaves shall sleep after their day's labour. The entrances shall be closed until morning with a large stone, on which I will have engraven this inscription: 'These are the dormitories invented by Gordian, bailiff of Saturninus, a nobleman, for the reception of refractory slaves.'

'Your plan is ingenious; but I suspect your slaves (so insensible to hardships are the brutal herd) will sleep as unconcernedly in their new dormitories as in their old.'

'Sleep! It will be a most original species of repose that they will taste there! The stench of the sulphur lake will breathe Sabian odours for them over a couch of mud! Their anointing oil will be the slime of attendant reptiles! Their liquid perfumes will be the stagnant oozings from their chamber roof! Their music will be the croaking of frogs and the humming of gnats; and as for their adornments, why, they will be decked forth with head-garlands of twining worms, and movable brooches of cockchafers and toads! Tell me now, most sagacious Socius, do you still think that amidst such luxuries as these my slaves will sleep?'

'No; they will die.'

'You are again wrong. They will curse and rave perhaps, but that is of no consequence. They will work the longer above ground to shorten the term of their repose beneath. They will wake at an instant's notice, and come forth at a moment's signal. I have no fear of their dying!'

'Do you leave Rome soon?'

'I go this evening, taking with me such a supply of trustworthy assistants as will enable me to execute my plan without delay. Farewell, Socius!'

'Most ingenious of bailiffs, I bid you farewell!'

As the worthy Gordian stalked off, big with the dignity of his new projects, the gestures and tones of a man who formed one of a little group collected in a remote part of the portico he was about to quit attracted his attention. Curiosity formed as conspicuous an ingredient in this man's character as cruelty. He stole behind the base of a neighbouring pillar; and, as the frequent repetition of the word 'Goths' struck his ear (the report of that nation's impending invasion having by this time reached Rome), he carefully disposed himself to listen with the most implicit attention to the speaker's voice.

'Goths!' cried the man, in the stern, concentrated accents of despair. 'Is there one among us to whom this report of their advance upon Rome does not speak of hope rather than of dread? Have we a chance of rising from the degradation forced on us by our superiors until this den of heartless triflers and shameless cowards is swept from the very earth that it pollutes!'

'Your sentiments on the evils of our condition are undoubtedly most just,' observed a fat, pompous man, to whom the preceding remarks had been addressed, 'but I cannot desire the reform you so ardently hope for. Think of the degradation of being conquered by barbarians!'

'I am the exile of my country's privileges. What interest have I in upholding her honour--if honour she really has!' replied the first speaker.

'Nay! Your expressions are too severe. You are too discontented to be just.'

'Am I! Hear me for a moment, and you will change your opinion. You see me now by my bearing and appearance superior to yonder plebeian herd. You doubtless think that I live at my ease in the world, that I can feel no anxiety for the future about my bodily necessities. What would you say were I to tell you that if I want another meal, a lodging for to- night, a fresh robe for tomorrow, I must rob or flatter some great man to gain them? Yet so it is. I am hopeless, friendless, destitute. In the whole of the Empire there is not an honest calling in which I can take refuge. I must become a pander or a parasite--a hired tyrant over slaves, or a chartered groveller beneath nobles--if I would not starve miserably in the streets, or rob openly in the woods! This is what I am. Now listen to what I was. I was born free. I inherited from my father a farm which he had successfully defended from the encroachments of the rich, at the expense of his comfort, his health, and his life. When I succeeded to his lands, I determined to protect them in my time as studiously as he had defended them in his. I worked unintermittingly: I enlarged my house, I improved my fields, I increased my flocks. One after another I despised the threats and defeated the wiles of my noble neighbours, who desired possession of my estate to swell their own territorial grandeur. In process of time I married and had a child. I believed that I was picked out from my race as a fortunate man--when one night I was attacked by robbers: slaves made desperate by the cruelty of their wealthy masters. They ravaged my cornfields, they deprived me of my flocks. When I demanded redress, I was told to sell my lands to those who could defend them--to those rich nobles whose tyranny had organised the band of wretches who had spoiled me of my possessions, and to whose fraud-gotten treasures the government were well pleased to grant that protection which they had denied to my honest hoards. In my pride I determined that I would still be independent. I planted new crops. With the little remnant of my money I hired fresh servants and bought more flocks. I had just recovered from my first disaster when I became the victim of a second. I was again attacked. This time we had arms, and we attempted to defend ourselves. My wife was slain before my eyes; my house was burnt to the ground; I myself only escaped, mutilated with wounds; my child soon afterwards pined and died. I had no wife, no offspring, no house, no money. My fields still stretched round me, but I had none to cultivate them. My walls still tottered at my feet, but I had none to rear them again, none to inhabit them if they were reared. My father's lands were now become a wilderness to me. I was too proud to sell them to my rich neighbour; I preferred to leave them before I saw them the prey of a tyrant, whose rank had triumphed over my industry, and who is now able to boast that he can travel over ten leagues of senatorial property untainted by the propinquity of a husbandman's farm. Houseless, homeless, friendless, I have come to Rome alone in my affliction, helpless in my degradation! Do you wonder now that I am careless about the honour of my country? I would have served her with my life and my possessions when she was worthy of my service; but she has cast me off, and I care not who conquers her. I say to the Goths--with thousands who suffer the same tribulation that I now undergo--"Enter our gates! Level our palaces to the ground! Confound, if you will, in one common slaughter, we that are victims with those that are tyrants! Your invasion will bring new lords to the land. They cannot crush it more--they may oppress it less. Our posterity may gain their rights by the sacrifice of lives that our country has made worthless. Romans though we are, we are ready to suffer and submit!"'

He stopped; for by this time he had lashed himself into fury. His eyes glared, his cheeks flushed, his voice rose. Could he then have seen the faintest vision of the destiny that future ages had in store for the posterity of the race that now suffered throughout civilised Europe, like him--could he have imagined how, in after years, the 'middle class', despised in his day, was to rise to priv lege and power; to hold in its just hands the balance of the prosperity of nations; o crush oppression and regulate rule; to soar in its mighty flight above thrones and principalities, and rank and riches, apparently obedient, but really commanding;--could he but have foreboded this, what a light must have burst upon his gloom, what a hope must have soothed him in his despair!

To what further extremities his anger might have carried him, to what proceedings the indignant Gordian, who still listened from his concealment, might have had recourse, it is difficult to say; for the complaints of the ill-fated landholder and the cogitations of the authoritative bailiff were alike suddenly suspended by an uproar raging at this moment round a carriage which had just emerged from the palace we have elsewhere described.

This vehicle looked one mass of silver. Embroidered silk curtains fluttered all around it, gold ornaments studded its polished sides, and it held no less a person than the nobleman who had feasted the people with baskets of meat. This fact had become known to the rabble before the palace gates. Such an opportunity of showing their exultation in their bondage, their real servility in their imaginary independence, was not to be lost; and accordingly they let loose such a torrent of clamorous gratitude on their entertainer's appearance, that a stranger in Rome would have thought the city in revolt. They leapt, they ran, they danced round the prancing horses, they flung their empty baskets into the air, and patted approvingly their 'fair round bellies'. From every side, as the carriage moved on, they gained fresh recruits and acquired new importance. The timid fled before them, the noisy shouted with them, the bold plunged into their ranks; and the constant burden of their rejoicing chorus was--'Health to the noble Pomponius! Prosperity to the senators of Rome, who feast us with their food and give us the freedom of their theatres! Glory to Pomponius! Glory to the senators!'

Fate seemed on this day to take pleasure in pampering the insatiable curiosity of Gordian, the bailiff. The cries of the multitude had scarcely died away in the distance, as they followed the departing carriage, when the voices of two men, pitched to a low, confidential tone, reached his ear from the opposite side of the pillar. He peeped cautiously round, and saw that they were priests.

'What an eternal jester is that Pomponius!' said one voice. 'He is going to receive absolution, and he journeys in his chariot of state, as if he were preparing to celebrate his triumph, instead of to confess his sins!'

'Has he committed, then, a fresh imprudence?'

'Alas, yes! For a senator he is dreadfully wanting in caution! A few days since, in a fit of passion, he flung a drinking-cup at one of his female slaves. The girl died on the spot, and her brother, who is also in his service, threatened immediate vengeance. To prevent disagreeable consequences to his body, Pomponius has sent the fellow to his estates in Egypt; and now, from the same precaution for the welfare of his soul, he goes to demand absolution from our holy and beneficent Church.'

'I am afraid these incessant absolutions, granted to men who are too careless even to make a show of repentance for their crimes, will prejudice us with the people at large.'

'Of what consequence are the sentiments of the people while we have their rulers on our side! Absolution is the sorcery that binds these libertines of Rome to our will. We know what converted Constantine--politic flattery and ready absolution; the people will tell you it was the sign of the Cross.'

'It is true this Pomponius is rich, and may increase our revenues, but still I fear the indignation of the people.'

'Fear nothing: think how long their old institutions imposed on them, and then doubt, if you can, that we may shape them to our wishes as we will. Any deceptions will be successful with a mob, if the instrument employed to forward them be a religion.'

The voices ceased. Gordian, who still cherished a vague intention of denouncing the fugitive landholder to the senatorial authorities, employed the liberty afforded to his attention by the silence of the priests in turning to look after his intended victim. To his surprise he saw that the man had left the auditors to whom he had before addressed himself, and was engaged in earnest conversation in another part of the portico, with an individual who seemed to have recently joined him, and whose appearance was so remarkable that the bailiff had moved a few steps forwards to gain a nearer view of him, when he was once more arrested by the voices of the priests.

Irresolute for an instant to which party to devote his unscrupulous attention, he returned mechanically to his old position. Ere long, however, his anxiety to hear the mysterious communications proceeding between the landholder and his friend overbalanced his delight in penetrating the theological secrets of the priests. He turned once more, but to his astonishment the objects of his curiosity had disappeared. He stepped to the outside of the portico and looked for them in every direction, but they were nowhere to be seen. Peevish and disappointed, he returned as a last resource to the pillar where he had left the priests, but the time consumed in his investigations after one party had been fatal to his reunion with the other. The churchmen were gone.

Sufficiently punished for his curiosity by his disappointment, the bailiff walked doggedly off towards the Pincian Hill. Had he turned in the contrary direction, towards the Basilica of St. Peter, he would have found himself once more in the neighbourhood of the landholder and his remarkable friend, and would have gained that acquaintance with the subjects of their conversation, which we intend that the reader shall acquire in the course of the next chapter.

Chapter 4

THE CHURCH

In the year 324, on the locality assigned by rumour to the martyrdom of St. Peter, and over the ruins of the Circus of Nero, Constantine erected the church called the Basilica of St. Peter.

For twelve centuries, this building, raised by a man infamous for his murders and his tyrannies, stood uninjured amid the shocks which during that long period devastated the rest of the city. After that time it was removed, tottering to its base from its own reverend and illustrious age, by Pope Julius II, to make way for the foundations of the modern church.

It is towards this structure of twelve hundred years' duration, erected by hands stained with blood, and yet preserved as a star of peace in the midst of stormy centuries of war, that we would direct the reader's attention. What art has done for the modern church, time has effected for the ancient. If the one is majestic to the eye by its grandeur, the other is hallowed to the memory by its age.

As this church by its rise commemorated the triumphant establishment of Christianity as the religion of Rome, so in its progress it reflected every change wrought in the spirit of the new worship by the ambition, the prodigality, or the frivolity of the priests. At first it stood awful and imposing, beautiful in all its parts as the religion for whose glory it was built. Vast porphyry colonnades decorated its approaches, and surrounded a fountain whose waters issued from the representation of a gigantic pine-tree in bronze. Its double rows of aisles were each supported by forty-eight columns of precious marble. Its flat ceiling was adorned with beams of gilt metal, rescued from the pollution of heathen temples. Its walls were decorated with large paintings of religious subjects, and its tribunal was studded with elegant mosaics. Thus it rose, simple and yet sublime, awful and yet alluring; in this its beginning, a type of the dawn of the worship which it was elevated to represent. But when, flushed with success, the priests seized on Christianity as their path to politics and their introduction to power, the aspect of the church gradually began to change. As, slowly and insensibly, ambitious man heaped the garbage of his mysteries, his doctrines, and his disputes, about the pristine purity of the structure given him by God, so, one by one, gaudy adornments and meretricious alterations arose to sully the once majestic basilica, until the threatening and reproving apparition of the pagan Julian, when both Church and churchmen received in their corrupt progress a sudden and impressive check.

The short period of the revival of idolatry once passed over, the priests, unmoved by the warning they had received, returned with renewed vigour to confuse that which both in their Gospel and their Church had been once simple. Day by day they put forth fresh treatises, aroused fierce controversies, subsided into new sects; and day by day they altered more and more the once noble aspect of the ancient basilica. They hung their nauseous relics on its mighty walls, they stuck their tiny tapers about its glorious pillars, they wreathed their tawdry fringes around its massive altars. Here they polished, there they embroidered. Wherever there was a window, they curtained it with gaudy cloths; wherever there was a statue, they bedizened it with artificial flowers; wherever there was a solemn recess, they outraged its religious gloom with intruding light; until (arriving at the period we write of) they succeeded so completely in changing the aspect of the building, that it looked, within, more like a vast pagan toyshop than a Christian church. Here and there, it is true, a pillar or an altar rose unencumbered as of old, appearing as much at variance with the frippery that surrounded it as a text of Scripture quoted in a sermon of the time. But as regarded the general aspect of the basilica, the decent glories of its earlier days seemed irrevocably departed and destroyed.

After what has been said of the edifice, the reader will have little difficulty in imagining that the square in which it stood lost whatever elevation of character it might once have possessed, with even greater rapidity than the church itself. If the cathedral now looked like an immense toyshop, assuredly its attendant colonnades had the appearance of the booths of an enormous fair.

The day, whose decline we have hinted at in the preceding chapter, was fast verging towards its close, as the inhabitants of the streets on the western bank of the Tiber prepared to join the crowds that they beheld passing by their windows in the direction of the Basilica of St. Peter. The cause of this sudden confluence of the popular current in once common direction was made sufficiently apparent to all inquirers who happened to be near a church or a public building, by the appearance in such situations of a large sheet of vellum elaborately illuminated, raised on a high pole, and guarded from contact with the inquisitive rabble by two armed soldiers. The announcements set forth in these strange placards were all of the same nature and directed to the same end. In each of them the Bishop of Rome informed his 'pious and honourable brethren', the inhabitants of the city, that, as the next days was the anniversary of the Martyrdom of St. Luke, the vigil would necessarily be held on that evening in the Basilica of St. Peter; and that, in consideration of the importance of the occasion, there would be exhibited, before the commencement of the ceremony, those precious relics connected with the death of the saint, which had become the inestimable inheritance of the Church; and which consisted of a branch of the olive-tree to which St. Luke was hung, a piece of the noose--including the knot--which had been passed round his neck, and a picture of the Apotheosis of the Virgin painted by his own hand. After some sentences expressive of lamentation for the sufferings of the saint, which nobody read, and which it is unnecessary to reproduce here, the proclamation went on to state that a sermon would be preached in the course of the vigil, and that at a later hour the great chandelier, containing two thousand four hundred lamps, would be lit to illuminate the church. Finally, the worthy bishop called upon all members of his flock, in consideration of the solemnity of the day, to abstain from sensual pleasures, in order that they might the more piously and worthily contemplate the sacred objects submitted to their view, and digest the spiritual nourishment to be offered to their understandings.

From the specimen we have already given of the character of the populace of Rome, it will perhaps be unnecessary to say that the great attractions presented by this theological bill of fare were the relics and the chandelier. Pulpit eloquence and vigil solemnities alone must have long exhibited their more sober allurements, before they could have drawn into the streets a fiftieth part of the immense crowd that now hurried towards the desecrated basilica. Indeed, so vast was the assemblage soon congregated, that the advanced ranks of sightseers had already filled the church to overflowing, before those in the rear had come within view of the colonnades.

However dissatisfied the unsuccessful portion of the citizens might feel at their exclusion from the church, they found a powerful counter- attraction in the amusements going forward in the Place, the occupants of which seemed thoroughly regardless of the bishop's admonitions upon the sobriety of behaviour due to the solemnity of the day. As if in utter defiance of the decency and order recommended by the clergy, popular exhibitions of all sorts were set up on the broad flagstones of the great space before the church. Street dancing-girls exercised at every available spot those 'gliding gyrations' so eloquently condemned by the worthy Ammianus Marcellinus of orderly and historical memory. Booths crammed with relics of doubtful authenticity, baskets filled with neat manuscript abstracts of furiously controversial pamphlets, pagan images regenerated into portraits of saints, pictorial representations of Arians writhing in damnation, and martyrs basking in haloes of celestial light, tempted, in every direction, the more pious among the spectators. Cooks perambulated with their shops on their backs; rival slave-merchants shouted petitions for patronage; wine-sellers taught Bacchanalian philosophy from the tops of their casks; poets recited compositions for sale; sophisters held arguments destined to convert the wavering and perplex the ignorant.

Incessant motion and incessant noise seemed to be the sole compensations sought by the multitude for the disappointment of exclusion from the church. If a stranger, after reading the proclamation of the day, had proceeded to the basilica, to feast his eyes on the contemplation of the illustrious aggregate of humanity, entitled by the bishop 'his pious and honourable brethren,' he must, on mixing at this moment with the assemblage, have either doubted the truth of the episcopal appellation, or have given the citizens credit for that refinement of intrinsic worth which is of too elevated a nature to influence the character of the outward man.

At the time when the sun set, nothing could be more picturesque than the distant view of this joyous scene. The deep red rays of the departing luminary cast their radiance, partly from behind the church, over the vast multitude in the Place. Brightly and rapidly the rich light roved over the waters that leaped towards it from the fountain in all the loveliness of natural and evanescent form. Bathed in that brilliant glow, the smooth porphyry colonnades reflected, chameleon like, ethereal and varying hues; the white marble statues became suffused in a delicate rose-colour, and the sober-tinted trees gleamed in the innermost of their leafy depths as if steeped in the exhalations of a golden mist. While, contrasting strangely with the wondrous radiance around them, the huge bronze pine-tree in the middle of the Place, and the wide front of the basilica, rose up in gloomy shadow, indefinite and exaggerated, lowering like evil spirits over the joyous beauty of the rest of the scene, and casting their great depths of shade into the midst of the light whose dominion they despised. Beheld from a distance, this wild combination of vivid brightness and solemn gloom; these buildings, at one place darkened till they looked gigantic, at another lightened till they appeared ethereal; these crowded groups, seeming one great moving mass gleaming at this point in radiant light, obscured at that in thick shadow, made up a whole so incongruous and yet so beautiful, so grotesque and yet so sublime, that the scene looked, for the moment, more like some inhabited meteor, half eclipsed by its propinquity to earth, than a mortal and material prospect.

The beauties of this atmospheric effect were of far too serious and sublime a nature to interest the multitude in the Place. Out of the whole assemblage, but two men watched that glorious sunset with even an appearance of the admiration and attention which it deserved. One was the landholder whose wrongs were related in the preceding chapter--the other his remarkable friend.

These two men formed a singular contrast to each other, both in demeanour and appearance, as they gazed forth upon the crimson heaven. The landholder was an under-sized, restless-looking man, whose features, naturally sharp, were now distorted by a fixed expression of misery and discontent. His quick, penetrating glance wandered incessantly from place to place, perceiving all things, but resting on none. In his attention to the scene before him, he appeared to have been led more by the influence of example than by his own spontaneous feelings; for ever and anon he looked impatiently round upon his friend as if expecting him to speak--but no word or movement escaped his thoughtful companion. Occupied exclusively in his own contemplations, he appeared wholly insensible to any ordinary outward appeal.

In age and appearance this individual was in the decline of life; for he had numbered sixty years, his hair was completely grey, and his face was covered with deep wrinkles. Yet, in spite of these disadvantages, he was in the highest sense of the word a handsome man. Though worn and thin, his features were still bold and regular; and there was an elevation about the habitual mournfulness of his expression, and an intelligence about his somewhat severe and earnest eyes, that bore eloquent testimony to the superiority of his intellectual powers. As he now stood gazing fixedly out into the glowing sky, his tall, meagre figure half supported upon his staff, his lips firmly compressed, his brow slightly frowning, and his attitude firm and motionless, the most superficial observer must have felt immediately that he looked on no ordinary being. The history of a life of deep thought--perhaps of long sorrow--seemed written in every lineament of his meditative countenance; and there was a natural dignity in his manner, which evidently restrained his restless companion from offering any determined interruption to the course of his reflections.

Slowly and gorgeously the sun had continued to wane in the horizon until he was now lost to view. As his last rays sunk behind the distant hills, the stranger started from his reverie and approached the landholder, pointing with his staff towards the fast-fading brightness of the western sky.

'Probus,' said he, in a low, melancholy voice, 'as I looked on that sunset I thought on the condition of the Church.'

'I see little in the Church to think of, or in the sunset to observe,' replied his companion.

'How pure, how vivid,' murmured the other, scarcely heeding the landholder's remark,' was the light which that sun cast upon this earth at our feet! How nobly for a time its brightness triumphed over the shadows around; and yet, in spite of the promise of that radiance, how swiftly did it fade ere long in its conflict with the gloom--how thoroughly, even now, has it departed from the earth, and withdrawn the beauty of its glory from the heavens! Already the shadows are lengthening around us, and shrouding in their darkness every object in the Place. But a short hour hence, and--should no moon arise--the gloom of night will stretch unresisted over Rome!'

'To what purpose do you tell me this?'

'Are you not reminded, by what we have observed, of the course of the worship which it is our privilege to profess? Does not that first beautiful light denote its pure and perfect rise; that short conflict between the radiance and the gloom, its successful preservation, by the Apostles and the Fathers; that rapid fading of the radiance, its desecration in later times; and the gloom which now surrounds us, the destruction which has encompassed it in this age we live in?--a destruction which nothing can avert but a return to that pure first faith that should now be the hope of our religion, as the moon is the hope of night!'

'How should we reform? Do people who have no liberties care about a religion? Who is to teach them?'

'I have--I will. It is the purpose of my life to restore to them the holiness of the ancient Church; to rescue them from the snare of traitors to the faith, whom men call priests. They shall learn through me that the Church knew no adornment once, but the presence of the pure; that the priest craved no finer vestment than his holiness; that the Gospel, which once taught humility and now raises dispute,

was in former days the rule of faith--sufficient for all wants, powerful over all difficulties. Through me they shall know that in times past it was the guardian of
the heart; through me they shall see that in times present it is the plaything of the
proud; through me they shall fear that in times future it may become the exile of
the Church! To this task I have vowed myself; to overthrow this idolatry--which,
like another paganism, rises among us with its images, its relics, its jewels, and its
gold--I will devote my child, my life, my energies, and my possessions. From this
attempt I will never turn aside--from this determination I will never flinch.
While I have a breath of life in me, I will persevere in restoring to this abandoned
city the true worship of the Most High!'

He ceased abruptly. The intensity of his agitation seemed suddenly to deny to
him the faculty of speech. Every muscle in the frame of that stern, melancholy
man quivered at the immortal promptings of the soul within him. There was
something almost feminine in his universal susceptibility to the influence of one
solitary emotion. Even the rough, desperate landholder felt awed by the enthusiasm of the being before him, and forgot his wrongs, terrible as they were--and his
misery, poignant as it was--as he gazed upon his companion's face.

For some minutes neither of the men said more. Soon, however, the last speaker
calmed his agitation with the facility of a man accustomed to stifle the emotions
that he cannot crush, and advancing to the landholder, took him sorrowfully by
the hand.

'I see, Probus, that I have amazed you,' said he; 'but the Church is the only subject on which I have no discretion. In all other matters I have conquered the rash-
ness of my early manhood; in this I have to wrestle with my hastier nature still.
When I look on the mockeries that are acting around us; when I behold a priesthood deceivers, a people deluded, a religion defiled, then, I confess it, my indignation overpowers my patience, and I burn to destroy, where I ought only to hope
to reform.'

'I knew you always violent of imagination; but when I last saw you your enthusiasm was love. Your wife--'

'Peace! She deceived me!'

'Your child--'

'Lives with me at Rome.'

'I remember her an infant, when, fourteen years since, I was your neighbour in Gaul. On my departure from the province, you had just returned from a journey into Italy, unsuccessful in your attempts to discover there a trace either of your parents, or of that elder brother whose absence you were wont so continually to lament. Tell me, have you, since that period, discovered the members of your ancient household? Hitherto you have been so occupied in listening to the history of my wrongs that you have scarcely spoken of the changes in your life since we last met.'

'If, Probus, I have been silent to you concerning myself, it is because for me retrospection has little that attracts. While yet it was in my power to return to those parents whom I deserted in my boyhood, I thought not of repentance; and now that they must be but too surely lost to me, my yearning towards them is of no avail. Of my brother, from whom I parted in a moment of childish jealousy and anger, and whose pardon and love I would give up even my ambition to acquire, I have never yet discovered a trace. Atonement to those whom I injured in early life is a privilege denied to the prayers of my age. From my parents and my brother I departed unblest, and unforgiven by them I feel that I am doomed to die! My life has been careless, useless, godless, passing from rapine and violence to luxury and indolence, and leading me to the marriage which I exulted in when I last saw you, but which I now feel was unworthy alike in its motives and its results. But blessed and thrice blessed by that last calamity of my wicked existence, for it opened my eyes to the truth--it made a Christian of me while I was yet alive!'

'Is it thus that the Christian can view his afflictions? I would, then, that I were a Christian like you!' murmured the landholder, in low, earnest tones.

'It was in those first days, Probus,' continued the other, 'when I found myself deserted and dishonoured, left alone to be the guardian of my helpless child, exiled for ever from a home that I had myself forsaken, that I repented me in earnest of my misdeeds, that I sought wisdom from the book of salvation, and the conduct of life from the Fathers of the Church. It was at that time that I determined to devote my child, like Samuel of old, to the service of heaven, and myself to the reformation of our degraded worship. As I have already told you, I forsook my abode and changed my name (remember it is as 'Numerian' that you must henceforth address me), that of my former self no remains might be left, that of my former companions not one might ever discover and tempt me again. With incessant care have I shielded my daughter from the contamination of the world. As a precious jewel in a miser's hands she has been watched and guarded in her father's house. Her destiny is to soothe the afflicted, to watch the sick, to succour the forlorn, when I, her teacher, have restored to the land the dominion of its ancient faith and the guidance of its faultless Gospel. We have neither of us an affection or a hope that can bind us to the things of earth. Our hearts look both towards heaven; our expectations are only from on high!'

'Do not set your hopes too firmly on your child. Remember how the nobles of Rome have destroyed the household I once had, and tremble for your own.'

'I have no fear for my daughter; she is cared for in my absence by one who is vowed to aid me in my labours for the Church. It is now nearly a year since I first met Ulpius, and from that time forth he has devoted himself to my service and watched over my child.'

'Who is this Ulpius, that you should put such faith in him?'

'He is a man of age like mine. I found him, like me, worn down by the calamities of his early life, and abandoned, as I had once been, to the delusions of the pagan gods. He was desolate, suffering, forlorn, and I had pity on him in his misery. I proved to him that the worship he still professed was banished for its iniquities from the land; that the religion which had succeeded it had become defiled by man, and that there remained but one faith for him to choose, if he would be saved--the faith of the early Church. He heard me and was converted. From that moment he has served my patiently and helped me willingly. Under the roof where I assemble the few who as yet are true believers, he is always the first to come and the last to remain. No word of anger has ever crossed his lips--no look of impatience has ever appeared in his eyes. Though sorrowful, he is gentle; though suffering, he is industrious. I have trusted him with all I possess, and I glory in my credulity! Ulpius is incorruptible!'

'And your daughter?--is Ulpius reverenced by her as he is respected by you?'

'She knows that her duty is to love whom I love, and to avoid whom I avoid. Can you imagine that a Christian virgin has any feelings disobedient to her father's wishes? Come to my house; judge with your own eyes of my daughter and my companion. You, whose misfortunes have left you no home, shall find one, if you will, with me. Come then and labour with me in my great undertaking! You will withdraw your mind from the contemplation of your woes, and merit by your devotion the favour of the Most High.'

'No, Numerian, I will still be independent, even of my friends! Nor Rome nor Italy are abiding-places for me. I go to another land to abide among another people, until the arms of a conqueror shall have restored freedom to the brave and protection to the honest throughout the countries of the Empire.'

'Probus, I implore you stay!'

'Never! My determination is taken, Numerian--farewell!'

For a few minutes Numerian stood motionless, gazing wistfully in the direction taken by his companion on his departure. At first an expression of grief and pity softened the austerity which seemed the habitual characteristic of his countenance when in repose, but soon these milder and tenderer feelings appeared to vanish from his heart as suddenly as they had arisen; his features reassumed their customary sternness, and he muttered to himself as he mixed with the crowd struggling onwards in the direction of the basilica: 'Let him depart unregretted; he has denied himself to the service of his Maker. He should no longer be my friend.'

In this sentence lay the index to the character of the man. His existence was one vast sacrifice, one scene of intrepid self-immolation. Although, in the brief hints at the events of his life which he had communicated to his friend, he had exaggerated the extent of his errors, he had by no means done justice to the fervour of his penitence--a penitence which outstripped the usual boundaries of repentance, and only began in despair to terminate in fanaticism. His desertion of his father's house (into the motives of which it is not our present intention to enter), and his long subsequent existence of violence and excess, indisposed his naturally strong passions to submit to the slightest restraint. In obedience to their first impulses, he contracted, at a mature age, a marriage with a woman thoroughly unworthy of the ardent admiration that she had inspired. When he found himself deceived and dishonoured by her, the shock of such an affliction thrilled through his whole being--crushed all his energies--struck him prostrate, heart and mind, at one blow. The errors of his youth, committed in his prosperity with moral impunity, reacted upon him in his adversity with an influence fatal to his future peace. His repentance was darkened by despondency; his resolutions were unbrightened by hope. He flew to religion as the suicide flies to the knife--in despair.

Leaving all remaining peculiarities in Numerian's character to be discussed at a future opportunity, we will now follow him in his passage through the crowd, to the entrance of the basilica--continuing to designate him, here and elsewhere, by the name which he had assumed on his conversion, and by which he had insisted on being addressed during his interview with the fugitive landholder.

Although at the commencement of his progress towards the church, our enthusiast found himself placed among the hindermost of the members of the advancing throng, he soon contrived so thoroughly to outstrip his dilatory and discursive neighbours as to gain, with little delay, the steps of the sacred building. Here, in common with many others, he was compelled to stop, while those nearest the basilica squeezed their way through its stately doors. In such a situation his remarkable figure could not fail to be noticed, and he was silently recognised by many of the bystanders, some of whom looked on him with wonder, and some with aversion. Nobody, however, approached or spoke to him. Every one felt the necessity of shunning a man whose bold and daily exposures of the abuses of the Church placed in incessant peril his liberty, and even his life.

Among the bystanders who surrounded Numerian, there were nevertheless two who did not remain content with carelessly avoiding any communication with the intrepid and suspected reformer. These two men belonged to the lowest order of the clergy, and appeared to be occupied in cautiously watching the actions and listening to the conversation of the individuals immediately around them. The instant they beheld Numerian they moved so as to elude his observation, taking care at the same time to occupy such a position as enabled them to keep in view the object of their evident distrust. 'Look, Osius,' said one, 'that man is here again!'

'And doubtless with the same motives which brought him here yesterday,' replied the other. 'You will see that he will again enter the church, listen to the service, retire to his little chapel near the Pincian Mount, and there, before his ragged mob of adherents, attack the doctrines which our brethren have preached, as we know he did last night, and as we suspect he will continue to do until the authorities think proper to give the signal for his imprisonment.'

'I marvel that he should have been permitted to persist so long a time as he has in his course of contumacy towards the Church. Have we not evidence enough in his writings alone to convict him of heresy? The carelessness of the bishop upon such a matter as this is quite inexplicable!'

'You should consider, Numerian not being a priest, that the carelessness about our interests lies more with the senate than the bishop. What time our nobles can spare from their debaucheries has been lately given to discussions on the conduct of the Emperor in retiring to Ravenna, and will now be dedicated to penetrating the basis of this rumour about the Goths. Besides, even were they at liberty, what care the senate about theological disputes? They only know this Numerian as a citizen of Rome, a man of some influence and possessions, and, consequently, a person of political importance as a member of the population. In addition to which, it would be no easy task for us at the present moment to impugn the doctrines broached by our assailant; for the fellow has a troublesome facility of supporting what he says by the Bible. Believe me, in this matter, our only way of righting ourselves will be to convict him of scandal against the highest dignitaries of the Church.'

'The order that we have lately received to track his movements and listen to his discourses, leads me to believe that our superiors are of your opinion.'

'Whether my convictions are correct or not, of this I feel assured--that his days of liberty are numbered. It was but a few hours ago that I saw the bishop's chamberlain's head-assistant, and he told me that he had heard, through the crevice of a door--'

'Hush! he moves; he is pressing forward to enter the church. You can tell me what you were about to say as we follow him. Quick! let us mix with the crowd.'

Ever enthusiastic in the performance of their loathsome duties, these two discreet pastors of a Christian flock followed Numerian with the most elaborate caution into the interior of the sacred building.

Although the sun still left a faint streak of red in the western sky, and the moon had as yet scarcely risen, the great chandelier of two thousand four hundred lamps, mentioned by the bishop in his address to the people, was already alight. In the days of its severe and sacred beauty, the appearance of the church would have suffered fatally by this blaze of artificial brilliancy; but now that the ancient character of the basilica was completely changed, now that from a solemn temple it had been altered to the semblance of a luxurious palace, it gained immensely by its gaudy illumination. Not an ornament along the vast extent of its glorious nave but glittered in vivid distinctness in the dazzling light that poured downwards from the roof. The gilded rafters, the smooth inlaid marble pillars, the rich hangings of the windows, the jewelled candlesticks on the altars, the pictures, the statues, the bronzes, the mosaics, each and all glowed with a steady and luxurious transparency absolutely intoxicating to the eye. Not a trace of wear, not a vestige of tarnish now appeared on any object. Each portion of the nave to which the attention was directed appeared too finely, spotlessly radiant, ever to have been touched by mortal hands. Entranced and bewildered, the observation roamed over the surface of the brilliant scene, until, wearied by the unbroken embellishment of the prospect, it wandered for repose upon the dimly lighted aisles, and dwelt with delight upon the soft shadows that hovered about their distant pillars, and the gliding forms that peopled their dusky recesses, or loitered past their lofty walls.

At the moment when Numerian entered the basilica, a part of the service had just concluded. The last faint echo from the voices of the choir still hung upon the incense-laden air, and the vast masses of the spectators were still grouped in their listening and various attitudes, as the devoted reformer looked forth upon the church. Even he, stern as he was, seemed for a moment subdued by the ineffable enchantment of the scene; but ere long, as if displeased with his own involuntary emotions of admiration, his brow contracted, and he sighed heavily, as (still followed by the attentive spies) he sought the comparative seclusion of the aisles.

During the interval between the divisions of the service, the congregation occupied themselves in staring at the relics, which were enclosed in a silver cabinet with crystal doors, and placed on the top of the high altar. Although it was impossible to obtain a satisfactory view of these ecclesiastical treasures, they nevertheless employed the attention of every one until the appearance of a priest in the pulpit gave signal of the commencement of the sermon, and admonished all those who had seats to secure them without delay.

Passing through the ranks of the auditors of the sermon--some of whom were engaged in counting the lights in the chandelier, to be certain that the bishop had not defrauded them of one out of the two thousand four hundred lamps; others in holding whispered conversations, and opening small boxes of sweetmeats--we again conduct the reader to the outside of the church.

The assemblage here had by this time much diminished; the shadows flung over the ground by the lofty colonnades had deepened and increased; and in many of the more remote recesses of the Place hardly a human being was to be observed. At one of these extremities, where the pillars terminated in the street and the obscurity was most intense, stood a solitary old man keeping himself cautiously concealed in the darkness, and looking out anxiously upon the public way immediately before him.

He had waited but a short time when a handsome chariot, preceded by a bodyguard of gaily-attired slaves, stopped within a few paces of his lurking-place, and the voice of the person it contained pronounced audibly the following words:--

'No! no! Drive on--we are later than I thought. If I stay to see this illumination of the basilica, I shall not be in time to receive my guests for to-night's banquet. Besides, this inestimable kitten of the breed most worshipped by the ancient Egyptians has already taken cold, and I would not for the world expose the susceptible animal any longer than is necessary to the dampness of the night-air. Drive on, good Carrio, drive on!'

The old man scarcely waited for the conclusion of this speech before he ran up to the chariot, where he was immediately confronted by two heads--one that of

Vetranio the senator, the other that of a glossy black kitten adorned with a collar of rubies, and half enveloped in its master's ample robes. Before the astonished noble could articulate a word, the man whispered in hoarse, hurried accents, 'I am Ulpius--dismiss your servants--I have something important to say!'

'Ha! my worthy Ulpius! You have a most unhappy faculty of delivering a message with the manner of an assassin! But I must pardon your unpleasant abruptness in consideration of your diligence. My excellent Carrio, If you value my approbation, remove your companions and yourself out of hearing!'

The freedman yielded instant obedience to his master's mandate. The following conversation then took place, the strange man opening it thus:--

'You remember your promise?'

'I do.'

'Upon your honour, as a nobleman and a senator, you are prepared to abide by it whenever it is necessary?'

'I am.'

'Then at the dawn of morning meet me at the private gate of your palace garden, and I will conduct you to Antonina's bedchamber.'

'The time will suit me. But why at the dawn of morning?'

'Because the Christian dotard will keep a vigil until midnight, which the girl will most probably attend. I wished to tell you this at your palace, but I heard there that you had gone to Aricia, and would return by way of the basilica; so I posted myself to intercept you thus.'

'Industrious Ulpius!'

'Remember your promise!'

Vetranio leaned forward to reply, but Ulpius was gone.

As the senator again commanded his equipage to move on, he looked anxiously around him, as if once more expecting to see his strange adherent still lurking near the chariot. He only perceived, however, a man whom he did not know, followed by two other, walking rapidly past him. They were Numerian and the spies.

'At last, my projects are approaching consummation,' exclaimed Vetranio to himself, as he and his kitten rolled off in the chariot. 'It is well that I thought of securing possession of Julia's villa to-day, for I shall now, assuredly, want to use it to-morrow. Jupiter! What a mass of dangers, contradictions, and mysteries encompass this affair! When I think that I, who pride myself on my philosophy, have quitted Ravenna, borrowed a private villa, leagued myself with an uncultivated plebeian, and all for the sake of a girl who has already deceived my expectations by gaining me as a music-master without admitting me as a lover, I am positively astonished at my own weakness! Still it must be owned that the complexion my adventure has lately assumed renders it of some interest in itself. The mere pleasure of penetrating the secrets of this Numerian's household is by no means the least among the numerous attraction of my design. How has he gained his influence over the girl? Why does he keep her in such strict seclusion? Who is this old half- frantic, unceremonious man-monster calling himself Ulpius; refusing all reward for his villainy; raving about a return to the old religion of the gods; and exulting in the promise he has extorted from me, as a good pagan, to support the first restoration of the ancient worship that may be attempted in Rome? Where does he come from? Why does he outwardly profess himself a Christian? What sent him into Numerian's service? By the girdle of Venus! everything connected with the girl is as incomprehensible as herself! But patience--patience! A few hours more, and these mysteries will be revealed. In the meantime, let me think of my banquet, and of its presiding deity, the Nightingale Sauce!'

Chapter 5

ANTONINA

Who that has been at Rome does not remember with delight the attractions of the Pincian Hill? Who, after toiling through the wonders of the dark, melancholy city, has not been revived by a visit to its shady walks, and by breathing its fragrant breezes? Amid the solemn mournfulness that reigns over declining Rome, this delightful elevation rises light, airy, and inviting, at once a refreshment to the body and a solace to the spirit. From its smooth summit the city is seen in its utmost majesty, and the surrounding country in its brightest aspect. The crimes and miseries of Rome seem deterred from approaching its favoured soil; it impresses the mind as a place set apart by common consent for the presence of the innocent and the joyful--as a scene that rest and recreation keep sacred from the intrusion of tumult and toil.

Its appearance in modern days is the picture of its character for ages past. Successive wars might dull its beauties for a time, but peace invariably restored them in all their pristine loveliness. The old Romans called it 'The Mount of Gardens'. Throughout the disasters of the Empire and the convulsions of the Middle Ages, it continued to merit its ancient appellation, and a 'Mount of Gardens' it still triumphantly remains to the present day.

At the commencement of the fifth century the magnificence of the Pincian Hill was at its zenith. Were it consistent with the conduct of our story to dwell upon the glories of its palaces and its groves, its temples and its theatres, such a glowing prospect of artificial splendour, aided by natural beauty, might be spread before the reader as would tax his credulity, while it excited his astonishment. This task, however, it is here unnecessary to attempt. It is not for the wonders of ancient luxury and taste, but for the abode of the zealous and religious Numerian, that we find it now requisite to arouse interest and engage attention.

At the back of the Flaminian extremity of the Pincian Hill, and immediately over-looking the city wall, stood, at the period of which we write, a small but elegant-ly built house, surrounded by a little garden of its own, and protected at the back by the lofty groves and outbuildings of the palace of Vetranio the senator. This abode had been at one time a sort of summer-house belonging to the former pro-prietor of a neighbouring mansion.

Profligate necessities, however, had obliged the owner to part with this portion of his possessions, which was purchased by a merchant well known to Numerian, who received it as a legacy at his friend's death. Disgusted, as soon as his reform-ing projects took possession of his mind, at the bare idea of propinquity to the ennobled libertines of Rome, the austere Christian determined to abandon his inheritance, and to sell it to another; but, at the repeated entreaties of his daugh-ter, he at length consented to change his purpose, and sacrifice his antipathy to his luxurious neighbours to his child's youthful attachment to the beauties of Nature as displayed in his legacy on the Pincian Mount. In this instance only did the natural affection of the father prevail over the acquired severity of the reformer. Here he condescended, for the first and the last time, to the sweet triv-ialities of youth. Here, indulgent in spite of himself, he fixed his little household, and permitted to his daughter her sole recreations of tending the flowers in the garden and luxuriating in the loveliness of the distant view.

******

The night has advanced an hour since the occurrence mentioned in the preced-ing chapter. The clear and brilliant moonlight of Italy now pervades every district of the glorious city, and bathes in its pure effulgence the groves and palaces on the Pincian Mount. From the garden of Numerian the irregular buildings of the great suburbs of Rome, the rich undulating country beyond, and the long ranges of mountains in the distance, are now all visible in the soft and luxurious light. Near the spot which commands this view, not a living creature is to be seen on a first examination; but on a more industrious and patient observation, you are subse-quently able to detect at one of the windows of Numerian's house, half hidden by a curtain, the figure of a young girl.

Soon this solitary form approaches nearer to the eye. The moonbeams, that have
hitherto shone only upon the window, now illuminate other objects. First they
display a small, white arm; then a light, simple robe; then a fair, graceful neck;
and finally a bright, youthful, innocent face, directed steadfastly towards the wide
moon-brightened prospect of the distant mountains.

For some time the girl remains in contemplation at her window. Then she leaves
her post, and almost immediately reappears at a door leading into the garden.
Her figure, as she advances towards the lawn before her, is light and small--a natural grace and propriety appear in her movements--she holds pressed to her
bosom and half concealed by her robe, a gilt lute. When she reaches a turf bank
commanding the same view as the window, she arranges her instrument upon her
knees, and with something of restraint in her manner gently touches the chords.
Then, as if alarmed at the sound she has produced, she glances anxiously around
her, apparently fearful of being overheard. Her large, dark, lustrous eyes have in
them an expression of apprehension; her delicate lips are half parted; a sudden
flush rises in her soft, olive complexion as she examines every corner of the garden. Having completed her survey without discovering any cause for the suspicions she seems to entertain, she again employs herself over her instrument. Once
more she strikes the chords, and now with a bolder hand. The notes she produces
resolve themselves into a wild, plaintive, irregular melody, alternately rising and
sinking, as if swayed by the fickle influence of a summer wind. These sounds are
soon harmoniously augmented by the young minstrel's voice, which is calm, still,
and mellow, and adapts itself with exquisite ingenuity to every arbitrary variation
in the tone of the accompaniment. The song that she has chosen is one of the
fanciful odes of the day. Its chief merit to her lies in its alliance to the strange
Eastern air which she heard at her first interview with the senator who presented
her with the lute. Paraphrased in English, the words of the composition would
run thus:--

THE ORIGIN OF MUSIC

I. Spirit, whose dominion reigns Over Music's thrilling strains, Whence may
be thy distant birth? Say what tempted thee to earth?

Mortal, listen: I was born In Creation's early years, Singing, 'mid the stars of
morn, 'To the music of the spheres.

Once as, within the realms of space, I view'd this mortal planet roll, A yearning towards they hapless race, Unbidden, filled my seraph soul!

Angels, who had watched my birth, Heard me sigh to sing to earth; 'Twas transgression ne'er forgiv'n To forget my native heav'n; So they sternly bade me go--Banish'd to the world below.

II. Exil'd here, I knew no fears; For, though darkness round me clung, Though none heard me in the spheres, Earth had listeners while I sung.

Young spirits of the Spring sweet breeze Came thronging round me, soft and coy, Light wood-nymphs sported in the trees, And laughing Echo leapt for joy!

Brooding Woe and writhing Pain Soften'd at my gentle strain; Bounding Joy, with footstep fleet, Ran to nestle at my feet; While, arous'd, delighted Love Softly kiss'd me from above!

III. Since those years of early time, Faithful still to earth I've sung; Flying through each distant clime, Ever welcome, ever young!

Still pleas'd, my solace I impart Where brightest hopes are scattered dead; 'Tis mine--sweet gift!--to charm the heart, Though all its other joys have fled!

Time, that withers all beside, Harmless past me loves to glide; Change, that mortals must obey, Ne'er shall shake my gentle sway; Still 'tis mine all hearts to move In eternity of love.

As the last sounds of her voice and her lute died softly away upon the still night air, an indescribable elevation appeared in the girl's countenance. She looked up rapturously into the far, star-bright sky; her lip quivered, her dark eyes filled with tears, and her bosom heaved with the excess of the emotions that the music and the scene inspired. Then she gazed slowly around her, dwelling tenderly upon the fragrant flower-beds that were the work of her own hands, and looking forth with an expression half reverential, half ecstatic over the long, smooth, shining plains, and the still, glorious mountains, that had so long been the inspiration of her most cherished thoughts, and that now glowed before her eyes, soft and beautiful as her dreams on her virgin couch. Then, overpowered by the artless thoughts and innocent recollections which on the magic wings of Nature and Night came wafted over her mind, she bent down her head upon her lute, pressed her round, dimpled cheek against its smooth frame, and drawing her fingers mechanically over its strings, abandoned herself unreservedly to the reveries of maidenhood and youth.

Such was the being devoted by her father's fatal ambition to a lifelong banishment from all that is attractive in human art and beautiful in human intellect! Such was the daughter whose existence was to be one long acquaintance with mortal woe, one unvaried refusal of mortal pleasure, whose thoughts were to be only of sermons and fasts, whose action were to be confined to the binding up of strangers' wounds and the drying of strangers' tears; whose life, in brief, was doomed to be the embodiment of her father's austere ideal of the austere virgins of the ancient Church!

Deprived of her mother, exiled from the companionship of others of her age, permitted no familiarity with any living being, no sympathies with any other heart, commanded but never indulged, rebuked but never applauded, she must have sunk beneath the severities imposed on her by her father, but for the venial disobedience committed in the pursuit of the solitary pleasure procured for her by her lute. Vainly, in her hours of study, did she read the fierce anathemas against love, liberty, and pleasure, poetry, painting, and music, gold, silver, and precious stones, which the ancient fathers had composed for the benefit of the submissive congregations of former days; vainly did she imagine, during those long hours of theological instruction, that her heart's forbidden longings were banished and destroyed--that her patient and childlike disposition was bowed in complete subserviency to the most rigorous of her father's commands. No sooner were her interviews with Numerian concluded than the promptings of that nature within us, which artifice may warp but can never destroy, lured her into a forgetfulness of all that she had heard and a longing for much that was forbidden. We live, in this existence, but by the companionship of some sympathy, aspiration, or pursuit, which serves us as our habitual refuge from the tribulations we inherit from the outer world. The same feeling which led Antonina in her childhood to beg for a flower-garden, in her girlhood induced her to gain possession of a lute.

The passion for music which prompted her visit to Vetranio, which alone saved her affections from pining in the solitude imposed on them, and which occupied her leisure hours in the manner we have already described, was an inheritance of her birth.

Her Spanish mother had sung to her, hour after hour, in her cradle, for the short time during which she was permitted to watch over her child. The impression thus made on the dawning faculties of the infant, nothing ever effaced. Though her earliest perception were greeted only by the sight of her father's misery; though the form which his despairing penitence soon assumed doomed her to a life of seclusion and an education of admonition, the passionate attachment to the melody of sound, inspired by her mother's voice--almost imbibed at her mother's

breast--lived through all neglect, and survived all opposition. It found its nourishment in childish recollections, in snatches of street minstrelsy heard through
her window, in the passage of the night winds of winter through the groves on the
Pincian Mount, and received its rapturous gratification in the first audible sounds
from the Roman senator's lute. How her possession of an instrument, and her
skill in playing, were subsequently gained, the reader already knows from
Vetranio's narrative at Ravenna. Could the frivolous senator have discovered the
real intensity of the emotions his art was raising in his pupil's bosom while he
taught her; could he have imagined how incessantly, during their lessons, her
sense of duty struggled with her love for music--how completely she was
absorbed, one moment by an agony of doubt and fear, another by an ecstasy of
enjoyment and hope--he would have felt little of that astonishment at her coldness towards himself which he so warmly expressed at his interview with Julia in
the gardens of the Court. In truth, nothing could be more complete than
Antonina's childish unconsciousness of the feelings with which Vetranio regarded her. In entering his presence, whatever remnant of her affections remained
unwithered by her fears was solely attracted and engrossed by the beloved and
beautiful lute. In receiving the instrument, she almost forgot the giver in the triumph of possession; or, if she thought of him at all, it was to be grateful for having escaped uninjured from a member of that class, for whom her father's reiterated admonitions had inspired her with a vague feeling of dread and distrust, and
to determine that, now she had acknowledged his kindness and departed from his
domains, nothing should ever induce her to risk discovery by her father and peril
to herself by ever entering them again.

Innocent in her isolation, almost infantine in her natural simplicity, a single
enjoyment was sufficient to satisfy all the passions of her age. Father, mother,
lover, and companion; liberties, amusements, and adornments--they were all
summed up for her in that simple lute. The archness, the liveliness, and the gentleness of her disposition; the poetry of her nature, and the affection of her heart;
the happy bloom of youth, which seclusion could not all wither nor distorted precept taint, were now entirely nourished, expanded, and freshened--such is the creative power of human emotion--by that inestimable possession. She could speak
to it, smile on it, caress it, and believe, in the ecstasy of her delight, in the carelessness of her self-delusion, that it sympathised with her joy. During her long
solitudes, when she was silently watched in her father's absence by the brooding,
melancholy stranger whom he had set over her, it became a companion dearer
than the flower-garden, dearer even that the plains and mountains which formed
her favourite view. When her father returned, and she was led forth to sit in a
dark place among strange, silent people, and to listen to interminable declama-
tions, it was a solace to think of the instrument as it lay hidden securely in her

chamber, and to ponder delightedly on what new music of her own she could play upon it next. And then, when evening arrived, and she was left alone in her garden--then came the hour of moonlight and song; the moment of rapture and melody that drew her out of herself, elevated her she felt not how, and transported her she knew not whither.

But, while we thus linger over reflection on motives and examinations into character, we are called back to the outer world of passing interests and events by the appearances of another figure on the scene. We left Antonina in the garden thinking over her lute. She still remains in her meditative position, but she is now no longer alone.

From the same steps by which she had descended, a man now advances into the garden, and walks towards the place she occupies. His gait is limping, his stature crooked, his proportions distorted. His large, angular features stand out in gaunt contrast to his shrivelled cheeks. His dry, matted hair has been burnt by the sun into a strange tawny brown. His expression is one of fixed, stern, mournful thought. As he steps stealthily along, advancing towards Antonina, he mutters to himself, and clutches mechanically at his garments with his lank, shapeless fingers. The radiant moonlight, falling fully upon his countenance, invests it with a livid, mysterious, spectral appearance: seen by a stranger at the present moment, he would have been almost awful to look upon.

This was the man who had intercepted Vetranio on his journey home, and who had now hurried back so as to regain his accustomed post before his master's return, for he was the same individual mentioned by Numerian as his aged convert, Ulpius, in his interview with the landholder at the Basilica of St. Peter.

When Ulpius had arrived within a few paces of the girl he stopped, saying in a hoarse, thick voice--

'Hide your toy--Numerian is at the gates!'

Antonina started violently as she listened to those repulsive accents. The blood rushed into her cheeks; she hastily covered the lute with her robe; paused an instant, as if intending to speak to the man, then shuddered violently, and hurried towards the house.

As she mounted the steps Numerian met her in the hall. There was now no chance of hiding the lute in its accustomed place.

'You stay too late in the garden,' said the father, looking proudly, in spite of all his austerity, upon his beautiful daughter as she stood by his side. 'But what affects you?' he added, noticing her confusion. 'You tremble; your colour comes and goes; your lips quiver. Give me your hand!'

As Antonina obeyed him, a fold of the treacherous robe slipped aside, and discovered a part of the frame of the lute. Numerian's quick eye discovered it immediately. He snatched the instrument from her feeble grasp. His astonishment on beholding it was too great for words, and for an instant he confronted the poor girl, whose pale face looked rigid with terror, in ominous and expressive silence.

'This thing,' said he at length, 'this invention of libertines in my house--in my daughter's possession!' and he dashed the lute into fragments on the floor.

For one moment Antonina looked incredulously on the ruins of the beloved companion, which was the centre of all her happiest expectations for future days. Then, as she began to estimate the reality of her deprivation, her eyes lost all their heaven-born brightness, and filled to overflowing with the tears of earth.

'To your chamber!' thundered Numerian, as she knelt, sobbing convulsively, over those hapless fragments. 'To your chamber! Tomorrow shall bring this mystery of iniquity to light!'

She rose humbly to obey him, for indignation had no part in the emotions that shook her gentle and affectionate nature. As she moved towards the room that no lute was henceforth to occupy, as she thought on the morrow that no lute was henceforth to enliven, her grief almost overpowered her. She turned back and looked imploringly at her father, as if entreating permission to pick up even the smallest of the fragments at his feet.

'To your chamber!' he reiterated sternly. 'Am I to be disobeyed to my face?'

Without any repetition of her silent remonstrance, she instantly retired. As soon as she was out of sight, Ulpius ascended the steps and stood before the angered father.

'Look, Ulpius,' cried Numerian, 'my daughter, whom I have so carefully cherished, whom I intended for an example to the world, has deceived me, even thus!'

He pointed, as he spoke, to the ruins of the unfortunate lute; but Ulpius did not address to him a word in reply, and he hastily continued:--

'I will not sully the solemn offices of tonight by interrupting them with my worldly affairs. To-morrow I will interrogate my disobedient child. In the meantime, do not imagine, Ulpius, that I connect you in any way with this wicked and unworthy deception! In you I have every confidence, in your faithfulness I have every hope.'

Again he paused, and again Ulpius kept silence. Any one less agitated, less confiding, than his unsuspicious master, would have remarked that a faint sinister smile was breaking forth upon his haggard countenance. But Numerian's indignation was still too violent to permit him to observed, and, spite of his efforts to control himself, he again broke forth in complaint.

'On this night too, of all others,' cried he, 'when I had hoped to lead her among my little assembly of the faithful, to join in their prayers, and to listen to my exhortations--on this night I am doomed to find her a player on a pagan lute, a possessor of the most wanton of the world's vanities! God give me patience to worship this night with unwandering thoughts, for my heart is vexed at the transgression of my child, as the heart of Eli of old at the iniquities of his sons!'

He was moving rapidly away, when, as if struck with a sudden recollection, he stopped abruptly, and again addressed his gloomy companion.

'I will go by myself to the chapel to-night,' said he. 'You, Ulpius, will stay to keep watch over my disobedient child. Be vigilant, good friend, over my house; for even now, on my return, I thought that two strangers were following my steps, and I forebode some evil in store for me as the chastisement for my sins, even greater than this misery of my daughter's transgression. Be watchful, good Ulpius--be watchful!'

And, as he hurried away, the stern, serious man felt as overwhelmed at the outrage that had been offered to his gloomy fanaticism, as the weak, timid girl at the destruction that had been wreaked upon her harmless lute.

After Numerian had departed, the sinister smile again appeared on the countenance of Ulpius. He stood for a short time fixed in thought, and then began slowly to descend a staircase near him which led to some subterranean apartments. He had not gone far when a slight noise became audible at an extremity of the corridor above. As he listened for a repetition of the sound, he heard a sob, and looking cautiously up, discovered, by the moonlight, Antonina stepping cautiously along the marble pavement of the hall.

She held in her hand a little lamp; her small, rosy feet were uncovered; the tears still streamed over her cheeks. She advanced with the greatest caution (as if fearful of being overheard) until she gained the part of the floor still strewn with the ruins of the broken lute. Here she knelt down, and pressed each fragment that lay before her separately to her lips. Then hurriedly concealing a single piece in her bosom, she arose and stole quickly away in the direction by which she had come.

'Be patient till the dawn,' muttered her faithless guardian, gazing after her from his concealment as she disappeared; 'it will bring to thy lute a restorer, and to Ulpius an ally!'

Chapter 6

AN APPRENTICESHIP TO THE TEMPLE

The action of our characters during the night included in the last two chapters has now come to a pause. Vetranio is awaiting his guests for the banquet; Numerian is in the chapel, preparing for the discourse that he is to deliver to his friends; Ulpius is meditating in his master's house; Antonina is stretched upon her couch, caressing the precious fragment that she had saved from the ruins of her lute. All the immediate agents of our story are, for the present, in repose.

It is our purpose to take advantage of this interval of inaction, and direct the reader's attention to a different country from that selected as the scene of our romance, and to such historical events of past years as connect themselves remarkably with the early life of Numerian's perfidious convert. This man will be found a person of great importance in the future conduct of our story. It is necessary to the comprehension of his character, and the penetration of such of his purposes as have been already hinted at, and may subsequently appear, that the long course of his existence should be traced upwards to its source.

It was in the reign of Julian, when the gods of the Pagan achieved their last victory over the Gospel of the Christian, that a decently attired man, leading by the hand a handsome boy of fifteen years of age, entered the gates of Alexandria, and proceeded hastily towards the high priest's dwelling in the Temple of Serapis.

After a stay of some hours at his destination, the man left the city alone as hastily as he entered it, and was never after seen at Alexandria. The boy remained in the abode of the high priest until the next day, when he was solemnly devoted to the service of the temple.

The boy was the young Emilius, afterwards called Ulpius. He was nephew to the high priest, to whom he had been confided by his father, a merchant of Rome.

Ambition was the ruling passion of the father of Emilius. It had prompted him to aspire to every distinction granted to the successful by the state, but it had not gifted him with the powers requisite to turn his aspirations in any instance into acquisitions. He passed through existence a disappointed man, planning but never performing, seeing his more fortunate brother rising to the highest distinction in the priesthood, and finding himself irretrievably condemned to exist in the affluent obscurity ensured to him by his mercantile pursuits.

When his brother Macrinus, on Julian's accession to the imperial throne, arrived at the pinnacle of power and celebrity as high priest of the Temple of Serapis, the unsuccessful merchant lost all hope of rivalling his relative in the pursuit of distinction. His insatiable ambition, discarded from himself, now settled on one of his infant sons. He determined that his child should be successful where he had failed. Now that his brother had secured the highest elevation in the temple, no calling could offer more direct advantages to a member of his household that the priesthood. His family had been from their earliest origin rigid Pagans. One of them had already attained to the most distinguished honours of his gorgeous worship. He determined that another should rival his kinsman, and that that other should be his eldest son.

Firm in this resolution, he at once devoted his child to the great design which he now held continually in view. He knew well that Paganism, revived though it was, was not the universal worship that it had been; that it was now secretly resisted, and might soon be openly opposed, by the persecuted Christians throughout the Empire; and that if the young generation were to guard it successfully from all future encroachments, and to rise securely to its highest honours, more must be exacted from them than the easy attachment to the ancient religion require from the votaries of former days. Then, the performance of the most important offices in the priesthood was compatible with the possession of military or political rank. Now, it was to the temple, and to the temple only, that the future servant of the gods should be devoted. Resolving thus, the father took care that all the son's occupations and rewards should, from his earliest years, be in some way connected with the career for which he was intended. His childish pleasures were to be conducted to sacrifices and auguries; his childish playthings and prizes were images of the deities. No opposition was offered on the boy's part to this plan of education. Far different from his younger brother, whose turbulent disposition defied all authority, he was naturally docile; and his imagination, vivid beyond his years, was easily led captive by any remarkable object presented to it. With such encouragement, his father became thoroughly engrossed by the occupation of forming him for his future existence. His mother's influence over him was jealously watched; the secret expression of her love, of her sorrow, at the prospect of parting with him, was ruthlessly suppressed whenever it was discovered; and his younger brother was neglected, almost forgotten, in order that the parental watchfulness might be entirely and invariably devoted to the eldest son.

When Emilius had numbered fifteen years, his father saw with delight that the time had come when he could witness the commencement of the realisation of all his projects. The boy was removed from home, taken to Alexandria, and gladly left, by his proud and triumphant father, under the especial guardianship of Macrinus, the high priest.

The chief of the temple full sympathised in his brother's designs for the young Emilius. As soon as the boy had entered on his new occupations, he was told that he must forget all that he had left behind him at Rome; that he must look upon the high priest as his father, and upon the temple, henceforth, as his home; and that the sole object of his present labours and future ambition must be to rise in the service of the gods. Nor did Macrinus stop here. So thoroughly anxious was he to stand to his pupil in the place of a parent, and to secure his allegiance by withdrawing him in every way from the world in which he had hitherto lived, that he even changed his name, giving to him one of his own appellations, and describing it as a privilege to stimulate him to future exertions. From the boy Emilius, he was now permanently transformed to the student Ulpius.

With such a natural disposition as we have already described, and under such guardianship as that of the high priest, there was little danger that Ulpius would disappoint the unusual expectations which had been formed of him. His attention to his new duties never relaxed; his obedience to his new masters never wavered. Whatever Macrinus demanded of him he was sure to perform. Whatever longings he might feel to return to home, he never discovered them; he never sought to gratify the tastes naturally peculiar to his age. The high priest and his colleagues were astonished at the extraordinary readiness with which the boy himself forwarded their intentions for him. Had they known how elaborately he had been prepared for his future employments at his father's house, they would have been less astonished at their pupil's unusual docility. Trained as he had been, he must have shown a more than human perversity had he displayed any opposition to his uncle's wishes. He had been permitted no childhood either of thought or action. His natural precocity had been seized as the engine to force his faculties into a perilous and unwholesome maturity; and when his new duties demanded his attention, he entered on them with the same sincerity of enthusiasm which his boyish coevals would have exhibited towards a new sport. His gradual initiation into the mysteries of his religion created a strange, voluptuous sensation of fear and interest in his mind. He heard the oracles, and he trembled; he attended the sacrifices and the auguries, and he wondered. All the poetry of the bold and beautiful superstition to which he was devoted flowed overwhelmingly into his young heart, absorbing the service of his fresh imagination, and transporting him incessantly from the vital realities of the outer world to the shadowy regions of aspiration and thought.

But his duties did not entirely occupy the attention of Ulpius. The boy had his peculiar pleasures as well as his peculiar occupations. When his employments were over for the day, it was a strange, unearthly, vital enjoyment to him to wander softly in the shade of the temple porticoes, looking down from his great mysterious eminence upon the populous and sun-brightened city at his feet; watching the brilliant expanse of the waters of the Nile glittering joyfully in the dazzling and pervading light; raising his eyes from the fields and woods, the palaces and garden, that stretched out before him below, to the lovely and cloudless sky that watched round him afar and above, and that awoke all that his new duties had left of the joyfulness, the affectionate sensibility, which his rare intervals of uninterrupted intercourse with his mother had implanted in his heart. Then, when the daylight began to wane, and the moon and stars already grew beautiful in their places in the firmament, he would pass into the subterranean vaults of the edifice, trembling as his little taper scarcely dispelled the dull, solemn gloom, and listening with breathless attention for the voices of those guardian spirits whose fabled habitation was made in the apartments of the sacred place. Or, when the multitude had departed for their amusements and their homes, he would steal into the lofty halls and wander round the pedestals of the mighty statues, breathing fearfully the still atmosphere of the temple, and watching the passage of the cold, melancholy moonbeams through the openings in the roof, and over the colossal limbs and features of the images of the pagan gods. Sometimes, when the services of Serapis and the cares attendant on his communications with the Emperor were concluded, Macrinus would lead his pupil into the garden of the priests, and praise him for his docility till his heart throbbed with gratitude and pride. Sometimes he would convey him cautiously outside the precincts of the sacred place, and show him, in the suburbs of the city, silent, pale, melancholy men, gliding suspiciously through the gay, crowded streets. Those fugitive figures, he would declare, were the enemies of the temple and all that it contained; conspirators against the Emperor and the gods; wretches who were to be driven forth as outcasts from humanity; whose appellation was 'Christian'; and whose impious worship, if tolerated, would deprive him of the uncle whom he loved, of the temple that he reverenced, and of the priestly dignity and renown which it should be his life's ambition to acquire.

Thus tutored in his duties by his guardian, and in his recreations by himself, as time wore on, the boy gradually lost every remaining characteristic of his age. Even the remembrance of his mother and his mother's love grew faint on his memory. Serious, solitary, thoughtful, he lived but to succeed in the temple; he laboured but to emulate the high priest. All his feelings and faculties were now enslaved by an ambition, at once unnatural at his present age, and ominous of affliction for his future life. The design that Macrinus had contemplated as the work of years was perfected in a few months. The hope that his father had scarce dared to entertain for his manhood was already accomplished in his youth.

In these preparations for future success passed three years of the life of Ulpius. At the expiration of that period the death of Julian darkened the brilliant prospects of the Pagan world. Scarcely had the priests of Serapis recovered the first shock of astonishment and grief consequent upon the fatal news of the vacancy in the imperial throne, when the edict of toleration issued by Jovian, the new Emperor, reached the city of Alexandria, and was elevated on the walls of the temple.

The first sight of this proclamation (permitting freedom of worship to the Christians) aroused in the highly wrought disposition of Ulpius the most violent emotions of anger and contempt. The enthusiasm of his character and age, guided invariably in the one direction of his worship, took the character of the wildest fanaticism when he discovered the Emperor's careless infringement of the supremacy of the temple. He volunteered in the first moments of his fury to tear down the edict from the walls, to lead an attack on the meetings of the triumphant Christians, or to travel to the imperial abode and exhort Jovian to withdraw his act of perilous leniency ere it was too late. With difficulty did his more cautious confederates restrain him from the execution of his impetuous designs. For two days he withdrew himself from his companions, and brooded in solitude over the injury offered to his beloved superstition, and the prospective augmentation of the influence of the Christian sect.

But the despair of the young enthusiast was destined to be further augmented by a private calamity, at once mysterious in its cause and overwhelming in its effect. Two days after the publication of the edict the high priest Macrinus, in the prime of vigour and manhood, suddenly died.

To narrate the confusion and horror within and without the temple on the discovery of this fatal even; to describe the execrations and tumults of the priests and
the populace, who at once suspected the favoured and ambitious Christians of
causing, by poison, the death of their spiritual ruler, might be interesting as a history of the manners of the times, but is immaterial to the object of this chapter.
We prefer rather to trace the effect on the mind of Ulpius of his personal and private bereavement; of this loss--irretrievable to him--of the master whom he loved
and the guardian whom it was his privilege to revere.

An illness of some months, during the latter part of which his attendants trembled for his life and reason, sufficiently attested the sincerity of the grief of Ulpius
for the loss of his protector. During his paroxysms of delirium the priests who
watched round his bed drew from his ravings many wise conclusions as to the
effects that his seizure and its causes were likely to produce on his future character; but, in spite of all their penetration, they were still far from appreciating to a
tithe of its extent the revolution that his bereavement had wrought in his disposition. The boy himself, until the moment of the high priest's death, had never
been aware of the depth of his devotion to his second father. Warped as they had
been by his natural parent, the affectionate qualities that were the mainspring of
his nature had never been entirely destroyed; and they seized on every kind word
and gentle action of Macrinus as food which had been grudged them since their
birth. Morally and intellectually, Macrinus had been to him the beacon that
pointed the direction of his course, the judge that regulated his conduct, the Muse
that he looked to for inspiration. And now, when this link which had connected
every ramification of his most cherished and governing ideas was suddenly
snapped asunder, a desolation sunk down upon his mind which at once paralysed
its elasticity and withered its freshness. He glanced back, and saw nothing but a
home from whose pleasures and affections his father's ambition had exiled him
for ever. He looked forward, and as he thought of his unfitness, both from character and education, to mix in the world as others mixed in it, he saw no guiding
star of social happiness for the conduct of his existence to come. There was now
no resource left for him but entirely to deliver himself up to those pursuits which
had made his home as a strange place to him, which were hallowed by their connection with the lost object of his attachment, and which would confer the sole
happiness and distinction that he could hope for in the wide world on his future
life.

In addition to this motive for labour in his vocation, there existed in the mind of
Ulpius a deep and settled feeling that animated him with unceasing ardour for the
prosecution of his cherished occupations. This governing principle was detesta-
tion of the Christian sect. The suspicion that others had entertained regarding

the death of the high priest was to his mind a certainty. He rejected every idea which opposed his determined persuasion that the jealousy of the Christians had prompted them to the murder, by poison, of the most powerful and zealous of the Pagan priests. To labour incessantly until he attained the influence and position formerly enjoyed by his relative, and to use that influence and position, when once acquired, as the means of avenging Macrinus, by sweeping every vestige of the Christian faith from the face of the earth, were now the settled purposes of his heart. Inspired by his determination with the deliberate wisdom which is in most men the result only of the experience of years, he employed the first days of his convalescence in cautiously maturing his future plans, and impartially calculating his chances of success. This self- examination completed, he devoted himself at once and for ever to his life's great design. Nothing wearied, nothing discouraged, nothing impeded him. Outward events passed by him unnoticed; the city's afflictions and the city's triumphs spoke no longer to his heart. Year succeeded to year, but Time had no tongue for him. Paganism gradually sank, and Christianity imperceptibly rose, but change spread no picture before his eyes. The whole outward world was a void to him, until the moment arrived that beheld him successful in his designs. His preparations for the future absorbed every faculty of his nature, and left him, as to the present, a mere automaton, reflecting no principle, and animated by no event--a machine that moved, but did not perceive--a body that acted, without a mind that thought.

Returning for a moment to the outward world, we find that on the death of Jovian, in 364, Valentinian, the new Emperor, continued the system of toleration adopted by his predecessor. On his death, in 375, Gratian, the successor to the imperial throne, so far improved on the example of the two former potentates as to range himself boldly on the side of the partisans of the new faith. Not content with merely encouraging, both by precept and by example, the growth of Christianity, the Emperor further testified to his zeal for the rising religion by inflicting incessant persecutions upon the rapidly decreasing advocates of the ancient worship; serving, by these acts of his reign, as pioneer to his successor, Theodosius the Great, in the religious revolution which that illustrious opponent of Paganism was destined to effect.

The death of Gratian, in 383, saw Ulpius enrolled among the chief priests of the temple, and pointed out as the next inheritor of the important office once held by the powerful and active Macrinus. Beholding himself thus secure of the distinction for which he had laboured, the aspiring priest found leisure, at length, to look forth upon the affairs of the passing day. From every side desolation darkened the prospect that he beheld. Already, throughout many provinces of the Empire, the temples of the gods had been overthrown by the destructive zeal of the triumphant Christians. Already hosts of the terrified people, fearing that the fate of their idols might ultimately be their own, finding themselves deserted by their disbanded priests, and surrounded by the implacable enemies of the ancient faith, had renounced their worship for the sake of saving their lives and securing their property. On the wide field of Pagan ruin there now rose but one structure entirely unimpaired. The Temple of Serapis still reared its head--unshaken, unbending, unpolluted. Here the sacrifice still prospered and the people still bowed in worship. Before this monument of the religious glories of ages, even the rising power of Christian supremacy quailed in dismay. Though the ranks of its once multitudinous congregations were now perceptibly thinned, though the new churches swarmed with converts, though the edicts from Rome denounced it as a blot on the face of the earth, its gloomy and solitary grandeur was still preserved. No unhallowed foot trod its secret recesses; no destroying hand was raised as yet against its ancient and glorious walls.

Indignation, but not despondency, filled the heart of Ulpius as he surveyed the situation of the Pagan world. A determination nourished as his had been by the reflections of years, and matured by incessant industry of deliberation, is above all those shocks which affect a hasty decision or destroy a wavering intention. Impervious to failure, disasters urge it into action, but never depress it to repose. Its existence is the air that preserves the vitality of the mind--the spring that moves the action of the thoughts. Never for a moment did Ulpius waver in his devotion to his great design, or despair of its ultimate execution and success. Though every succeeding day brought the news of fresh misfortunes for the Pagans and fresh triumphs for the Christians, still, with a few of his more zealous comrades, he persisted in expecting the advent of another Julian, and a day of restoration for the dismantled shrines of the deities that he served. While the Temple of Serapis stood uninjured, to give encouragement to his labours and refuge to his persecuted brethren, there existed for him such an earnest of success as would spur him to any exertion, and nerve him against any peril.

And now, to the astonishment of priests and congregations, the silent, thoughtful, solitary Ulpius suddenly started from his long repose, and stood forth the fiery advocate of the rights of his invaded worship. In a few days the fame of his addresses to the Pagans who still attended the rites of Serapis spread throughout the whole city. The boldest among the Christians, as they passed the temple walls, involuntarily trembled when they heard the vehemence of the applause which arose from the audience of the inspired priest. Addressed to all varieties of age and character, these harangues woke an echo in every breast they reached. To the young they were clothed in all the poetry of the worship for which they pleaded. They dwelt on the altars of Venus that the Christians would lay waste; on the woodlands that the Christians would disenchant of their Dryads; on the hallowed Arts that the Christians would arise and destroy. To the aged they called up remembrances of the glories of the past achieved through the favour of the gods; of ancestors who had died in their service; of old forgotten loves, and joys, and successes that had grown and prospered under the gentle guardianship of the deities of old--while the unvarying burden of their conclusion to all was the reiterated assertion that the illustrious Macrinus had died a victim to the toleration of the Christian sect.

But the efforts of Ulpius were not confined to the delivery of orations. Every moment of his leisure time was dedicated to secret pilgrimages into Alexandria. Careless of peril, regardless of threats, the undaunted enthusiast penetrated into the most private meeting-places of the Christians; reclaiming on every side apostates to the Pagan creed, and defying the hostility of half the city from the stronghold of the temple walls. Day after day fresh recruits arrived to swell the ranks of the worshippers of Serapis. The few members of the scattered congregations of the provinces who still remained faithful to the ancient worship were gathered together in Alexandria by the private messengers of the unwearied Ulpius. Already tumults began to take place between the Pagans and the Christians; and even now the priest of Serapis prepared to address a protest to the new Emperor in behalf of the ancient religion of the land. At this moment it seemed probable that the heroic attempts of one man to prop the structure of superstition, whose foundations were undermined throughout, and whose walls were attacked by brigands, might actually be crowned with success. But Time rolled on; and with him came inexorable change, trampling over the little barriers set up against it by human opposition, and erecting its strange and transitory fabrics triumphantly in their stead. In vain did the devoted priest exert all his powers to augment and combine his scattered band; in vain did the mighty temple display its ancient majesty, its gorgeous sacrifices, its mysterious auguries. The spirit of Christianity was forth for triumph on the earth--the last destinies of Paganism were fast accomplishing. Yet a few seasons more of unavailing resistance passed by, and then the Archbishop of Alexandria issued his decree that the Temple of Serapis should be destroyed.

At the rumour of their Primate's determination, the Christian fanatics rose by swarms from every corner of Egypt, and hurried into Alexandria to be present at the work of demolition. From the arid solitudes of the desert, from their convents on rocks and their caverns in the earth, hosts of rejoicing monks flew to the city gates, and ranged themselves with the soldiery and the citizens, impatient for the assault. At the dawn of morning this assembly of destroyers was convened, and as the sun rose over Alexandria they arrived before the temple walls.

The gates of the glorious structure were barred; the walls were crowded with their Pagan defenders. A still, dead, mysterious silence reigned over the whole edifice; and, of all the men who thronged it, one only moved from his appointed place-- one only wandered incessantly from point to point, wherever the building was open to assault. Those among the besiegers who were nearest the temple saw in this presiding genius of the preparations for defence the object at once of their most malignant hatred and their most ungovernable dread--Ulpius the priest.

As soon as the Archbishop gave the signal for the assault, a band of monks--their harsh, discordant voices screaming fragments of psalms, their tattered garments waving in the air, their cadaverous faces gleaming with ferocious joy--led the way, placed the first ladders against the walls, and began the attack. From all sides the temple was assailed by the infuriated besiegers, and on all sides it was successfully defended by the resolute besieged. Shock after shock fell upon the massive gates without forcing them to recede; missile after missile was hurled at the building, but no breach was made in its solid surface. Multitudes scaled the walls, gained the outer porticoes, and slaughtered their Pagan defenders, but were incessantly repulsed in their turn ere they could make their advantage good. Over and over again did the assailants seem on the point of storming the temple successfully, but the figure of Ulpius, invariably appearing at the critical moment among his disheartened followers, acted like a fatality in destroying the effect of the most daring exertions and the most important triumphs. Wherever there was danger, wherever there was carnage, wherever there was despair, thither strode the undaunted priest, inspiring the bold, succouring the wounded, reanimating the feeble. Blinded by no stratagem, wearied by no fatigue, there was something almost demoniac in his activity for destruction, in his determination under defeat. The besiegers marked his course round the temple by the calamities that befell them at his every step. If the bodies of slaughtered Christians were flung down upon them from the walls, they felt that Ulpius was there. If the bravest of the soldiery hesitated at mounting the ladders, it was known that Ulpius was directing the defeat of their comrades above. If a sally from the temple drove back the advanced guard upon the reserves in the rear, it was pleaded as their excuse that Ulpius was fighting at the head of his Pagan bands. Crowd on crowd of Christian warriors still pressed forward to the attack; but though the ranks of the unbelievers were perceptibly thinned, though the gates that defended them at last began to quiver before the reiterated blows by which they were assailed, every court of the sacred edifice yet remained in the possession of the besieged, and was at the disposal of the unconquered captain who organised the defence.

Depressed by the failure of his efforts, and horrified at the carnage already perpetrated among his adherents, the Archbishop suddenly commanded a cessation of hostilities, and proposed to the defenders of the temple a short and favourable truce. After some delay, and apparently at the expense of some discord among their ranks, the Pagans sent to the Primate an assurance of their acceptance of his terms, which were that both parties should abstain from any further struggle for the ascendancy until an edict from Theodosius determining the ultimate fate of the temple should be applied for and obtained.

The truce once agreed on, the wide space before the respited edifice was gradually cleared of its occupants. Slowly and sadly the Archbishop and his followers departed from the ancient walls whose summits they had assaulted in vain; and when the sun went down, of the great multitude congregated in the morning a few corpses were all that remained. Within the sacred building, Death and Repose ruled with the night, where morning had brightly glittered on Life and Action. The wounded, the wearied, and the cold, all now lay hushed alike, fanned by the night breezes that wandered through the lofty porticoes, or soothed by the obscurity that reigned over the silent halls. Among the ranks of the Pagan devotees but one man still toiled and thought. Round and round the temple, restless as a wild beast that is threatened in his lair, watchful as a lonely spirit in a city of strange tombs, wandered the solitary and brooding Ulpius. For him there was no rest of body--no tranquility of mind. On the events of the next few days hovered the fearful chance that was soon, either for misery or happiness, to influence irretrievably the years of his future life. Round and round the mighty walls he watched with mechanical and useless anxiety. Every stone in the building was eloquent to his lonely heart--beautiful to his wild imagination. On those barren structures stretched for him the loved and fertile home; there was the shrine for whose glory his intellect had been enslaved, for whose honour his youth had been sacrificed! Round and round the secret recesses and sacred courts he paced with hurried footstep, cleansing with gentle and industrious hand the stains of blood and the defilements of warfare from the statues at his side. Sad, solitary, thoughtful, as in the first days of his apprenticeship to the gods, he now roved in the same moonlit recesses where Macrinus had taught him in his youth. As the menacing tumults of the day had aroused his fierceness, so the stillness of the quiet night awakened his gentleness. He had combated for the temple in the morning as a son for a parent, and he now watched over it at night as a miser over his treasure, as a lover over his mistress, as a mother over her child!

The days passed on; and at length the memorable morning arrived which was to determine the fate of the last temple that Christian fanaticism had spared to the admiration of the world. At an early hour of the morning the diminished numbers of the Pagan zealots met their reinforced and determined opponents--both sides being alike unarmed--in the great square of Alexandria. The imperial prescript was then publicly read. It began by assuring the Pagans that their priest's plea for protection for the temple had received the same consideration which had been bestowed on the petition against the gods presented by the Christian Archbishop, and ended by proclaiming the commands of the Emperor that Serapis and all other idols in Alexandria should immediately be destroyed.

The shout of triumph which followed the conclusion of the imperial edict still rose from the Christian ranks when the advanced guard of the soldiers appointed to ensure the execution of the Emperor's designs appeared in the square. For a few minutes the forsaken Pagans stood rooted to the spot where they had assembled, gazing at the warlike preparations around them in a stupor of bewilderment and despair. Then as they recollected how diminished were their numbers, how arduous had been their first defence against a few, and how impossible would be a second defence against many--from the boldest to the feeblest, a panic seized on them; and, regardless of Ulpius, regardless of honour, regardless of the gods, they turned with one accord and fled from the place.

With the flight of the Pagans the work of demolition began. Even women and children hurried to join in the welcome task of indiscriminate destruction. No defenders on this occasion barred the gates of the temple to the Christian hosts. The sublime solitude of the tenantless building was outraged and invaded in an instant. Statues were broken, gold was carried off, doors were splintered into fragments; but here for a while the progress of demolition was delayed. Those to whom the labour of ruining the outward structure had been confided were less successful than their neighbours who had pillaged its contents. The ponderous stones of the pillars, the massive surfaces of the walls, resisted the most vigorous of their puny efforts, and forced them to remain contented with mutilating that which they could not destroy--with tearing off roofs, defacing marbles, and demolishing capitals. The rest of the buildings remained uninjured, and grander even now in the wildness of ruin than ever it had been in the stateliness of perfection and strength.

But the most important achievement still remained, the death-wound of Paganism was yet to be struck--the idol Serapis, which had ruled the hearts of millions, and was renowned in the remotest corners of the Empire, was to be destroyed! A breathless silence pervaded the Christian ranks as they filled the hall of the god. A superstitious dread, to which they had hitherto thought themselves superior, overcame their hearts, as a single soldier, bolder than his fellows, mounted by a ladder to the head of the colossal statue, and struck at its cheek with an axe. The blow had scarcely been dealt when a deep groan was heard from the opposite wall of the apartment, succeeded by a noise of retreating footsteps, and then all was silent again. For a few minutes this incident stayed the feet of those who were about to join their companion in the mutilation of the idol; but after an interval their hesitation vanished, they dealt blow after blow at the statue, and no more groans followed--no more sounds were heard, save the wild echoes of the stroke of hammer, crowbar, and club, resounding through the lofty hall. In an incredibly short space of time the image of Serapis lay in great fragments on the marble floor. The multitude seized on the limbs of the idol and ran forth to drag them in triumph through the streets. Yet a few minutes more, and the ruins were untenanted, the temple was silent--Paganism was destroyed!

Throughout the ravaging course of the Christians over the temple, they had been followed with dogged perseverance, and at the same time with the most perfect impunity, by the only Pagan of all his brethren who had not sought safety by flight. This man, being acquainted with every private passage and staircase in the sacred building, was enabled to be secretly present at each fresh act of demolition, in whatever part of the edifice it might be perpetrated. From hall to hall, and from room to room, he tracked with noiseless step and glaring eye the movements of the Christian mob--now hiding himself behind a pillar, now passing into concealed cavities in the walls, now looking down from imperceptible fissures in the roof; but, whatever his situation, invariably watching from it, with the same industry of attention and the same silence of emotion, the minutest acts of spoliation committed by the most humble follower of the Christian ranks. It was only when he entered with the victorious ravagers into the vast apartment occupied by the idol Serapis that the man's countenance began to give evidence of the agony under which his heart was writhing within him. He mounted a private staircase cut in the hollow of the massive wall of the room, and gaining a passage that ran round the extremities of the ceiling, looked through a sort of lattice concealed in the ornaments of the cornice. As he gazed down and saw the soldier mounting, axe in hand, to the idol's head, great drops of perspiration trickled from his forehead. His hot, thick breath hissed through his closed teeth, and his hands strained at the strong metal supports of the lattice until they bent beneath his grasp. When the stroke descended on the image, he closed his eyes. When the fragment detached by the blow fell on the floor, a groan burst from his quivering lips. For one moment more he glared down with a gaze of horror upon the multitude at his feet, and then with frantic speed he descended the steep stairs by which he had mounted to the roof, and fled from the temple.

The same night this man was again seen by some shepherds whom curiosity led to visit the desecrated building, weeping bitterly in its ruined and deserted porticoes. As they approached to address him, he raised his head, and with a supplicating action signed to them to leave the place. For the few moments during which he confronted them, the moonlight shone full upon his countenance, and the shepherds, who had in former days attended the ceremonies of the temple, saw with astonishment that the solitary mourner whose meditations they had disturbed was no other than Ulpius the priest.

At the dawn of day these shepherds had again occasion to pass the walls of the pillaged temple. Throughout the hours of the night the remembrance of the scene of unsolaced, unpartaken grief that they had beheld--of the awful loneliness of misery in which they had seen the heart-broken and forsaken man, whose lightest words they had once delighted to revere--inspired them with a feeling of pity for the deserted Pagan, widely at variance with the spirit of persecution which the spurious Christianity of their day would fain have instilled in the bosoms of its humblest votaries. Bent on consolation, anxious to afford help, these men, like the Samaritan of old, went up at their own peril to succour a brother in affliction. They searched every portion of the empty building, but the object of their sympathy was nowhere to be seen. They called, but heard no answering sound, save the dirging of the winds of early morning through the ruined halls, which but a short time since had resounded with the eloquence of the once illustrious priest. Except a few night-birds, already sheltered by the deserted edifice, not a living being moved in what was once the temple of the Eastern world. Ulpius was gone.

These events took place in the year 389. In 390, Pagan ceremonies were made treason by the laws throughout the whole Roman Empire.

From that period the scattered few who still adhered to the ancient faith became divided into three parties; each alike insignificant, whether considered as openly or secretly inimical to the new religion of the State at large.

The first party unsuccessfully endeavoured to elude the laws prohibitory of sacrifices and divinations by concealing their religious ceremonies under the form of convivial meetings.

The second preserved their ancient respect for the theory of Paganism, but abandoned all hope and intention of ever again accomplishing its practice. By such timely concessions many were enabled to preserve--and some even to attain--high and lucrative employments as officers of the State.

The third retired to their homes, the voluntary exiles of every religion; resigning the practice of their old worship as a necessity, and shunning the communion of Christians as a matter of choice.

Such were the unimportant divisions into which the last remnants of the once powerful Pagan community now subsided; but to none of them was the ruined and degraded Ulpius ever attached.

For five weary years--dating from the epoch of the prohibition of Paganism--he wandered through the Empire, visiting in every country the ruined shrines of his deserted worship--a friendless, hopeless, solitary man!

Throughout the whole of Europe, and all of Asia and the East that still belonged to Rome, he bent his slow and toilsome course. In the fertile valleys of Gaul, over the burning sands of Africa, through the sun- bright cities of Spain, he travelled--unfriended as a man under a curse, lonely as a second Cain. Never for an instant did the remembrance of his ruined projects desert his memory, or his mad determination to revive his worship abandon his mind. At every relic of Paganism, however slight, that he encountered on his way, he found a nourishment for his fierce anguish, and employment for his vengeful thoughts. Often, in the little villages, children were frightened from their sports in a deserted temple by the apparition of his gaunt, rigid figure among the tottering pillars, or the sound of his hollow voice as he muttered to himself among the ruins of the Pagan tombs. Often, in crowded cities, groups of men, congregated to talk over the fall of Paganism, found him listening at their sides, and comforting them, when they carelessly regretted their ancient faith, with a smiling and whispered assurance that a time of restitution would yet come. By all opinions and in all places he was regarded as a harmless madman, whose strange delusions and predilections were not to be combated, but to be indulged. Thus he wandered through the Christian world; regardless alike of lapse of time and change of climate; living within himself; mourning, as a luxury, over the fall of his worship; patient of wrongs, insults, and disappointments; watching for the opportunity that he still persisted in believing was yet to arrive; holding by his fatal determination with all the recklessness of ambition and all the perseverance of revenge.

The five years passed away unheeded, uncalculated, unregretted by Ulpius. For him, living but in the past, hoping but for the future, space held no obstacles--time was an oblivion. Years pass as days, hours as moments, when the varying emotions which mark their existence on the memory, and distinguish their succession on the dial of the heart, exist no longer either for happiness or woe. Dead to all freshness of feeling, the mind of Ulpius, during the whole term of his wanderings, lay numbed beneath the one idea that possessed it. It was only at the expiration of those unheeded years, when the chances of travel turned his footsteps towards Alexandria, that his faculties burst from the long bondage which had oppressed them. Then--when he passed through those gates which he had entered in former years a proud, ambitious boy, when he walked ungreeted through the ruined temple where he had once lived illustrious and revered--his dull, cold thoughts arose strong and vital within him. The spectacle of the scene of his former glories, which might have awakened despair in others, aroused the dormant passions, emancipated the stifled energies in him. The projects of vengeance and the visions of restoration which he had brooded over for five long years, now rose before him as realised already under the vivid influence of the desecrated scenes around. As he stood beneath the shattered porticoes of the sacred place, not a stone crumbling at his feet but rebuked him for his past inaction, and strengthened him for daring, for conspiracy, for revenge, in the service of the outrage gods. The ruined temples he had visited in his gloomy pilgrimages now became revived by his fancy, as one by one they rose on his toiling memory. Broken pillars soared from the ground; desecrated idols reoccupied their vacant pedestals; and he, the exile and the mourner, stood forth once again the ruler, the teacher, and the priest. The time of restitution was come; though his understanding supplied him with no distinct projects, his heart urged him to rush blindly on the execution of his reform. The moment had arrived--Macrinus should yet be avenged; the temple should at last be restored.

He descended into the city; he hurried--neither welcomed nor recognised--through the crowded streets; he entered the house of a man who had once been his friend and colleague in the days that were past, and poured forth to him his wild determinations and disjointed plans, entreating his assistance, and promising him a glorious success. But his old companion had become, by a timely conversion to Christianity, a man of property and reputation in Alexandria, and he turned from the friendless enthusiast with indignation and contempt. Repulsed, but not disheartened, Ulpius sought others who he had known in his prosperity and renown. They had all renounced their ancient worship--they all received him with studied coldness or careless disdain; but he still persisted in his useless efforts. He blinded his eyes to their contemptuous looks; he shut his ears to their derisive words. Persevering in his self-delusion, he appointed them messengers to their brethren in other countries, captains of the conspiracy that was to commence in Alexandria, orators before the people when the memorable revolution had once begun. It was in vain that they refused all participation in his designs; he left them as the expressions of refusal rose to their lips, and hurried elsewhere, as industrious in his efforts, as devoted to his unwelcome mission, as if half the population of the city had vowed themselves joyfully to aid him in his frantic attempt.

Thus during the whole day he continued his labour of useless persuasion among those in the city who had once been his friends. When the evening came, he repaired, weary but not despondent, to the earthly paradise that he was determined to regain--to the temple where he had once taught, and where he still imagined that he was again destined to preside. Here he proceeded, ignorant of the new laws, careless of discovery and danger, to ascertain by divination, as in the days of old, whether failure or success awaited him ultimately in his great design.

Meanwhile the friends whose assistance Ulpius had determined to extort were far from remaining inactive on their parts after the departure of the aspiring priest. They remembered with terror that the laws affected as severely those concealing their knowledge of a Pagan intrigue as those actually engaged in directing a Pagan conspiracy; and their anxiety for their personal safety overcoming every consideration of the dues of honour or the claims of ancient friendship, they repaired in a body to the Prefect of the city, and informed him, with all the eagerness of apprehension, of the presence of Ulpius in Alexandria, and of the culpability of the schemes that he had proposed.

A search after the devoted Pagan was immediately commenced. He was found the same night before a ruined altar, brooding over the entrails of an animal that he had just sacrificed. Further proof of his guilt could not be required. He was taken prisoner; led forth the next morning to be judged, amid the execrations of the very people who had almost adored him once; and condemned the following day to suffer the penalty of death.

At the appointed hour the populace assembled to behold the execution. To their indignation and disappointment, however, when the officers of the city appeared before the prison, it was only to inform the spectators that the performance of the fatal ceremony had been adjourned. After a mysterious delay of some weeks, they were again convened, not to witness the execution, but the receive the extraordinary announcement that the culprit's life had been spared, and that his amended sentence now condemned him to labour as a slave for life in the copper-mines of Spain.

What powerful influence induced the Prefect to risk the odium of reprieving a prisoner whose guilt was so satisfactorily ascertained as that of Ulpius never was disclosed. Some declared that the city magistrate was still at heart a Pagan, and that he consequently shrunk from authorising the death of a man who had once been the most illustrious among the professors of the ancient creed. Others reported that Ulpius had secured the leniency of his judges by acquainting them with the position of one of those secret repositories of enormous treasure supposed to exist beneath the foundations of the dismantled Temple of Serapis. But the truth of either of these rumours could never be satisfactorily proved. Nothing more was accurately discovered than that Ulpius was removed from Alexandria to the place of earthly torment set apart for him by the zealous authorities, at the dead of night; and that the sentry at the gate through which he departed heard him mutter to himself, as he was hurried onward, that his divinations had prepared him for defeat, but that the great day of Pagan restoration would yet arrive.

In the year 407, twelve years after the events above narrated, Ulpius entered the city of Rome.

He had not advanced far, before the gaiety and confusion in the streets appeared completely to bewilder him. He hastened to the nearest public garden that he could perceive, and avoiding the frequented paths, flung himself down, apparently fainting with exhaustion, at the foot of a tree.

For some time he lay on the shady resting-place which he had chosen, gasping painfully for breath, his frame ever and anon shaken to its centre by sudden spasms, and his lips quivering with an agitation which he vainly endeavoured to suppress. So changed was his aspect, that the guards who had removed him from Alexandria, wretched as was his appearance even then, would have found it impossible to recognise him now as the same man whom they had formerly abandoned to slavery in the mines of Spain. The effluvia exhaled from the copper ore in which he had been buried for twelve years had not only withered the flesh upon his bones, but had imparted to its surface a livid hue, almost death- like in its dulness. His limbs, wasted by age and distorted by suffering, bent and trembled beneath him; and his form, once so majestic in its noble proportions, was now so crooked and misshapen, that whoever beheld him could only have imagined that he must have been deformed from his birth. Of the former man no characteristic remained but the expression of the stern, mournful eyes; and these, the truthful interpreters of the indomitable mind whose emotions they seemed created to express, preserved, unaltered by suffering and unimpaired by time, the same look, partly of reflection, partly of defiance, and partly of despair, which had marked them in those past days when the temple was destroyed and the congregations of the Pagans dispersed.

But the repose at this moment demanded by his worn-out body was even yet denied to it by his untamed, unwearied mind, and, as the voice of his old delusion spoke within him again, the devoted priest rose from his solitary resting-place, and looked forth upon the great city, whose new worship he was vowed to overthrow.

'By years of patient watchfulness,' he whispered to himself, 'have I succeeded in escaping successfully from my dungeon among the mines. Yet a little more cun-

ning, a little more endurance, a little more vigilance, and I shall still live to people, by my own exertions, the deserted temples of Rome.'

As he spoke he emerged from the grove into the street. The joyous sunlight--a
stranger to him for years--shone warmly down upon his face, as if to welcome him
to liberty and the world. The sounds of gay laughter rang in his ears, as if to woo
him back to the blest enjoyments and amenities of life; but Nature's influence and
man's example were now silent alike to his lonely heart. Over its dreary wastes
still reigned the ruthless ambition which had exiled love from his youth, and
friendship from his manhood, and which was destined to end its mission of
destruction by banishing tranquility from his age. Scowling fiercely at all around
and above him, he sought the loneliest and shadiest streets. Solitude had now
become a necessity to his heart. The 'great gulph' of his unshared aspirations had
long since socially separated him for ever from his fellow-men. He thought,
laboured, and suffered for himself alone.

To describe the years of unrewarded labour and unalleviated hardship endured by
Ulpius in the place of his punishment; to dwell on the day that brought with it-
-whatever the season in the world above--the same unwearying inheritance of
exertion and fatigue; to chronicle the history of night after night of broken slumber one hour, of wearying thought the next, would be to produce a picture from
the mournful monotony of which the attention of the reader would recoil with
disgust. It will be here sufficient to observe, that the influence of the same infat-
uation which had nerved him to the defence of the assaulted temple, and encouraged him to attempt his ill-planned restoration of Paganism, had preserved him
through sufferings under which stronger and younger men would have sunk for
ever; had prompted his determination to escape from his slavery, and had now
brought him to Rome--old, forsaken, and feeble as he was--to risk new perils and
suffer new afflictions for the cause to which, body and soul, he had ruthlessly
devoted himself for ever.

Urged, therefore, by his miserable delusion, he had now entered a city where even
his name was unknown, faithful to his frantic project of opposing himself, as a
helpless, solitary man, against the people and government of an Empire. During
his term of slavery, regardless of his advanced years, he had arranged a series of
projects, the gradual execution of which would have demanded the advantages of
a long and vigorous life. He no more desired, as in his former attempt at
Alexandria, to precipitate at all hazards the success of his designs. He was now prepared to watch, wait, plot, and contrive for years on years; he was resigned to be
contented with the poorest and slowest advancement--to be encouraged by the
smallest prospect of ultimate triumph. Acting under this determination, he start-

ed his project by devoting all that remained of his enfeebled energies to cautiously informing himself, by every means in his power, of the private, political, and religious sentiments of all men of influence in Rome. Wherever there was a popular assemblage, he attended it to gather the scandalous gossip of the day; wherever there was a chance of overhearing a private conversation, he contrived to listen to it unobserved. About the doors of taverns and the haunts of discharged servants he lurked noiseless as a shadow, attentive alike to the careless revelations of intoxication or the scurrility of malignant slaves. Day after day passed on, and still saw him devoted to his occupation (which, servile as it was in itself, was to his eyes ennobled by its lofty end), until at the expiration of some months he found himself in possession of a vague and inaccurate fund of information, which he stored up as a priceless treasure in his mind. He next discovered the name and abode of every nobleman in Rome suspected even of the most careless attachment to the ancient form of worship. He attended Christian churches, mastered the intricacies of different sects, and estimated the importance of contending schisms; gaining this collection of heterogeneous facts under the combined disadvantages of poverty, solitude, and age; dependent for support on the poorest public charities, and for shelter on the meanest public asylums. Every conclusion that he drew from all he learned partook of the sanguine character of the fatal self-deception which had embittered his whole life. He believed that the dissensions which he saw raging in the Church would speedily effect the destruction of Christianity itself; that, when such a period should arrive, the public mind would require but the guidance of some superior intellect to return to its old religious predilections; and that to lay the foundation for effecting in such a manner the desired revolution, it was necessary for him--impossible though it might seem in his present degraded condition--to gain access to the disaffected nobles of Rome, and discover the secret of acquiring such an influence over them as would enable him to infect them with his enthusiasm, and fire them with his determination. Greater difficulties even than these had been overcome by other men. Solitary individuals had, ere this, originated revolutions. The gods would favour him; his own cunning would protect him. Yet a little more patience, a little more determination, and he might still, after all his misfortunes, be assured of success.

It was about this period that he first heard, while pursuing his investigations, of an obscure man who had suddenly arisen to undertake a reformation in the Christian Church, whose declared aim was to rescue the new worship from that very degeneracy on the fatal progress of which rested all his hopes of triumph. It was reported that this man had been for some time devoted to his reforming labours, but that the difficulties attendant on the task that he had appointed for himself had hitherto prevented him from attaining all the notoriety essential to the satisfactory prosecution of his plans. On hearing this rumour, Ulpius immediately joined the few who attended the new orator's discourses, and there heard enough to convince him that he listened to the most determined zealot for Christianity in the city of Rome. To gain this man's confidence, to frustrate every effort that he might make in his new vocation, to ruin his credit with his hearers, and to threaten his personal safety by betraying his inmost secrets to his powerful enemies in the Church, were determinations instantly adopted by the Pagan as duties demanded by the exigencies of his creed. From that moment he seized every opportunity of favourably attracting the new reformer's attention to himself, and, as the reader already knows, he was at length rewarded for his cunning and perseverance by being received into the household of the charitable and unsuspicious Numerian as a pious convert to the Christianity of the early Church.

Once installed under Numerian's roof, the treacherous Pagan saw in the Christian's daughter an instrument admirably adapted, in his unscrupulous hands, for forwarding his wild project of obtaining the ear of a Roman of power and station who was disaffected to the established worship. Among the patricians of whose anti-Christian predilections report had informed him, was Numerian's neighbour, Vetranio the senator. To such a man, renowned for his life of luxury, a girl so beautiful as Antonina would be a bribe rich enough to enable him to extort any promise required as a reward for betraying her while under the protection of her father's house. In addition to this advantage to be drawn from her ruin, was the certainty that her loss would so affect Numerian as to render him, for a time at least, incapable of pursuing his labours in the cause of Christianity. Fixed then in his detestable purpose, the ruthless priest patiently awaited the opportunity of commencing his machinations. Nor did he watch in vain. The victim innocently fell into the very trap that he had prepared for her when she first listened to the music of Vetranio's lute, and permitted her treacherous guardian to become the friend who concealed her disobedience from her father's ear. After that first fatal step every day brought the projects of Ulpius nearer to success. The long-sought interview with the senator was at length obtained; the engagement imperatively demanded on the one side was, as we have already related, carelessly accepted on the other; the day that was to bring success to the schemes of the betrayer, and degradation to the honour of the betrayed, was appointed; and once more the cold heart of the fanatic warmed to the touch of joy. No doubts upon the validity of his engagement with Vetranio ever entered his mind. He never imagined that powerful senator could with perfect impunity deny him the impracticable assistance he had demanded as his reward, and thrust him as an ignorant madman from his palace gates. Firmly and sincerely he believed that Vetranio was so satisfied with his readiness in pandering to his profligate designs, and so dazzled by the prospect of the glory which would attend success in the great enterprise, that he would gladly hold to the performance of his promise whenever it should be required of him. In the meantime the work was begun. Numerian was already, through his agency, watched by the spies of a jealous and unscrupulous Church. Feuds, schisms, treacheries, and dissensions marched bravely onward through the Christian ranks. All things combined to make it certain that the time was near at hand when, through his exertions and the friendly senator's help, the restoration of Paganism might be assured.

With the widest diversity of pursuit and difference of design, there was still a strange and mysterious analogy between the temporary positions of Ulpius and Numerian. One was prepared to be a martyr for the temple; the other to be a martyr for the Church. Both were enthusiasts in an unwelcome cause; both had suffered more than a life's wonted share of affliction; and both were old, passing irretrievably from their fading present on earth to the eternal future awaiting them in the unknown spheres beyond.

But here--with their position--the comparison between them ends. The Christian's principle of action, drawn from the Divinity he served, was love; the Pagan's, born of the superstition that was destroying him, was hate. The one laboured for mankind; the other for himself. And thus the aspirations of Numerian, founded on the general good, nourished by offices of kindness, and nobly directed to a generous end, might lead him into indiscretion, but could never degrade him into crime--might trouble the serenity of his life, but could never deprive him of the consolation of hope. While, on the contrary, the ambition of Ulpius, originating in revenge and directed to destruction, exacted cruelty from his heart and duplicity from his mind; and, as the reward for his service, mocked him alternately throughout his whole life with delusion and despair.

Chapter 7

THE BED-CHAMBER

It is now time to resume our chronicle of the eventful night which marked the destruction of Antonina's lute and the conspiracy against Antonina's honour.

The gates of Vetranio's palace were closed, and the noises in it were all hushed; the banquet was over, the triumph of the Nightingale Sauce had been achieved, and the daybreak was already glimmering in the eastern sky, when the senator's favoured servant, the freedman Carrio, drew back the shutter of the porter's lodge, where he had been dozing since the conclusion of the feast, and looked out lazily into the street. The dull, faint light of dawn was now strengthening slowly over the lonely roadway and on the walls of the lofty houses. Of the groups of idlers of the lowest class who had assembled during the evening in the street to snuff the fragrant odours which steamed afar from Vetranio's kitchens, not one remained; men, women, and children had long since departed to seek shelter wherever they could find it, and to fatten their lean bodies on what had been charitable bestowed on them of the coarser relics of the banquet. The mysterious solitude and tranquility of daybreak in a great city prevailed over all things. Nothing impressed, however, by the peculiar and solemn attraction of the scene at this moment, the freedman apostrophised the fresh morning air, as it blew over him, in strong terms of disgust, and even ventured in lowered tones to rail against his master's uncomfortable fancy for being awakened after a feast at the approach of dawn. Far too well aware, nevertheless, of the necessity of yielding the most implicit obedience to the commands he had received to resign himself any longer to the pleasant temptations of repose, Carrio, after yawning, rubbing his eyes, and indulging for a few moments more in the luxury of complaint, set forth in earnest to follow the corridors leading to the interior of the palace, and to awaken Vetranio without further delay.

He had not advanced more than a few steps when a proclamation, written in letters of gold on a blue-coloured board, and hung against the wall at his side, attracted his attention. This public notice, which delayed his progress at the very outset, and which was intended for the special edification of all the inhabitants of Rome, was thus expressed:--

'ON THIS DAY, AND FOR TEN DAYS FOLLOWING, THE AFFAIRS OF OUR PATRON OBLIGE HIM TO BE ABSENT FROM ROME.'

Here the proclamation ended, without descending to particulars. It had been put forth, in accordance with the easy fashion of the age, to answer at once all applications at Vetranio's palace during the senator's absence. Although the colouring of the board, the writing of the letters, and the composition of the sentence were the work of his own ingenuity, the worthy Carrio could not prevail upon himself to pass the proclamation without contemplating is magnificence anew. For some time he stood regarding it with the same expression of lofty and complacent approbation which we see in these modern days illuminating the countenance of a connoisseur before one of his own old pictures which he has bought as a great bargain, or dawning over the bland features of a linen-draper as he surveys from the pavement his morning's arrangement of the window of the shop. All things, however, have their limits, even a man's approval of an effort of his own skill. Accordingly, after a prolonged review of the proclamation, some faint ideas of the necessity of immediately obeying his master's commands revived in the mind of the judicious Carrio, and counselled him to turn his steps at once in the direction of the palace sleeping apartments.

Greatly wondering what new caprice had induced the senator to contemplate leaving Rome at the dawn of day--for Vetranio had divulged to no one the object of his departure--the freedman cautiously entered his master's bed-chamber. He drew aside the ample silken curtains suspended around and over the sleeping couch, from the hands of Graces and Cupids sculptured in marble; but the statues surrounded an empty bed. Vetranio was not there. Carrio next entered the bathroom; the perfumed water was steaming in its long marble basin, and the soft wrapping-cloths lay ready for use; the attendant slave, with his instruments of ablution, waited, half asleep, in his accustomed place; but here also no signs of the master's presence appeared. Somewhat perplexed, the freedman examined several other apartments. He found guests, dancing girls, parasites, poets, painters--a motley crew--occupying every kind of dormitory, and all peacefully engaged in sleeping off the effects of the wine they had drunk at the banquet; but the great object of his search still eluded him as before. At last it occurred to him that the senator, in an excess of convivial enthusiasm and jovial hospitality, might yet be detaining some favoured guest at the table of the feast.

Pausing, therefore, at some carved doors which stood ajar at one extremity of a spacious hall, he pushed them open, and hurriedly entered the banqueting-room beyond.

A soft, dim, luxurious light reigned over this apartment, which now presented, as far as the eye could discern, an aspect of confusion that was at once graceful and picturesque. Of the various lamps, of every variety of pattern, hanging from the ceiling, but few remained alight. From those, however, which were still unextinguished there shone a mild brightness, admirably adapted to display the objects immediately around them. The golden garlands and the alabaster pots of sweet ointment which had been suspended before the guests during the banquet, still hung from the painted ceiling. On the massive table, composed partly of ebony and partly of silver, yet lay, in the wildest confusion, fragments of gastronomic delicacies, grotesque dinner services, vases of flowers, musical instruments, and crystal dice; while towering over all rose the glittering dish which had contained the nightingales consumed by the feasters, with the four golden Cupids which had spouted over them that illustrious invention--the Nightingale Sauce. Around the couches, of violet and rose colour, ranged along the table, the perfumed and gaily- tinted powders that had been strewn in patterns over the marble floor were perceptible for a few yards; but beyond this point nothing more was plainly distinguishable. The eye roved down the sides of the glorious chamber, catching dim glimpses of gorgeous draperies, crowded statues, and marble columns, but discerning nothing accurately, until it reached the half-opened windows, and rested upon the fresh dewy verdure now faintly visible in the shady gardens without. There--waving in the morning breezes, charged on every leaf with their burden of pure and welcome moisture--rose the lofty pine-trees, basking in the recurrence of the new day's beautiful and undying youth, and rising in reproving contrast before the exhausted allurements of luxury and the perverted creations of art which burdened the tables of the hall within.

After a hasty survey of the apartment, the freedman appeared to be on the point of quitting it in despair, when the noise of a falling dish, followed by several partly suppressed and wholly confused exclamations of affright, caught his ear. He once more approached the banqueting- table, retrimmed a lamp that hung near him, and taking it in his hand, passed to the side of the room whence the disturbance proceeded. A hideous little negro, staring in ludicrous terror at a silver oven, half filled with bread, which had just fallen beside him, was the first object he discovered. A few paces beyond the negro reposed a beautiful boy, crowned with vine leaves and ivy, still sleeping by the side of his lyre; and farther yet, stretched in an uneasy slumber on a silken couch, lay the identical object of the freedman's search--the illustrious author of the Nightingale Sauce.

Immediately above the sleeping senator hung his portrait, in which he was modestly represented as rising by the assistance of Minerva to the top of Parnassus, the nine Muses standing round him rejoicing. At his feet reposed a magnificent white cat, whose head rested in all the luxurious laziness of satiety on the edge of a golden saucer half filled with dormice stewed in milk. The most indubitable evidences of the night's debauch appeared in Vetranio's disordered dress and flushed countenance as the freedman regarded him. For some minutes the worthy Carrio stood uncertain whether to awaken his master or not, deciding finally, however, on obeying the commands he had received, and disturbing the slumbers of the wearied voluptuary before him. To effect this purpose, it was necessary to call in the aid of the singing-boy; for, by a refinement of luxury, Vetranio had forbidden his attendants to awaken him by any other method than the agency of musical sounds.

With some difficulty the boy was sufficiently aroused to comprehend the service that was required of him. For a short time the notes of the lyre sounded in vain. At last, when the melody took a louder and more martial character, the sleeping patrician slowly opened his eyes and stared vacantly around him.

'My respected patron,' said the polite Carrio in apologetic tones, 'commanded that I should awaken him with the dawn; the daybreak has already appeared.'

When the freedman had ceased speaking, Vetranio sat up on the couch, called for a basin of water, dipped his fingers in the refreshing liquid, dried them abstractedly on the long silky curls of the singing- boy who stood beside him, gazed about him once more, repeated interrogatively the word 'daybreak', and sunk gently back upon his couch. We are grieved to confess it--but the author of the Nightingale Sauce was moderately inebriated.

A short pause followed, during which the freedman and the singing-boy stared upon each other in mutual perplexity. At length the one resumed his address of apology, and the other resumed his efforts on the lyre. Once more, after an interval, the eyes of Vetranio lazily unclosed, and this time he began to speak; but his thoughts--if thoughts they could be called--were as yet wholly occupied by the 'table-talk' at the past night's banquet.

'The ancient Egyptians--oh, sprightly and enchanting Camilla--were a wise nation!' murmured the senator drowsily. 'I am myself descended from the ancient Egyptians; and, therefore, I hold in high veneration that cat in your lap, and all cats besides. Herodotus--an historian whose works I feel a certain gratification in publicly mentioning as good--informs us, that when a cat died in the dwelling of an ancient Egyptian, the owner shaved his eyebrows as a mark of grief, embalmed the defunct animal in a consecrated house, and carried it to be interred in a con-siderable city of Lower Egypt, called 'Bubastis'--an Egyptian word which I have discovered to mean The Sepulchre of all the Cats; whence it is scarcely erroneous to infer--'

At this point the speaker's power of recollection and articulation suddenly failed him, and Carrio--who had listened with perfect gravity to his master's oration upon cats--took immediate advantage of the opportunity now afforded him to speak again.

'The equipage which my patron was pleased to command to carry him to Aricia,' said he, with a strong emphasis on the last word, 'now stands in readiness at the private gate of the palace gardens.'

As he heard the word 'Aricia', the senator's powers of recollection and perception seemed suddenly to return to him. Among that high order of drinkers who can imbibe to the point of perfect enjoyment, and stop short scientifically before the point of perfect oblivion, Vetranio occupied an exalted rank. The wine he had swallowed during the night had disordered his memory and slightly troubled his self-possession, but had not deprived him of his understanding. There was noth-ing plebeian even in his debauchery; there was an art and a refinement in his very excesses.

'Aricia--Aricia!' he repeated to himself, 'ah! the villa that Julia lent to me at Ravenna! The pleasures of the table must have obscured for a moment the image of my beautiful pupil of other days, which now revives before me again as Love resumes the dominion that Bacchus usurped! My excellent Carrio,' he continued, speaking to the freedman, 'you have done perfectly right in awakening me; delay not a moment more in ordering my bath to be prepared, or my man-monster Ulpius, the king of conspirators and high priest of all that is mysterious, will wait for me in vain! And you, Glyco,' he pursued, when Carrio had departed, address-ing the singing-boy, 'array yourself for a journey, and wait with my equipage at the garden-gate. I shall require you to accompany me in my expedition to Aricia. But first, oh! gifted and valued songster, let me reward you for the harmonious symphony that has just awakened me. Of what rank of my musicians are you at present, Glyco?'

'Of the fifth,' replied the boy.

'Were you bought, or born in my house?' asked Vetranio.

'Neither; but bequeathed to you by Geta's testament,' rejoined the gratified Glyco.

'I advance you,' continued Vetranio, 'to the privileges and the pay of the first rank of my musicians; and I give you, as a proof of my continued favour, this ring. In return for these obligations, I desire to keep secret whatever concerns my approaching expedition; to employ your softest music in soothing the ear of a young girl who will accompany us--in calming her terrors if she is afraid, in drying her tears if she weeps; and finally, to exercise your voice and your lute incessantly in uniting the name 'Antonina' to the sweetest harmonies of sound that your imagination can suggest.'

Pronouncing these words with an easy and benevolent smile, and looking round complacently on the display of luxurious confusion about him, Vetranio retired to the bath that was to prepare him for his approaching triumph.

Meanwhile a scene of a very different nature was proceeding without, at Numerian's garden-gate. Here were no singing-boys, no freedmen, no profusion of rich treasures--here appeared only the solitary and deformed figure of Ulpius, half hidden among surrounding trees, while he waited at his appointed post. As time wore on, and still Vetranio did not appear, the Pagan's self-possession began to desert him. He moved restlessly backwards and forwards over the soft dewy grass, sometimes in low tones calling upon his gods to hasten the tardy footsteps of the libertine patrician, who was to be made the instrument of restoring to the temples the worship of other days--sometimes cursing the reckless delay of the senator, or exulting in the treachery by which he madly believed his ambition was at last to be fulfilled; but still, whatever his words or thoughts, wrought up to the same pitch of fierce, fanatic enthusiasm which had strengthened him for the defence of his idols at Alexandria, and had nerved him against the torment and misery of years in his slavery in the copper mines of Spain.

The precious moments were speeding irrevocably onwards. His impatience was rapidly changing to rage and despair as he strained his eyes for the last time in the direction of the palace gardens, and now at length discerned a white robe among the distant trees. Vetranio was rapidly approaching him.

Restored by his bath, no effect of the night's festivity but its exhilaration remained in the senator's brain. But for a slight uncertainty in his gait, and an unusual vacancy in his smile, the elegant gastronome might now have appeared to the closest observer guiltless of the influence of intoxicating drinks. He advanced, radiant with exultation, prepared for conquest, to the place where Ulpius awaited him, and was about to address the Pagan with that satirical familiarity so fashionable among the nobles of Rome in their communications with the people, when the object of his intended pleasantries sternly interrupted him, saying, in tones more of command than of advice, 'Be silent! If you would succeed in your purpose, follow me without uttering a word!'

There was something so fierce and determined in the tones of the old man's voice--low, tremulous, and husky though they were--as he uttered those words, that the bold, confident senator instinctively held his peace as he followed his stern guide into Numerian's house. Avoiding the regular entrance, which at that early hour of the morning was necessarily closed, Ulpius conducted the patrician through a small wicket into the subterranean apartment, or rather outhouse, which was his customary, though comfortless, retreat in his leisure hours, and which was hardly ever entered by the other members of the Christian's household.

From the low, arched brick ceiling of this place hung an earthenware lamp, whose light, small and tremulous, left all the corners of the apartment in perfect obscurity. The thick buttresses that projected inwards from the walls, made visible by their prominence, displayed on their surfaces rude representations of idols and temples drawn in chalk, and covered with strange, mysterious hieroglyphics. On a block of stone which served as a table lay some fragments of small statues, which Vetranio recognised as having belonged to the old, accredited representations of Pagan idols. Over the sides of the table itself were scrawled in Latin characters these two words, 'Serapis', 'Macrinus'; and about its base lay some pieces of torn, soiled linen, which still retained enough of their former character, both in shape, size, and colour, to convince Vetranio that they had once served as the vestments of a Pagan priest. Further than this the senator's observation did not carry him, for the close, almost mephitic atmosphere of the place already began to affect him unfavourably. He felt a suffocating sensation in his throat and a dizziness in his head. The restorative influence of his recent bath declined rapidly. The fumes of the wine he had drunk in the night, far from having been, as he imagined, permanently dispersed, again mounted to his head. He was obliged to lean against the stone table to preserved his equilibrium as he faintly desired the Pagan to shorten their sojourn in his miserable retreat.

Without even noticing the request, Ulpius hurriedly proceeded to erase the drawings on the buttresses and the inscriptions on the table. Then collecting the fragments of statues and the pieces of linen, he deposited them in a hiding-place in the corner of the apartment. This done, he returned to the stone against which Vetranio supported himself, and for a few minutes silently regarded the senator with a firm, earnest, and penetrating gaze.

A dark suspicion that he had betrayed himself into the hands of a villain, who was then plotting some atrocious project connected with his safety or honour, began to rise on the senator's bewildered brain as he unwillingly submitted to the penetrating examination of the Pagan's glance. At that moment, however, the withered lips of the old man slowly parted, and he began to speak. Whether as he looked on Vetranio's disturbed countenance, and marked his unsteady gait, the heart of Ulpius, for the first time since his introduction to the senator, misgave him when he thought of their monstrous engagement; or whether the near approach of the moment that was henceforth, as he wildly imagined, to fix Vetranio as his assistant and ally, so powerfully affected his mind that it instinctively sought to vent its agitation through the natural medium of words, it is useless to inquire. Whatever his motives for speech, the impressive earnestness of his manner gave evidence of the depth and intensity of his emotions as he addressed the senator thus:--

'I have submitted to servitude in a Christian's house, I have suffered the contamination of a Christian's prayers, to gain the use of your power and station when the time to employ them should arrive. The hour has now come when my part of the conditions of our engagement is to be performed; the hour will yet come when your part shall be exacted from you in turn! Do you wonder at what I have done and what I will do? Do you marvel that a household drudge should speak thus to a nobleman of Rome? Are you astonished that I risk so much as to venture on enlisting you--by the sacrifice of the girl who now slumbers above--in the cause whose end is the restoration of our fathers' gods, and in whose service I have suffered and grown old? Listen, and you shall hear from what I have fallen--you shall know what I once was!' 'I adjure you by all the gods and goddesses of our ancient worship, let me hear you where I can breathe--in the garden, on the housetop, anywhere but in this dungeon!' murmured the senator in entreating accents.

'My birth, my parents, my education, my ancient abode--these I will not disclose,' interrupted the Pagan, raising one arm authoritatively, as if to obstruct Vetranio from approaching the door. 'I have sworn by my gods, that until the day of restitution these secrets of my past life shall remain unrevealed to strangers' ears.

Unknown I entered Rome, and unknown I will labour in Rome until the projects I have lived for are crowned with success! It is enough that I confess to you that with those sacred images whose fragments you have just beheld, I was once lodged; that those sacred vestments whose remains you discerned at your feet, I once wore. To attain the glories of the priesthood there was nothing that I did not resign, to preserve them there was nothing I did not perform, to recover them there is nothing that I will not attempt! I was once illustrious, prosperous, beloved; of my glory, my happiness, my popularity, the Christians have robbed me, and I will yet live to requite it heavily at their hands! I had a guardian who loved me in my youth; the Christians murdered him! A temple was under the rule of my manhood; the Christians destroyed it! The people of a whole nation once listened to my voice; the Christians have dispersed them! The wise, the great, the beautiful, the good, were once devoted to me; the Christians have made me a stranger at their doors, and outcast of their affections and thoughts! For all this shall I take no vengeance? Shall I not plot to rebuild my ruined temple, and win back, in my age, the honours that adorned me in my youth?'

'Assuredly!--at once--without delay!' stammered Vetranio, returning the stern and inquiring gaze of the Pagan with a bewildered, uneasy stare.

'To mount over the bodies of the Christian slain,' continued the old man, his sinister eyes dilating in anticipated triumph as he whispered close at the senator's ear, 'to rebuild the altars that the Christians have overthrown, is the ambition that has made light to me the sufferings of my whole life. I have battled, and it has sustained me in the midst of carnage; I have wandered, and it has been my home in the desert; I have failed, and it has supported me; I have been threatened with death, and it has preserved me from fear; I have been cast into slavery, and it has made my fetters light. You see me now, old, degraded, lonely--believe that I long neither for wife, children, tranquility, nor possessions; that I desire no companion but my cherished and exalted purpose! Remember, then, in the hour of performance the promise you have now made to aid me in the achievement of that purpose! Remember that you are a Pagan yourself! Feast, laugh, carouse with your compeers; be still the airy jester, the gay companion; but never forget the end to which you are vowed--the destiny of glory that the restoration of our deities has in store for us both!'

He ceased. Though his voice, while he spoke, never rose beyond a hoarse, monotonous, half-whispering tone, all the ferocity of his abused and degraded nature was for the instant thoroughly aroused by his recapitulation of his wrongs. Had Vetranio at this moment shown any symptoms of indecision, or spoken any words of discouragement, he would have murdered him on the spot where they stood.

Every feature in the Pagan's seared and livid countenance expressed the stormy emotions that were rushing over his heart as he now confronted his bewildered yet attentive listener. His firm, menacing position; his poor and scanty garments; his wild, shaggy hair; his crooked, distorted form; his stern, solemn, unwavering gaze--opposed as they were (under the fitful illumination of the expiring lamp and the advancing daylight) to the unsteady gait, the vacant countenance, the rich robes, the youthful grace of form and delicacy of feature of the object of his steady contemplation, made so wild and strange a contrast between his patrician ally and himself that they scarcely looked like beings of the same race. Nothing could be more immense than the difference, more wild than the incongruity between them. It was sickness hand-in-hand with health; pain marshalled face to face with enjoyment; darkness ranged in monstrous discordance by the very side of light.

The next instant--just as the astonished senator was endeavouring to frame a suitable answer to the solemn adjuration that had been addressed to him--Ulpius seized his arm, and opening a door at the inner extremity of the apartment, led him up some stairs that conducted to the interior of the house.

They passed the hall, on the floor of which still lay the fragments of the broken lute, dimly distinguishable in the soft light of daybreak; and ascending another staircase, paused at a little door at the top, which Ulpius cautiously opened, and in a moment afterwards Vetranio was admitted into Antonina's bed-chamber.

The room was of no great extent; its scanty furniture was of the most ordinary description; no ornaments glittered on its walls; no frescoes adorned its ceiling; and yet there was a simple elegance in its appearance, an unobtrusive propriety in its minutest details, which made it at once interesting and attractive to the eye. From the white curtains at the window to the vase of flowers standing by the bedside, the same natural refinement of taste appeared in the arrangement of all that the apartment contained. No sound broke the deep silence of the place, save the low, soft breathing, occasionally interrupted by a long, trembling sigh, of its sleeping occupant. The sole light in the room consisted of a little lamp, so placed in the middle of the flowers round the sides of the vase that no extended or steady illumination was cast upon any object. There was something in the decent propriety of all that was visible in the bed-chamber; in the soft obscurity of its atmosphere; in the gentle and musical sound that alone interrupted its magical stillness, impressive enough, it might have been imagined, to have awakened some hesitation in the bosom of the boldest libertine ere he deliberately proceeded to intrude on the unprotected slumbers of its occupant. No such feeling of indecision, however, troubled the thoughts of Vetranio as he cast a rapid glance round the apartment which he had venture so treacherously to invade. The fumes of the wine he had imbibed at the banquet had been so thoroughly resuscitated by the oppressive atmosphere of the subterranean retreat he had just quitted, as to have left him nothing of his more refined nature. All that was honourable or intellectual in his character had now completely ceded to all that was base and animal. He looked round, and perceiving that Ulpius had silently quitted him, softly closed the door. Then advancing to the bedside with the utmost caution compatible with the involuntary unsteadiness of an intoxicated man, he took the lamp from the vase in which it was half concealed, and earnestly surveyed by its light the figure of the sleeping girl.

The head of Antonina was thrown back and rested rather over than on her pillow. Her light linen dress had become so disordered during the night that it displayed her throat and part of her bosom, in all the dawning beauties of their youthful formation, to the gaze of the licentious Roman. One hand half supported her head, and was almost entirely hidden in the locks of her long black hair, which had escaped from the white cincture intended to confine it, and now streamed over the pillow in dazzling contrast to the light bed-furniture around it. The other hand held tightly clasped to her bosom the precious fragment of her broken lute. The deep repose expressed in her position had not thoroughly communicated itself to her face. Now and then her slightly parted lips moved and trembled, and ever and anon a change, so faint and fugitive that it was hardly perceptible, appeared in her complexion, breathing on the soft olive that was its natural hue, the light rosy flush which the emotions of the past night had impressed on it ere she slept. Her position, in its voluptuous negligence, seemed the very type of Oriental loveliness; while her face, calm and sorrowful in its expression, displayed the more refined and sober graces of the European model. And thus these two characteristics of two different orders of beauty, appearing conjointly under one form, produced a whole so various and yet so harmonious, so impressive and yet so attractive, that the senator, as he bent over the couch, though the warm, soft breath of the young girl played on his cheeks and waved the tips of his perfumed locks, could hardly imagine that the scene before him was more than a bright, delusive dream.

While Vetranio was yet absorbed in admiration of her charms, Antonina's form slightly moved, as if agitated by the influence of a passing dream. The change thus accomplished in her position broke the spell that its former stillness and beauty had unconsciously wrought to restrain the unhallowed ardour of the profligate Roman. He now passed his arm round her warm, slender figure, and gently raising her till her head rested on his shoulder as he sat by the bed, imprinted kiss after kiss on the pure lips that sleep had innocently abandoned to him.

As he had foreseen, Antonina instantly awoke, but, to his unmeasured astonishment, neither started nor shrieked. The moment she had opened her eyes she had recognised the person of Vetranio; and that overwhelming terror which suspends in its victims the use of every faculty, whether of the body or the mind, had immediately possessed itself of her heart. Too innocent to imagine the real motive that prompted the senator's intrusion on her slumbers, where others of her sex would have foreboded dishonour, she feared death. All her father's vague denunciations against the enormities of the nobles of Rome rushed in an instant over her mind, and her childish imagination pictured Vetranio as armed with some terrible and mysterious vengeance to be wreaked on her for having avoided all communication with him as soon as she had gained possession of her lute. Prostrate beneath the petrifying influence of her fears, motionless and powerless before him as its prey before the serpent, she made no effort to move or speak; but looked up steadfastly into the senator's face, her large eyes fixed and dilated in a gaze of overpowering terror.

Intoxicated though he was, the affrighted expression of the poor girl's pale, rigid countenance did not escape Vetranio's notice; and he taxed his bewildered brain for such soothing and reassuring expressions as would enable him to introduce his profligate proposals with some chance that they would be listened to and understood.

'Dearest pupil! Most beautiful of Roman maidens,' he began in the husky, monotonous tones of inebriety, 'abandon your fears! I come hither, wafted by the breath of love, to restore the worship of the--I would say to bear you on my bosom to a villa--the name of which has for the moment escaped my remembrance. You cannot have forgotten that it was I who taught you to compose the Nightingale Sauce--or, no--let me rather say to play upon the lute. Love, music, pleasure, all await you in the arms of your attached Vetranio. Your eloquent silence speaks encouragement to my heart. Beloved Anto--'

Here the senator suddenly paused; for the eyes of the girl, which had hitherto been fixed on him with the same expression of blank dismay that had characterised them from the first, slowly moved in the direction of the door. The instant afterwards a slight noise caught Vetranio's ear, and Antonina shuddered so violently as he pressed her to his side that he felt it through his whole frame. Slowly and unwillingly he withdrew his gaze from the pale yet lovely countenance on which it had been fixed, and looked up.

At the open door, pale, silent, motionless, stood the master of the house.

Incapable, from the confusion of his ideas, of any other feeling than the animal instinct of self-defence, Vetranio no sooner beheld Numerian's figure than he rose, and drawing a small dagger from his bosom, attempted to advance on the intruder. He found himself, however, restrained by Antonina, who had fallen on her knees before him, and grasped his robe with a strength which seemed utterly incompatible with the slenderness of her form and the feebleness of her sex and age.

The first voice that broke the silence which ensued was Numerian's. He advanced, his face ghastly with anguish, his lip quivering with suppressed emotions, to the senator's side, and addressed him thus:--

'Put up your weapon; I come but to ask a favour at your hands.'

Vetranio mechanically obeyed him. There was something in the stern calmness, frightful at such a moment, of the Christian's manner that awed him in spite of himself.

'The favour I would petition for,' continued Numerian, in low, steady, bitter tones, 'is that you would remove your harlot there, to your own abode. Here are no singing-boys, no banqueting-halls, no perfumed couches. The retreat of a solitary old man is no place for such an one as she. I beseech you, remove her to a more congenial home. She is well fitted for her trade; her mother was a harlot before her!'

He laughed scornfully, and pointed, as he spoke, to the figure of the unhappy girl kneeling with outstretched arms at his feet.

'Father, father!' she cried, in accents bereft of their native softness and melody, 'have you forgotten me?'

'I know you not!' he replied, thrusting her from him. 'Return to his bosom; you shall never more be pressed to mine. Go to his palace; my house is yours no longer! You are his harlot, not my daughter! I command you--go!'

As he advanced towards her with fierce glance and threatening demeanour, she suddenly rose up. Her reason seemed crushed within her as she looked with frantic earnestness from Vetranio to her father, and then back again from her father to Vetranio. On one side she saw an enemy who had ruined her she knew not how, and who threatened her with she knew not what; on the other, a parent who had cast her off. For one instant she directed a final look on the room, that, sad and lonely though it was, had still been a home to her; and then, without a word or a sigh, she turned, and crouching like a beaten dog, fled from the house.

During the whole of the scene Vetranio had stood so fixed in the helpless astonishment of intoxication as to be incapable of moving or uttering a word. All that took place during the short and terrible interview between father and child utterly perplexed him. He heard no loud, violent anger on one side, no clamorous petitioning for forgiveness on the other. The stern old man whom Antonina had called father, and who had been pointed out to him as the most austere Christian in Rome, far from avenging his intrusion on Antonina's slumber, had voluntarily abandoned his daughter to his licentious will. That the anger or irony of so severe a man should inspire such an action as this, or that Numerian, like his servant, was plotting to obtain some strange mysterious favour from him by using Antonina as a bribe, seemed perfectly impossible. all that passed before the senator was, to his bewildered imagination, thoroughly incomprehensible. Frivolous, thoughtless, profligate as he might be, his nature was not radically base, and when the scene of which he had been the astounded witness was abruptly terminated by the flight of Antonina, the look of frantic misery fixed on him by the unfortunate girl at the moment of her departure, almost sobered him for the instant, as he stood before the now solitary father gazing vacantly around him with emotions of uncontrollable confusion and dismay.

Meanwhile a third person was now approaching to join the two occupants of the bedchamber abandoned by its ill-fated mistress. Although in the subterranean retreat to which he had retired on leaving Vetranio, Ulpius had not noticed the silent entrance of the master of the house, he had heard through the open doors the sound, low though it was, of the Christian's voice. As he rose, suspecting all things and prepared for every emergency, to ascend to the bedchamber, he saw, while he mounted the lowest range of stairs, a figure in white pass rapidly through the hall and disappear by the principal entrance of the house. He hesitated for an instant and looked after it, but the fugitive figure had passed so swiftly in the uncertain light of early morning that he was unable to identify it, and he determined to ascertain the progress of events, now that Numerian must have discovered a portion at least of the plot against his daughter and himself, by ascending immediately to Antonina's apartment, whatever might be the consequences of his intrusion at such an hour on her father's wrath.

As soon as the Pagan appeared before him, a sensible change took place in Vetranio. The presence of Ulpius in the chamber was a positive relief to the senator's perturbed faculties, after the mysterious, overpowering influence that the moral command expressed in the mere presence of the father and the master of

the house, at such an hour, had exercised over them. Over Ulpius he had an
absolute right, Ulpius was his dependant; and he determined, therefore, to extort
from the servant whom he despised an explanation of the mysteries in the conduct of the master whom he feared, and the daughter whom he began to doubt.

'Where is Antonina?' he cried, starting as if from a trance, and advancing fiercely
towards the treacherous Pagan. 'She has left the room--she must have taken
refuge with you.'

With a slow and penetrating gaze Ulpius looked round the apartment. A faint
agitation was perceptible in his livid countenance, but he uttered not a word.

The senator's face became pale and red with alternate emotions of apprehension
and rage. He seized the Pagan by the throat, his eyes sparkled, his blood boiled,
he began to suspect even then that Antonina was lost to him for ever.

'I ask you again where is she?' he shouted in a voice of fury. 'If through this
night's work she is lost or harmed, I will revenge it on you. Is this the performance of your promise? Do you think that I will direct your desired restoration of
the gods of old for this? If evil comes to Antonina through your treachery, sooner than assist in your secret projects, I would see you and your accursed deities all
burning together in the Christians' hell! Where is the girl, you slave? Villain,
where was your vigilance, when you let that man surprise u⸱ at our first interview?'

He turned towards Numerian as he spoke. Trouble and emergency gift the faculties with a more than mortal penetration. Every word that he had uttered had
eaten its burning way into the father's heart. Hours of narrative could not have
convinced him how fatally he had been deceived, more thoroughly than the few
hasty expressions he had just heard. No word passed his lips--no action betrayed
his misery. He stood before the spoilers of his home, changed in an instant from
the courageous enthusiast to the feeble, helpless, heart-broken man.

Though all the ferocity of his old Roman blood had been roused in Vetranio, as
he threatened Ulpius, the father's look of cold, silent, frightful despair froze it in
his young veins in an instant. His heart was still the impressible heart of youth;
and, struck for the first time in his life with emotions of horror and remorse, he
advanced a step to offer such explanation and atonement as he best might, when
the voice of Ulpius suspended his intentions, and made him pause to listen.

'She passed me in the hall,' muttered the Pagan, doggedly. 'I did my part in
betraying her into your power--it was for you to hinder her in her flight. Why

did you not strike him to the earth,' he continued, pointing with a mocking smile to Numerian, 'when he surprised you? You are wealthy and a noble of Rome; murder would have been no crime in you!'

'Stand back!' cried the senator, thrusting him from the position he had hitherto occupied in the door-way. 'She may be recovered even yet! All Rome shall be searched for her!'

The next instant he disappeared from the room, and the master and servant were left together alone.

The silence that now reigned in the apartment was broken by distant sounds of uproar and confusion in the streets of the city beneath. These ominous noises had arisen with the dawn of day, but the different emotions of the occupants of Numerian's abode had so engrossed them, that the turmoil in the outer world had passed unheeded by all. No sooner, however, had Vetranio departed than it caught the attention of Ulpius, and he advanced to the window. What he there saw and heard was of no ordinary importance, for it at once fixed him to the spot where he stood in mute and ungovernable surprise.

While Ulpius was occupied at the window, Numerian had staggered to the side of the bed which his ill-timed severity had made vacant, perhaps for ever. The power of action, the capacity to go forth and seek his child himself, was entirely suspended in the agony of her loss, as the miserable man fell on his knees, and in the anguish of his heart endeavoured to find solace in prayer. In the positions they severally occupied the servant and the master long remained--the betrayer watching at the window, the betrayed mourning at his lost daughter's bed--both alike silent, both alike unconscious of the lapse of time.

At length, apparently unaware at first that he was not alone in the room, Numerian spoke. In his low, broken, tremulous accents, none of his adherents would have recognised the voice of the eloquent preacher--the bold chastiser of the vices of the Church. The whole nature of the man--moral, intellectual, phys-ical--seemed fatally and completely changed.

'She was innocent, she was innocent!' he whispered to himself. 'And even had she been guilty, was it for me to drive her from my doors! My part, like my Redeemer's, was to teach repentance, and to show mercy! Accursed be the pride and anger that drove justice and patience from my heart, when I beheld her, as I thought, submitting herself without a struggle or a cry, to my dishonour, and hers! Could I not have imagined her terror, could I not have remembered her purity? Alas, my beloved, if I myself have been the dupe of the wicked, what marvel is it that you should have been betrayed as well! And I have driven you from me, you, from whose mouth no word of anger ever dropped! I have thrust you from my bosom, you, who were the adornment of my age! My death approaches, and you will not be by to pardon my heavy offence, to close my weary eyes, to mourn by my solitary tomb! God--oh God! If I am left thus lonely on the earth, thou hast punished me beyond what I can bear!'

He paused--his emotions for the instant bereft him of speech. After an interval, he muttered to himself in a low, moaning voice--'I called her harlot! My pure, innocent child! I called her harlot--I called her harlot!'

In a paroxysm of despair, he started up and looked distractedly around him. Ulpius still stood motionless at the window. At the sight of the ruthless Pagan he trembled in every limb. All those infirmities of age that had been hitherto spared him, seemed to overwhelm him in an instant. He feebly advanced to his betrayer's side, and addressed him thus:--

'I have lodged you, taught you, cared for you; I have never intruded on your secrets, never doubted your word, and for all this, you have repaid me by plotting against my daughter and deceiving me! If your end was to harm me by assailing my child's happiness and honour you have succeeded! If you would banish me from Rome, if you would plunge me into obscurity, to serve some mysterious ambition of your own, you may dispose of me as you will! I bow before the terrible power of your treachery! I will renounce whatever you command, if you will restore me to my child! I am helpless and miserable; I have neither heart nor strength to seek her myself! You, who know all things and can dare all dangers, may restore her to pardon and bless me, if you will! Remember, whoever you really are, that you were once helpless and alone, and that you are still old, like me! Remember that I have promised to abandon to you whatever you desire! Remember that no woman's voice can cheer me, no woman's heart feel for me, now that I am old and lonely, but my daughter's! I have guessed from the words of the nobleman whom you serve, what are the designs you cherish and the faith you profess; I will neither betray the one nor assault the other! I thought that my labours for the Church were more to me than anything on earth, but now, that through my fault, my daughter is driven from her father's roof, I know that she is dearer to me than the greatest of my designs; I must gain her pardon; I must win back her affection before I die! You are powerful and can recover her! Ulpius! Ulpius!'

As he spoke, the Christian knelt at the Pagan's feet. It was terrible to see the man of affection and integrity thus humbled before the man of heartlessness and crime.

Ulpius turned to behold him, then without a word he raised him from the ground, and thrusting him to the window, pointed with flashing eyes to the wide view without.

The sun had arisen high in the heaven and beamed in dazzling brilliancy over Rome and the suburbs. A vague, fearful, mysterious desolation seemed to have suddenly overwhelmed the whole range of dwellings beyond the walls. No sounds rose from the gardens, no population idled in the streets. The ramparts on the other hand were crowded at every visible point with people of all ranks, and the distant squares and amphitheatres of the city itself, swarmed like ant-hills to the eye with the crowds that struggled within them. Confused cries and strange wild noises rose at all points from these masses of human beings. The whole of Rome seemed the prey of a vast and universal revolt.

Extraordinary and affrighting as was the scene at the moment when he beheld it, it passed unheeded before the eyes of the scarce conscious father. He was blind to all sights but his daughter's form, deaf to all sounds but her voice; and he murmured as he looked vacantly forth upon the wild view before him, 'Where is my child!--where is my child!'

'What is your child to me? What are the fortunes of affections of man or woman, at such an hour as this?' cried the Pagan, as he stood by Numerian, with features horribly animated by the emotions of fierce delight and triumph that were raging within him at the prospect he beheld. 'Dotard, look from this window! Listen to those voices! The gods whom I serve, the god whom you and your worship would fain have destroyed, have risen to avenge themselves at last! Behold those suburbs, they are left desolate! Hear those cries--they are from Roman lips! While your household's puny troubles have run their course, this city of apostates has been doomed! In the world's annals this morning will never be forgotten! THE GOTHS ARE AT THE GATES OF ROME!'

Chapter 8

THE GOTHS

It was no false rumour that had driven the populace of the suburbs to fly to the security of the city walls. It was no ill-founded cry of terror that struck the ear of Ulpius, as he stood at Numerian's window. The name of Rome had really lost its pristine terrors; the walls of Rome, those walls which had morally guarded the Empire by their renown, as they had actually guarded its capital by their strength, were deprived at length of their ancient inviolability. An army of barbarians had indeed penetrated for conquest and for vengeance to the City of the World! The achievement which the invasions of six hundred years had hitherto attempted in vain, was now accomplished, and accomplished by the men whose forefathers had once fled like hunted beasts to their native fastnesses, before the legions of the Caesars--'The Goths were at the gates of Rome!'

And now, as his warriors encamped around him, as he saw the arrayed hosts whom his summons had gathered together, and his energy led on, threatening at their doors the corrupt senate who had deceived, and the boastful populace who had despised him, what emotions stirred within the heart of Alaric! As the words of martial command fell from his lips, and his eyes watched the movements of the multitudes around him, what exalted aspirations, what daring resolves, grew and strengthened in the mind of the man who was the pioneer of that mighty revolution, which swept from one quarter of the world the sway, the civilisation, the very life and spirit of centuries of ancient rule! High thoughts gathered fast in his mind; a daring ambition expanded within him--the ambition not of the barbarian plunderer, but of the avenger who had come to punish; not of the warrior who combated for combat's sake, but of the hero who was vowed to conquer and to sway. From the far-distant days when Odin was driven from his territories by the romans, to the night polluted by the massacre of the hostages in Aquileia, the hour of just and terrible retribution for Gothic wrongs had been delayed through the weary lapse of years, and the warning convulsion of bitter strifes, to approach at last under him. He looked on the towering walls before him, the only invader since Hannibal by whom they had been beheld; and he felt as he looked, that his new aspirations did not deceive him, that his dreams of dominion were brightening into proud reality, that his destiny was gloriously linked with the overthrow of Imperial Rome!

But even in the moment of approaching triumph, the leader of the Goths was still wily in purpose and moderate in action. His impatient warriors waited but the word to commence the assault, to pillage the city, and to slaughter the inhabitants; but he withheld it. Scarcely had the army halted before the gates of Rome, when the news was promulgated among their ranks, that Alaric, for purposes of his own, had determined to reduce the city by a blockade.

The numbers of his forces, increased during his march by the accession of thirty thousand auxiliaries, were now divided into battalions, varying in strength according to the service that was required of them. These divisions stretched round the city walls, and though occupying separate posts, and devoted to separate duties, were so arranged as to be capable of uniting at a signal in any numbers, on any given point. Each body of men was commanded by a tried and veteran warrior, in whose fidelity Alaric could place the most implicit trust, and to whom he committed the duty of enforcing the strictest military discipline that had ever prevailed among the Gothic ranks. Before each of the twelve principal gates a separate encampment was raised. Multitudes watched the navigation of the Tiber in every possible direction, with untiring vigilance; and not one of the ordinary inlets to Rome, however apparently unimportant, was overlooked. By these means, every mode of communication between the beleaguered city and the wide and fertile tracts of land around it, was effectually prevented. When it is remembered that this elaborate plan of blockade was enforced against a place containing, at the lowest possible computation, twelve hundred thousand inhabitants, destitute of magazines for food within its walls, dependent for supplies on its regular contributions from the country without, governed by an irresolute senate, and defended by an enervated army, the horrors that now impended over the besieged Romans are as easily imagined as described.

Among the ranks of the army that now surrounded the doomed city, the division appointed to guard the Pincian Gate will be found, at this juncture, most worthy of the reader's attention: for one of the warriors appointed to its subordinate command was the young chieftain Hermanric, who had been accompanied by Goisvintha through all the toils and dangers of the march, since the time when we left him at the Italian Alps.

The watch had been set, the tents had been pitched, the defences had been raised on the portion of ground selected to occupy every possible approach to the Pincian Gate, as Hermanric retired to await by Goisvintha's side, whatever further commands he might yet be entrusted with, by his superiors in the Gothic camp. The spot occupied by the young warrior's simple tent was on a slight eminence, apart from the positions chosen by his comrades, eastward of the city gate, and overlooking at some distance the deserted gardens of the suburbs, and the stately palaces of the Pincian Hill. Behind his temporary dwelling was the open country, reduced to a fertile solitude by the flight of its terrified inhabitants; and at each side lay one unvarying prospect of military strength and preparation, stretching out its animated confusion of soldiers, tents, and engines of warfare, as far as the sight could reach. It was now evening. The walls of Rome, enshrouded in a rising mist, showed dim and majestic to the eyes of the Goths. The noises in the beleaguered city softened and deepened, seeming to be muffled in the growing darkness of the autumn night, and becoming less and less audible as the vigilant besiegers listened to them from their respective posts. One by one, lights broke wildly forth at irregular distances, in the Gothic camp. Harshly and fitfully the shrill call of the signal trumpets rang from rank to rank; and through the dim thick air rose, in the intervals of the more important noises, the clash of heavy hammers and the shout of martial command. Wherever the preparations for the blockade were still incomplete, neither the approach of night nor the pretext of weariness were suffered for an instant to hinder their continued progress. Alaric's indomitable will conquered every obstacle of nature, and every deficiency of man. Darkness had no obscurity that forced him to repose, and lassitude no eloquence that lured him to delay.

In no part of the army had the commands of the Gothic king been so quickly and intelligently executed, as in that appointed to watch the Pincian Gate. The interview of Hermanric and Goisvintha in the young chieftain's tent, was, consequently, uninterrupted for a considerable space of time by any fresh mandate from the head-quarters of the camp.

In outward appearance, both the brother and sister had undergone a change remarkable enough to be visible, even by the uncertain light of the torch which now shone on them as they stood together at the door of the tent. The features of Goisvintha--which at the period when we first beheld her on the shores of the mountain lake, retained, in spite of her poignant sufferings, much of the lofty and imposing beauty that had been their natural characteristic in her happier days-- now preserved not the slightest traces of their former attractions. Its freshness had withered from her complexion, its fulness had departed from her form. Her eyes had contracted an unvarying sinister expression of malignant despair, and her manner had become sullen, repulsive, and distrustful. This alteration in her out- ward aspect, was but the result of a more perilous change in the disposition of her heart. The death of her last child at the very moment when her flight had suc- cessfully directed her to the protection of her people, had affected her more fatal- ly than all the losses she had previously sustained. The difficulties and dangers that she had encountered in saving her offspring from the massacre; the dismal certainty that the child was the only one, out of all the former objects of her affec- tion, left to her to love; the wild sense of triumph that she experienced in remem- bering, that in this single instance her solitary efforts had thwarted the savage treachery of the Court of Rome, had inspired her with feelings of devotion towards the last of her household which almost bordered on insanity. And, now that her beloved charge, her innocent victim, her future warrior, had, after all her struggles for his preservation, pined and died; now that she was childless indeed; now that Roman cruelty had won its end in spite of all her patience, all her courage, all her endurance; every noble feeling within her sunk, annihilated at the shock. Her sorrow took the fatal form which irretrievable destroys, in women, all the softer and better emotions;--it changed to the despair that asks no sympathy, to the grief that holds no communion with tears.

Less elevated in intellect and less susceptible in disposition, the change to sullen- ness of expression and abruptness of manner now visible in Hermanric, resulted rather from his constant contemplation of Goisvintha's gloomy despair, tan from any actual revolution in his own character. In truth, however many might be the points of outward resemblance now discernible between the brother and sister, the difference in degree of their moral positions, implied of itself the difference in degree of the inward sorrow of each. Whatever the trials and afflictions that might assail him, Hermanric possessed the healthful elasticity of youth and the martial occupations of manhood to support them. Goisvintha could repose on neither. With no employment but bitter remembrance to engage her thoughts, with no kindly aspiration, no soothing hope to fill her heart, she was abandoned irrevocably to the influence of unpartaken sorrow and vindictive despair.

Both the woman and the warrior stood together in silence for some time. At length, without taking his eyes from the dusky, irregular mass before him, which was all that night now left visible of the ill-fated city, Hermanric addressed Goisvintha thus:--

'Have you no words of triumph, as you look on the ramparts that your people have fought for generations to behold at their mercy, as we now behold them? Can a woman of the Goths be silent when she stands before the city of Rome?'

'I came hither to behold Rome pillaged, and Romans slaughtered; what is Rome blockaded to me?' replied Goisvintha fiercely. 'The treasures within that city will buy its safety from our King, as soon as the tremblers on the ramparts gain heart enough to penetrate a Gothic camp. Where is the vengeance that you promised me among those distant palaces? Do I behold you carrying that destruction through the dwellings of Rome, which the soldiers of yonder city carried through the dwellings of the Goths? Is it for plunder or for glory that the army is here? I thought, in my woman's delusion, that it was for revenge!'

'Dishonour will avenge you--Famine will avenge you--Pestilence will avenge you!'

'They will avenge my nation; they will not avenge me. I have seen the blood of Gothic women spilt around me--I have looked on my children's corpses bleeding at my feet! Will a famine that I cannot see, and a pestilence that I cannot watch, give me vengeance for this? Look! Here is the helmet-crest of my husband and your brother--the helmet-crest that was flung to me as a witness that the Romans had slain him! Since the massacre of Aquileia it has never quitted my bosom. I have sworn that the blood which stains and darkens it, shall be washed off in the blood of the people of Rome. Though I should perish under those accursed walls; though you in your soulless patience should refuse me protection and aid; I, widowed, weakened, forsaken as I am, will hold to the fulfilment of my oath!'

As she ceased she folded the crest in her mantle, and turned abruptly from Hermanric in bitter and undissembled scorn. All the attributes of her sex, in thought, expression, and manner, seemed to have deserted her. The very tones she spoke in were harsh and unwomanly.

Every word she had uttered, every action she had displayed, had sunk into the inmost heart, had stirred the fiercest passions of the young warrior whom she addressed. The first national sentiment discoverable in the day-spring of the ages of Gothic history, is the love of war; but the second is the reverence of woman. This latter feeling--especially remarkable among so fierce and unsusceptible a people as the ancient Scandinavians--was entirely unconnected with those strong attaching ties, which are the natural consequence of the warm temperaments of more southern nations; for love was numbered with the base inferior passions, in the frigid and hardy composition of the warrior of the north. It was the offspring of reasoning and observation, not of instinctive sentiment and momentary impulse. In the wild, poetical code of the old Gothic superstition was one axiom, closely and strangely approximating to an important theory in the Christian scheme--the watchfulness of an omnipotent Creator over a finite creature. Every action of the body, every impulse of the mind, was the immediate result, in the system of worship among the Goths of the direct, though invisible interference of the divinities they adored. When, therefore, they observed that women were more submitted in body to the mysterious laws of nature and temperament, and more swayed in mind by the native and universal instincts of humanity than themselves, they inferred as an inevitable conclusion, that the female sex was more incessantly regarded, and more constantly and remarkably influenced by the gods of their worship, than the male. Acting under this persuasion, they committed the study of medicine, the interpretation of dreams, and in many instances, the mysteries of communication with the invisible world, to the care of their women. The gentler sex became their counsellors in difficulty, and their physicians in sickness--their companions rather than their mistresses,--the objects of their veneration rather than the purveyors of their pleasures. Although in after years, the national migrations of the Goths changed the national temperament, although their ancient mythology was exchanged for the worship of Christ, this prevailing sentiment of their earliest existence as a people never entirely deserted them; but, with different modifications and in different forms, maintained much of its old supremacy through all changes of manners and varieties of customs, descending finally to their posterity among the present nations of Europe, in the shape of that established code of universal courtesy to women, which is admitted to be one great distinguishing mark between the social systems of the inhabitants of civilised and uncivilised lands.

This powerful and remarkable ascendancy of the woman over the man, among the Goths, could hardly be more strikingly displayed than in the instance of Hermanric. It appeared, not only in the deteriorating effect of the constant companionship of Goisvintha on his naturally manly character, but also in the strong influence over his mind of the last words of fury and disdain that she had spoken. His eyes gleamed with anger, his cheeks flushed with shame, as he listened to those passages in her wrathful remonstrance which reflected most bitterly on himself. She had scarcely ceased, and turned to retire into the tent, when he arrested her progress, and replied, in heightened and accusing tones:--

'You wrong me by your words! When I saw you among the Alps, did I refuse you protection? When the child was wounded, did I leave him to suffer unaided? When he died, did I forsake him to rot upon the earth, or abandon to his mother the digging of his grave? When we approached Aquileia, and marched past

Ravenna, did I forget that the sword hung at my shoulder? Was it at my will that it remained sheathed, or that I entered not the gates of the Roman towns, but passed by them in haste? Was it not the command of the king that withheld me? and could I, his warrior, disobey? I swear it to you, the vengeance that I promised, I yearn to perform,--but is it for me to alter the counsels of Alaric? Can I alone assault the city which it is his command that we should blockade? What would you have of me?'

'I would have you remember,' retorted Goisvintha, indignantly, 'that Romans slew your brother, and made me childless! I would have you remember that a public warfare of years on years, is powerless to stay one hour's craving of private vengeance! I would have you less submitted to your general's wisdom, and more devoted to your own wrongs! I would have you--like me--thirst for the blood of the first inhabitant of yonder den of traitors, who--whether for peace or for war--passes the precincts of its sheltering walls!'

She paused abruptly for an answer, but Hermanric uttered not a word. The courageous heart of the young chieftain recoiled at the deliberate act of assassination, pressed upon him in

Goisvintha's veiled yet expressive speech. To act with his comrades in taking the city by assault, to outdo in the heat of battle the worst horrors of the massacre of Aquileia, would have been achievements in harmony with his wild disposition and warlike education; but, to submit himself to Goisvintha's projects, was a sacrifice, that the very peculiarities of his martial character made repugnant to his thoughts. Emotions such as these he would have communicated to his companion, as they passed through his mind; but there was something in the fearful and ominous change that had occurred in her disposition since he had met her among the Alps,--in her frantic, unnatural craving for bloodshed and revenge, that gave her a mysterious and powerful influence over his thoughts, his words, and even his actions. He hesitated and was silent.

'Have I not been patient?' continued Goisvintha, lowering her voice to tones of earnest, agitated entreaty, which jarred upon Hermanric's ear, as he thought who was the petitioner, and what would be the object of the petition,--' Have I not been patient throughout the weary journey from the Alps? Have I not waited for the hour of retribution, even before the defenceless cities that we passed on the march? Have I not at you instigation governed my yearning for vengeance, until the day that should see you mounting those walls with the warriors of the Goths, to scourge with fire and sword the haughty traitors of Rome? Has that day come? Is it by this blockade that the requital you promised me over the corpse of my murdered child, is to be performed? Remember the perils I dared, to preserved the life of that last one of my household,--and will you risk nothing to avenge his death? His sepulchre is untended and solitary. Far from the dwellings of his people, lost in the dawn of his beauty, slaughtered in the beginning of his strength, lies the offspring of your brother's blood. And the rest--the two children, who were yet infants; the father, who was brave in battle and wise in council--where are they? Their bones whiten on the shelterless plain, or rot unburied by the ocean shore! Think--had they lived--how happily your days would have passed with them in the time of peace! how gladly your brother would have gone forth with you to the chase! how joyfully his boys would have nestled at your knees, to gather from your lips the first lessons that should form them for the warrior's life! Think of such enjoyments as these, and then think that Roman swords have deprived you of them all!'

Her voice trembled, she ceased for a moment, and looked mournfully up into Hermanric's averted face. Every feature in the young chieftain's countenance expressed the tumult that her words had aroused within him. He attempted to reply, but his voice was powerless in that trying moment. His head drooped upon his heaving breast, and he sighed heavily as, without speaking, he grasped Goisvintha by the hand. The object she had pleaded for was nearly attained;--he was fast sinking beneath the tempter's well-spread toils!

'Are you silent still?' she gloomily resumed. 'Do you wonder at this longing for vengeance, at this craving for Roman blood? I tell you that my desire has arisen within me, at promptings from the voices of an unknown world. They urge me to seek requital on the nation who have widowed and bereaved me--yonder, in their vaunted city, from their pampered citizens, among their cherished homes-- in the spot where their shameful counsels take root, and whence their ruthless treacheries derive their bloody source! In the book that our teachers worship, I have heard it read, that "the voice of blood crieth from the ground!" This is the voice--Hermanric, this is the voice that I have heard! I have dreamed that I walked on a shore of corpses, by a sea of blood--I have seen, arising from that sea, my husband's and my children's bodies, gashed throughout with Roman wounds! They have called to me through the vapour of carnage that was around them;-- 'Are we yet unavenged? Is the sword of Hermanric yet sheathed?' Night after night have I seen this vision and heard those voice, and hoped for no respite until the day that saw the army encamped beneath the walls of Rome, and raising the scaling ladders for the assault! And now, after all my endurance, how has that day arrived? Accursed be the lust of treasure! It is more to the warriors, and to you, than the justice of revenge!'

'Listen! listen!' cried Hermanric entreatingly.

'I listen no longer!' interrupted Goisvintha. 'The tongue of my people is as a strange language in my ears; for it talks but of plunder and of peace, of obedience, of patience, and of hope! I listen no longer; for the kindred are gone that I loved to listen to--they are all slain by the Romans but you--and you I renounce!'

Deprived of all power of consideration by the violence of the emotions awakened in his heart by Goisvintha's wild revelations of the evil passion that consumed her, the young Goth, shuddering throughout his whole frame, and still averting his face, murmured in hoarse, unsteady accents: 'Ask of me what you will. I have no words to deny, no power to rebuke you--ask of me what you will!'

'Promise me,' cried Goisvintha, seizing the hand of Hermanric, and gazing with a look of fierce triumph on his disordered countenance, 'that this blockade of the city shall not hinder my vengeance! Promise me that the first victim of our righteous revenge, shall be the first one that appears before you--whether in war or peace--of the inhabitants of Rome!'

'I promise,' cried the Goth. And those two words sealed the destiny of his future life.

During the silence that now ensued between Goisvintha and Hermanric, and while each stood absorbed in deep meditation, the dark prospect spread around them began to brighten slowly under a soft, clear light. The moon, whose dull broad disk had risen among the evening mists arrayed in gloomy red, had now topped the highest of the exhalations of earth, and beamed in the wide heaven, adorned once more in her pale, accustomed hue. Gradually, yet perceptibly, the vapour rolled,--layer by layer,--from the lofty summits of the palaces of Rome, and the high places of the mighty city began to dawn, as it were, in the soft, peaceful, mysterious light; while the lower divisions of the walls, the desolate suburbs, and parts of the Gothic camp, lay still plunged in the dusky obscurity of the mist, in grand and gloomy contrast to the prospect of glowing brightness, that almost appeared to hover about them from above and around. Patches of ground behind the tent of Hermanric, began to grow partially visible in raised and open positions; and the song of the nightingale was now faintly audible at intervals, among the solitary and distant trees. In whatever direction it was observed, the aspect of nature gave promise of the cloudless, tranquil night, of the autumnal climate of ancient Italy.

Hermanric was the first to return to the contemplation of the outward world. Perceiving that the torch which still burnt by the side of his tent, had become useless, now that the moon had arisen and dispelled the mists, he advance and extinguished it; pausing afterwards to look forth over the plains, as they brightened slowly before him. He had been thus occupied but a short time, when he thought he discerned a human figure moving slowly over a spot of partially lightened and hilly ground, at a short distance from him. It was impossible that this wandering form could be one of his own people;--they were all collected at their respective posts, and his tent he knew was on the outermost boundary of the encampment before the Pincian Gate.

He looked again. The figure still advanced, but at too great a distance to allow him a chance of discovering, in the uncertain light around him, either its nation, its sex, or its age. His heart misgave him as he remembered his promise to Goisvintha, and contemplated the possibility that it was some miserable slave, abandoned by the fugitives who had quitted the suburbs in the morning, who now approached as a last resource, to ask mercy and protection from his enemies in the camp. He turned towards Goisvintha as the idea crossed his mind, and observed that she was still occupied in meditation. Assured by the sight, that she had not yet observed the fugitive figure, he again directed his attention--with an excess of anxiety which he could hardly account for--in the direction where he had first beheld it, but it was no more to be seen. It had either retired to concealment, or was now still advancing towards his tent through a clump of trees that clothed the descent of the hill.

Silently and patiently he continued to look forth over the landscape; and still no living thing was to be seen. At length, just as he began to doubt whether his senses had not deceived him, the fugitive figure suddenly appeared from the trees, hurried with wavering gait over the patch of low, damp ground that still separated it from the young Goth, gained his tent, and then with a feeble cry fell helplessly upon the earth at his feet.

That cry, faint as it was, attracted Goisvintha's attention. She turned in an instant, thrust Hermanric aside, and raised the stranger in her arms. The light, slender form, the fair hand and arm hanging motionless towards the ground, the long locks of deep black hair, heavy with the moisture of the night atmosphere, betrayed the wanderer's sex and age in an instant. The solitary fugitive was a young girl.

Signing to Hermanric to kindle the extinguished torch at a neighbouring watch-fire, Goisvintha carried the still insensible girl into the tent. As the Goth silently

proceeded to obey her, a vague, horrid suspicion, that he shrunk from embody-
ing, passed across his mind. His hand shook so that he could hardly light the
torch, and bold and vigorous as he was, his limbs trembled beneath him as he
slowly returned to the tent.

When he had gained the interior of his temporary abode, the light of his torch
illuminated a strange and impressive scene.

Goisvintha was seated on a rude oaken chest, supporting on her knees the form
of the young girl, and gazing with an expression of the most intense and
enthralling interest upon her pale, wasted countenance. The tattered robe that
had hitherto enveloped the fugitive had fallen back, and disclosed the white dress,
which was the only other garment she wore. Her face, throat, and arms, had been
turned, by exposure to the cold, to the pure whiteness of marble. Her eyes were
closed, and her small, delicate features were locked in a rigid repose. But for her
deep black hair, which heightened the ghastly aspect of her face, she might have
been mistaken, as she lay in the woman's arms, for an exquisitely chiseled statue
of youth in death! When the figure of the young warrior, arrayed in his martial
habiliments, and standing near the insensible girl with evident emotions of wonder and anxiety, was added to the group thus produced,--when Goisvintha's tall,
powerful frame, clothed in dark garments, and bent over the fragile form and
white dress of the fugitive, was illuminated by the wild, fitful glare of the torch,-
-when the heightened colour, worn features, and eager expression of the woman
were beheld, here shadowed, there brightened, in close opposition to the pale,
youthful, reposing countenance of the girl, such an assemblage of violent lights
and deep shades was produced, as gave the whole scene a character at once mysterious and sublime. It presented an harmonious variety of solemn colours, united by the exquisite artifice of Nature to a grand, yet simple disposition of form.
It was a picture executed by the hand of Rembrandt, and imagined by the mind
of Raphael.

Starting abruptly from her long, earnest examination of the fugitive, Goisvintha
proceeded to employ herself in restoring animation to her insensible charge.
While thus occupied, she preserved unbroken silence. A breathless expectation,
that absorbed all her senses in one direction, seemed to have possessed itself of her
heart. She laboured at her task with the mechanical, unwavering energy of those,
whose attention is occupied by their thoughts rather than their actions. Slowly
and unwillingly the first faint flush of returning animation dawned, in the ten-
derest delicacy of hue, upon the girl's colourless cheek. Gradually and softly, her
quickening respiration fluttered a thin lock of hair that had fallen over her face.
A little interval more, and then the closed, peaceful eyes suddenly opened, and

glance quickly round the tent with a wild expression of bewilderment and terror. Then, as Goisvintha rose, and attempted to place her on a seat, she tore herself from her grasp, looked on her for a moment with fearful intentness, and then falling on her knees, murmured, in a plaintive voice,--

'Have mercy upon me. I am forsaken by my father,--I know not why. The gates of the city are shut against me. My habitation in Rome is closed to me for ever!'

She had scarcely spoken these few words, before an ominous change appeared in Goisvintha's countenance. Its former expression of ardent curiosity changed to a look of malignant triumph. Her eyes fixed themselves on the girl's upturned face, in glaring, steady, spell-bound contemplation. She gloated over the helpless creature before her, as the wild beast gloats over the prey that it has secured. Her form dilated, a scornful smile appeared on her lips, a hot flush rose on her cheeks, and ever and anon she whispered softly to herself, 'I knew she was Roman! Aha! I knew she was Roman!'

During this space of time Hermanric was silent. His breath came short and thick, his face grew pale, and his glance, after resting for an instant on the woman and the girl, travelled slowly and anxiously round the tent. In one corner of it lay a heavy battle-axe. He looked for a moment from the weapon to Goisvintha, with a vivid expression of horror, and then moving slowly across the tent, with a firm, yet trembling grasp, he possessed himself of the arm.

As he looked up, Goisvintha approached him. In one hand she held the bloody helmet-crest, while she pointed with the other to the crouching form of the girl. Her lips were still parted with their unnatural smile, and she whispered softly to the Goth--'Remember your promise!--remember your kindred!--remember the massacre of Aquileia!'

The young warrior made no answer. He moved rapidly forward a few steps, and signed hurriedly to the young girl to fly by the door; but her terror had by this time divested her of all her ordinary powers of perception and comprehension. She looked up vacantly at Hermanric, and then shuddering violently, crept into a corner of the tent. During the short silence that now ensued, the Goth could hear her shiver and sigh, as he stood watching, with all the anxiety of apprehension, Goisvintha's darkening brow.

'She is Roman--she is the first dweller in the city who has appeared before you!--remember your promise!--remember your kindred!--remember the massacre of Aquileia!' said the woman in fierce, quick, concentrated tones.

'I remember that I am a warrior and a Goth,' replied Hermanric, disdainfully. 'I have promised to avenge you, but it must be on a man that my promise must be fulfilled--an armed man, who can come forth with weapons in his hand--a strong man of courage whom I will slay in single combat before your eyes! The girl is too young to die, too weak to be assailed!'

Not a syllable that he had spoken had passed unheeded by the fugitive, every word seemed to revive her torpid faculties. As he ceased she arose, and with the quick instinct of terror, ran up to the side of the young Goth. Then seizing his hand-- the hand that still grasped the battle-axe--she knelt down and kissed it, uttering hurried broken ejaculations, as she clasped it to her bosom, which the tremu- lousness of her voice rendered completely unintelligible.

'Did the Romans think my children too young to die, or too weak to be assailed?' cried Goisvintha. 'By the Lord God of Heaven, they murdered them the more willingly because they were young, and wounded them the more fiercely because they were weak! My heart leaps within me as I look on the girl! I am doubly avenged, if I am avenged on the innocent and the youthful! Her bones shall rot on the plains of Rome, as the bones of my offspring rot on the plains of Aquileia! Shed me her blood!--Remember your promise!--Shed me her blood!'

She advanced with extended arms and gleaming eyes towards the fugitive. She gasped for breath, her face turned suddenly to a livid paleness, the torchlight fell upon her distorted features, she looked unearthly at that fearful moment; but the divinity of mercy had now braced the determination of the young Goth to meet all emergencies. His bright steady eye quailed not for an instant, as he encoun- tered the frantic glance of the fury before him. With one hand he barred Goisvintha from advancing another step; the other, he could not disengage from the girl, who now clasped and kissed it more eagerly than before.

'You do this but to tempt me to anger,' said Goisvintha, altering her manner with sudden and palpable cunning, more ominous of peril to the fugitive than the fury she had hitherto displayed. 'You jest at me, because I have failed in patience, like a child! But you will shed her blood--you are honourable and will hold to your promise--you will shed her blood! And I,' she continued, exultingly, seating her- self on the oaken chest that she had previously occupied, and resting her clenched hands on her knees; 'I will wait to see it!'

At this moment voices and steps were heard outside the tent. Hermanric instant- ly raised the trembling girl from the ground, and supporting her by his arm, advanced to ascertain the cause of the disturbance. He was confronted the next instant by an old warrior of superior rank, attached to the person of Alaric, who was followed by a small party of the ordinary soldiery of the camp.

'Among the women appointed by the king to the office of tending, for this night, those sick and wounded on the march, is Goisvintha, sister of Hermanric. If she is here, let her approach and follow me;' said the chief of the party in authoritative tones, pausing at the door of the tent.

Goisvintha rose. For an instant she stood irresolute. To quit Hermanric at such a time as this, was a sacrifice that wrung her savage heart;--but she remembered the severity of Alaric's discipline, she saw the armed men awaiting her, and yielded after a struggle to the imperious necessity of obedience to the king's commands. Trembling with suppressed anger and bitter disappointment, she whispered to Hermanric as she passed him:--

'You cannot save her if you would! You dare not commit her to the charge of your companions, she is too young and too fair to be abandoned to their doubtful protection. You cannot escape with her, for you must remain here on the watch at your post. You will not let her depart by herself, for you know that she would perish with cold and privation before the morning rises. When I return on the morrow I shall see her in the tent. You cannot escape from your promise;--you cannot forget it,--you must shed her blood!'

'The commands of the king,' said the old warrior, signing to his party to depart with Goisvintha, who now stood with forced calmness awaiting their guidance: 'will be communicated to the chieftain Hermanric on the morrow. Remember,' he continued in a lower tone, pointing contemptuously to the trembling girl; 'that the vigilance you have shown in setting the watch before yonder gate, will not excuse any negligence your prize there may now cause you to commit! Consult your youthful pleasures as you please, but remember your duties! Farewell!'

Uttering these words in a stern, serious tone, the veteran departed. Soon the last sound of the footsteps of his escort died away, and Hermanric and the fugitive were left alone in the tent.

During the address of the old warrior to the chieftain, the girl had silently detached herself from her protector's support, and retired hastily to the interior of the tent. When she saw that they were left together again, she advanced hesitatingly towards the young Goth, and looked up with an expression of mute inquiry into his face.

'I am very miserable,' said she, after an interval of silence, in soft, clear, melancholy accents. 'If you forsake me now, I must die--and I have lived so short a time on the earth, I have known so little happiness and so little love, that I am not fit to die! But you will protect me! You are good and brave, strong with weapons in your hands, and full of pity. You have defended me, and spoken kindly of me--I love you for the compassion you have shown me.'

Her language and actions, simple as they were, were yet so new to Hermanric, whose experience of her sex had been almost entirely limited to the women of his own stern impassive nation, that he could only reply by a brief assurance of protection, when the suppliant awaited his answer. A new page in the history of humanity was opening before his eyes, and he scanned it in wondering silence.

'If that woman should return,' pursued the girl, fixing her dark, eloquent eyes intently upon the Goth's countenance, 'take me quickly where she cannot come. My heart grows cold as I look on her! She will kill me if she can approach me again! My father's anger is very fearful, but hers is horrible--horrible--horrible! Hush! already I hear her coming back--let us go--I will follow you wherever you please--but let us not delay while there is time to depart! She will destroy me if she sees me now, and I cannot die yet! Oh my preserver, my compassionate defender, I cannot die yet!'

'No one shall harm you--no on shall approach you to-night--you are secure from all dangers in this tent,' said the Goth, gazing on her with undissembled astonishment and admiration.

'I will tell you why death is so dreadful to me,' she continued, and her voice deepened as she spoke, to tones of mournful solemnity, strangely impressive in a creature so young. 'I have lived much alone, and have had no companions but my thoughts, and the sky that I could look up to, and the things on the earth that I could watch. As I have seen the clear heaven and the soft fields, and smelt the perfume of flowers, and heard the voices of singing-birds afar off, I have wondered why the same God who made all this, and made me, should have made grief and pain and hell--the dread eternal hell that my father speaks of in his church. I never looked at the sun-light, or woke from my sleep to look on and to think of the distant stars, but I longed to love something that might listen to my joy. But my father forbade me to be happy! He frowned even when he gave me my flower-garden--though God made flowers. He destroyed my lute--though God made music. My life has been a longing in loneliness for the voices of friends! My heart has swelled and trembled within my, because when I walked in the garden and looked on the plains and woods and high, bright mountains that were round me,

I knew that I loved them alone! Do you know now why I dare not die? It is because I must find first the happiness which I feel God has made for me. It is because I must live to praise this wonderful, beautiful world with others who enjoy it as I could! It is because my home has been among those who sigh, and never among those who smile! It is for this that I fear to die! I must find companions whose prayers are in singing and in happiness, before I go to the terrible hereafter that all dread. I dare not die! I dare not die!'

As she uttered these last words she began to weep bitterly. Between amazement and compassion the young Goth was speechless. He looked down upon the small, soft hand that she had placed on his arm while she spoke, and saw that it trembled; he pressed it, and felt that it was cold; and in the first impulse of pity produced by the action, he found the readiness of speech which he had hitherto striven for in vain.

'You shiver and look pale,' said he; 'a fire shall be kindled at the door of the tent. I will bring you garments that will warm you, and food that will give you strength; you shall sleep, and I will watch that no one harms you.'

The girl hastily looked up. An expression of ineffable gratitude overspread her sorrowful countenance. She murmured in a broken voice, 'Oh, how merciful, how merciful you are!' And then, after an evident struggle with herself, she covered her face with her hands, and again burst into tears.

More and more embarrassed, Hermanric mechanically busied himself in procuring from such of his attendants as the necessities of the blockade left free, the supplies of fire, food and raiment, which he had promised. She received the coverings, approached the blazing fuel, and partook of the simple refreshment, which the young warrior offered her, with eagerness. After that she sat for some time silent, absorbed in deep meditation, and cowering over the fire, apparently unconscious of the curiosity with which she was still regarded by the Goth. At length she suddenly looked up, and observing his eyes fixed on her, arose and beckoned him to the seat that she occupied.

'Did you know how utterly forsaken I am,' said she, 'you would not wonder as you do, that I, a stranger and a Roman, have sought you thus. I have told you how lonely was my home; but yet that home was a refuge and a protection to me until the morning of this long day that is past, when I was expelled from it for ever! I was suddenly awakened in my bed by--my father entered in anger--he called me--'

She hesitated, blushed, and then paused at the very outset of her narrative. Innocent as she was, the natural instincts of her sex spoke, though in a mysterious yet in a warning tone, within her heart, abruptly imposing on her motives for silence that she could neither penetrate nor explain. She clasped her trembling hands over her bosom as if to repress its heaving, and casting down her eyes, continued in a lower tone:--

I cannot tell you why my father drove me from his doors. He has always been silent and sorrowful to me; setting me long tasks in mournful books; commanding that I should not quit the precincts of his abode, and forbidding me to speak to him when I have sometimes asked him to tell me of my mother whom I have lost. Yet he never threatened me or drove me from his side, until the morning of which I have told you. Then his wrath was terrible; his eyes were fierce; his voice was threatening! He bade me begone, and I obeyed him in affright, for I thought he would have slain me if I stayed! I fled from the house, knowing not where I went, and ran through yonder gate, which is hard by our abode. As I entered the suburbs, I met great crowds, all hurrying into Rome. I was bewildered by my fears and the confusion all around, yet I remember that they called loudly to me to fly to the city, ere the gates were closed against the assault of the Goths. And others jostled and scoffed at me, as they passed by and saw me in the thin night garments in which I was banished from my home!'

Here she paused and listened intently for a few moments. Every accidental noise that she heard still awakened in her the apprehension of Goisvintha's return. Reassured by Hermanric and by her own observation of all that was passing outside the tent, she resumed her narrative after an interval, speaking now in a steadier voice. 'I thought my heart would burst within me,' she continued, 'as I tried to escape them. All things whirled before my eyes. I could not speak--I could not stop--I could not weep. I fled and fled I knew not whither, until I sank down exhausted at the door of a small house on the outskirts of the suburbs. Then I called for aid, but no one was by to hear me. I crept--for I could stand no longer--into the house. It was empty. I looked from the windows: no human figure passed through the silent streets. The roar of a mighty confusion still rose from the walls of the city, but I was left to listen to it alone. In the house I saw scattered on the floor some fragments of bread and an old garment. I took them both, and then rose and departed; for the silence of the place was horrible to me, and I remembered the fields and the plains that I had once loved to look on, and I thought that I might find there the refuge that had been denied to me at Rome! So I set forth once more; and when I gained the soft grass, and sat down beside the shady trees, and saw the sunlight brightening over the earth, my heart grew sad, and I wept as I thought on my loneliness and remembered my father's anger.

'I had not long remained in my resting-place, when I heard a sound of trumpets in the distance, and looking forth, I saw far off, advancing over the plains, a mighty multitude with arms that glittered in the sun. I strove, as I beheld them, to arise and return even to those suburbs whose solitude had affrighted me. But my limbs failed me. I saw a little hollow hidden among the trees around. I entered it, and there throughout the lonely day I lay concealed. I heard the long tramp of footsteps, as your army passed me on the roads beneath; and then, after those hours of fear came the weary hours of solitude!

'Oh, those--lonely--lonely--lonely hours! I have lived without companions, but those hours were more terrible to me than all the years of my former life! I dared not venture to leave my hiding-place--I dared not call! Alone in the world, I crouched in my refuge till the sun went down! Then came the mist, and the darkness, and the cold. The bitter winds of night thrilled through and through me! The lonely obscurity around me seemed filled with phantoms whom I could not behold, who touched me and rustled over the surface of my skin! They half maddened me! I rose to depart; to meet my wrathful father, or the army that had passed me, or solitude in the cold, bright meadows--I cared not which!--when I discerned the light of your torch, the moment ere it was extinguished. Dark though it then was, I found your tent. And now I know that I have found yet more--a companion and a friend!'

She looked up at the young Goth as she pronounced these words with the same grateful expression that had appeared on her countenance before; but this time her eyes were not by tears. Already her disposition--poor as was the prospect of happiness which now lay before it--had begun to return, with an almost infantine facility of change, to the restoring influences of the brighter emotions. Already the short tranquilities of the present began to exert for her their effacing charm over the long agitations of the past. Despair was unnumbered among the emotions that grew round that child-like heart; shame, fear, and grief, however they might overshadow it for a time, left no taint of their presence on its bright, fine surface. Tender, perilously alive to sensation, strangely retentive of kindness as she was by nature, the very solitude to which she had been condemned had gifted her, young as she was, with a martyr's endurance of ill, and with a stoic's patience under pain.

'Do not mourn for me now,' she pursued, gently interrupting some broken expressions of compassion which fell from the lips of the young Goth. 'If you are merciful to me, I shall forget all that I have suffered! Though your nation is at enmity with mine, while you remain my friend, I fear nothing! I can look on your great stature, and heavy sword, and bright armour now without trembling! You are not like to the soldiers of Rome;--you are taller, stronger, more gloriously arrayed! You are like a statue I once saw by chance of a warrior of the Greeks! You have a look of conquest and a presence of command!'

She gazed on the manly and powerful frame of the young warrior, clothed as it was in the accoutrements of his warlike nation, with an expression of childish interest and astonishment, asking him the appellation and use of each part of his equipment, as it attracted her attention, and ending her inquiries by eagerly demanding his name.

'Hermanric,' she repeated, as he answered her, pronouncing with some difficulty the harsh Gothic syllables--'Hermanric!--that is a stern, solemn name--a name fit for a warrior and a man! Mine sounds worthless, after such a name as that! It is only Antonina!'

Deeply as he was interested in every word uttered by the girl, Hermanric could no longer fail to perceive the evident traces of exhaustion that now appeared in the slightest of her actions. Producing some furs from a corner of the tent, he made a sort of rude couch by the side of the fire, heaped fresh fuel on the flames, and then gently counselled her to recruit her wasted energies by repose. There was something so candid in his manner, so sincere in the tones of his voice, as he made his simple offer of hospitality to the stranger who had taken refuge with him, that the most distrustful woman would have accepted with as little hesitation as Antonina; who, gratefully and unhesitatingly, laid down on the bed that he had been spreading for her at her feet.

As soon as he had carefully covered her with a cloak, and rearranged her couch in the position best calculated to insure her all the warmth of the burning fuel, Hermanric retired to the other side of the fire; and, leaning on his sword, abandoned himself to the new and absorbing reflections which the presence of the girl naturally aroused.

He thought not one the duties demanded of him by the blockade; he remembered neither the scene of rage and ferocity that had followed his evasion of his reckless promise; nor the fierce determination that Goisvintha had expressed as she quitted him for the night. The cares and toils to come with the new morning, which would oblige him to expose the fugitive to the malignity of her revengeful enemy; the thousand contingencies that the difference of their sexes, their nations, and their lives, might create to oppose the continuance of the permanent protection that he had promised to her, caused him no forebodings. Antonina, and Antonina alone, occupied every faculty of his mind, and every feeling of his heart. There was a softness and a melody to his ear in her very name!

His early life had made him well acquainted with the Latin tongue, but he had never discovered all its native smoothness of sound, and elegance of structure, until he had heard it spoken by Antonina. Word by word, he passed over in his mind her varied, natural, and happy turns of expression; recalling, as he was thus employed, the eloquent looks, the rapid gesticulations, the changing tones which had accompanied those words, and thinking how wide was the difference between this young daughter of Rome, and the cold and taciturn women of his own nation. The very mystery enveloping her story, which would have excited the suspicion or contempt of more civilised men, aroused in him no other emotions than those of wonder and compassion. No feelings of a lower nature than these entered his heart towards the girl. She was safe under the protection of the enemy and the barbarian, after having been lost through the interference of the Roman and the senator.

To the simple perceptions of the Goth, the discovery of so much intelligence united to such extreme youth, of so much beauty doomed to such utter loneliness, was the discovery of an apparition that dazzled, and not of a woman who charmed him. He could not even have touched the hand of the helpless creature, who now reposed under his tent, unless she had extended it to him of her own accord. He could only think--with a delight whose excess he was far from estimating himself--on this solitary mysterious being who had come to him for shelter and for aid; who had awakened in him already new sources of sensation; and who seemed to his startled imagination to have suddenly twined herself for ever about the destinies of his future life.

He was still deep in meditation, when he was startled by a hand suddenly laid on his arm. He looked up and saw that Antonina, whom he had imagined to be slumbering on her couch, was standing by his side.

'I cannot sleep,' said the girl in a low, awe-struck voice, 'until I have asked you to spare my father when you enter Rome. I know that you are here to ravage the city; and, for aught I can tell, you may assault and destroy it to-night. Will you promise to warn me before the walls are assailed? I will then tell you my father's name and abode, and you will spare him as you have mercifully spared me? He has denied me his protection, but he is my father still; and I remember that I disobeyed him once, when I possessed myself of a lute! Will you promise me to spare him? My mother, whom I have never seen and who must therefore be dead, may love me in another world for pleading for my father's life!'

In a few words, Hermanric quieted her agitation by explaining to her the nature and intention of the Gothic blockade, and she silently returned to the couch. After a short interval, her slow, regular breathing announced to the young warrior, as he watched by the side of the fire, that she had at length forgotten the day's heritage of misfortune in the welcome oblivion of sleep.

Chapter 9

THE TWO INTERVIEWS

The time, is the evening of the first day of the Gothic blockade; the place, is Vetranio's palace at Rome. In one of the private apartments of his mansion is seated its all-accomplished owner, released at length from the long sitting convened by the Senate on the occasion of the unexpected siege of the city. Although the same complete discipline, the same elegant regularity, and the same luxurious pomp, which distinguished the senator's abode in times of security, still prevail over it in the time of imminent danger which now threatens rich and poor alike in Rome, Vetranio himself appears far from partaking the tranquility of his patrician household. His manner displays an unusual sternness, and his face an unwonted displeasure, as he sits, occupied by his silent reflections and thoroughly unregardful of whatever occurs around him. Two ladies who are his companions in the apartment, exert all their blandishments to win him back to hilarity, but in vain. The services of his expectant musicians are not put into requisition, the delicacies on his table remain untouched, and even 'the inestimable kitten of the breed most worshipped by the ancient Egyptians' gambols unnoticed and unapplauded at his feet. All its wonted philosophical equanimity has evidently departed, for the time at least, from the senator's mind.

Silence--hitherto a stranger to the palace apartments--had reigned uninterruptedly over them for some time, when the freedman Carrio dissipated Vetranio's meditations, and put the ladies who were with him to flight, by announcing in an important voice, that the Prefect Pompeianus desired a private interview with the Senator Vetranio.

The next instant the chief magistrate of Rome entered the apartment. He was a short, fat, undignified man. Indolence and vacillation were legibly impressed on his appearance and expression. You saw, in a moment, that his mind, like a shuttlecock, might be urged in any direction by the efforts of others, but was utterly incapable of volition by itself. But once in his life had the Prefect Pompeianus been known to arrive unaided at a positive determination, and that was in deciding a fierce argument between a bishop and a general, regarding the relative merits of two rival rope-dancers of equal renown.

'I have come, my beloved friend,' said the Prefect in agitated tones, 'to ask your opinion, at this period of awful responsibility for us all, on the plan of operations proposed by the Senate at the sitting of to- day! But first,' he hastily continued, perceiving with the unerring instinct of an old gastronome, that the inviting refreshments on Vetranio's table had remained untouched, 'permit me to fortify my exhausted energies by a visit to your ever-luxurious board. Alas, my friend, when I consider the present fearful scarcity of our provision stores in the city, and the length of time that this accursed blockade may be expected to last, I am inclined to think that the gods alone know (I mean St. Peter) how much longer we may be enabled to give occupation to our digestions and employment to our cooks.

'I have observed,' pursued the Prefect, after an interval, speaking with his mouth full of stewed peacock; 'I have observed, oh esteemed colleague! the melancholy of your manner and your absolute silence during your attendance to-day at our deliberations. Have we, in your opinion, decided erroneously? It is not impossible! Our confusion at this unexpected appearance of the barbarians may have blinded our usual penetration! If by any chance you dissent from our plans, I beseech you communicate your objections to me without reserve!'

'I dissent from nothing, because I have heard nothing,' replied Vetranio sullenly. 'I was so occupied by a private matter of importance during my attendance at the sitting of the Senate, that I was deaf to their deliberations. I know that we are besieged by the Goths--why are they not driven from before the walls?'

'Deaf to our deliberations! Drive the Goths from the walls!' repeated the Prefect faintly. 'Can you think of any private matter at such a moment as this? Do you know our danger? Do you know that our friends are so astonished at this frightful calamity, that they move about like men half awakened from a dream? Have you not seen the streets filled with terrified and indignant crowds? Have you not mounted the ramparts and beheld the innumerable multitudes of pitiless Goths surrounding us on all sides, intercepting our supplies of provisions from the country, and menacing us with a speedy famine, unless our hoped-for auxiliaries arrive from Ravenna?'

'I have neither mounted the ramparts, nor viewed with any attention the crowds in the streets,' replied Vetranio, carelessly.

'But if you have seen nothing yourself, you must have heard what others saw,' persisted the Prefect; 'you must know at least that the legions we have in the city are not sufficient to guard more than half the circuit of the walls. Has no one informed you that if it should please the leader of the barbarians to change his blockade into an assault, it is more than probable that we should be unable to repulse him successfully? Are you still deaf to our deliberations, when your palace may to-morrow be burnt over your head, when we may be staved to death, when we may be doomed to eternal dishonour by being driven to conclude a peace? Deaf to our deliberations, when such an unimaginable calamity as this invasion has fallen like a thunderbolt under our very walls! You amaze me! You overwhelm me! You horrify me!'

And in the excess of his astonishment the bewildered Prefect actually abandoned his stewed peacock, and advanced, wine-cup in hand, to obtain a nearer view of the features of his imperturbable host.

'If we are not strong enough to drive the Goths out of Italy,' rejoined Vetranio coolly, 'you and the Senate know that we are rich enough to bribe them to depart to the remotest confines of the empire. If we have not swords enough to fight, we have gold and silver enough to pay.'

'You are jesting! Remember our honour and the auxiliaries we still hope for from Ravenna,' said the Prefect reprovingly.

'Honour has lost the signification now, that it had in the time of the Caesars,' retorted the Senator. 'Our fighting days are over. We have had heroes enough for our reputation. As for the auxiliaries you still hope for, you will have none! While the Emperor is safe in Ravenna, he will care nothing for the worst extremities that can be suffered by the people of Rome.'

'But you forget your duties,' urged the astonished Pompeianus, turning from rebuke to expostulation. 'You forget that it is a time when all private interests must be abandoned! You forget that I have come here to ask your advice, that I am bewildered by a thousand projects, forced on me from all sides, for ruling the city successfully during the blockade; that I look to you, as a friend and a man of reputation, to aid me in deciding on a choice out of the varied counsels submitted to me in the Senate to-day.'

'Write down the advice of each senator on a separate strip of vellum; shake all the strips together in an urn; and then, let the first you take out by chance, be your guide to govern by in the present condition of the city!' said Vetranio with a sneer.

'Oh friend, friend! it is cruel to jest with me thus!' cried the Prefect, in tones of lament; 'Would you really persuade me that you are ignorant that what sentinels we have, are doubled already on the walls? Would you attempt to declare seriously to me, that you never heard the project of Saturninus for reducing imperceptibly the diurnal allowance of provisions? Or the recommendation of Emilianus, that the people should be kept from thinking on the dangers and extremities which now threaten them, by being provided incessantly with public amusements at the theatres and hippodromes? Do you really mean that you are indifferent to the horrors of our present situation? By the souls of the Apostles, Vetranio, I begin to think that you do not believe in the Goths!'

'I have already told you that private affairs occupy me at present, to the exclusion of public,' said Vetranio impatiently. 'Debate as you choose--approve what projects you will--I withdraw myself from interference in your deliberations!'

'This,' murmured the repulsed Prefect in soliloquy, as he mechanically resumed his place at the refreshment table, 'this is the very end and climax of all calamities! Now, when advice and assistance are more precious than jewels in my estimation, I receive neither! I gain from none, the wise and saving counsels which, as chief magistrate of this Imperial City, it is my right to demand from all; and the man on whom I most depended is the man who fails me most! Yet hear me, oh Vetranio, once again,' he continued, addressing the Senator, 'if our perils beyond the walls affect you not, there is a weighty matter that has been settled within them, which must move you. After you had quitted the Senate, Serena, the widow of Stilicho, was accused, as her husband was accused before her, of secret and treasonable correspondence with the Goths; and has been condemned, as her husband was condemned, to suffer the penalty of death. I myself discerned no evidence to convict her; but the populace cried out, in universal frenzy, that she was guilty, that she should die; and that the barbarians, when they heard of the punishment inflicted on their secret adherent, would retire in dismay from Rome. This also was a moot point of argument, on which I vainly endeavoured to decide; but the Senate and the people were wiser than I; and Serena was condemned to be strangled to-morrow by the public executioner. She was a woman of good report before this time, and is the adopted mother of the Emperor. It is now doubted by many whether Stilicho, her husband, was ever guilty of the correspondence with the Goths, of which he was accused; and I, on my part, doubt much that Serena has deserved the punishment of death at our hands. I beseech you, Vetranio, let me be enlightened by your opinion on this one point at least!'

The Prefect waited anxiously for an answer, but Vetranio neither looked at him nor replied. It was evident that the Senator had not listened to a word that he had said!

This reception of his final appeal for assistance, produced the effect on the petitioner, which it was perhaps designed to convey--the Prefect Pompeianus quitted the room in despair.

He had not long departed, when Carrio again entered the apartment, and addressed his master thus:

'It is grievous for me, revered patron, to disclose it to you, but your slaves have returned unsuccessful from the search!'

'Give the description of the girl to a fresh division of them, and let them continue their efforts throughout the night, not only in the streets, but in all the houses of public entertainment in the city. She must be in Rome, and she must be found!' said the senator gloomily.

Carrio bowed profoundly, and was about to depart, when he was arrested at the door by his master's voice.

'If an old man, calling himself Numerian, should desire to see me,' said Vetranio, 'admit him instantly.'

'She had quitted the room but a short time when I attempted to reclaim her,' pursued the senator, speaking to himself; 'and yet when I gained the open air, she was nowhere to be seen! She must have mingled unintentionally with the crowds whom the Goths drove into the city, and thus have eluded my observation! So young and so innocent! She must be found! She must be found!'

He paused, once more engrossed in deep and melancholy thought. After a long interval, he was roused form his abstraction by the sound of footsteps on the marble floor. He looked up. The door had been opened without his perceiving it, and an old man was advancing with slow and trembling steps towards his silken couch. It was the bereaved and broken-hearted Numerian.

'Where is she? Is she found?' asked the father, gazing anxiously round the room, as if he had expected to see his daughter there.

'My slaves still search for her,' said Vetranio, mournfully.

'Ah, woe--woe--woe! How I wronged her! How I wronged her!' cried the old man, turning to depart.

'Listen to me ere you go,' said Vetranio, gently detaining him. 'I have done you a great wrong, but I will yet atone for it by finding for you your child! While there were women who would have triumphed in my admiration, I should not have attempted to deprive you of your daughter! Remember when you recover her--and you shall recover her--that from the time when I first decoyed her into listening to my lute, to the night when your traitorous servant led me to her bed-chamber, she has been innocent in this ill-considered matter. I alone have been guilty! She was scarcely awakened when you discovered her in my arms, and my entry into her chamber, was as little expected by her, as it was by you. I was bewildered by the fumes of wine and the astonishment of your sudden appearance, or I should have rescued her from your anger, ere it was too late! The events which have passed this morning, confused though they were, have yet convinced me that I had mistaken you both. I now know that your child was too pure to be an object fitted for my pursuit; and I believe that in secluding her as you did, however ill-advised you might appear, you were honest in your design! Never in my pursuit of pleasure did I commit so fatal an error, as when I entered the doors of your house!'

In pronouncing these words, Vetranio but gave expression to the sentiments by which they were really inspired. As we have before observed, profligate as he was by thoughtlessness of character and license of social position, he was neither heartless nor criminal by nature. Fathers had stormed, but his generosity had hitherto invariably pacified them. Daughters had wept, but had found consolation on all previous occasions in the splendour of his palace and the amiability of his disposition. In attempting, therefore, the abduction of Antonina, though he had prepared for unusual obstacles, he had expected no worse results of his new conquest, than those that had followed, as yet, his gallantries that were past. But, when--in the solitude of his own home, and in the complete possession of his faculties--he recalled all the circumstances of his attempt, from the time when he had stolen on the girl's slumbers, to the moment when she had fled from the house; when he remembered the stern concentrated anger of Numerian, and the agony and despair of Antonina; when he thought on the spirit-broken repentance of the deceived father, and the fatal departure of the injured daughter, he felt as a man who had not merely committed an indiscretion, but had been guilty of a crime; he became convinced that he had incurred the fearful responsibility of destroying the happiness of a parent who was really virtuous, and a child who was truly innocent. To a man, the business of whose whole life was to procure for himself a heritage of unalloyed pleasure, whose sole occupation was to pamper that refined sensuality which the habits of a life had made the very material of his heart, by diffusing luxury and awakening smiles wherever he turned his steps, the mere mental disquietude attending the ill-success of his intrusion into Numerian's dwelling, was as painful in its influence, as the bitterest remorse that could have afflicted a more highly-principled mind. He now, therefore, instituted the search after Antonina, and expressed his contrition to her father, from a genuine persuasion that nothing but the completest atonement for the error he had committed, could restore to him that luxurious tranquility, the loss of which had, as he had himself expressed it, rendered him deaf to the deliberations of the Senate, and regardless of the invasion of the Goths.

'Tell me,' he continued, after a pause, 'whither has Ulpius betaken himself? It is necessary that he should be discovered. He may enlighten us upon the place of Antonina's retreat. He shall be secured and questioned.'

'He left me suddenly; I saw him as I stood at the window, mix with the multitude in the street, but I know not whither he is gone,' replied Numerian; and a tremor passed over his whole frame as he spoke of the remorseless Pagan.

Again there was a short silence. The grief of the broken-spirited father, possessed in its humility and despair, a voice of rebuke, before which the senator, careless and profligate as he was, instinctively quailed. For some time he endeavoured in vain to combat the silencing and reproving influence, exerted over him by the very presence of the sorrowing man whom he had so fatally wronged. At length, after an interval, he recovered self-possession enough to address to Numerian some further expressions of consolation and hope; but he spoke to ears that listened not. The father had relapsed into his mournful abstraction; and when the senator paused, he merely muttered to himself--'She is lost! Alas, she is lost for ever!'

'No, she is not lost for ever,' cried Vetranio, warmly. 'I have wealth and power enough to cause her to be sought for to the ends of the earth! Ulpius shall be secured and questioned--imprisoned, tortured, if it is necessary. Your daughter shall be recovered. Nothing is impossible to a senator of Rome!'

'I knew not that I loved her, until the morning when I wronged and banished her!' continued the old man, still speaking to himself. 'I have lost all traces of my parents and my brother--my wife is parted from me for ever--I have nothing left but Antonina; and now too she is gone! Even my ambition, that I once thought my all in all, is no comfort to my soul; for I loved it--alas! unconsciously loved it--through the being of my child! I destroyed her lute--I thought her shameless--I drove her from my doors! Oh, how I wronged her!--how I wronged her!'

'Remain here, and repose yourself in one of the sleeping apartments, until my slaves return in the morning. You will then hear without delay of the result of their search to-night,' said Vetranio, in kindly and compassionate tones.

'It grows dark--dark!' groaned the father, tottering towards the door; 'but that is nothing; daylight itself now looks darkness to me! I must go: I have duties at the chapel to perform. Night is repose for you--for me, it is tribulation and prayer!'

He departed as he spoke. Slowly he paced along the streets that led to his chapel, glancing with penetrating eye at each inhabitant of the besieged city who passed him on his way. With some difficulty he arrived at his destination; for Rome was still thronged with armed men hurrying backwards and forwards, and with crowds of disorderly citizens pouring forth, wherever there was space enough for them to assemble. The report of the affliction that had befallen him had already gone abroad among his hearers, and they whispered anxiously to each other as he entered the plain, dimly-lighted chapel, and slowly mounted the pulpit to open the service, by reading the chapter in the Bible which had been appointed for perusal that night, and which happened to be the fifth of the Gospel of St. Mark. His voice trembled, his face was ghastly pale, and his hands shook perceptibly as he began; but he read on, in low, broken tones, and with evident pain and difficulty, until he came to the verse containing these words: 'My little daughter lieth at the point of death.' Here he stopped suddenly, endeavoured vainly for a few minutes to proceed, and then, covering his face with his hands, sank down in the pulpit and sobbed aloud. His sorrowing and startled audience immediately gathered round him, raised him in their arms, and prepared to conduct him to his own abode. When, however, they had gained the door of the chapel, he desired them gently, to leave him and return to the performance of the service among themselves. Ever implicitly obedient to his slightest wishes, the persons of his little assembly, moved to tears by the sight of their teacher's suffering, obeyed him, by retiring silently to their former places. As soon as he found that he was alone, he passed the door; and whispering to himself, 'I must join those who seek her! I must aid them myself in the search!'--he mingled once more with the disorderly citizens who thronged the darkened streets.

Chapter 10

THE RIFT IN THE WALL

When Ulpius suddenly departed from Numerian's house on the morning of the siege, it was with no distinct intention of betaking himself to any particular place, or devoting himself to any immediate employment. It was to give vent to his joy--to the ecstacy that now filled his heart to bursting--that he sought the open streets. His whole moral being was exalted by that overwhelming sense of triumph, which urges the physical nature into action. He hurried into the free air, as a child runs on a bright day in the wide fields; his delight was too wild to expand under a roof; his excess of bliss swelled irrepressibly beyond all artificial limits of space.

The Goths were in sight! A few hours more, and their scaling ladders would be planted against the walls. On a city so weakly guarded as Rome, their assault must be almost instantaneously successful. Thirsting for plunder, they would descend in infuriated multitudes on the defenceless streets. Christians though they were, the restraints of religion would, in that moment of fierce triumph, be powerless with such a nation of marauders against the temptations to pillage. Churches would be ravaged and destroyed; priests would be murdered in attempting the defence of their ecclesiastical treasures; fire and sword would waste to its remotest confines the stronghold of Christianity, and overwhelm in death and oblivion the boldest of Christianity's devotees! Then, when the hurricane of ruin and crime had passed over the city, when a new people were ripe for another government and another religion--then would be the time to invest the banished gods of old Rome with their former rule; to bid the survivors of the stricken mul-

titude remember the judgment that their apostacy to their ancient faith had
demanded and incurred; to strike the very remembrance of the Cross out of the
memory of man; and to reinstate Paganism on her throne of sacrifices, and under
her roof of gold, more powerful from her past persecutions; more universal in her
sudden restoration, than in all the glories of her ancient rule!

Such thoughts as these passed through the Pagan's toiling mind as, unobservant
of all outward events, he paced through the streets of the beleaguered city.
Already he beheld the array of the Goths preparing the way, as the unconscious
pioneers of the returning gods, for the march of that mighty revolution which he
was determined to lead. The warmth of his past eloquence, the glow of his old
courage, thrilled through his heart, as he figured to himself the prospect that
would soon stretch before him--a city laid waste, a people terrified, a government
distracted, a religion destroyed. Then, arising amid this darkness and ruin; amid
this solitude, desolation, and decay, it would be his glorious privilege to summon
an unfaithful people to return to the mistress of their ancient love; to rise from
prostration beneath a dismantled Church; and to seek prosperity in temples
repeopled and at shrines restored!

All remembrance of late events now entirely vanished from his mind. Numerian,
Vetranio, Antonina, they were all forgotten in this memorable advent of the
Goths! His slavery in the mines, his last visit to Alexandria, his earlier wander-
ings--even these, so present to his memory until the morning of the siege, were
swept from its very surface now. Age, solitude, infirmity--hitherto the mournful
sensations which were proofs to him that he still continued to exist--suddenly
vanished from his perceptions, as things that were not; and now at length he forgot that he was an outcast, and remembered triumphantly that he was still a
priest. He felt animated by the same hopes, elevated by the same aspirations, as
in those early days when he had harangued the wavering Pagans in the Temple,
and first plotted the overthrow of the Christian Church.

It was a terrible and warning proof of the omnipotent influence that a single idea
may exercise over a whole life, to see that old man wandering among the crowds
around him, still enslaved, after years of suffering and solitude, degradation, and
crime, by the same ruling ambition, which had crushed the promise of his early
youth! It was an awful testimony to the eternal and mysterious nature of thought,
to behold that wasted and weakened frame; and then to observe how the unassailable mind within still swayed the wreck of body yet left to it--how faithfully
the last exhausted resources of failing vigour rallied into action at its fierce com-
mand--how quickly, at its mocking voice, the sunken eye lightened again with a
gleam of hope, and the pale, thin lips parted mechanically with an exulting smile!

The hours passed, but he still walked on--whither or among whom he neither knew nor cared. No remorse touched his heart for the destruction that he had wreaked on the Christian who had sheltered him; no terror appalled his soul at the contemplation of the miseries that he believed to be in preparation for the city from the enemy at its gates. The end that had hallowed to him the long series of his former offences and former sufferings, now obliterated iniquities just passed, and stripped of all their horrors, atrocities immediately to come.

The Goths might be destroyers to others, but they were benefactors to him; for they were harbingers of the ruin which would be the material of his reform, and the source of his triumph. It never entered his imagination that, as an inhabitant of Rome, he shared the approaching perils of the citizens, and in the moment of the assault might share their doom. He beheld only the new and gorgeous prospect that war and rapine were opening before him. He thought only of the time that must elapse ere his new efforts could be commenced--of the orders of the people among whom he should successively make his voice heard--of the temples which he should select for restoration--of the quarter of Rome which should first be chosen for the reception of his daring reform.

At length he paused; his exhausted energies yielded under the exertions imposed on them, and obliged him to bethink himself of refreshment and repose. It was now noon. The course of his wanderings had insensibly conducted him again to the precincts of his old, familiar dwelling- place; he found himself at the back of the Pincian Mount, and only separated by a strip of uneven woody ground, from the base of the city wall. The place was very solitary. It was divided from the streets and mansions above by thick groves and extensive gardens, which stretched along the undulating descent of the hill. A short distance to the westward lay the Pincian Gate, but an abrupt turn in the wall and some olive trees which grew near it, shut out all view of objects in that direction. On the other side, towards the eastward, the ramparts were discernible, running in a straight line of some length, until they suddenly turned inwards at a right angle and were concealed from further observation by the walls of a distant palace and the pine trees of a public garden. The only living figure discernible near this lonely spot, was that of a sentinel, who occasionally passed over the ramparts above, which--situated as they were between two stations of soldiery, one at the Pincian Gate and the other where the wall made the angle already described--were untenanted, save by the guard within the limits of whose watch they happened to be placed. Here, for a short space of time, the Pagan rested his weary frame, and aroused himself insensibly from the enthralling meditations which had hitherto blinded him to the troubled aspect of the world around him.

He now for the first time heard on all sides distinctly, the confused noises which still rose from every quarter of Rome. The same incessant strife of struggling voices and hurrying footsteps, which had caught his ear in the early morning, attracted his attention now; but no shrieks of distress, no clash of weapons, no shouts of fury and defiance, were mingled with them; although, as he perceived by the position of the sun, the day had sufficiently advanced to have brought the Gothic army long since to the foot of the walls. What could be the cause of this delay in the assault; of this ominous tranquillity on the ramparts above him? Had the impetuosity of the Goths suddenly vanished at the sight of Rome? Had negotiations for peace been organised with the first appearance of the invaders? He listened again. No sounds caught his ear differing in character from those he had just heard. Though besieged, the city was evidently--from some mysterious cause--not even threatened by an assault.

Suddenly there appeared from a little pathway near him, which led round the base of the wall, a woman preceded by a child, who called to her impatiently, as he ran on, 'Hasten, mother, hasten! There is no crowd here. Yonder is the Gate. We shall have a noble view of the Goths!'

There was something in the address of the child to the woman that gave Ulpius a suspicion, even then, of the discovery that flushed upon him soon after. He rose and followed them. They passed onward by the wall, through the olive trees beyond, and then gained the open space before the Pincian Gate. Here a great concourse of people had assembled, and were suffered, in their proper turn, to ascend the ramparts in divisions, by some soldiers who guarded the steps by which they were approached. After a short delay, Ulpius and those around him were permitted to gratify their curiosity, as others had done before them. They mounted the walls, and beheld, stretched over the ground within and beyond the suburbs, the vast circumference of the Gothic lines.

Terrible and almost sublime as was the prospect of that immense multitude, seen under the brilliant illumination of the noontide sun, it was not impressive enough to silence the turbulent loquacity rooted in the dispositions of the people of Rome. Men, women, and children, all made their noisy and conflicting observations on the sight before them, in every variety of tone, from the tremulous accents of terror, to the loud vociferations of bravado.

Some spoke boastfully of the achievements that would be performed by the Romans, when their expected auxiliaries arrived from Ravenna. Others foreboded, in undissembled terror, an assault under cover of the night. Here, a group abused, in low confidential tones, the policy of the government in its relations with the Goths. There, a company of ragged vagabonds amused themselves by pompously confiding to each other their positive conviction, that at that very moment the barbarians must be trembling in their camp, at the mere sight of the all-powerful Capital of the World. In one direction, people were heard noisily speculating whether the Goths would be driven from the walls by the soldiers of Rome, or be honoured by an invitation to conclude a peace with the august Empire, which they had so treasonably ventured to invade. In another, the more sober and reputable among the spectators audibly expressed their apprehensions of starvation, dishonour, and defeat, should the authorities of the city be fool-hardy enough to venture a resistance to Alaric and his barbarian hosts. But wide as was the difference of the particular opinions hazarded among the citizens, they all agreed in one unavoidable conviction, that Rome had escaped the immediate horrors of an assault, to be threatened--if unaided by the legions at Ravenna--by the prospective miseries of a blockade.

Amid the confusion of voices around him, that word 'blockade' alone reached the Pagan's ear. It brought with it a flood of emotions that overwhelmed him. All that he saw, all that he heard, connected itself imperceptibly with that expression. a sudden darkness, neither to be dissipated nor escaped, seemed to obscure his faculties in an instant. He struggled mechanically through the crowd, descended the steps of the ramparts, and returned to the solitary spot where he had first beheld the woman and the child.

The city was blockaded! The Goths were bent then, on obtaining a peace and not on achieving a conquest! The city was blockaded! It was no error of the ignorant multitude--he had seen with his own eyes the tents and positions of the enemy, he had heard the soldiers on the wall discoursing on the admirable disposition of Alaric's forces, on the impossibility of obtaining the smallest communication with the surrounding country, on the vigilant watch that had been set over the navigation of the Tiber. There was no doubt on the matter--the barbarians had determined on a blockade!

There was even less uncertainty upon the results which would be produced by this unimaginable policy of the Goths--the city would be saved! Rome had not scrupled in former years to purchase the withdrawal of all enemies from her distant provinces; and now that the very centre of her glory, the very pinnacle of her declining power, was threatened with sudden and unexpected ruin, she would lavish on the Goths the treasures of the whole empire, to bribe them to peace and to tempt them to retreat. The Senate might possibly delay the necessary concessions, from hopes of assistance that would never be realised; but sooner or later the hour of negotiation would arrive; northern rapacity would be satisfied with southern wealth; and in the very moment when it seemed inevitable, the ruin from which the Pagan revolution was to derive its vigorous source, would be diverted from the churches of Rome.

Could the old renown of the Roman name have retained so much of its ancient influence as to daunt the hardy Goths, after they had so successfully penetrated the empire as to have reached the walls of its vaunted capital? Could Alaric have conceived so exaggerated an idea of the strength of the forces in the city as to despair, with all his multitudes, of storming it with success? It could not be otherwise! No other consideration could have induced the barbarian general to abandon such an achievement as the destruction of Rome. With the chance of an assault the prospects of Paganism had brightened--with the certainty of a blockade, they sunk immediately into disheartening gloom!

Filled with these thoughts, Ulpius paced backwards and forwards in his solitary retreat, utterly abandoned by the exaltation of feeling which had restored to his faculties in the morning, the long-lost vigour of their former youth. Once more, he experienced the infirmities of his age; once more he remembered the miseries that had made his existence one unending martyrdom; once more he felt the presence of his ambition within him, like a judgment that he was doomed to welcome, like a curse that he was created to cherish. To say that his sensations at this moment were those of the culprit who hears the order for his execution when he had been assured of a reprieve, is to convey but a faint idea of the fierce emotions of rage, grief, and despair, that now united to rend the Pagan's heart.

Overpowered with weariness both of body and mind, he flung himself down under the shade of some bushes that clothed the base of the wall above him. As he lay there--so still in his heavy lassitude that life itself seemed to have left him--one of the long green lizards, common to Italy, crawled over his shoulder. He seized the animal--doubtful for the moment whether it might not be of the poisonous species--and examined it. At the first glance he discovered that it was of the harmless order of its race, and would have flung it carelessly from him, but for something in its appearance which, in the wayward irritability of his present mood, he felt a strange and sudden pleasure in contemplating.

Through its exquisitely marked and transparent skin he could perceive the action of the creature's heart, and saw that it was beating violently, in the agony of fear caused to the animal by its imprisonment in his hand. As he looked on it, and thought how continually a being so timid must be thwarted in its humble anxieties, in its small efforts, in its little journeys from one patch of grass to another, by a hundred obstacles, which, trifles though they might be to animals of a high-er species, were yet of fatal importance to creatures constituted like itself, he began to find an imperfect, yet remarkable analogy between his own destiny and that of this small unit of creation. He felt that, in its petty sphere, the short life of the humble animal before him must have been the prey of crosses and disappoint-ments, as serious to it, as the more severed and destructive afflictions of which he, in his existence, had been the victim; and, as he watched the shadow-like move-ment of the little fluttering heart of the lizard, he experienced a cruel pleasure in perceiving that there were other beings in the creation, even down to the most insignificant, who inherited a part of his misery, and suffered a portion of his despair.

Ere long, however, his emotions took a sterner and a darker hue. The sight of the animal wearied him, and he flung it contemptuously aside. It disappeared in the direction of the ramparts; and almost at the same moment he heard a slight sound, resembling the falling of several minute particles of brick or light stone, which seemed to come from the wall behind him.

That such a noise should proceed from so massive a structure appeared unac-countable. He rose, and, parting the bushes before him, advanced close to the surface of the lofty wall. To his astonishment, he found that the brickwork had in many places so completely mouldered away, that he could move it easily with his fingers. The cause of the trifling noise that he had heard was now fully explained: hundreds of lizards had made their homes between the fissures of the bricks; the animal that he had permitted to escape had taken refuge in one of these cavities, and in the hurry of its flight had detached several of the loose crum-bling fragments that surrounded its hiding-place.

No content, however, with the discovery he had already made, he retired a little, and, looking stedfastly up through some trees which in this particular place grew at the foot of the wall, he saw that its surface was pierced in many places by great irregular rifts, some of which extended nearly to its whole height. In addition to this, he perceived that the mass of the structure at one particular point, leaned considerably out of the perpendicular. Astounded at what he beheld, he took a stick from the ground, and inserting it in one of the lowest and smallest of the cracks, easily succeeded in forcing it entirely into the wall, part of which seemed to be hollow, and part composed of the same rotten brickwork which had at first attracted his attention.

It was now evident that the whole structure, over a breadth of several yards, had been either weakly and carelessly built, or had at some former period suffered a sudden and violent shock. He left the stick in the wall to mark the place; and was about to retire, when he heard the footstep of the sentinel on the rampart immediately above. Suddenly cautious, though from what motive he would have been at that moment hardly able to explain, he remained in the concealment of the trees and bushes, until the guard had passed onward; then he cautiously emerged from the place; and, retiring to some distance, fell into a train of earnest and absorbing thought.

To account to the reader for the phenomenon which now engrossed the Pagan's attention, it will be necessary to make a brief digression to the history of the walls of Rome.

The circumference of the first fortifications of the city, built by Romulus, was thirteen miles. The greater part, however, of this large area was occupied by fields and gardens, which it was the object of the founder of the empire to preserve for arable purposes, from the incursions of the different enemies by whom he was threatened from without. As Rome gradually increased in size, its walls were progressively enlarged and altered by subsequent rulers. But it was not until the reign of the Emperor Aurelian (A.D. 270), that any extraordinary or important change was effected in the defences of the city. That potentate commenced the erection of walls, twenty-one miles in circumference, which were finally completed in the reign of Probus (A.D. 276), were restored by Belisarius (A.D. 537), and are to be seen in detached portions, in the fortifications of the modern city, to the present day.

At the date of our story, then (A.D. 408), the walls remained precisely as they had been constructed in the reigns of Aurelian and Probus. They were for the most part made of brick; and in a few places, probably, a sort of soft sandstone might have been added to the pervading material. At several points in their circumference, and particularly in the part behind the Pincian Hill, these walls were built in arches, forming deep recesses, and occasionally disposed in double rows. The method of building employed in their erection, was generally that mentioned by Vitruvius, in whose time it originated, as 'opus reticulatum'.

The 'opus reticulatum' was composed of small bricks (or stones) set together on their angles, instead of horizontally, and giving the surface of a wall the appearance of a sort of solid network. This was considered by some architects of antiquity a perishable mode of construction; and Vitruvius asserts that some buildings where he had seen it used, had fallen down. From the imperfect specimens of it which remain in modern times, it would be difficult to decide upon its merits. That it was assuredly insufficient to support the weight of the bank of the Pincian

Mount, which rose immediately behind it, in the solitary spot described some pages back, is still made evident by the appearance of the wall at that part of the city, which remains in modern times bent out of the perpendicular, and cracked in some places almost from top to bottom. This ruin is now known to the present race of Italians, under the expressive title of 'Il Muro Torto' or, The Crooked Wall.

We may here observe that it is extremely improbable that the existence of this natural breach in the fortifications of Rome was noticed, or if noticed, regarded with the slightest anxiety or attention by the majority of the careless and indolent inhabitants, at the period of the present romance. It is supposed to have been visible as early as the time of Aurelian, but is only particularly mentioned by Procopius, an historian of the sixth century, who relates that Belisarius, in strengthening the city against a siege of the Goths, attempted to repair this weak point in the wall, but was hindered in his intended labour by the devout populace, who declared that it was under the peculiar protection of St. Peter, and that it would be consequently impious to meddle with it. The general submitted without remonstrance to the decision of the inhabitants, and found no cause afterwards to repent of his facility of compliance; for, to use the translated words of the writer above-mentioned, 'During the siege neither the enemy nor the Romans regarded this place.' It is to be supposed that so extraordinary an event as this, gave the wall that sacred character, which deterred subsequent rulers from attempting its repair; which permitted it to remain crooked and rent through the convulsions of the middle ages; and which still preserves it, to attest the veracity of historians, by appealing to the antiquarian curiosity of the traveller of modern times.

We now return to Ulpius. It is a peculiarity observable in the characters of men living under the ascendancy of one ruling idea, that they intuitively distort whatever attracts their attention in the outer world, into a connection more or less intimate with the single object of their mental contemplation. since the time when he had been exiled from the Temple, the Pagan's faculties had, unconsciously to himself, acted solely in reference to the daring design which it was the business of his whole existence to entertain. Influenced, therefore, by this obliquity of moral feeling, he had scarcely reflected on the discovery that he had just made at the base of the city wall, ere his mind instantly reverted to the ambitious meditations which had occupied it in the morning; and the next moment, the first dawning conception of a bold and perilous project began to absorb his restless thoughts.

He reflected on the peculiarities and position of the wall before him. Although the widest and most important of the rents which he had observed in it, existed too near the rampart to be reached without the assistance of a ladder, there were others as low as the ground, which he knew, by the result of the trial he had already made, might be successfully and immensely widened by the most ordinary exertion and perseverance. The interior of the wall, if judged by the condition of the surface, could offer no insuperable obstacles to an attempt at penetration so partial as to be limited to a height and width of a few feet. The ramparts, from their position between two guard-houses, would be unencumbered by an inquisitive populace. The sentinel, within the limits of whose allotted watch it happened to fall, would, when night came on, be the only human being likely to pass the spot; and at such an hour his attention must necessarily be fixed--in the circumstances under which the city was now placed--on the prospect beyond, rather than on the ground below and behind him. It seemed, therefore, almost a matter of certainty, that a cautious man, labouring under cover of the night, might pursue whatever investigations he pleased at the base of the wall.

He examined the ground where he now stood. Nothing could be more lonely than its present appearance. The private gardens on the hill above it shut out all communication from that quarter. It could only be approached by the foot-path that ran round the Pincian Mount, and along the base of the walls. In the state of affairs now existing in the city, it was not probable that any one would seek this solitary place, whence nothing could be seen, and where little could be heard, in preference to mixing with the spirit-stirring confusion in the streets, or observing the Gothic encampment from such positions on the ramparts as were easily attainable to all. In addition to the secresy offered by the loneliness of this patch of ground to whatever employments were undertaken on it, was the further advantage afforded by the trees and thickets which covered its lower end, and which would effectually screen an intruder, during the darkness of night, from the most penetrating observation directed from the wall above.

Reflecting thus, he doubted not that a cunning and determined man might with impunity so far widen any one of the inferior breaches in the lower part of the wall as to make a cavity (large enough to admit a human figure) that should pierce to its outer surface, and afford that liberty of departing from the city and penetrating the Gothic camp which the closed gates now denied to all the inhabitants alike. To discover the practicability of such an attempt as this was, to a mind filled with such aspirations as the Pagan's, to determine irrevocably on its immediate execution. He resolved as soon as night approached to begin his labours on the wall; to seek--if the breach were made good, and the darkness favoured him--the tent of Alaric; and once arrived there, to acquaint the Gothic King with the weakness of the materials for defence within the city, and dilapidated condition of the fortifications below the Pincian Mount, insisting, as the condition of his treachery, on an assurance from the barbarian leader (which he doubted not would be gladly and instantly accorded) of the destruction of the Christian churches, the pillage of the Christian possessions, and the massacre of the Christian priests.

He retired cautiously from the lonely place that had now become the centre of his new hopes; and entering the streets of the city, proceeded to provide himself with an instrument that would facilitate his approaching labours, and food that would give him strength to prosecute his intended efforts, unthreatened by the hindrance of fatigue. As he thought on the daring treachery of his project, his morning's exultation began to return to him again. All his previous attempts to organise the restoration of Paganism sunk into sudden insignificance before his present design. His defence of the Temple of Serapis, his conspiracy at Alexandria, his intrigue with Vetranio, were the efforts of a man; but this projected destruction of the priests, the churches, and the treasures of a whole city, through the agency of a mighty army, moved by the unaided machinations of a single individual, would be the dazzling achievement of a god!

The hours loitered slowly onward. The sun waned in the gorgeous heaven, and set, surrounded by red and murky clouds. Then came silence and darkness. The Gothic watch-fires flamed one by one into the dusky air. The guards were doubled at the different posts. The populace were driven from the ramparts, and the fortifications of the great city echoed to no sound now but the tramp of the restless sentinel, or the clash of arms from the distant guard-houses that dotted the long line of the lofty walls.

It was then that Ulpius, passing cautiously along the least-frequented streets, gained unnoticed the place of his destination. A thick vapour lay over the lonely and marshy spot. Nothing was now visible from it but the dim, uncertain outline of the palaces above, and the mass, so sunk in obscurity that it looked like a dark layer of mist itself, of the rifted fortifications. A smile of exultation passed over the Pagan's countenance, as he perceived the shrouding and welcome thickness of the atmosphere. Groping his way softly through the thickets, he arrived at the base of the wall. For some time he passed slowly along it, feeling the width of the different rents wherever he could stretch his hand. At length he paused at one more extensive than the rest, drew from its concealment in his garments a thick bar of iron sharpened at one end, and began to labour at the breach.

Chance had led him to the place best adapted to his purpose. The ground he stood on was only encumbered close to the wall by rank weeds and low thickets, and was principally composed of damp, soft turf. The bricks, therefore, as he carefully detached them, made no greater noise in falling than the slight rustling caused by their sudden contact with the boughs through which they descended. Insignificant as this sound was, it aroused the apprehension of the wary Pagan. He laid down his iron bar, and removed the thickets by dragging them up, or breaking them at the roots, until he had cleared a space of some feet in extent before the base of the wall. He then returned to his toilsome task, and with hands bleeding from the wounds inflicted by the thorns he had grasped in removing the thickets continued his labour at the brick-work. He pursued his employment with perfect impunity; the darkness covered him from observation; no one disturbed him by approaching the solitary scene of his operations; and of the two sentinels who were placed near the part of the wall which was the centre of all his exertions, one remained motionless at the most distant extremity of his post, and the other paced restlessly backwards and forwards on the rampart, singing a wild, rambling son about war, and women, and wine, which, whatever liberty it might allow to his organs of perception, effectually hindered the vigilant exercise of his faculties of hearing.

Brick after brick yielded to the vigorous and well-timed efforts of Ulpius. He had already made a cavity, in an oblique direction, large enough to creep through, and was preparing to penetrate still further, when a portion of the rotten material of the interior of the wall suddenly yielded in a mass to a chance pressure of his iron bar, and slowly sunk down inwards into a bed which, judging by such faint sounds as were audible at the moment, must have been partly water, and partly marshy earth and rotten brick-work. After having first listened, to be sure that the slight noise caused by this event had not reached the ears or excited the suspicions of the careless sentinels, Ulpius crept into the cavity he had made, groping his way with his bar, until he reached the brink of a chasm, the depth of which he could not probe, and the breadth of which he could not ascertain.

He lingered irresolute; the darkness around him was impenetrable; he could feel toads and noisome animals crawling over his limbs. The damp atmosphere of the place began to thrill through him to his very bones; his whole frame trembled under the excess of his past exertions. Without light, he could neither attempt to proceed, nor hope to discover the size and extent of the chasm which he had partially laid open. The mist was fast vanishing as the night advanced: it was necessary to arrive at a resolution ere it would be too late.

He crept out of the cavity. Just as he had gained the open air, the sentinel halted over the very spot where the Pagan stood, and paused suddenly in his song. There was an instant's interval of silence, during which the inmost soul of Ulpius quailed beneath an apprehension as vivid, as that which had throbbed in the heart of the despised lizard, whose flight had guided him to his discovery at the wall.

Soon, however, he heard the voice of the soldier calling cheerfully to his fellow sentinel, 'Comrade, do you see the moon? She is rising to cheer our watch!'

Nothing had been discovered!--he was still safe! But if he stayed at the cavity till the mists faded before the moonlight, could he be certain of preserving his security? He felt that he could not!

What mattered a night more or a night less, to such a project as his? Months might elapse before the Goths retired from the walls. It was better to suffer delay than to risk discovery. He determined to leave the place, and to return on the following night provided with a lantern, the light of which he would conceal until he entered the cavity. Once there, it could not be perceived by the sentinels above--it would guide him through all obstacles, preserve him through all dangers. Massive as it was, he felt convinced that the interior of the wall was in as ruinous a condition as the outside. Caution and perseverance were sufficient of themselves to insure to his efforts the speediest and completest success.

He waited until the sentinel had again betaken himself to the furthest limits of his watch, and then softly gathering up the brushwood that lay round him, he concealed with it the mouth of the cavity in the outer wall, and the fragments of brick-work that had fallen on the turf beneath. This done, he again listened, to assure himself that he had been unobserved; then, stepping with the utmost caution, he departed by the path that led round the slope of the Pincian Hill.

'Strength--patience--and to-morrow night!' muttered the Pagan to himself, as he entered the streets, and congregated once more with the citizens of Rome.

Chapter 11

GOISVINTHA'S RETURN

It was morning. The sun had risen, but his beams were partially obscured by thick heavy clouds, which scowled already over the struggling brightness of the eastern horizon. The bustle and animation of the new day gradually overspread the Gothic encampment in all directions. The only tent whose curtain remained still closed, and round which no busy crowds congregated in discussion or mingled in labour, was that of Hermanric. By the dying embers of his watchfire stood the young chieftain, with two warriors, to whom he appeared to be giving some hurried directions. His countenance expressed emotions of anxiety and discontent, which, though partially repressed while he was in the presence of his companions, became thoroughly visible, not only in his features, but in his manner, when they left him to watch alone before his tent.

For some time he walked regularly backwards and forwards, looking anxiously down the westward lines of the encampment, and occasionally whispering to himself a hasty exclamation of doubt and impatience. With the first breath of the new morning, the delighting meditations which had occupied him by his watchfire during the darkness of the night had begun to subside. And now, as the hour of her expécted return gradually approached, the image of Goisvintha banished from his mind whatever remained of those peaceful and happy contemplation in which he had hitherto been absorbed. The more he thought on his fatal promise--on the nation of Antonina--on his duties to the army and the people to whom he belonged, the more doubtful appeared to him his chance of permanently protecting the young Roman without risking his degradation as a Goth, and his ruin as a warrior; and the more sternly and ominously ran in his ears the unassailable truth of Goisvintha's parting taunt--'You must remember your promise, you cannot save her if you would!'

Wearied of persisting in deliberations which only deepened his melancholy and increased his doubts; bent on sinking in a temporary and delusive oblivion the boding reflections that overcame him in spite of himself, by seeking--while its enjoyment was yet left to him--the society of his ill-fated charge, he turned towards his tent, drew aside the thick, heavy curtains of skins which closed its opening, and approached the rude couch on which Antonina was still sleeping.

A ray of sunlight, fitful and struggling, burst at this moment through the heavy clouds, and stole into the opening of the tent as he contemplated the slumbering girl. It ran its flowing course up her uncovered hand and arm, flew over her bosom and neck, and bathed in a bright fresh glow, her still and reposing features. Gradually her limbs began to move, her lips parted gently and half smiled, as if in welcome to the greeting of the light; her eyes slightly opened, then dazzled by the brightness that flowed through their raised lids, tremblingly closed again. At length thoroughly awakened, she shaded her face with her hands, and sitting up on the couch, met the gaze of Hermanric fixed on her in sorrowful examination.

'Your bright armour, and your glorious name, and your merciful words, have remained with me even in my sleep,' said she, wonderingly; 'and now, when I awake, I see you before me again! It is a happiness to be aroused by the sun which has gladdened me all my life, to look upon you who have given me shelter in my distress! But why,' she continued, in altered and enquiring tones, 'why do you gaze upon me with doubting and mournful eyes?'

'You have slept well and safely,' said Hermanric, evasively, 'I closed the opening of the tent to preserve you from the night-damps, but I have raised it now, for the air is warming under the rising sun--'

'Are you wearied with watching?' she interrupted, rising to her feet, and looking anxiously into his face. But he spoke not in reply. His head was turned towards the door of the tent. He seemed to be listening for some expected sound. It was evident that he had not heard her question. She followed the direction of his eyes. The sight of the great city, half brightened, half darkened, as its myriad buildings reflected the light of the sun, or retained the shadows of the clouds, brought back to her remembrance her last night's petition for her father's safety. She laid her hand upon her companion's arm to awaken his attention, and hastily resumed:--

'You have not forgotten what I said to you last night? My father's name is Numerian. He lives on the Pincian Mount. You will save him, Hermanric--you will save him! You will remember your promise!'

The young warrior's eyes fell as she spoke, and an irrepressible shudder shook his whole frame. The last part of Antonina's address to him, was expressed in the same terms as a past appeal from other lips, and in other accents, which still clung to his memory. The same demand, 'Remember your promise,' which had been advanced to urge him to bloodshed, by Goisvintha, was now proffered by Antonina, to lure him to pity. The petition of affection was concluded in the same terms as the petition of revenge. As he thought on both, the human pity of the one, and the fiend-like cruelty of the other, rose in sinister and significant contrast on the mind of the Goth, realising in all its perils the struggle that was to come when Goisvintha returned, and dispelling instantaneously the last hopes that he had yet ventured to cherish for the fugitive at his side.

'No assault of the city is commanded--no assault is intended. Your father's life is safe from the swords of the Goths,' he gloomily replied, in answer to Antonina's last words.

The girl moved back from him a few steps as he spoke, and looked thoughtfully round the tent. The battle-axe that Hermanric had secured during the scene of the past evening, still lay on the ground, in a corner. The sight of it brought back a flood of terrible recollections to her mind. She started violently; a sudden change overspread her features, and when she again addressed Hermanric, it was with quivering lips and in almost inarticulate words.

'I know now why you look on me so gloomily,' said she; 'that woman is coming back! I was so occupied by my dreams and my thoughts of my father and of you, and my hopes for days to come, that I had forgotten her when I awoke! But I remember all now! She is coming back--I see it in your sorrowful eyes--she is coming back to murder me! I shall die at the moment when I had such hope in my life! There is no happiness for me! None!--none!'

The Goth's countenance began to darken. He whispered to himself several times, 'How can I save her?' For a few minutes there was a deep silence, broken only by the sobs of Antonina. He looked round at her after an interval. She held her hands clasped over her eyes. The tears were streaming through her parted fingers; her bosom heaved as if her emotions would burst their way through it in some palpable form; and her limbs trembled so, that she could scarcely support herself. Unconsciously, as he looked on her, he passed his arm round her slender form, drew her hands gently from her face, and said to her, though his heart belied his words as he spoke, 'Do not be afraid--trust in me!'

'How can I be calm?' she cried, looking up at him entreatingly; 'I was so happy last night, so sure that you could preserve me, so hopeful about to-morrow--and now I see by your mournful looks, I know by your doubting voice, that to soothe my anguish you have promised me more than you can perform! The woman who is your companion, has a power over us both, that it is terrible even to think of! She will return, she will withdraw all mercy from your heart, she will glare upon me with her fearful eyes, she will kill me at your feet! I shall die after all I have suffered and all I have hoped! Oh, Hermanric, while there is yet time let us escape! You were not made to shed blood--you are too merciful! God never made you to destroy! You cannot yearn towards cruelty and woe, for you have aided and protected me! Let us escape! I will follow you wherever you wish! I will do whatever you ask! I will go with you beyond those far, bright mountains behind us, to any strange and distant land; for there is beauty everywhere; there are woods that may be dwelt in, and valleys that may be loved, on all the surface of this wide great earth!'

The Goth looked sadly on her as she paused; but he gave her no answer--the gloom was deepening over his heart--the false words of consolation were silenced on his lips.

'Think how many pleasures we should enjoy, how much we might see!' continued the girl, in soft, appealing tones. 'We should be free to wander wherever we pleased; we should never be lonely; never be mournful; never be wearied! I could listen to you day after day, while you told me of the country where your people were born! I could sing you sweet songs that I have learned upon the lute! Oh, how I have wept in my loneliness to lead such a life as this! How I have longed that such freedom and joy might be mine! How I have thought of the distant lands that I would visit, of the happy nations that I would discover, of the mountain breezes that I would breathe, of the shady places that I would repose in, of the rivers that I would follow in their course, of the flowers I would plant, and the fruits I would gather! How I have hoped for such an existence as this! How I have longed for a companion who might enjoy it as I should! Have you never felt this joy that I have imagined to myself, you who have been free to wander wherever you pleased? Let us leave this place, and I will teach it to you if you have not. I will be so patient, so obedient, so happy! I will never be sorrowful; never repining--but let us escape--Oh, Hermanric, let us escape while there is yet time! Will you keep me here to be slain? Can you drive me forth into the world alone? Remember that the gates of the city and the doors of my home are now closed to me! Remember that I have no mother, and that my father has forsaken me! Remember that I am a stranger on the earth which was made for me to be joyful in! Think how soon the woman who has vowed that she will murder me will return; think how terrible it is to be in the fear of death; and while there is time let us depart--Hermanric, Hermanric, if you have pity for me, let us depart!'

She clasped her hands, and looked up in his face imploringly. The manner of Hermanric had expressed more to her senses, sharpened as they were by peril, than his words could have conveyed, even had he confessed to her the cause of the emotions of doubt and apprehension that oppressed his mind. Nothing could more strikingly testify to the innocence of her character and the seclusion of her life, than her attempt to combine with her escape from Goisvintha's fury, the acquisition of such a companion as the Goth. But to the forlorn and affectionate girl who saw herself--a stranger to the laws of the social existence of her fellow creatures--suddenly thrust forth friendless into the unfriendly world, could the heart have naturally prompted any other desire, than anxiety to secure the companion after having discovered the protector? In the guilelessness of her character, in her absolute ignorance of humanity, of the influence of custom, of the adaptation of difference of feeling to difference of sex, she vainly imagined that the tranquil existence she had urged on Hermanric, would suffice for the attainment of her end, by presenting the same allurements to him, a warrior and a Goth, that it contained for her--a lonely, thoughtful, visionary girl! And yet, so wonderful was the ascendancy that she had acquired by the magic of her presence, the freshness of her beauty, and the novelty of her manner, over the heart of the young chieftain, that he, who would have spurned from him with contempt any other woman who might have addressed to him such a petition as Antonina's, looked down sorrowfully at the girl as she ceased speaking, and for an instant hesitated in his choice.

At that moment, when the attention of each was fixed on the other, a third person stealthily approached the opening of the tent, and beholding them together thus, burst into a bitter, taunting laugh. Hermanric raised his eyes instantly; but the sound of that harsh unwomanly voice was all-eloquent to Antonina's senses. She hid her face against the Goth's breast, and murmured breathlessly--'She has returned! I must die! I must die!'

She had returned! She perceived Hermanric and Antonina in a position, which left no doubt that a stronger feeling than the mere wish to protect the victim of her intended revenge, had arisen, during her absence, in the heart of her kinsman. Hour after hour, while she had fulfilled her duties by the beds of Alaric's invalided soldiery, had she brooded over her projects of vengeance and blood. Neither the sickness nor the death which she had beheld around her, had possessed an influence powerful enough over the stubborn ferocity which now alone animated her nature, to lure it to mercy or awe it to repentance. Invigorated by delay, and enlarged by disappointment, the evil passion that consumed her had strengthened its power, and aroused the most latent of its energies, during the silent vigil that she had just held. She had detested the girl on the evening before, for her nation; she now hated her for herself.

'What have you to do with the trappings of a Gothic warrior?' she cried, in mocking accents, pointing at Hermanric with a long hunting-knife which she held in her hand. 'Why are you here in a Gothic encampment? Go, knock at the gates of Rome, implore her guards on your knees to admit you among the citizens, and when they ask you why--show them the girl there! Tell them that you love her, that you would wed her, that it is nothing to you that her people have murdered your brother and his children! And then, when you yourself have begotten sons, Gothic bastards infected with Roman blood, be a Roman at heart yourself, send your children forth to complete what your wife's people left undone at Aquileia--by murdering me!'

She paused and laughed scornfully. Then her humour suddenly changed, she advanced a few steps, and continued in a louder and sterner tone:--

'You have broken your faith; you have lied to me; you have forgotten your wrongs and mine; but you have not yet forgotten my parting words when I left you last night! I told you that she should be slain, and now that you have refused to avenge me, I will make good my words by killing her with my own hand! If you would defend her, you must murder me. You must shed her blood or mine!'

She stepped forward, her towering form was stretched to its highest stature, the muscles started into action on her bare arms as she raised them above her head. For one instant, she fixed her glaring eyes steadily on the girl's shrinking form-- the next, she rushed up and struck furiously with the knife at her bare neck. As the weapon descended, Hermanric caught her wrist. She struggled violently to disengage herself from his grasp, but in vain.

The countenance of the young warrior grew deadly pale, as he held her. For a few minutes he glanced eagerly round the tent, in an agony of bewilderment and despair. The conflicting interests of his duty towards his sister, and his anxiety for Antonina's preservation, filled his heart to distraction. A moment more he hesitated, and during that short delay, the despotism of custom had yet power enough to prevail over the promptings of pity. He called to the girl--withdrawing his arm which had hitherto been her support,--'Go, have mercy on me, go!'

But she neither heeded nor heard him. She fell on her knees at the woman's feet, and in a low moaning voice faltered out:--

'What have I done that I deserve to be slain? I never murdered your children; I never yet saw a child but I loved it; if I had seen your children, I should have loved them!'

'If I had preserved to this time the child that I saved from the massacre, and you had approached him,' returned the woman fiercely, 'I would have taught him to strike at you with his little hands! When you spoke to him, he should have spat upon you for answer--even thus!'

Trembling, exhausted, terrified as she was, the girl's Roman blood rushed over her pale cheeks as she felt the insult. She turned towards Hermanric, looked up at him appealingly, attempted to speak, and then sinking lower upon the ground, wept bitterly.

'Why do you weep and pray and mouth it at him?' shrieked Goisvintha, pointing to Hermanric with her disengaged hand. 'He has neither courage to protect you, nor honour to aid me. Do you think that I am to be moved by your tears and entreaties? I tell you that your people have slain my husband and my children, and that I hate you for that. I tell you that you have lured Hermanric into love for a Roman and unfaithfulness to me, and I will slay you for doing it! I tell you that there is not a living thing of the blood of your country, or the name of your nation, throughout the length and breadth of this empire, that I would not destroy if I had the power! If the very trees on the road hither could have had feeling, I would have torn the bark from their stems with my own hands! If a bird, native of your skies, had flown into my bosom from very tameness and sport, I would have crushed it dead at my feet! And do you think that you shall escape? Do you think that I will not avenge the deaths of my husband and my children upon you, after this?'

As she spoke, she mechanically unclenched her hands. The knife dropped to the ground. Hermanric instantly stooped and secured it. For a moment she stood before him released from his grasp, motionless and speechless. Then, starting as if struck by a sudden idea, she moved towards the opening of the tent, and, in tones of malignant triumph, addressed him thus:--

'You shall not save her yet! You are unworthy of your nation and your name! I will betray your cowardice and treachery to your brethren in the camp!' And she ran to the outside of the tent, calling in a loud voice to a group of young warriors who happened to be passing at a short distance. 'Stay, stay! Fritigern--Athanaric-

-Colias--Suerid--Witheric--Fravitta! Hasten hitherward! Hermanric has a captive in his tent--a prisoner whom it will rejoice to see! Hitherward! hitherward!'

The group she addressed contained some of the most turbulent and careless spirits of the whole Gothic army. They had just been released from their duties of the past night, and were at leisure to comply with Goisvintha's request. She had scarcely concluded her address before they turned and hurried eagerly up to the tent, shouting to Hermanric, as they advanced, to make his prisoner visible to them in the open air.

They had probably expected to be regaled by the ludicrous terror of some Roman slave whom their comrade had discovered lurking in the empty suburbs; for when they entered the tent, and saw nothing but the shrinking figure of the unhappy girl, as she crouched on the earth at Hermanric's feet, they all paused with one accord, and looked round on each other in speechless astonishment.

'Behold her!' cried Goisvintha, breaking the momentary silence. 'She is the Roman prisoner that your man of valour there has secured for himself! For that trembling child he has forgotten the enmities of his people! She is more to him already than army, general, or companions. You have watched before the city during the night; but he has stood sentinel by the maiden of Rome! Hope not that he will share in your toils, or mix in your pleasures more. Alaric and the warriors have lost his services--his future king cringes there at his feet!'

She had expected to arouse the anger and excite the jealousy of the rough audience she addressed; but the result of her envenomed jeers disappointed her hopes. The humour of the moment prompted the Goths to ridicule, a course infinitely more inimical to Antonina's interests with Hermanric than menaces or recrimination. Recovered from their first astonishment, they burst into a loud and universal laugh.

'Mars and Venus caught together! But, by St. Peter, I see not Vulcan and the net!' cried Fravitta, who having served in the armies of Rome, and acquired a vague knowledge there of the ancient mythology, and the modern politics of the Empire, was considered by his companions as the wit of the battalion to which he was attached.

'I like her figure,' growled Fritigern, a heavy, phlegmatic giant, renowned for his imperturbable good humour and his prowess in drinking. 'What little there is of it looks so limp that Hermanric might pack her into his light baggage and carry her about with him on his shoulders wherever he goes!'

'By which process you would say, old sucker of wine-skins, that he will attain the double advantage of always keeping her to himself, and always keeping her warm,' interrupted Colias, a ruddy, reckless boy of sixteen, privileged to be impertinent in consideration of his years.

'Is she Orthodox or Arian?' gravely demanded Athanaric, who piqued himself on his theological accomplishments and his extraordinary piety.

'What hair she has!' exclaimed Suerid, sarcastically. 'It is as black as the horse-hides of a squadron of Huns!'

'Show us her face! Whose tent will she visit next?' cried Witheric, with an insolent laugh.

'Mine!' replied Fritigern, complacently. 'What says the chorus of the song?

'Money and wine Make beauty mine!

I have more of both than any of you. She will come to my tent!'

During the delivery of these clumsy jests, which followed one upon another with instantaneous rapidity, the scorn at first expressed in Hermanric's countenance became gradually replaced by a look of irrepressible anger. As Fritigern spoke, he lost all command over himself, and seizing his sword, advanced threateningly towards the easy- tempered giant, who made no attempt to recede or defend himself, but called out soothingly, 'Patience, man! patience! Would you kill an old comrade for jesting? I envy you your good luck as a friend, not as an enemy!'

Yielding to the necessity of lowering his sword before a defenceless man, Hermanric was about to reply angrily to Fritigern, when his voice was drowned in the blast of a trumpet, sounding close by the tent. The signal that it gave was understood at once by the group of jesters still surrounding the young Goth. They turned, and retired without an instant's delay. The last of their number had scarcely disappeared, when the same veteran who had spoken with Hermanric, on the departure of Goisvintha the evening before, entered and thus addressed him:--

'You are commanded to post yourself with the division that now awaits you, at a place eastward of your present position, which will be shown you by a guide. Make ready at once--you have not an instant to delay.'

As the words passed the old man's lips, Hermanric turned and looked on Goisvintha. During the presence of the Goths in the tent, she had sat listening to their rough jeers in suppressed wrath and speechless disdain; now she rose and advanced a few steps. But there suddenly appeared an unwonted hesitation in her gait; her face was pale; she breathed fast and heavily. 'Where will you shelter her now?' she cried, addressing Hermanric, and threatening the girl with her out-stretched hands. 'Abandon her to your companions, or leave her to me; she is lost either way! I shall triumph--triumph!'--

At this moment her voice sank to an unintelligible murmur; she tottered where she stood. It was evident that the long strife of passions during her past night of watching, and the fierce and varying emotions of the morning, suddenly brought to a crisis, as they had been, by her exultation when she heard the old warrior's fatal message, had at length overtasked the energies even of her powerful frame. Yet one moment more she endeavoured to advance, to speak, to snatch the hunting knife from Hermanric's hand; the next she fell insensible at his feet.

Goaded almost to madness by the successive trials that he had undergone; Goisvintha's furious determination to thwart him, still present to his mind; the scornful words of his companions yet ringing in his ears; his inexorable duties demanding his attention without reserve or delay; Hermanric succumbed at last under the difficulties of his position, and despairingly abandoned all further hope of effecting the girl's preservation. Pointing to some food that lay in a corner of the tent, and to the country behind, he said to her, in broken and gloomy accents, 'Furnish yourself with those provisions, and fly, while Goisvintha is yet unable to pursue you. I can protect you no longer!'

Until this moment, Antonina had kept her face hidden, and had remained still crouching on the ground; motionless, save when a shudder ran through her frame as she listened to the loud, coarse jesting of the Goths; and speechless, except that when Goisvintha sank senseless to the earth, she uttered an exclamation of terror. But now, when she heard the sentence of her banishment proclaimed by the very lips which but the evening before had assured her of shelter and protection, she rose up instantly, cast on the young Goth a glance of such speechless misery and despair, that he involuntarily quailed before it; and then, without a tear or a sigh, without a look of reproach, or a word of entreaty, petrified and bowed down beneath a perfect trance of terror and grief, she left the tent.

Hurrying his actions with the reckless energy of a man determined on banishing his thoughts by his employments, Hermanric placed himself at the head of his troop, and marched quickly onwards in an eastward direction past the Pincian

Gate. Two of his attendants who happened to enter the tent after his departure, observing Goisvintha still extended on the earth, proceeded to transport her to part of the camp occupied by the women who were attached to the army; and then, the little sheltering canopy which made the abode of the Goth, and which had witnessed so large a share of human misery and so fierce a war of human contention in so few hours, was left as silent and lonely as the deserted country in which Antonina was now fated to seek a refuge and a home.

Chapter 12

THE PASSAGE OF THE WALL

'A fair night this, Balbus! All moonlight and no mist! I was posted last evening at the Ostian Gate, and was half choked by the fog.'

'If you were posted last night at the Ostian Gate, you were better placed than you are now. The ramparts here are as lonely as a ruin in the provinces. Nothing behind us but the back of the Pincian Mount; nothing before us but the empty suburbs; nothing at each side of us but brick and stone; nothing at our posts but ourselves. May I be crucified like St. Peter, if I believe that there is another place on the whole round of the walls possessed of such solitary dulness as this!'

'You are a man to find something to complain of, if you were lodged in one of the palaces yonder. The place is solitary enough, it is true; but whether it is dull or not depends on ourselves, its most honourable occupants. I, for one, am determined to promote its joviality by the very praiseworthy exertion of obliging you, my discontented friend, with an inexhaustible series of those stories for which, I may say, without arrogance, I am celebrated throughout the length and breadth of all the barracks of Rome.'

'You may tell as many stories as you please, but do not imagine that I will make one of your audience.'

'You are welcome to attend to me or not, as you choose. Though you do not listen, I shall still relate my stories by way of practice. I will address them to the walls, or to the air, or to the defunct gods and goddesses of antiquity, should they happen at this moment to be hovering over the city in a rage, as some of the unconverted would have us believe; or to our neighbours the Goths, if they are seized with a sudden desire to quite their encampments, and obtain a near view of the fortifications that they are so discreetly unwilling to assault. Or, these materials for a fit and decent auditory failing me, I will tell my stories to the most attentive of all listeners--myself.'

And the sentinel, without further delay, opened his budget of anecdotes, with the easy fluency of of a man who possessed a well-placed confidence in the perfection of his capacities for narration. Determined that his saturnine colleague should hear him, though he would not give him his attention, he talked in a raised voice, pacing briskly backwards and forwards over the space of his allotted limits, and laughing with ludicrous regularity and complacency at every jest that he happened to make in the course of his ill-rewarded narrative. He little thought, as he continued to proceed in his tale that its commencement had been welcomed by an unseen hearer, with emotions widely different from those which had dictated the observations of the unfriendly companion of his watch.

True to his determination, Ulpius, with part of the wages which he had hoarded in Numerian's service, had procured a small lantern from a shop in one of the distant quarters of Rome; and veiling its light in a piece of coarse, thick cloth, had proceeded by the solitary pathway to his second night's labour at the wall. He arrived at the breach, at the commencement of the dialogue above related, and heard with delight the sentinel's noisy resolution to amuse his companion in spite of himself. The louder and the longer the man talked, the less probable was the chance that the Pagan's labours in the interior of the wall would be suspected or overheard.

Softly clearing away the brushwood at the entrance of the hole that he had made the night before, Ulpius crept in as far as he had penetrated on that occasion; and then, with mingled emotions of expectation and apprehension which affected him so powerfully, that he was for the moment hardly master of his actions, he slowly and cautiously uncovered his light.

His first glance was intuitively directed to the cavity that opened beneath him. He saw immediately that it was less important, both in size and depth, than he had imagined it to be. The earth at this particular place had given way beneath the foundations of the wall, which had sunk down, deepening the chasm by their weight, into the yielding ground beneath them. A small spring of water (probably the first cause of the sinking in the earth) had bubbled up into the space in the brick-work, which bit by bit, and year by year, it had gradually undermined. Nor did it remain stagnant at this place. It trickled merrily and quietly onward--a tiny rivulet, emancipated from one prison in the ground only to enter another in the wall, bounded by no grassy banks, brightened by no cheerful light, admired by no human eye, followed in its small course through the inner fissures in the brick by no living thing but a bloated toad, or a solitary lizard: yet wending as happily on its way through darkness and ruin, as its sisters who were basking in the sunlight of the meadows, or leaping in the fresh breezes of the open mountain side.

Raising his eyes from the little spring, Ulpius next directed his attention to the prospect above him.

Immediately over his head, the material of the interior of the wall presented a smooth, flat, hard surface, which seemed capable of resisting the most vigorous attempts at its destruction; but on looking round, he perceived at one side of him and further inwards, an appearance of dark, dimly-defined irregularity, which promised encouragingly for his intended efforts. He descended into the chasm of the rivulet, crawled up on a heap of crumbling brick-work, and gained a hole above it, which he immediately began to widen, to admit of his passage through. Inch by inch, he enlarged the rift, crept into it, and found himself on a fragment of the bow of one of the foundation arches, which, though partly destroyed, still supported itself, isolated from all connection with the part of the upper wall which it had once sustained, and which had gradually crumbled away into the cavities below.

He looked up. An immense rift soared above him, stretching its tortuous ramifications, at different points, into every part of the wall that was immediately visible. The whole structure seemed, at this place, to have received a sudden and tremendous wrench. But for the support of the sounder fortifications at each side of it, it could not have sustained itself after the shock. The Pagan gazed aloft, into the fearful breaches which yawned above him, with ungovernable awe. His small, fitful light was not sufficient to show him any of their terminations. They looked, as he beheld them in dark relief against the rest of the hollow part of the wall, like mighty serpents twining their desolating path right upward to the ramparts above; and he, himself, as he crouched on his pinnacle with his little light by his side, was reduced by the wild grandeur, the vast, solemn gloom of the obscure, dusky, and fantastic objects around him, to the stature of a pigmy. Could he have been seen from the ramparts high overhead, as he now peered down behind his lantern into the cavities and irregularities below him, he would have looked, with his flickering light, like a mole led by a glow-worm.

He paused to consider his next movements. In a stationary position, the damp coldness of the atmosphere was almost insupportable, but he attained a great advantage by his present stillness: he could listen undisturbed by the noises made by the bricks which crumbled from under him, if he advanced.

Ere long, he heard a thin, winding, long-drawn sound, now louder, now softer; now approaching, now retreating; now verging towards shrillness, now quickly returning to a faint, gentle swell. Suddenly this strange unearthly music was interrupted by a succession of long, deep, rolling sounds, which travelled grandly about the fissures above, like prisoned thunderbolts striving to escape. Utterly ignorant that the first of these noises was occasioned by the night wind winding through the rents in the brick of the outer wall beyond him; and the second, by the echoes produced in the irregular cavities above, by the footfall of the sentries overhead--roused by the influence of the place, and the mystery of his employment, to a pitch of fanatic exaltation, which for the moment absolutely unsteadied his reason--filled with the frantic enthusiasm of his designs, and the fearful legends of invisible beings and worlds which made the foundation of his worship, Ulpius conceived, as he listened to the sounds around and above, that the gods of antiquity were now in viewless congregation hovering about him, and calling to him in unearthly voices and in an unknown tongue, to proceed upon his daring enterprise, in the full assurance of its near and glorious success.

'Roar and mutter, and make your hurricane music in my ears!' exclaimed the Pagan, raising his withered hands, and addressing in a savage ecstacy his imagined deities. 'Your servant Ulpius stops not on the journey that leads him to your repeopled shrines! Blood, crime, danger, pain--pride and honour, joy and rest, have I strewn like sacrifices at your altars' feet! Time has whirled past me; youth and manhood have lain long since buried in the hidden Lethe which is the portion of life; age has wreathed his coils over my body's strength, but still I watch by your temples and serve your mighty cause! Your vengeance is near! Monarchs of the world, your triumph is at hand!'

He remained for some time in the same position, looking fixedly up into the trackless darkness above him, drinking in the sounds which--alternately rising and sinking--still floated round him. The trembling gleam of his lantern fell red and wild upon his livid countenance. His shaggy hair floated in the cold breezes that blew by him. At this moment he would have appeared from a distance, like a phantom of fire perishing in a mist of darkness; like a Gnome in adoration in the bowels of the earth; like a forsaken spirit in a solitary purgatory, watching for the advent of a glimpse of beauty, or a breath of air.

At length he aroused himself from his trance, trimmed with careful hand his guiding lantern, and set forward to penetrate the breadth of the great rift he had just entered.

He moved on in an oblique direction several feet, now creeping over the tops of the foundation arches, now skirting the extremities of protrusions in the ruined brick-work, now descending into dark slimy rubbish-choked chasms, until the rift suddenly diminished in all directions.

The atmosphere was warmer in the place he now occupied; he could faintly distinguish patches of dark moss, dotted here and there over the uneven surface of the wall; and once or twice, some blades of long flat grass, that grew from a prominence immediately above his head, were waved in his face by the wind, which he could now feel blowing through the narrow fissure that he was preparing to enlarge. It was evident that he had by this time advanced to within a few feet of the outer extremity of the wall.

'Numerian wanders after his child through the streets,' muttered the Pagan, as he deposited his lantern by his side, bared his trembling arms, and raised his iron bar, 'the slaves of his neighbour the senator are forth to pursue me. On all sides my enemies are out after me; but, posted here, I mock their strictest search! If they would track me to my hiding-place, they must penetrate the walls of Rome! If they would hunt me down in my lair, they must assail me to-night in the camp of the Goths! Fools! let them look to themselves! I seal the doom of their city, with the last brick that I tear from their defenceless walls!'

He laughed to himself as he thrust his bar boldly into the crevice before him. In some places the bricks yielded easily to his efforts; in others, their resistance was only to be overcome by the exertion of his utmost strength. Resolutely and unceasingly he continued his labours; now wounding his hands against the jagged surfaces presented by the widening fissure; now involuntarily dropping his instrument from ungovernable exhaustion; but, still working bravely on, in defiance of every hindrance that opposed him, until he gained the interior of the new rift.

As he drew his lantern after him into the cavity that he had made, he perceived that, unless it was heightened immediately over him, he could proceed no further, even in a creeping position. Irritated at this unexpected necessity for more violent exertion, desperate in his determination to get through the wall at all hazards on that very night, he recklessly struck his bar upwards with all his strength, instead of gradually and softly loosening the material of the surface that opposed him, as he had done before.

A few moments of this labour had scarcely elapsed, when a considerable portion of the brick-work, consolidated into one firm mass, fell with lightning suddenness from above. It hurled him under it, prostrate on the foundation arch which had been his support; crushed and dislocated his right shoulder; and shivered his lantern into fragments. A groan of irrepressible anguish burst from his lips. He was left in impenetrable darkness.

The mass of brick-work, after it had struck him, rolled a little to one side. By a desperate exertion he extricated himself from under it--only to swoon from the fresh anguish caused to him by the effort.

For a short time he lay insensible in his cold dark solitude. Then, reviving after this first shock, he began to experience in all their severity, the fierce spasms, the dull gnawings, the throbbing torments, that were the miserable consequences of the injury he received. His arm lay motionless by his side--he had neither strength nor resolution to move any one of the other sound limbs in his body. At one moment his deep, sobbing, stifled respirations, syllabled horrible and half-formed curses--at another, his panting breaths suddenly died away within him; and then he could hear the blood dripping slowly from his shoulder, with dismal regularity, into a little pool that it had formed already by his side.

The shrill breezes which wound through the crevices in the wall before him, were now felt only on his wounded limb. They touched its surface like innumerable splinters of thin, sharp ice; they penetrated his flesh like rushing sparks struck out of a sea of molten lead. There were moments, during the first pangs of this agony, when if he had been possessed of a weapon and of the strength to use it, he would have sacrificed his ambition for ever by depriving himself of life.

But this desire to end his torments with his existence lasted not long. Gradually, the anguish in his body awakened a wilder and stronger distemper in his mind, and then the two agonies, physical and mental, rioted over him together in fierce rivalry, divesting him of all thoughts but such as were by their own agency created or aroused.

For some time he lay helpless in his misery, alternately venting by stifled groans the unalleviated torment of his wounds, and lamenting with curses the failure of his enterprise, at the very moment of its apparent success. At length, the pangs that struck through him seemed to grow gradually less frequent; he hardly knew now from what part of his frame they more immediately proceeded. Insensibly, his faculties of thinking and feeling grew blunted; then he remained a little while

in a mysterious unrefreshing repose of body and mind; and then his disordered
senses, left unguided and unrestrained, became the victims of a sudden and terrible delusion.

The blank darkness around him appeared, after an interval, to be gradually dawning into a dull light, thick and misty, like the reflections on clouds which threat-
en a thunderstorm at the close of evening. Soon, this atmosphere seemed to be
crossed and streaked with a fantastic trellis-work of white, seething vapour. Then
the mass of brick-work which had struck him down, grew visible at his side,
enlarged to an enormous bulk, and endued with a power of self-motion, by which
it mysteriously swelled and shrank, and raised and depressed itself, without quitting for a moment its position near him. And then, from its dark and toiling surface there rose a long stream of dusky shapes, which twined themselves about the
misty trellis-work above, and took the prominent and palpable form of human
countenances, marked by every difference of age and distorted by every variety of
suffering.

There were infantine faces, wreathed about with grave-worms that hung round
them like locks of filthy hair; aged faces, dabbled with gore and slashed with
wounds; youthful faces, seamed with livid channels, along which ran unceasing
tears; lovely faces, distorted into fixed expressions of raging pain, wild malignity,
and despairing gloom. Not one of these countenances exactly resembled the
other. Each was distinguished by a revolting character of its own. Yet, however
deformed might be their other features, the eyes of all were preserved unimpaired.
Speechless and bodiless, they floated in unceasing myriads up to the fantastic trellis-work, which seemed to swell its wild proportions to receive them. There they
clustered, in their goblin amphitheatre, and fixed and silently they all glared
down, without one exception, on the Pagan's face!

Meanwhile, the walls at the side began to gleam out with a light of their own,
making jagged boundaries to the midway scene of phantom faces. Then the rifts
in their surfaces widened, and disgorged misshapen figures of priests and idols of
the old time, which came forth in every hideous deformity of aspect, mocking at
the faces on the trellis-work; while behind and over the whole, soared shapes of
gigantic darkness, robed in grim cloudy resemblances of skins such as were worn
by the Goths, and wielding through the quivering vapour, mighty and shadow-
like weapons of war. From the whole of this ghastly assemblage there rose not the
slightest sound. A stillness, as of a dead and ruined world, possessed in all its quarters the appalling scene. The deep echoes of the sentries' footsteps and the faint
dirging of the melancholy winds were no more. The blood that had as yet
dripped from his wound, made no sound now in the Pagan's ear; even his own

agony of terror was as silent as were the visionary demons who had aroused it.
Days, years, centuries, seemed to pass, as he lay gazing up, in a trance of horror,
into his realm of peopled and ghostly darkness. At last nature yielded under the
trial; the phantom prospect suddenly whirled round him with fearful velocity, and
his senses sought refuge from the thraldom of their own creation in a deep and
welcome swoon.

Time had moved wearily onward, the chiding winds had many times waved the
dry locks of his hair to and fro about his brow, as if to bid him awaken and arise,
ere he again recovered his consciousness. Once more aroused to the knowledge
of his position and the sensation of his wound, he slowly raised himself upon his
uninjured arm, and looked wildly around for the faintest appearance of a gleam
of light. But the winding and uneven nature of the track which he had formed
to lead him through the wall, effectually prevented the moonbeams, then floating
into the outermost of the cavities that he had made, from reaching the place
where he now lay. Not a single object was even faintly distinguishable around
him. Darkness hemmed him in, in rayless and triumphant obscurity, on every
side.

The first agonies of the injury he had received had resolved themselves into one
dull, heavy, unchanging sensation of pain. The vision that had overwhelmed his
senses was now, in a vast and shadowy form, present only to his memory, filling
the darkness with fearful recollections, and not with dismal forms; and urging on
him a restless, headlong yearning to effect his escape from the lonely and unhallowed sepulchre, the prison of solitude and death, that his own fatal exertions
threatened him with, should he linger much longer in the caverns of the wall.

'I must pass from this darkness into light--I must breathe the air of the sky, or I
shall perish in the damps of this vault,' he exclaimed in a hoarse, moaning voice,
as he raised himself gradually and painfully into a creeping position; and turning
round slowly, commenced his meditated retreat.

His brain still whirled with the emotions that had so lately overwhelmed his
mind; his right hand hung helplessly by his side, dragged after him like a prisoner's chain, and lacerated by the uneven surface of the ground over which it was
slowly drawn, as--supporting himself on his left arm, and creeping forward a few
inches at a time--he set forth on his toilsome journey.

Here, he paused bewildered in the darkness; there, he either checked himself by a
convulsive effort from falling headlong into the unknown deeps beneath him, or
lost the little ground he had gained in labour and agony, by retracing his way at

the bidding of some unexpected obstacle. Now he gnashed his teeth in anguish, now he cursed in despair, now he was breathless with exhaustion; but still, with an obstinacy that had in it something of the heroic, he never failed in his fierce resolution to effect his escape.

Slowly and painfully, moving with the pace and the perseverance of the tortoise, hopeless yet determined as a navigator in a strange sea, he writhed onward and onward upon his unguided course, until he reaped at length the reward of his long suffering, by the sudden discovery of a thin ray of moonlight toiling through a crevice in the murky brickwork before him. Hardly did the hearts of the Magi when the vision of 'the star in the East' first dawned on their eyes, leap within them with a more vivid transport, than that which animated the heart of Ulpius at the moment when he beheld the inspiring and guiding light.

Yet a little more exertion, a little more patience, a little more anguish; and he stood once again, a ghastly and crippled figure, before the outer cavity in the wall.

It was near daybreak; the moon shone faintly in the dull, grey heaven; a small, vaporous rain was sinking from the shapeless clouds; the waning night showed bleak and cheerless to the earth, but cast no mournful or reproving influence over the Pagan's mind. He looked round on his solitary lurking place, and beheld no human figure in its lonely recesses. He looked up at the ramparts, and saw that the sentinels stood silent and apart, wrapped in their heavy watch-cloaks, and supported on their trusty weapons. It was perfectly apparent that the events of his night of suffering and despair had passed unheeded by the outer world.

He glanced back with a shudder upon his wounded and helpless limb; then his eyes fixed themselves upon the wall. After surveying it with an earnest and defiant gaze, he slowly moved the brushwood with his foot, against the small cavity in its outer surface.

'Days pass, wounds heal, chances change,' muttered the old man, departing from his haunt with slow and uncertain steps. 'In the mines I have borne lashes without a murmur--I have felt my chains widening, with each succeeding day, the ulcers that their teeth of iron first gnawed in my flesh, and have yet lived to loosen my fetters, and to close my sores! Shall this new agony have a power to conquer me greater than the others that are past? I will even yet return in time to overcome the resistance of the wall! My arm is crushed, but my purpose is whole!'

Chapter 13

THE HOUSE IN THE SUBURBS

Retracing some hours, we turn from the rifted wall to the suburbs and the country which its ramparts overlook; abandoning the footsteps of the maimed and darkly-plotting Ulpius, our attention now fixes itself on the fortunes of Hermanric, and the fate of Antonina.

Although the evening had as yet scarcely closed, the Goth had allotted to the warriors under his command their different stations for the night in the lonely suburbs of the city. This duty performed, he was left to the unbroken solitude of the deserted tenement which now served him as a temporary abode.

The house he occupied was the last of the wide and irregular street in which it stood; it looked towards the wall beneath the Pincian Mount, from which it was separated by a public garden about half a mile in extent. This once well-thronged place of recreation was now totally unoccupied. Its dull groves were brightened by no human forms; the chambers of its gay summer houses were dark and desolate; the booths of its fruit and flower-sellers stood vacant on its untrodden lawns. Melancholy and forsaken, it stretched forth as a fertile solitude under the very walls of a crowded city.

And yet there was a charm inexpressibly solemn and soothing in the prospect of loneliness that it presented, as its flower-beds and trees were now gradually obscured to the eye in the shadows of the advancing night. It gained in its present refinement as much as it had lost of its former gaiety; it had its own simple

attraction still, though it failed to sparkle to the eye with its accustomed illumi-
nations, or to please the ear by the music and laughter, which rose from it in times
of peace. As he looked forth over the view from the terrace of his new abode, the
remembrance of the employments of his past and busy hours deserted the memory of the young Goth, leaving his faculties free to welcome the reflections which
night began insensibly to awaken and create.

Employed under such auspices, whither would the thoughts of Hermanric naturally stray?

From the moonlight that already began to ripple over the topmost trembling
leaves of the trees beyond him, to the delicate and shadowy flowers that twined
up the pillars of the deserted terrace where he now stood, every object he beheld
connected itself, to his vivid and uncultured imagination, with the one being of
whom all that was beautiful in nature, seemed to him the eloquent and befitting
type. He thought of Antonina whom he had once protected; of Antonina whom
he had afterwards abandoned; of Antonina whom he had now lost!

Strong in the imaginative and weak in the reasoning faculties; gifted with large
moral perception and little moral firmness; too easy to be influenced and too difficult to be resolved, Hermanric had deserted the girl's interests from an infirmity of disposition, rather than from a determination of will. Now, therefore, when
the employments of the day had ceased to absorb his attention; now when silence
and solitude led his memory back to his morning's abandonment of his helpless
charge, that act of fatal impatience and irresolution inspired him with the
strongest emotions of sorrow and remorse. If during her sojourn under his care,
Antonina had insensibly influenced his heart, her image, now that he reflected on
his guilty share in their parting scene, filled all his thoughts, at once saddening
and shaming him, as he remembered her banishment from the shelter of his tent.

Every feeling which had animated his reflections on Antonina on the previous
night, was doubled in intensity as he thought on her now. Again he recalled her
eloquent words, and remembered the charm of her gentle and innocent manner;
again he dwelt on the beauties of her outward form. Each warm expression; each
varying intonation of voice that had accompanied her petition to him for safety
and companionship; every persuasion that she had used to melt him, now revived
in his memory and moved in his heart with steady influence and increasing
power. All the hurried and imperfect pictures of happiness which she had drawn
to allure him, now expanded and brightened, until his mind began to figure to
him visions that had been hitherto unknown to faculties occupied by no other
images than those of rivalry, turbulence, and strife. Scenes called into being by

Antonina's lightest and hastiest expressions, now rose vague and shadowy before his brooding spirit. Lovely places of earth that he had visited and forgotten now returned to his recollection, idealised and refined as he thought of her. She appeared to his mind in every allurement of action, fulfilling all the duties and enjoying all the pleasures that she had proposed to him. He imagined her happy and healthful, journeying gaily by his side in the fresh morning, with rosy cheek and elastic step; he imagined her delighting him by her promised songs, enlivening him by her eloquent words, in the mellow stillness of evening; he imagined her sleeping, soft and warm and still, in his protecting arms--ever happy and ever gentle; girl in years, and woman in capacities; at once lover and companion, teacher and pupil, follower and guide!

Such she might have been once! What was she now?

Was she sinking under her loneliness, perishing from exposure and fatigue, repulsed by the cruel, or mocked by the unthinking? To all these perils and miseries had he exposed her; and to what end? To maintain the uncertain favour, to preserve the unwelcome friendship, of a woman abandoned even by the most common and intuitive virtues of her sex; whose frantic craving for revenge, confounded justice with treachery, innocence with guilt, helplessness with tyranny; whose claims of nation and relationship should have been forfeited in his estimation, by the openly-confessed malignity of her designs, at the fatal moment when she had communicated them to him in all their atrocity, before the walls of Rome. He groaned in despair, as he thought on this, the most unworthy of the necessities, to which the forsaken girl had been sacrificed.

Soon, however, his mind reverted from such reflections as these, to his own duties and his own renown; and here his remorse became partially lightened, though his sorrow remained unchanged.

Wonderful as had been the influence of Antonina's presence and Antonina's words over the Goth, they had not yet acquired power enough to smother in him entirely the warlike instincts of his sex and nation, or to vanquish the strong and hostile promptings of education and custom. She had gifted him with new emotions, and awakened him to new thought; she had aroused all the dormant gentleness of his disposition to war against the rugged indifference, the reckless energy, that teaching and example had hitherto made a second nature to his heart. She had wound her way into his mind, brightening its dark places, enlarging its narrow recesses, beautifying its unpolished treasures. She had created, she had refined, during her short hours of communication with him, but she had not lured his disposition entirely from its old habits and its old attachments; she had not yet stripped off the false glitter from barbarian strife, or the pomp from martial renown; she had not elevated the inferior intellectual, to the height of the superior moral faculties, in his inward composition. Submitted almost impartially to the alternate and conflicting dominion of the two masters, Love and Duty, he at once regretted Antonina, and yet clung mechanically to his old obedience to those tyrannic requirements of nation and name, which had occasioned her loss.

Oppressed by his varying emotions, destitute alike of consolation and advice, the very inaction of his present position sensibly depressed him. He rose impatiently, and buckling on his weapons, sought to escape from his thoughts, by abandoning the scene under the influence of which they had been first aroused. Turning his back upon the city, he directed his steps at random, through the complicated labyrinth of streets, composing the extent of the deserted suburbs.

After he had passed through the dwellings comprised in the occupation of the Gothic lines, and had gained those situated nearer to the desolate country beyond, the scene around him became impressive enough to have absorbed the attention of any man not wholly occupied by other and more important objects of contemplation.

The loneliness he now beheld on all sides, was not the loneliness of ruin--the buildings near him were in perfect repair; it was not the loneliness of pestilence-- there were no corpses strewn over the untrodden pavements of the streets; it was not the loneliness of seclusion--there were no barred windows, and few closed doors; it was a solitude of human annihilation. The open halls were unapproached; the benches before the wine-shops were unoccupied; remains of gaudy household wares still stood on the counters of the street booths, watched by none, bought by none; particles of bread and meat (treasures, fated to become soon of greater value than silver and gold, to beleaguered Rome) rotted here in the open air, like garbage upon dunghills; children's toys, women's ornaments, purses, money, love- tokens, precious manuscripts, lay scattered hither and thither in the public ways, dropped and abandoned by their different owners, in the hurry of their sudden and universal flight. Every deserted street was eloquent of darling projects desperately resigned, of valued labours miserably deserted, of delighting enjoyments irretrievably lost. The place was forsaken even by those household gods of rich and poor, its domestic animals. They had either followed their owners into the city, or strayed, unhindered and unwatched, into the country beyond. Mansion, bath, and circus, displayed their gaudy pomp and luxurious comfort in vain; not even a wandering Goth was to be seen near their empty halls. For, with such a prospect before them as the subjugation of Rome, the army had caught the infection of its leader's enthusiasm for his exalted task, and willingly obeyed his commands for suspending the pillage of the suburbs, disdaining the comparatively worthless treasures around them, attainable at any time, when they felt that the rich coffers of Rome herself were now fast opening to their eager hands. Voiceless and noiseless, unpeopled and unravaged, lay the far-famed suburbs of the greatest city of the universe, sunk alike in the night of Nature, the night of Fortune, and the night of Glory!

Saddening and impressive as was the prospect thus presented to the eyes of the young Goth, it failed to weaken the powerful influence that his evening's meditations yet held over his mind. As, during the hours that were passed, the image of the forsaken girl had dissipated the remembrance of the duties he had performed, and opposed the contemplation of the commands he was yet to fulfil, so it now denied to his faculties any impressions from the lonely scene, beheld, yet unnoticed, which spread around him. Still, as he passed through the gloomy streets, his vain regrets and self-accusations, his natural predilections and acquired attachments, ruled over him and contended within him, as sternly and as unceasingly as in the first moments when they had arisen with the evening, during his sojourn in the terrace of the deserted house.

He had now arrived at the extremest boundary of the buildings in the suburbs. Before him lay an uninterrupted prospect of smooth, shining fields, and soft, hazy, indefinable woods. At one side of him were some vineyards and cottage gardens; at the other was a solitary house, the outermost of all the abodes in his immediate vicinity. Dark and cheerless as it was, he regarded it for some time with the mechanical attention of a man more occupied in thought than observation,--gradually advancing towards it in the moody abstraction of his reflections, until he unconsciously paused before the low range of irregular steps which led to its entrance door.

Startled from its meditations by his sudden propinquity to the object that he had unwittingly approached, he now, for the first time, examined the lonely abode before him with real attention.

There was nothing remarkable about the house, save the extreme desolateness of its appearance, which seemed to arise partly from its isolated position, and partly from the unusual absence of all decoration on its external front. It was too extensive to have been the dwelling of a poor man, too void of pomp and ornament to have been a mansion of the rich. It might, perhaps, have belonged to some citizen, or foreigner, or the middle class--some moody Northman, some solitary Egyptian, some scheming Jew. Yet, though it was not possessed, in itself, of any remarkable or decided character, the Goth experienced a mysterious, almost an eager curiosity to examine its interior. He could assign no cause, discover no excuse for the act, as he slowly mounted the steps before him. Some invisible and incomprehensible magnet attracted him to the dwelling. If his return had been suddenly commanded by Alaric himself; if evidences of indubitable treachery had lurked about the solitary place, at the moment when he thrust open its unbarred door, he felt that he must still have proceeded upon his onward course. The next instant he entered the house. The light streamed through the open entrance into the gloomy hall; the night-wind, rushing upon its track, blew shrill and dreary among the stone pillars, and in the hidden crevices and untenanted chambers above. Not a sign of life appeared, not a sound of a footstep was audible, not even an article of household use was to be seen. The deserted suburbs rose without, like a wilderness; and this empty house looked within, like a sepulchre--void of corpses, and yet eloquent of death!

There was an inexplicable fascination to the eyes of the Goth about this vault-like, solitary hall. He stood motionless at its entrance, gazing dreamily at the gloomy prospect before him, until a strong gust of wind suddenly forced the outer door further backwards, and at the same moment admitted a larger stream of light.

The place was not empty. In a corner of the hall, hitherto sunk in darkness, crouched a shadowy form. It was enveloped in a dark garment, and huddled up into an indefinable and unfamiliar shape. Nothing appeared on it, as a denoting sign of humanity, but one pale hand, holding the black drapery together, and relieved against it in almost ghastly contrast under the cold light of the moon.

Vague remembrances of the awful superstitions of his nation's ancient worship, hurried over the memory of the young Goth, at the first moment of his discovery of the ghost-like occupant of the hall. As he stood in fixed attention before the motionless figure, it soon began to be endowed with the same strange influence over his will, that the lonely house had already exerted. He advanced slowly towards the crouching form.

It never stirred at the noise of his approach. The pale hand still held the mantle over the compressed figure, with the same rigid immobility of grasp. Brave as he was, Hermanric shuddered as he bent down and touched the bloodless, icy fingers. At that action, as if endowed with instant vitality from contact with a living being, the figure suddenly started up.

Then, the folds of the dark mantle fell back, disclosing a face as pale in hue as the stone pillars around it; and the voice of the solitary being became audible, uttering in faint, monotonous accents, these words:--

'He has forgotten and abandoned me!--slay me if you will!--I am ready to die!'

Broken, untuned as it was, there yet lurked in that voice a tone of its old music,
there beamed in that vacant and heavy eye a ray of its native gentleness. With a
sudden exclamation of compassion and surprise, the Goth stepped forward, raised
the trembling outcast in his arms; and, in the impulse of the moment quitting the
solitary house, stood the next instant on the firm earth, and under the starry sky,
once more united to the charge that he had abandoned--to Antonina whom he
had lost.

He spoke to her, caressed her, entreated her pardon, assured her of his future care;
but she neither answered nor recognised him. She never looked in his face, never
moved in his arms, never petitioned for mercy. She gave no sign of life or being,
saving that she moaned at regular intervals in piteous accents:--'He has forgotten
and abandoned me!' as if that one simple expression comprised in itself, her
acknowledgment of the uselessness of her life, and her dirge for her expected
death.

The Goth's countenance whitened to his very lips. He began to fear that her faculties had sunk under her trials. He hurried on with her with trembling steps
towards the open country, for he nourished a dreamy, intuitive hope, that the
sight of those woods and fields and mountains which she had extolled to him, in
her morning's entreaty for protection, might aid in restoring her suspended consciousness, if she now looked on them.

He ran forward, until he had left the suburbs at least half a mile behind him, and
had reached an eminence, bounded on each side by high grass banks and clustering woods, and commanding a narrow, yet various prospect, of the valley ground
beneath, and the fertile plains that extended beyond.

Here the warrior paused with his burden; and, seating himself on the bank, once
more attempted to calm the girl's continued bewilderment and terror. He
thought not on his sentinels, whom he had abandoned--on his absence from the
suburbs, which might be perceived and punished by an unexpected visit, at his
deserted quarters, from his superiors in the camp. The social influence that sways
the world; the fragile idol at whose shrine pride learns to bow, and insensibility to
feel; the soft, grateful influence of yielding nature yet eternal rule--the influence
of woman, source alike of virtues and crimes, of earthly glories and earthly disas-
ters--had, in this moment of anguish and expectation, silenced in him every
appeal of duty, and overthrown every obstacle of selfish doubt. He now spoke to
Antonina as alluringly as a woman, as gently as a child. He caressed her as warm-

ly as a lover, as cheerfully as a brother, as kindly as a father. He--the rough, northern warrior, whose education had been of arms, and whose youthful aspirations
had been taught to point towards strife and bloodshed and glory--even he was
now endowed with the tender eloquence of pity and love--with untiring, skilful
care--with calm, enduring patience.

Gently and unceasingly he plied his soothing task; and soon, to his joy and triumph, he beheld the approaching reward of his efforts, in the slow changes that
became gradually perceptible in the girl's face and manner. She raised herself in
his arms, looked up fixedly and vacantly into his face, then round upon the
bright, quiet landscape, then back again more stedfastly upon her companion;
and at length, trembling violently, she whispered softly and several times the
young Goth's name, glancing at him anxiously and apprehensively, as if she feared
and doubted while she recognised him.

'You are bearing me to my death,'--said she suddenly. 'You, who once protected
me--you, who forsook me!--You are luring me into the power of the woman who
thirsts for my blood!--Oh, it is horrible--horrible!'

She paused, averted her face, and shuddering violently, disengaged herself from
his arms. After an interval, she continued:--

'Through the long day, and in the beginning of the cold night, I have waited in
one solitary place for the death that is in store for me! I have suffered all the loneliness of my hours of expectation, without complaint; I have listened with little
dread, and no grief, for the approach of my enemy who has sworn that she will
shed my blood! Having none to love me, and being a stranger in the land of my
own nation, I have nothing to live for! But it is a bitter misery to me to behold
in you the fulfiller of my doom; to be snatched by the hand of Hermanric from
the heritage of life that I have so long struggled to preserve!'

Her voice had altered, as she pronounced these words, to an impressive lowness
and mournfulness of tone. Its quiet, saddened accents were expressive of an
almost divine resignation and sorrow; they seemed to be attuned to a mysterious
and untraceable harmony with the melancholy stillness of the night-landscape.
As she now stood looking up with pale, calm countenance, and gentle, tearless
eyes, into the sky whose moonlight brightness shone softly over her form, the
Virgin watching the approach of her angel messenger could hardly have been
adorned with a more pure and simple loveliness, than now dwelt over the features
of Numerian's forsaken child.

No longer master of his agitation; filled with awe, grief, and despair, as he looked on the victim of his heartless impatience; Hermanric bowed himself at the girl's feet, and, in the passionate utterance of real remorse, offered up his supplications for pardon and his assurances of protection and love. All that the reader has already learned--the bitter self-upbraidings of his evening, the sorrowful wanderings of his night, the mysterious attraction that led him to the solitary house, his joy at once more discovering his lost charge--all these confessions he now poured forth in the simple yet powerful eloquence of strong emotion and true regret.

Gradually and amazedly, as she listened to his words, Antonina awoke from her abstraction. Even the expression of his countenance and the earnestness of his manner, viewed by the intuitive penetration of her sex, wrought with kind and healing influence on her mind. She started suddenly, a bright flush flew over her colourless cheeks; she bent down, and looked earnestly and wistfully into the Goth's face. Her lips moved, but her quick convulsive breathing stifled the words that she vainly endeavoured to form.

'Yes,' continued Hermanric, rising and drawing her towards him again, 'you shall never mourn, never fear, never weep more! Though you have lost your father, and the people of your nation are as strangers to you, though you have been threatened and forsaken, you shall still be beautiful--still be happy; for I will watch you, and you shall never be harmed; I will labour for you, and you shall never want! People and kindred--fame and duty, I will abandon them all to make atonement to you!'

Its youthful freshness and hope returned to the girl's heart, as water to the long-parched spring, when the young warrior ceased. The tears stood in her eyes, but she neither sighed nor spoke. Her frame trembled all over with the excess of her astonishment and delight, as she still steadfastly looked on him and still listened intently as he proceeded:--

'Fear, then, no longer for your safety--Goisvintha, whom you dread, is far from us; she knows not that we are here; she cannot track our footsteps now, to threaten or to harm you! Remember no more how you have suffered and I have sinned! Think only how bitterly I have repented our morning's separation, and how gladly I welcome our meeting of to-night! Oh, Antonina! you are beautiful with a wondrous loveliness, you are young with a perfected and unchildlike youth, your words fall upon my ear with the music of a song of the olden time; it is like a dream of the spirits that my fathers worshipped, when I look up and behold you at my side!'

An expression of mingled confusion, pleasure, and surprise, flushed the girl's half-averted countenance as she listened to the Goth. She rose with a smile of ineffable gratitude and delight, and pointed to the prospect beyond, as she softly rejoined:--

'Let us go a little further onward, where the moonlight shines over the meadow below. My heart is bursting in this shadowy place! Let us seek the light that is yonder; it seems happy like me!'

They walked forward; and as they went, she told him again of the sorrows of her past day; of her lonely and despairing progress from his tent to the solitary house where he had found her in the night, and where she had resigned herself from the first to meet a death that had little horror for her then. There was no thought of reproach, no utterance of complaint, in this renewal of her melancholy narration. It was solely that she might luxuriate afresh in those delighting expressions of repentance and devotion, which she knew that it would call forth from the lips of Hermanric, that she now thought of addressing him once more with the tale of her grief.

As they still went onward; as she listened to the rude fervent eloquence of the language of the Goth; as she looked on the deep repose of the landscape, and the soft transparency of the night sky; her mind, ever elastic under the shock of the most violent emotions, ever ready to regain its wonted healthfulness and hope--now recovered its old tone, and re-assumed its accustomed balance. Again her memory began to store itself with its beloved remembrances, and her heart to rejoice in its artless longings and visionary thoughts. In spite of all her fears and all her sufferings, she now walked on blest in a disposition that woe had no shadow to darken long, and neglect no influence to warp; still as happy in herself; even yet as forgetful of her past, as hopeful for her future, as on that first evening when we beheld her in her father's garden, singing to the music of her lute.

Insensibly as they proceeded, they had diverged from the road, had entered a bye-path, and now stood before a gate which led to a small farm house, surrounded by its gardens and vineyards, and, like the suburbs that they had quitted, deserted by its inhabitants on the approach of the Goths. They passed through the gate, and arriving at the plot of ground in front of the house, paused for a moment to look around them.

The meadows had been already stripped of their grass, and the young trees of their branches by the foragers of the invading army, but here the destruction of the little property had been stayed. The house with its neat thatched roof and shutters of variegated wood, the garden with its small stock of fruit and its carefully tended beds of rare flowers, designed probably to grace the feast of a nobleman or the statue of a martyr, had presented no allurements to the rough tastes of Alaric's soldiery. Not a mark of a footstep appeared on the turf before the house door; the ivy crept in its wonted luxuriance about the pillars of the lowly porch; and as Hermanric and Antonina walked towards the fish- pond at the extremity of the garden, the few water-fowl placed there by the owners of the cottage, came swimming towards the bank, as if to welcome in their solitude the appearance of a human form.

Far from being melancholy, there was something soothing and attractive about the loneliness of the deserted farm. Its ravaged outhouses and plundered meadows, which might have appeared desolate by day, were so distanced, softened, and obscured, by the atmosphere of night, that they presented no harsh contrast to the prevailing smoothness and luxuriance of the landscape around. As Antonina beheld the brightened fields and the shadowed woods, here mingled, there succeeding each other, stretched far onward and onward until they joined the distant mountains, that eloquent voice of nature, whose audience is the human heart, and whose theme is eternal love, spoke inspiringly to her attentive senses. She stretched out her arms as she looked with steady and enraptured gaze upon the bright view before her, as if she longed to see its beauties resolved into a single and living form--into a spirit human enough to be addressed, and visible enough to be adored.

'Beautiful earth!' she murmured softly to herself, 'Thy mountains are the watch-towers of angels, thy moonlight is the shadow of God!'

Her eyes filled with bright, happy tears; she turned to Hermanric, who stood watching her, and continued:--

'Have you never thought that light, and air, and the perfume of flowers, might contain some relics of the beauties of Eden that escaped with Eve, when she wandered into the lonely world? They glowed and breathed for her, and she lived and was beautiful in them! They were united to one another, as the sunbeam is united to the earth that it warms; and could the sword of the cherubim have sundered them at once? When Eve went forth, did the closed gates shut back in the empty Paradise, all the beauty that had clung, and grown, and shone round her? Did no ray of her native light steal forth after her into the desolateness of the world? Did no print of her lost flowers remain on the bosom they must once have pressed? It cannot be! A part of her possessions of Eden must have been spared to her with a part of her life. She must have refined the void air of the earth when she entered it, with a breath of the fragrant breezes, and gleam of the truant sunshine of her lost Paradise! They must have strengthened and brightened, and must now be strengthening and brightening with the slow lapse of mortal years, until, in the time when earth itself will be an Eden, they shall be made one again with the hidden world of perfection, from which they are yet separated. So that, even now, as I look forth over the landscape, the light that I behold has in it a glow of Paradise, and this flower that I gather a breath of the fragrance that once stole over the senses of my first mother, Eve!'

Though she paused here, as if in expectation of an answer, the Goth preserved an unbroken silence. Neither by nature nor position was he capable of partaking the wild fancies and aspiring thoughts, drawn by the influences of the external world from their concealment in Antonina's heart.

The mystery of his present situation; his vague remembrance of the duties he had abandoned; the uncertainty of his future fortunes and future fate; the presence of the lonely being so inseparably connected with his past emotions and his existence to come, so strangely attractive by her sex, her age, her person, her misfortunes, and her endowments; all contributed to bewilder his faculties. Goisvintha, the army, the besieged city, the abandoned suburbs, seemed to hem him in like a circle of shadowy and threatening judgments; and in the midst of them stood the young denizen of Rome, with her eloquent countenance and her inspiring words, ready to hurry him, he knew not whither, and able to influence him, he felt not how.

Unconsciously interpreting her companion's silence into a wish to change the scene and the discourse, Antonina, after lingering over the view from the garden for a moment longer, led the way back towards the untenanted house. They removed the wooden padlock from the door of the dwelling, and guided by the brilliant moonlight, entered its principal apartment.

The homely adornments of the little room had remained undisturbed, and dimly distinguishable though they now were, gave it to the eyes of the two strangers, the same aspect of humble comfort which had probably once endeared it to its exiled occupants. As Hermanric seated himself by Antonina's side on the simple couch which made the principal piece of furniture in the place, and looked forth from the window over the same view that they had beheld in the garden, the magic stillness and novelty of the scene now began to affect his slow perceptions, as they had already influenced the finer and more sensitive faculties of the thoughtful girl. New hopes and tranquil ideas arose in his young mind, and communicated an unusual gentleness to his expression, an unusual softness to his voice, as he thus addressed his silent companion:--

'With such a home as this, with this garden, with that country beyond, with no warfare, no stern teachers, no enemy to threaten you; with companions and occupations that you loved--tell me, Antonina, would not your happiness be complete?'

As he looked round at the girl to listen to her reply, he saw that her countenance had changed. Their past expression of deep grief had again returned to her features. Her eyes were fixed on the short dagger that hung over the Goth's breast, which seemed to have suddenly aroused in her a train of melancholy and unwelcome thoughts. When she at length spoke, it was in a mournful and altered voice, and with a mingled expression of resignation and despair.

'You must leave me--we must be parted again,' said she; 'the sight of your weapons has reminded me of all that until now I had forgotten, of all that I have left in Rome, of all that you have abandoned before the city walls. Once I thought we might have escaped together from the turmoil and the danger around us, but now I know that it is better that you should depart! Alas! for my hopes and my happiness, I must be left alone once more!'

She paused for an instant, struggling to retain her self-possession, and then continued:--

'Yes, you must quit me, and return to your post before the city; for in the day of assault there will be none to care for my father but you! Until I know that he is safe, until I can see him once more, and ask him for pardon, and entreat him for love, I dare not remove from the perilous precincts of Rome! Return, then, to your duties, and your companions, and your occupations of martial renown; and do not forget Numerian when the city is assailed, nor Antonina, who is left to think on you in the solitary plains!'

She rose from her place, as if to set the example of departing; but her strength and resolution both failed her, and she sank down again on the couch, incapable of making another movement, or uttering another word.

Strong and conflicting emotions passed over the heart of the Goth. The language of the girl had quickened the remembrance of his half-forgotten duties, and strengthened the failing influence of his old predilections of education and race. Both conscience and inclination now opposed his disputing her urgent and unselfish request. For a few minutes he remained in deep reflection; then he rose and looked earnestly from the window; then back again upon Antonina and the room they occupied. At length, as if animated by a sudden determination, he again approached his companion, and thus addressed her:--

'It is right that I should return. I will do your bidding, and depart for the camp (but not till the break of day), while you, Antonina, remain in concealment and in safety here. None can come hither to disturb you. The Goths will not revisit the fields they have already stripped; the husbandman who owns this dwelling is imprisoned in the beleaguered city; the peasants from the country beyond dare not approach so near to the invading hosts; and Goisvintha, whom you dread, knows not even of the existence of such a refuge as this. Here, though lonely, you will be secure; here you can await my return, when each succeeding night gives me the opportunity of departing from the camp; and here I will warn you before-hand, if the city is devoted to an assault. Though solitary, you will not be abandoned--we shall not be parted one from the other. Often and often I shall return to look on you, and to listen to you, and to love you! You will be happier here, even in this lonely place, than in the former home that you have lost through your father's wrath!'

'Oh! I will willingly remain--I will joyfully await you!' cried the girl, raising her beaming eyes to Hermanric's face. 'I will never speak mournfully to you again; I will never remind you more of all that I have suffered, and all that I have lost! How merciful you were to me, when I first saw you in your tent--how doubly merciful you are to me here! I am proud when I look on your stature, and your strength, and your heavy weapons, and know that you are happy in remaining with me; that you will succour my father; that you will return from your glittering encampments to this farm-house, where I am left to await you! Already I have forgotten all that has happened to me of woe; already I am more joyful than ever I was in my life before! See, I am no longer weeping in sorrow! If there are any tears still on my cheeks, they are the tears of gladness that every one welcomes-- tears to sing and rejoice in!'

She ceased abruptly, as if words failed to give expression to her new delight. All the gloomy emotions that had oppressed her but a short time before had now completely vanished; and the young, fresh heart, superior still to despair and woe, basked as happily again in its native atmosphere of joy as a bird in the sunlight of morning and spring.

Then, when after an interval of delay their former tranquility had returned to them, how softly and lightly the quiet hours of the remaining night flowed onward to the two watchers in the lonely house! How gladly the delighted girl disclosed her hidden thoughts, and poured forth her innocent confessions, to the dweller among other nations and the child of other impressions than her own! All the various reflections aroused in her mind by the natural objects she had secretly studied, by the mighty imagery of her Bible lore, by the gloomy histories of saints' visions and martyrs' sufferings, which she had learnt and pondered over by her father's side, were now drawn from their treasured places in her memory, and addressed to the ear of the Goth. As the child flies to the nurse with the story of its first toy; as the girl resorts to the sister with the confession of her first love; as the poet hurries to the friend with the plan of his first composition; so did Antonina seek the attention of Hermanric with the first outward revealings enjoyed by her faculties and the first acknowledgment of her emotions liberated from her heart.

The longer the Goth listened to her, the more perfect became the enchantment of her words, half struggling into poetry, and her voice half gliding into music. As her low, still, varying tones wound smoothly into his ear, his thoughts suddenly and intuitively reverted to her formerly expressed remembrances of her lost lute, inciting him to ask her, with new interest and animation, of the manner of her acquisition of that knowledge of song, which she had already assured him that she possessed.

'I have learned many odes of many poets,' said she, quickly and confusedly avoiding the mention of Vetranio, which a direct answer to Hermanric's question must have produced, 'but I remember none perfectly, save those whose theme is of spirits and of other worlds, and of the invisible beauty that we think of but cannot see. Of the few that I know of these, there is one that I first learned and loved most. I will sing it, that you may be assured I will not fail to you in my promised art.'

She hesitated for a moment. Sorrowful remembrances of the events that had followed the utterance of the last notes she sang in her father's garden, swelled within her, and held her speechless. Soon, however, after a short interval of silence, she recovered her self-possession, and began to sing, in low tremulous tones, that harmonised well with the character of the words and the strain of the melody which she had chosen.

THE MISSION OF THE TEAR

I.

The skies were its birth-place--the TEAR was the child Of the dark maiden SORROW, by young JOY beguil'd; It was born in convulsion; 'twas nurtur'd in woe; And the world was yet young when it wander'd below.

II.

No angel-bright guardians watch'd over its birth, Ere yet it was suffer'd to roam upon earth; No spirits of gladness its soft form caress'd; SIGHS mourned round its cradle, and hush'd it to rest.

III.

Though JOY might endeavour, with kisses and wiles, To lure it away to his household of smiles: From the daylight he lived in it turn'd in affright, To nestle with SORROW in climates of night.

IV.

When it came upon earth, 'twas to choose a career, The brightest and best that is left to a TEAR; To hallow delight, and bestow the relief Denied by despair to the fulness of grief.

V.

Few repell'd it--some bless'd it--wherever it came; Whether soft'ning their sorrow, or soothing their shame; And the joyful themselves, though its name they might fear, Oft welcom'd the calming approach of the TEAR!

VI.

Years on years have worn onward, as--watch'd from above--Speeds that meek spirit yet on its labour of love; Still the exile of Heav'n, it ne'er shall away, Every heart has a home for it, roam where it may!

For the first few minutes after she had concluded the ode, Hermanric was hardly conscious that she had ceased; and when at length she looked up at him, her mute petition for approval had an eloquence which would have been marred to the Goth at that moment, by the utterance of single word. A rapture, an inspiration, a new life moved within him. The hour and the scene completed what the magic of the song had begun. His expression now glowed with a southern warmth; his words assumed a Roman fervour. Gradually, as they discoursed, the voice of the girl was less frequently audible. A change was passing over her spirit; from the teacher, she was now becoming the pupil.

As she still listened to the Goth, as she felt the birth of new feelings within her while he spoke, her cheeks glowed, her features lightened up, her very form seemed to freshen and expand. No intruding thought or awakening remembrance disturbed her rapt attention. No cold doubt, no gloomy hesitation, appeared in her companion's words. The one listened, the other spoke, with the whole heart, the undivided soul. While a world-wide revolution was concentrating its hurricane forces around them; while the city of an Empire tottered already to its tremendous fall; while Goisvintha plotted new revenge; while Ulpius toiled for his revolution of bloodshed and ruin; while all these dark materials of public misery and private strife seethed and strengthened around them, they could as completely forget the stormy outward world, in themselves; they could think as serenely of tranquil love; the kiss could be given as passionately and returned as tenderly, as if the lot of their existence had been cast in the pastoral days of the shepherd poets, and the future of their duties and enjoyments was securely awaiting them in a land of eternal peace!

Chapter 14

THE FAMINE

The end of November is approaching. Nearly a month has elapsed since the occurrence of the events mentioned in the last chapter, yet still the Gothic lines stretch round the city walls. Rome, that we left haughty and luxurious even while ruin threatened her at her gates, has now suffered a terrible and warning change. As we approach her again, woe, horror, and desolation have already gone forth to shadow her lofty palaces and to darken her brilliant streets.

Over Pomp that spurned it, over Pleasure that defied it, over Plenty that scared it in its secret rounds, the spectre Hunger has now risen triumphant at last. Day by day has the city's insufficient allowance of food been more and more sparingly doled out; higher and higher has risen the value of the coarsest and simplest provision; the hoarded supplies that pity and charity have already bestowed to cheer the sinking people have reached their utmost limits. For the rich, there is still corn in the city--treasure of food to be bartered for treasure of gold. For the poor, man's natural nourishment exists no more; the season of famine's loathsome feasts, the first days of the sacrifice of choice to necessity have darkly and irretrievably begun.

It is morning. A sad and noiseless throng is advancing over the cold flagstones of the great square before the Basilica of St. John Lateran. The members of the assembly speak in whispers. The weak are tearful--the strong are gloomy--they all move with slow and languid gait, and hold in their arms their dogs or other domestic animals. On the outskirts of the crowd march the enfeebled guards of the city, grasping in their rough hands rare favourite birds of gaudy plumage and melodious note, and followed by children and young girls vainly and piteously entreating that their favourites may be restored.

This strange procession pauses, at length, before a mighty caldron slung over a great fire in the middle of the square, round which stand the city butchers with bare knives, and the trustiest men of the Roman legions with threatening weapons. A proclamation is then repeated, commanding the populace who have no money left to purchase food, to bring up their domestic animals to be boiled together over the public furnace, for the sake of contributing to the public support.

The next minute, in pursuance of this edict, the dumb favourites of the crowd passed from the owner's caressing hand into the butcher's ready grasp. The faint cries of the animals, starved like their masters, mingled for a few moments with the sobs and lamentations of the women and children, to whom the greater part of them belonged. For, in this the first stage of their calamities, that severity of hunger which extinguishes pity and estranges grief was unknown to the populace; and though fast losing spirit, they had not yet sunk to the depths of ferocious despair which even now were invisibly opening between them. A thousand pangs were felt, a thousand humble tragedies were acted, in the brief moments of separation between guardian and charge. The child snatched its last kiss of the bird that had sung over its bed; the dog looked its last entreaty for protection from the mistress who had once never met it without a caress. Then came the short interval of agony and death, then the steam rose fiercely from the greedy caldron, and then the people for a time dispersed; the sorrowful to linger near the confines of the fire, and the hungry to calm their impatience by a visit to the neighbouring church.

The marble aisles of the noble basilica held a gloomy congregation. Three small candles were alone lighted on the high altar. No sweet voices sang melodious anthems or exulting hymns. The monks, in hoarse tones and monotonous harmonics, chanted the penitential psalms. Here and there knelt a figure clothed in mourning robes, and absorbed in secret prayer; but over the majority of the assembly either blank despondency or sullen inattention universally prevailed.

As the last dull notes of the last psalm died away among the lofty recesses of the church, a procession of pious Christians appeared at the door and advanced slowly to the altar. It was composed both of men and women barefooted, clothed in black garments, and with ashes scattered over their dishevelled hair. Tears flowed from their eyes, and they beat their breasts as they bowed their foreheads on the marble pavement of the altar steps.

This humble public expression of penitence under the calamity that had now fallen on the city was, however, confined only to its few really religious inhabitants, and commanded neither sympathy nor attention from the heartless and obstinate population of Rome. Some still cherished the delusive hope of assistance from the court at Ravenna; others believed that the Goths would ere long impatiently abandon their protracted blockade, to stretch their ravages over the rich and unprotected fields of Southern Italy. But the same blind confidence in the lost terrors of the Roman name, the same fierce and reckless determination to defy the Goths to the very last, sustained the sinking courage and suppressed the despondent emotions of the great mass of the suffering people, from the beggar who prowled for garbage, to the patrician who sighed over his new and unwelcome nourishment of simple bread.

While the penitents who formed the procession above described were yet engaged in the performance of their unnoticed and unshared duties of penance and prayer, a priest ascended the great pulpit of the basilica, to attempt the ungrateful task of preaching patience and piety to the hungry multitude at his feet.

He began his sermon by retracing the principal occurrences in Rome since the beginning of the Gothic blockade. He touched cautiously upon the first event that stained the annals of the besieged city--the execution of the widow of the Roman general Stilicho, on the unauthorised suspicion that she had held treasonable communication with Alaric and the invading army; he noticed lengthily the promises of assistance transmitted from Ravenna, after the perpetration of that ill-omened act. He spoke admiringly of the skill displayed by the government in making the necessary and immediate reductions in the daily supplies of food; he lamented the terrible scarcity which followed, too inevitably, those seasonable reductions. He pronounced an eloquent eulogium on the noble charity of Laeta, the widow of the Emperor Gratian, who, with her mother, devoted the store of provisions obtained by their imperial revenues to succouring, at that important juncture, the starving and desponding poor: he admitted the new scarcity, consequent on the dissipation of Laeta's stores; deplored the present necessity of sacrificing the domestic animals of the citizens; condemned the enormous prices now demanded for the last remnants of wholesome food that were garnered up; announced it as the firm persuasion of every one that a few days more would bring help from Ravenna; and ended his address by informing his auditory that, as they had suffered so much already, they could patiently suffer a little more, and that if, after this, they were so ill-fated as to sink under their calamities, they would feel it a noble consolation to die in the cause of Catholic and Apostolic Rome, and would assuredly be canonised as saints and martyrs by the next generation of the pious in the first interval of fertile and restoring peace.

Flowing as was the eloquence of this oration, it yet possessed not the power of inducing one among those whom it addressed to forget the sensation of his present suffering, and to fix his attention on the vision of future advantage, spread before all listeners by the fluent priest. With the same murmurs of querulous complaint, and the same expressions of impotent hatred and and defiance of the Goths which had fallen from them as they entered the church, the populace now departed from it, to receive from the city officers the stinted allowance of repugnant food, prepared for their hunger from the caldron in the public square:

And see, already from other haunts in the neighbouring quarter of Rome their fellow-citizens press onward at the given signal, to meet them round the caldron's sides! The languid sentinel, released from duty, turns his gaze from the sickening prospect of the Gothic camp, and hastens to share the public meal; the baker starts from sleeping on his empty counter, the beggar rises from his kennel in the butcher's vacant out-house, the slave deserts his place by the smouldering kitchen-fire--all hurry to swell the numbers of the guests that are bidden to the wretched feast. Rapidly and confusedly, the congregation in the basilica pours through its lofty gates; the priests and penitents retire from the altar's foot, and in the great church, so crowded by a few moments before, there now only remains the figure of a solitary man.

Since the commencement of the service, neither addressed nor observed, this lonely being has faltered round the circle of the congregation, gazing long and wistfully over the faces that met his view. Now that the sermon is ended, and the last lingerer has quitted the church, he turns from the spot whence he has anxiously watched the different members of the departing throng, and feebly crouches down on his knees at the base of a pillar that is near him. His eyes are hollow, and his cheeks are wan; his thin grey hairs are few and fading on his aged head. He makes no effort to follow the crowd and partake their sustenance; no one is left behind to urge, no one returns to lead him to the public meal. Though weak and old, he is perfectly forsaken in his loneliness, perfectly unsolaced in his grief; his friends have lost all trace of him; his enemies have ceased to fear or to hate him now. As he crouches by the pillar alone, he covers his forehead with his pale, palsied hands, his dim eyes fill with bitter tears, and such expressions as these are ever and anon faintly audible in the intervals of his heavy sighs: 'Day after day! Day after day! And my lost one is not found! my loved and wronged one is not restored! Antonina! Antonina!'

Some days after the public distribution of food in the square of St. John Lateran, Vetranio's favourite freedman might have been observed pursuing his way homeward, sadly and slowly, to his master's palace.

It was not without cause that the pace of the intelligent Carrio was funereal and his expression disconsolate. Even during the short period that had elapsed since the scene in the basilica already described, the condition of the city had altered fearfully for the worse. The famine advanced with giant strides; every succeeding hour endued it with new vigour, every effort to repel it served but to increase its spreading and overwhelming influence. One after another the pleasures and pursuits of the city declined beneath the dismal oppression of the universal ill, until the public spirit in Rome became moved alike in all classes by one gloomy inspiration--a despairing defiance of the famine and the Goths.

The freedman entered his master's palace neither saluted nor welcomed by the once obsequious slaves in the outer lodge. Neither harps nor singing-boys, neither woman's ringing laughter nor man's bacchanalian glee, now woke the echoes in the lonely halls. The pulse of pleasure seemed to have throbbed its last in the joyless being of Vetranio's altered household.

Hastening his steps as he entered the mansion, Carrio passed into the chamber where the senator awaited him.

On two couches, separated by a small table, reclined the lord of the palace and his pupil and companion at Ravenna, the once sprightly Camilla. Vetranio's open brow had contracted a clouded and severe expression, and he neither regarded nor addressed his visitor, who, on her part, remained as silent and as melancholy as himself. Every trace of the former characteristics of the gay, elegant voluptuary and the lively, prattling girl seemed to have completely vanished. On the table between them stood a large bottle containing Falernian wine, and a vase filled with a little watery soup, in the middle of which floated a small dough cake, sparingly sprinkled with common herbs. As for the usual accompaniments of Vetranio's luxurious privacy, they were nowhere to be seen. Poems, pictures, trinkets, lutes, all were absent. Even the 'inestimable kitten of the breed most worshipped by the ancient Egyptians' appeared no more. It had been stolen, cooked, and eaten by a runaway slave, who had already bartered its ruby collar for a lean parrot and the unroasted half of the carcase of a dog.

'I lament to confess it, O estimable patron, but my mission has failed,' observed Carrio, producing from his cloak several bags of money and boxes of jewels, which he carefully deposited on the table. 'The Prefect has himself assisted in searching the public and private granaries, and has arrived at the conclusion that not a handful of corn is left in the city. I offered publicly in the market-place five thousand sestertii for a living cock and hen, but was told that the race had long since been exterminated, and that, as money would no longer buy food, money was no longer desired by the poorest beggar in Rome. There is no more even of the hay I yesterday purchased to be obtained for the most extravagant bribes. Those still possessing the smallest supplies of provision guard and hide them with the most jealous care. I have done nothing but obtain for the consumption of the few slaves who yet remain faithful in the house this small store of dogs' hides, reserved from the public distribution of some days since in the square of the Basilica of St. John.'

And the freedman, with an air of mingled triumph and disgust, produced as he spoke his provision of dirty skins.

'What supplies have we still left in our possession?' demanded Vetranio, after drinking a deep draught of the Falernian, and motioning his servant to place his treasured burden out of sight.

'I have hidden in a secure receptacle, for I know not how soon hunger may drive the slaves to disobedience,' rejoined Carrio, 'seven bags of hay, three baskets stocked with salted horse-flesh, a sweetmeat-box filled with oats, and another with dried parsley; the rare Indian singing birds are still preserved inviolate in their aviary; there is a great store of spices, and some bottles of the Nightingale Sauce yet remain.'

'What is the present aspect of the city?' interrupted Vetranio impatiently.

'Rome is as gloomy as a subterranean sepulchre,' replied Carrio, with a shudder. 'The people congregate in speechless and hungry mobs at the doors of their hous-es and the corners of the streets, the sentinels at the ramparts totter on their posts, women and children are sleeping exhausted on the very pavements of the church-es, the theatres are emptied of actors and audience alike, the baths resound with cries for food and curses on the Goths, thefts are already committed in the open and unguarded shops, and the barbarians remain fixed in their encampments, unapproached by our promised legions from Ravenna, neither assaulting us in our weakness, nor preparing to raise the blockade! Our situation grows more and more perilous. I have great hopes in our store of provisions; but--'

'Cast your hopes to the court at Ravenna, and your beasts' provender to the howl-ing mob!' cried Vetranio with sudden energy. 'It is now too late to yield; if the next few days bring us no assistance, the city will be a human shambles! And think you that I, who have already lost in this public suspension of social joys my pleasures, my employments, and my companions, will wait serenely for the lin-gering and ignoble death that must then threaten us all? No, it shall never be said that I died starving with the herd, like a slave that his master deserts! Though the plates in my banqueting hall must now be empty, my vases and wine-cups shall yet sparkle for my guests! There is still wine in the cellar, and spices and perfumes remain in the larder stores! I will invite my friends to a last feast; a saturnalia in a city of famine; a banquet of death, spread by the jovial labours of Silenus and his fauns! Though the Parcae have woven for me the destiny of a dog, it is the hand of Bacchus that shall sever the fatal thread!'

His cheeks were flushed, his eyes sparkled; all the mad energy of his determination appeared in his face as he spoke. He was no longer the light, amiable, smooth-tongued trifler, but a moody, reckless, desperate man, careless of every obligation and pursuit which had hitherto influenced the easy surface of his patrician life. The startled Camilla, who had as yet preserved a melancholy silence, ran towards him with affrighted looks and undissembled tears. Carrio stared in vacant astonishment on his master's disordered countenance; and, forgetting his bundle of dogskins, suffered them to drop unheeded on the floor. A momentary silence followed, which was suddenly interrupted by the abrupt entrance of a fourth person, pale, trembling and breathless, who was no other than Vetranio's former visitor, the Prefect Pompeianus.

'I bid you welcome to my approaching feast of brimming wine-cups and empty dishes!' cried Vetranio, pouring the sparkling Falernian into his empty glass. 'The last banquet given in Rome, ere the city is annihilated, will be mine! The Goths and the famine shall have no part in my death! Pleasure shall preside at my last moments, as it has presided at my whole life! I will die like Sardanapalus, with my loves and my treasures around me, and the last of my guests who remains proof against our festivity shall set fire to my palace, as the kingly Assyrian set fire to his!'

'This is no season for jesting,' exclaimed the Prefect, staring round him with bewildered eyes and colourless cheeks. 'Our miseries are but dawning as yet! In the next street lies the corpse of a woman, and--horrible omen!--a coil of serpents is wreathed about her neck! We have no burial-place to receive her, and the thousands who may die like her, ere assistance arrives. The city sepulchres outside the walls are in the hands of the Goths. The people stand round the body in a trance of horror, for they have now discovered a fatal truth we would fain have concealed from them;' here the Prefect paused, looked round affrightedly on his listeners, and then added in low trembling tones--

'The citizens are lying dead from famine in the streets of Rome!'

Chapter 15

THE CITY AND THE GODS

We return once more to the Gothic encampment in the suburbs eastward of the Pincian Gate, and to Hermanric and the warriors under his command, who are still posted at that particular position on the great circle of the blockade.

The movements of the young chieftain from place to place expressed, in their variety and rapidity, the restlessness that was agitating his mind. He glanced back frequently from the warriors around him to the remote and opposite quarter of the suburbs, occasionally directing his eyes towards the western horizon, as if anxiously awaiting the approach of some particular hour of the coming night. Weary at length of pursuing occupations which evidently irritated rather than soothed his impatience, he turned abruptly from his companions, and advancing towards the city, paced slowly backwards and forwards over the waste ground between the suburbs and the walls of Rome.

At intervals he still continued to examine the scene around him. A more dreary prospect than now met his view, whether in earth or sky, can hardly be conceived.

The dull sunless day was fast closing, and the portentous heaven gave promise of a stormy night. Thick, black layers of shapeless cloud hung over the whole firmament, save at the western point; and here lay a streak of pale, yellow light, enclosed on all sides by the firm, ungraduated, irregular edges of the masses of gloomy vapour around it. A deep silence hung over the whole atmosphere. The wind was voiceless among the steady trees. The stir and action in the being of nature and the life of man seemed enthralled, suspended, stifled. The air was laden with a burdensome heat; and all things on earth, animate and inanimate, felt the oppression that weighed on them from the higher elements. The people who lay gasping for breath in the famine-stricken city, and the blades of grass that drooped languidly on the dry sward beyond the walls, owned the enfeebling influence alike.

As the hours wore on and night stealthily and gradually advanced, a monotonous darkness overspread, one after another, the objects discernible to Hermanric from the solitary ground he still occupied. Soon the great city faded into one vast, impenetrable shadow, while the suburbs and the low country around them vanished in the thick darkness that gathered almost perceptibly over the earth. And now the sole object distinctly visible was the figure of a weary sentinel, who stood on the frowning rampart immediately above the rifted wall, and whose drooping figure, propped upon his weapon, was indicated in hard relief against the thin, solitary streak of light still shining in the cold and cloudy wastes of the western sky.

But as the night still deepened, this one space of light faded, contracted, vanished, and with it disappeared the sentinel and the line of rampart on which he was posted. The rule of the darkness now became universal. Densely and rapidly it overspread the whole city with startling suddenness; as if the fearful destiny now working its fulfilment in Rome had forced the external appearances of the night into harmony with its own woe-boding nature.

Then, as the young Goth still lingered at his post of observation, the long, low, tremulous, absorbing roll of thunder afar off became grandly audible. It seemed to proceed from a distance almost incalculable; to be sounding from its cradle in the frozen north; to be journeying about its ice-girdled chambers in the lonely poles. It deepened rather than interrupted the dreary, mysterious stillness of the atmosphere. The lightning, too, had a summer softness in its noiseless and frequent gleam. It was not the fierce lightning of winter, but a warm, fitful brightness, almost fascinating in its light, rapid recurrence, tinged with the glow of heaven, and not with the glare of hell.

There was no wind--no rain; and the air was as hushed as if it slept over chaos in the infancy of a new creation.

Among the various objects displayed, instant by instant, by the rapid lightning to the eyes of Hermanric, the most easily and most distinctly visible was the broad surface of the rifted wall. The large, loose stones, scattered here and there at its

base, and the overhanging lid of its broad rampart, became plainly though fitfully apparent in the brief moments of their illumination. The lightning had played
for some time over that structure of the fortifications, and the bare ground that
stretched immediately beyond them, when the smooth prospect which it thus
gave by glimpses to view, was suddenly chequered by a flight of birds appearing
from one of the lower divisions of the wall, and flitting uneasily to and fro at one
spot before its surface.

As moment after moment the lightning continued to gleam, so the black forms
of the birds were visible to the practised eye of the Goth--perceptible, yet evanescent, as sparks of fire or flakes of snow--whirling confusedly and continually
about the spot whence they had evidently been startled by some unimaginable
interruption. At length, after a lapse of some time, they vanished as suddenly as
they had appeared, with shrill notes of affright which were audible even above the
continuous rolling of the thunder; and immediately afterwards, when the lightning alternated with the darkness, there appeared to Hermanric, in the part of the
wall where the birds had been first disturbed, a small red gleam, like a spark of
fire lodged in the surface of the structure. Then this was lost; a longer obscurity
than usual prevailed in the atmosphere, and when the Goth gazed eagerly through
the next succession of flashes, they showed him the momentary and doubtful
semblance of a human figure, standing erect on the stones at the base of the wall.

Hermanric started with astonishment. Again the lightning ceased. In the ardour
of his anxiety to behold more, he strained his eyes with the vain hope of penetrating the obscurity around him. The darkness seemed interminable. Once
again the lightning flashed brilliantly out. He looked eagerly towards the wall--
the figure was still there.

His heart throbbed quickly within him, as he stood irresolute on the spot he had
occupied since the first peal of thunder had struck upon his ear. Were the light
and the man--one seen but for an instant, the other still perceptible--mere phantoms of his erring sight, dazzled by the quick recurrence of atmospheric changes
through which it had acted? Or did he indubitably behold a human form, and
had he really observed a material light? Some strange treachery, some dangerous
mystery might be engendering in the besieged city, which it would be his duty to
observe and unmask. He drew his sword, and, at the risk of being observed
through the lightning, and heard during the pauses in the thunder, by the sentinel
on the wall, resolutely advanced to the very foot of the fortifications of hostile
Rome.

He heard no sound, perceived no light, observed no figure, as, after several unsuccessful attempts to reach the place where they stood, he at length paused at the

loose stones which he knew were heaped at the base of the wall. The next moment he was so close to it, that he could pass his sword-point over parts of its rugged surface. He had scarcely examined thus a space of more than ten yards, before his weapon encountered a sharp, jagged edge; and a sudden presentiment assured him instantly that he had found the spot where he had beheld the momentary light, and that he stood on the same stone which had been occupied by the figure of the man.

After an instant's hesitation, he was about to mount higher on the loose stones, and examine more closely the irregularity he had just discovered in the wall, when a vivid flash of lightning, unusually prolonged, showed him, obstructing at scarcely a yard's distance his onward path, the figure he had already distantly beheld from the plain behind.

There was something inexpressibly fearful in his viewless vicinity, during the next moment of darkness, to this silent, mysterious form, so imperfectly shown by the lightning that quivered over its half-revealed proportions. Every pulse in the body of the Goth seemed to pause as he stood, with ready weapon, looking into the gloomy darkness, and wafting for the next flash. It came, and displayed to him the man's fierce eyes glaring steadily down upon his face; another gleam, and he beheld his haggard finger placed upon his lip in token of silence; a third, and he saw the arm of the figure pointing towards the plain behind him; and then in the darkness that followed, a hot breath played upon his ear, and a voice whispered to him, through a pause in the rolling of the thunder--'Follow me.'

The next instant Hermanric felt the momentary contact of the man's body, as with noiseless steps he passed him on the stones. It was no time to deliberate or to doubt. He followed close upon the stranger's footsteps, gaining glimpses of his dark form moving onward before, whenever the lightning briefly illuminated the scene, until they arrived at a clump of trees, not far distant from the houses in the suburbs that were occupied by the Goths under his own command.

Here the stranger paused before the trunk of a tree which stood between the city wall and himself, and drew from beneath his ragged cloak a small lantern, carefully covered with a piece of cloth, which he now removed, and holding the light high above his head, regarded the Goth with a steady and anxious scrutiny.

Hermanric attempted to address him first, but the appearance of the man, barely visible though it was by the feeble light of his lantern, was so startling and repulsive, that the half-formed words died away on his lips. The face of the stranger was of a ghastly paleness; his hollow cheeks were seamed with deep wrinkles; and his eyes glared with an expression of ferocious suspicion. One of his arms was covered with old bandages, stiff with coagulated blood, and hung paralysed at his side. The hand that held the light trembled, so that the lantern containing it vibrated continuously in his unsteady grasp. His limbs were lank and shrivelled almost to deformity, and it was with evident difficulty that he stood upright on his feet. Every member of his body seemed to be wasting with a gradual death, while his expression, ardent and forbidding, was stamped with all the energy of manhood, and all the daring of youth.

It was Ulpius! The wall was passed! The breach was made good!

After a protracted examination of Hermanric's countenance and attire, the man, with an imperious expression, strangely at variance with his faltering voice, thus addressed him:--

'You are a Goth?'

'I am,' rejoined the young chief; 'and you are--'

'A friend of the Goths,' was the quick answer.

An instant of silence followed. The dialogue was then again begun by the stranger.

'What brought you alone to the base of the ramparts?' he demanded, and an expression of ungovernable apprehension shot from his eyes as he spoke.

'I saw the appearance of a man in the gleam of the lightning,' answered Hermanric. 'I approached it, to assure myself that my eyes had not deluded me, to discover--'

'There is but one man of your nation who shall discover whence I came and what I would obtain,' interrupted the stranger fiercely; 'that man is Alaric, your king.'

Surprise, indignation, and contempt appeared in the features of the Goth, as he listened to such a declaration from the helpless outcast before him. The man perceived it, and motioning him to be silent, again addressed him.

'Listen!' cried he. 'I have that to reveal to the leader of your forces which will stir the heart of every man in your encampment, if you are trusted with the secret after your king has heard it from my lips! Do you still refuse to guide me to his tent?'

Hermanric laughed scornfully.

'Look on me,' pursued the man, bending forward, and fixing his eyes with savage earnestness upon his listener's face. 'I am alone, old, wounded, weak,--a stranger to your nation,--a famished and a helpless man! Should I venture into your camp--should I risk being slain for a Roman by your comrades--should I dare the wrath of your imperious ruler without a cause?'

He paused; and then, still keeping his eyes on the Goth, continued in lower and more agitated tones--

'Deny me your help, I will wander through your camp till I find your king? Imprison me, your violence will not open my lips! Slay me, you will gain nothing by my death! But aid me, and to the latest moment of your life you will rejoice in the deed! I have words of terrible import for Alaric's ear,--a secret in the gaining of which I have paid the penalty thus!'

He pointed to his wounded arm. The solemnity of his voice, the rough energy of his words, the stern determination of his aspect, the darkness of the night that was round them, the rolling thunder that seemed to join itself to their discourse, the impressive mystery of their meeting under the city walls, all began to exert their powerful and different influences over the mind of the Goth, changing insensibly the sentiments at first inspired in him by the man's communications. He hesitated, and looked round doubtfully towards the lines of the camp.

There was a long silence, which was again interrupted by the stranger.

'Guard me, chain me, mock at me if you will,' he cried, with raised voice and flashing eyes, 'but lead me to Alaric's tent! I swear to you by the thunder pealing over our heads, that the words I would speak to him will be more precious in his eyes than the brightest jewel he could ravish from the coffers of Rome.'

Though visibly troubled and impressed, Hermanric still hesitated.

'Do you yet delay?' exclaimed the man, with contemptuous impatience. 'Stand back! I will pass on by myself into the very heart of your camp! I entered on my project alone--I will work its fulfilment without help! Stand back!'

And he moved past Hermanric in the direction of the suburbs, with the same look of fierce energy on his withered features which had marked them so strikingly at the outset of his extraordinary interview with the young chieftain.

The daring devotion to his purpose, the reckless toiling after a dangerous and doubtful success, manifested in the words and actions of one so feeble and unaided as the stranger, aroused in the Goth that sentiment of irrepressible admiration which the union of moral and physical courage inevitably awakens. In addition to the incentive to aid the man thus created, an ardent curiosity to discover his secret filled the mind of Hermanric, and further powerfully inclined him to conduct his determined companion into Alaric's presence--for by such proceeding only could he hope, after the man's firm declaration that he would communicate in the first instance to no one but the king, to penetrate ultimately the object of his mysterious errand. Animated, therefore, by such motives as these, he called to the stranger to stop, and briefly communicated to him his willingness to conduct him instantly to the presence of the leader of the Goths.

The man intimated by a sign his readiness to accept the offer. His physical powers were now evidently fast failing, but he still tottered painfully onward as they moved to the headquarters of the camp, muttering and gesticulating to himself almost incessantly. Once only did he address his conductor during their progress; and then with a startling abruptness of manner, and in tones of vehement anxiety and suspicion, he demanded of the young Goth if he had ever examined the surface of the city wall before that night. Hermanric replied in the negative; and they then proceeded in perfect silence.

Their way lay through the line of encampment to the westward, and was imperfectly lighted by the flame of an occasional torch or the glow of a distant watch-fire. The thunder had diminished in frequency, but had increased in volume; faint breaths of wind soared up fitfully from the west, and already a few raindrops fell slowly to the thirsty earth. The warriors not actually on duty at the different posts of observation had retired to the shelter of their tents; none of the thousand idlers and attendants attached to the great army appeared at their usual haunts; even the few voices that were audible sounded distant and low. The night-scene here, among the ranks of the invaders of Italy, was as gloomy and repelling as on the solitary plains before the walls of Rome.

Ere long the stranger perceived that they had reached a part of the camp more thickly peopled, more carefully illuminated, more strongly fortified, than that through which they had already passed; and the liquid, rushing sound of the waters of the rapid Tiber now caught his suspicious and attentive ear. They still moved onward a few yards; and then paused suddenly before a tent, immediately surrounded by many others, and occupied at all its approaches by groups of richly-armed warriors. Here Hermanric stopped an instant to parley with the sentinel, who, after a short delay, raised the outer covering of the entrance to the tent, and the moment after the Roman adventurer beheld himself standing by his conductor's side in the presence of the Gothic king.

The interior of Alaric's tent was lined with skins, and illuminated by one small lamp, fastened to the centre pole that supported its roof. The only articles of furniture in the place were some bundles of furs flung down loosely on the ground, and a large, rudely-carved wooden chest, on which stood a polished human skull, hollowed into a sort of clumsy wine-cup. A thoroughly Gothic ruggedness of aspect, a stately Northern simplicity prevailed over the spacious tent, and was indicated not merely in its thick shadows, its calm lights, and its freedom from pomp and glitter, but even in the appearance and employment of its remarkable occupant.

Alaric was seated alone on the wooden chest already described, contemplating with bent brow and abstracted gaze some old Runic characters, traced upon the carved surface of a brass and silver shield, full five feet high, which rested against the side of the tent. The light of the lamp falling upon the polished surface of the weapon--rendered doubly bright by the dark skins behind it--was reflected back upon the figure of the Goth chief. It glowed upon his ample cuirass; it revealed his firm lips, slightly curled by an expression of scornful triumph; it displayed the grand, muscular formation of his arm, which rested--clothed in tightly-fitting leather--upon his knee; it partly brightened over his short, light hair, and glittered steadily in his fixed, thoughtful, manly eyes, which were just perceptible beneath the partial shadow of his contracted brow; while it left the lower part of his body and his right hand, which was supported on the head of a huge, shaggy dog couching at his side, shadowed almost completely by the thick skins heaped confusedly against the sides of the wooden chest. He was so completely absorbed in the contemplation of the Runic characters, traced among the carved figures on his immense shield, that he did not notice the entry of Hermanric and the stranger until the growl of the watchful dog suddenly disturbed him in his occupation. He looked up instantly, his quick, penetrating glance dwelling for a moment on the young chieftain, and then resting steadily and inquiringly on his companion's feeble and mutilated form.

Accustomed to the military brevity and promptitude exacted by his commander in all communications addressed to him by his inferiors, Hermanric, without waiting to be interrogated or attempting to preface or excuse his narrative, shortly related the conversation that had taken place between the stranger and himself on the plain near the Pincian Gate; and then waited respectfully to receive the commendation or incur the rebuke of the king, as the chance of the moment might happen to decide.

After again fixing his eyes in severe scrutiny on the person of the Roman, Alaric spoke to the young warrior in the Gothic language thus:--

'Leave the man with me--return to your post, and there await whatever commands it may be necessary that I should despatch to you to-night.'

Hermanric immediately departed. Then, addressing the stranger for the first time, and speaking in the Latin language, the Gothic leader briefly and significantly intimated to his unknown visitant that they were now alone.

The man's parched lips moved, opened, quivered; his wild, hollow eyes brightened till they absolutely gleamed, but he seemed incapable of uttering a word; his features became horribly convulsed, the foam gathered about his lips, he staggered forward and would have fallen to the ground, had not the king instantly caught him in his strong grasp, and placed him on the wooden chest that he had hitherto occupied himself.

'Can a starving Roman have escaped from the beleaguered city?' muttered Alaric, as he took the skull cup, and poured some of the wine it contained down the stranger's throat.

The liquor was immediately successful in restoring composure to the man's features and consciousness to his mind. He raised himself from the seat, dashed off the cold perspiration that overspread his forehead, and stood upright before the king--the solitary, powerless old man before the vigorous lord of thousands, in the midst of his warriors--without a tremor in his steady eye or a prayer for protection on his haughty lip.

'I, a Roman,' he began, 'come from Rome, against which the invader wars with the weapon of famine, to deliver the city, her people, her palaces, and her treasures into the hands of Alaric the Goth.'

The king started, looked on the speaker for a moment, and then turned from him in impatience and contempt.

'I lie not,' pursued the enthusiast, with a calm dignity that affected even the hardy sensibilities of the Gothic hero. 'Eye me again! Could I come starved, shrivelled, withered thus from any place but Rome? Since I quitted the city an hour has hardly passed, and by the way that I left it the forces of the Goths may enter it to-night.'

'The proof of the harvest is in the quantity of the grain, not in the tongue of the husbandman. Show me your open gates, and I will believe that you have spoken truth,' retorted the king, with a rough laugh.

'I betray the city,' resumed the man sternly, 'but on one condition; grant it me, and--'

'I will grant you your life,' interrupted Alaric haughtily.

'My life!' cried the Roman, and his shrunken form seemed to expand, and his tremulous voice to grow firm and steady in the very bitterness of his contempt, as he spoke. 'My life! I ask it not of your power! The wreck of my body is scarce strong enough to preserve it to me a single day! I have no home, no loves, no friends, no possessions! I live in Rome a solitary in the midst of the multitude, a pagan in a city of apostates! What is my life to me? I cherish it but for the service of the gods, whose instruments of vengeance against the nation that has denied them I would make you and your hosts! If you slay me, it is a sign to me from them that I am worthless in their cause. I shall die content.'

He ceased. The king's manner, as he listened to him, gradually lost the bluntness and carelessness that had hitherto characterised it, and assumed an attention and a seriousness more in accordance with his high station and important responsibilities. He began to regard the stranger as no common renegade, no ordinary spy, no shallow impostor, who might be driven from his tent with disdain; but as a man important enough to be heard, and ambitious enough to be distrusted. Accordingly, he resumed the seat from which he had risen during the interview, and calmly desired his new ally to explain the condition, on the granting of which depended the promised betrayal of the city of Rome.

The pain-worn and despondent features of Ulpius became animated by a glow of triumph as he heard the sudden mildness and moderation of the king's demand; he raised his head proudly, and advanced a few steps, as he thus loudly and abruptly resumed:--

'Assure to me the overthrow of the Christian churches, the extermination of the Christian priests, and the universal revival of the worship of the gods, and this night shall make you master of the chief city of the empire you are labouring to subvert!'

The boldness, the comprehensiveness, the insanity of wickedness displayed in such a proposition, and emanating from such a source, so astounded the mind of

Alaric, as to deprive him for the moment of speech. The stranger, perceiving his temporary inability to answer him, broke the silence which ensued and continued--

'Is my condition a hard one? A conqueror is all-powerful; he can overthrow the worship, as he can overthrow the government of a nation. What matters it to you, while empire, renown, and treasure are yours, what deities the people adore? Is it a great price to pay for an easy conquest, to make a change which threatens neither your power, your fame, nor your wealth? Do you marvel that I desire from you such a revolution as this? I was born for the gods, in their service I inherited rank and renown, for their cause I have suffered degradation and woe, for their restoration I will plot, combat, die! Assure me then by oath, that with a new rule you will erect our ancient worship, and through my secret inlet to the city I will introduce men enough of the Goths to murder with security the sentinels at the guard-houses, and open the gates of Rome to the numbers of your whole invading forces. Think not to despise the aid of a man unprotected and unknown! The citizens will never yield to your blockade; you shrink from risking the dangers of an assault; the legions of Ravenna are reported on their way hitherward. Outcast as I am, I tell it to you here, in the midst of your camp--your speediest assurance of success rests on my discovery and on me!'

The king started suddenly from his seat. 'What fool or madman!' he cried, fixing his eyes in furious scorn and indignation on the stranger's face, 'prates to me about the legions of Ravenna and the dangers of an assault! Think you, renegade, that your city could have resisted me had I chosen to storm it on the first day when I encamped before its walls? Know you that your effeminate soldiery have laid aside the armour of their ancestors, because their puny bodies are too feeble to bear its weight, and that the half of my army here trebles the whole number of the guards of Rome? Now, while you stand before me, I have but to command, and the city shall be annihilated with fire and sword, without the aid of one of the herd of traitors cowering beneath the shelter of its ill-defended walls!'

As Alaric spoke thus, some invisible agency seemed to crush, body and mind, the lost wretch whom he addressed. The shock of such an answer as he now heard seemed to strike him idiotic, as a flash of lightning strikes with blindness. He regarded the king with a bewildered stare, waving his hand tremulously backwards and forwards before his face, as if to clear some imaginary darkness off his eyes; then his arm fell helpless by his side, his head drooped upon his breast, and he moaned out in low, vacant tones, 'The restoration of the gods--that is the condition of conquest--the restoration of the gods!'

'I come not hither to be the tool of a frantic and forgotten priesthood,' cried Alaric disdainfully. 'Wherever I meet with your accursed idols I will melt them down into armour for my warriors and shoes for my horses; I will turn your temples into granaries and cut your images of wood into billets for the watchfires of my hosts!'

'Slay me and be silent!' groaned the man, staggering back against the side of the tent, and shrinking under the merciless words of the Goth like a slave under the lash.

'I leave the shedding of such blood as yours to your fellow Romans,' answered the king; 'they alone are worthy of the deed.'

No syllable of reply now escaped the stranger's lips, and after an interval of silence Alaric resumed, in tones divested of their former fiery irritation, and marked by a solemn earnestness that conferred irresistible dignity and force on every word that he uttered.

'Behold the characters engraven there!' said he, pointing to the shield; 'they trace the curse denounced by Odin against the great oppressor, Rome! Once these words made part of the worship of our fathers; the worship has long since vanished, but the words remain; they seal the eternal hatred of the people of the North to the people of the South; they contain the spirit of the great destiny that has brought me to the walls of Rome. Citizen of a fallen empire, the measure of your crimes is full! The voice of a new nation calls through me for the freedom of the earth, which was made for man, and not for Romans! The rule that your ancestors won by strength their posterity shall no longer keep by fraud. For two hundred years, hollow and unlasting truces have alternated with long and bloody wars between your people and mine. Remembering this, remembering the wrongs of the Goths in their settlements in Thrace, the murder of the Gothic youths in the towns of Asia, the massacre of the Gothic hostages in Aquileia, I come--chosen by the supernatural decrees of Heaven--to assure the freedom and satisfy the wrath of my nation, by humbling at its feet the power of tyrannic Rome! It is not for battle and bloodshed that I am encamped before yonder walls. It is to crush to the earth, by famine and woe, the pride of your people and the spirit of your rulers; to tear from you your hidden wealth, and to strip you of your boasted honour; to overthrow by oppression the oppressors of the world; to deny you the glories of a resistance, and to impose on you the shame of a submission. It is for this that I now abstain from storming your city, to encircle it with an immovable blockade!'

As the declaration of his great mission burst thus from the lips of the Gothic king, the spirit of his lofty ambition seemed to diffuse itself over his outward form. His noble stature, his fine proportions, his commanding features, became invested with a simple, primeval grandeur. Contrasted as he now was with the shrunken figure of the spirit-broken stranger, he looked almost sublime.

A succession of protracted shuddering ran through the Pagan's frame, but he neither wept nor spoke. The unavailing defence of the Temple of Serapis, the defeated revolution at Alexandria, and the abortive intrigue with Vetranio, were now rising on his memory, to heighten the horror of his present and worst overthrow. Every circumstance connected with his desperate passage through the rifted wall revived, fearfully vivid, on his mind. He remembered all the emotions of his first night's labour in the darkness, all the miseries of his second night's torture under the fallen brickwork, all the woe, danger, and despondency that accompanied his subsequent toil--persevered in under the obstructions of a famine-weakened body and a helpless arm--until he passed, in delusive triumph, the last of the hindrances in the long-laboured breach. One after another these banished recollections returned to his memory as he listened to Alaric's rebuking words--reviving past infirmities, opening old wounds, inflicting new lacerations. But, saving the shudderings that still shook his body, no outward witness betrayed the inward torment that assailed him. It was too strong for human words, too terrible for human sympathy;--he suffered it in brute silence. Monstrous as was his plot, the moral punishment of its attempted consummation was severe enough to be worthy of the projected crime.

After watching the man for a few minutes more, with a glance of pitiless disdain, Alaric summoned one of the warriors in attendance; and, having previously commanded him to pass the word to the sentinels, authorising the stranger's free passage through the encampment, he then turned, and, for the last time, addressed him as follows:--

'Return to Rome, through the hole whence, reptile-like, you emerged!--and feed your starving citizens with the words you have heard in the barbarian's tent!'

The guard approached, led him from the presence of the king, issued the necessary directions to the sentinels, and left him to himself. Once he raised his eyes in despairing appeal to the heaven that frowned over his head; but still, no word, or tear, or groan, escaped him. He moved slowly on through the thick darkness; and turning his back on the city, passed, careless whither he strayed, into the streets of the desolate and dispeopled suburbs.

Chapter 16

LOVE MEETINGS

Who that has looked on a threatening and tempestuous sky, has not felt the pleasure of discovering unexpectedly a small spot of serene blue, still shining among the stormy clouds? The more unwillingly the eye has wandered over the gloomy expanse of the rest of the firmament, the more gladly does it finally rest on the little oasis of light which meets at length its weary gaze, and which, when it was dispersed over the whole heaven, was perhaps only briefly regarded with a careless glance. Contrasted with the dark and mournful hues around it, even that small spot of blue gradually acquires the power of investing the wider and sadder prospect with a certain interest and animation that it did not before possess--until the mind recognises in the surrounding atmosphere of storm an object adding variety to the view--a spectacle whose mournfulness may interest as well as repel.

Was it with sensations resembling these (applied, however, rather to the mind than to the eye) that the reader perused those pages devoted to Hermanric and Antonina? Does the happiness there described now appear to him to beam through the stormy progress of the narrative as the spot of blue beams through the gathering clouds? Did that small prospect of brightness present itself, at the time, like a garden of repose amid the waste of fierce emotions which encompassed it? Did it encourage him, when contrasted with what had gone before, to enter on the field of gloomier interest which was to follow? If, indeed, it has thus affected him, if he can still remember the scene at the farm-house beyond the suburbs with emotions such as these, he will not now be unwilling to turn again for a moment from the gathering clouds to the spot of blue,--he will not deny us an instant's digression from Ulpius and the city of famine to Antonina and the lonely plains.

During the period that has elapsed since we left her, Antonina has remained secure in her solitude, happy in her well-chosen concealment. The few straggling Goths who at rare intervals appeared in the neighbourhood of her sanctuary never intruded on its peaceful limits. The sight of the ravaged fields and emptied granaries of the deserted little property sufficed invariably to turn their marauding steps in other directions. Day by day ran smoothly and swiftly onwards for the gentle usurper of the abandoned farm-house. In the narrow round of its gardens and protecting woods was comprised for her the whole circle of the pleasures and occupations of her new life.

The simple stores left in the house, the fruits and vegetables to be gathered in the garden, sufficed amply for her support. The pastoral solitude of the place had in it a quiet, dreamy fascination, a novelty, an unwearying charm, after the austere loneliness to which her former existence had been subjected in Rome. And when evening came, and the sun began to burnish the tops of the western tress, then, after the calm emotions of the solitary day, came the hour of absorbing cares and happy expectations--ever the same, yet ever delighting and ever new. Then the rude shutters were carefully closed; the open door was shut and barred; the small light--now invisible to the world without--was joyfully kindled; and then, the mistress and author of these preparations resigned herself to await, with pleased anxiety, the approach of the guest for whose welcome they were designed.

And never did she expect the arrival of that treasured companion in vain. Hermanric remembered his promise to repair constantly to the farm-house, and performed it with all the constancy of love and all the enthusiasm of youth. When the sentinels under his command were arranged in their order of watching for the night, and the trust reposed in him by his superiors exempted his actions from superintendence during the hours of darkness that followed, he left the camp, passed through the desolate suburbs, and gained the dwelling where the young Roman awaited him--returning before daybreak to receive the communication s regularly addressed to him, at that hour, by his inferior in the command.

Thus, false to his nation, yet true to the new Egeria of his thoughts and actions--traitor to the requirements of vengeance and war, yet faithful to the interests of tranquility and love--did he seek, night after night, Antonina's presence. His passion, though it denied him to his warrior duties, wrought not deteriorating change in his disposition. All that it altered in him it altered nobly. It varied and exalted his rude emotions, for it was inspired, not alone by the beauty and youth that he saw, but by the pure thoughts, the artless eloquence that he heard. And she--the forsaken daughter, the source whence the Northern warrior derived those new and higher sensations that had never animated him until now--regarded her protector, her first friend and companion, as her first love, with a devotion which, in its mingled and exalted nature, may be imagined by the mind, but can be but imperfectly depicted by the pen. It was a devotion created of innocence and gratitude, of joy and sorrow, of apprehension and hope. It was too fresh, too unworldly to own any upbraidings of artificial shame, any self- reproaches of artificial propriety. It resembled in its essence, though not in its application, the devotion of the first daughters of the Fall to their brother-lords.

But it is now time that we return to the course of our narrative; although, ere we again enter on the stirring and rapid present, it will be necessary for a moment more to look back in another direction to the eventful past.

But it is not on peace, beauty, and pleasure that our observation now fixes itself. It is to anger, disease, and crime--to the unappeasable and unwomanly Goisvintha, that we now revert.

Since the day when the violence of her conflicting emotions had deprived her of consciousness, at the moment of her decisive triumph over the scruples of Hermanric and the destiny of Antonina, a raging fever had visited on her some part of those bitter sufferings that she would fain have inflicted on others. Part of the time she lay in a raving delirium; part of the time in helpless exhaustion; but she never forgot, whatever the form assumed by her disease, the desperate purpose in the pursuit of which she had first incurred it. Slowly and doubtfully her vigour at length returned to her, and with it strengthened and increased the fierce ambition of vengeance that absorbed her lightest thoughts and governed her most careless actions.

Report informed her of the new position, on the line of blockade, on which Hermanric was posted, and only enumerated as the companions of his sojourn the warriors sent thither under his command. But, though thus persuaded of the separation of Antonina and the Goth, her ignorance of the girl's fate rankled unintermittingly in her savage heart. Doubtful whether she had permanently reclaimed Hermanric to the interests of vengeance and bloodshed; vaguely suspecting that he might have informed himself in her absence of Antonina's place of refuge or direction of flight; still resolutely bent on securing the death of her victim, wherever she might have strayed, she awaited with trembling eagerness that day of restoration to available activity and strength which would enable her to resume her influence over the Goth, and her machinations against the safety of the fugitive girl. The time of her final and long- expected recovery, was the very day preceding the stormy night we have already described, and her first employment of her renewed energy was to send word to the young Goth of her intention of seeking him at his encampment ere the evening closed.

It was this intimation which caused the inquietude mentioned as characteristic of the manner of Hermanric at the commencement of the preceding chapter. The evening there described was the first that saw him deprived, through the threatened visit of Goisvintha, of the anticipation of repairing to Antonina, as had been his wont, under cover of the night; for to slight his kinswoman's ominous message was to risk the most fatal of discoveries. Trusting to the delusive security of her sickness, he had hitherto banished the unwelcome remembrance of her existence from his thoughts. But, now that she was once more capable of exertion and of crime, he felt that if he would preserve the secret of Antonina's hiding-place and the security of Antonina's life, he must remain to oppose force to force and stratagem to stratagem, when Goisvintha sought him at his post, even at the risk of inflicting, by his absence from the farm-house, all the pangs of anxiety and apprehension on the lonely girl.

Absorbed in such reflections as these, longing to depart, yet determined to remain, he impatiently awaited Goisvintha's approach, until the rising of the storm with its mysterious and all-engrossing train of events forced his thoughts and actions into a new channel. When, however, his interviews with the stranger and the Gothic king were past, and he had returned as he had been bidden to his appointed sojourn in the camp, his old anxieties, displaced but not destroyed, resumed their influence over him. He demanded eagerly of his comrades if Goisvintha had arrived in his absence, and received the same answer in the negative from each.

As he now listened to the melancholy rising of the wind and the increasing loudness of the thunder, to the shrill cries of the distant night-birds hurrying to shelter, emotions of mournfulness and awe possessed themselves of his heart. He now wondered that any events, however startling, however appalling, should have had the power to turn his mind for a moment from the dreary contemplations that had engaged it at the close of day. He thought of Antonina, solitary and helpless, listening to the tempest in affright, and watching vainly for his long- delayed approach. His fancy arrayed before him dangers, plots, and crimes, robed in all the horrible exaggerations of a dream. Even the quick, monotonous dripping of the rain-drops outside aroused within him dark and indefinable forebodings of ill. The passion that had hitherto created for him new pleasures was now fulfilling the other half of its earthly mission, and causing him new pains.

As the storm strengthened, as the darkness lowered deeper and deeper, so did his inquietude increase, until at length it mastered the last feeble resistance of his wavering firmness.   Persuading himself that, after having delayed so long, Goisvintha would now refrain from seeking him until the morrow, and that all communications from Alaric, had they been despatched, would have reached him ere this; unable any longer to combat his anxiety for the safety of Antonina; determined to risk the worst possibilities rather than be absent at such a time of tempest and peril from the farm-house, he made a last visit to the stations of the watchful sentinels, and quitted the camp for the night.

Chapter 17

THE HUNS

More than an hour after Hermanric had left the encampment, a man hurriedly entered the house set apart for the young chieftain's occupation. He made no attempt to kindle either light or fire, but sat down in the principal apartment, occasionally whispering to himself in a strange and barbarous tongue.

He had remained but a short time in possession of his comfortless solitude, when he was intruded on by a camp-follower, bearing a small lamp, and followed closely by a woman, who, as he started up and confronted her, announced herself as Hermanric's kinswoman, and eagerly demanded an interview with the Goth.

Haggard and ghastly though it was from recent suffering and long agitation, the countenance of Goisvintha (for it was she) appeared absolutely attractive as it was now opposed by the lamp-light to the face and figure of the individual she addressed. A flat nose, a swarthy complexion, long, coarse, tangled locks of deep black hair, a beardless, retreating chin, and small, savage, sunken eyes, gave a character almost bestial to this man's physiognomy. His broad, brawny shoulders overhung a form that was as low in stature as it was athletic in build; you looked on him and saw the sinews of a giant strung in the body of a dwarf. And yet this deformed Hercules was no solitary error of Nature--no extraordinary exception to his fellow-beings, but the actual type of a whole race, stunted and repulsive as himself. He was a Hun.

This savage people, the terror even of their barbarous neighbours, living without government, laws, or religion, possessed but one feeling in common with the human race--the instinct of war. Their historical career may be said to have begun with their early conquests in China, and to have proceeded in their first victories over the Goths, who regarded them as demons, and fled at their approach. The hostilities thus commenced between the two nations were at length suspended by the temporary alliance of the conquered people with the empire, and subsequently ceased in the gradual fusion of the interests of each in one animating spirit--detestation of Rome.

By this bond of brotherhood, the Goths and the Huns became publicly united, though still privately at enmity--for the one nation remembered its former defeats as vividly as the other remembered its former victories. With various disasters, dissensions, and successes, they ran their career of battle and rapine, sometimes separate, sometimes together, until the period of our romance, when Alaric's besieging forces numbered among the ranks of their barbarian auxiliaries a body of Huns, who, unwillingly admitted to the title of Gothic allies, were dispersed about the army in subordinate stations, and of whom the individual above described was one of those contemptuously favoured by promotion to an inferior command, under Hermanric, as a Gothic chief.

An expression of aversion, but not of terror, passed over Goisvintha's worn features as she approached the barbarian, and repeated her desire to be conducted to Hermanric's presence. For the second time, however, the man gave her no answer. He burst into a shrill, short laugh, and shook his huge shoulders in clumsy derision.

The woman's cheek reddened for an instant, and then turned again to livid paleness as she thus resumed--

'I came not hither to be mocked by a barbarian, but to be welcomed by a Goth! Again I ask you, where is my kinsman, Hermanric?'

'Gone!' cried the Hun. And his laughter grew more wild and discordant as he spoke.

A sudden tremor ran through Goisvintha's frame as she marked the manner of the barbarian and heard his reply. Repressing with difficulty her anger and agitation, she continued, with apprehension in her eyes and entreaty in her tones--

'Whither has he gone? Wherefore has he departed? I know that the hour I appointed for our meeting here has long passed; but I have suffered a sickness of many weeks, and when, at evening, I prepared to set forth, my banished infirmities seemed suddenly to return to me again. I was borne to my bed. But, though the woman who succoured me bid me remain and repose, I found strength in the night to escape them, and through storm and darkness to come hither alone--for I was determined, though I should perish for it, to seek the presence of Hermanric, as I had promised by my messengers. You, that are the companion of his watch, must know whither he is gone. Go to him, and tell him what I have spoken. I will await his return!'

'His business is secret,' sneered the Hun. 'He has departed, but without telling me whither. How should I, that am a barbarian, know the whereabouts of an illustrious Goth? It is not for me to know his actions, but to obey his words!'

'Jeer not about your obedience,' returned Goisvintha with breathless eagerness. 'I say to you again, you know whither he is gone, and you must tell me for what he has departed. You obey him--there is money to make you obey me!'

'When I said his business was secret, I lied not,' said the Hun, picking up with avidity the coins she flung to him--'but he has not kept it secret from me! The Huns are cunning! Aha, ugly and cunning!'

Suspicion, the only refined emotion in a criminal heart, half discovered to Goisvintha, at this moment, the intelligence that was yet to be communicated. No word, however, escaped her, while she signed the barbarian to proceed.

'He has gone to a farm-house on the plains beyond the suburbs behind us. He will not return till daybreak,' continued the Hun, tossing his money carelessly in his great, horny hands.

'Did you see him go?' gasped the woman.

'I tracked him to the house,' returned the barbarian. 'For many nights I watched and suspected him--to-night I saw him depart. It is but a short time since I returned from following him. The darkness did not delude me; the place is on the high-road from the suburbs--the first by- path to the westward leads to its garden gate. I know it! I have discovered his secret! I am more cunning than he!'

'For what did he seek the farm-house at night?' demanded Goisvintha after an interval, during which she appeared to be silently fixing the man's last speech in her memory; 'are you cunning enough to tell me that?'

'For what do men venture their safety and their lives, their money and their renown?' laughed the barbarian. 'They venture them for women! There is a girl at the farm-house; I saw her at the door when the chief went in!'

He paused; but Goisvintha made no answer. Remembering that she was descended from a race of women who slew their wounded husbands, brothers, and sons with their own hands when they sought them after battle dishonoured by a defeat; remembering that the fire of the old ferocity of such ancestors as these still burnt at her heart; remembering all that she had hoped from Hermanric, and had plotted against Antonina; estimating in all its importance the shock of the intelligence she now received, we are alike unwilling and unable to describe her emotions at this moment. For some time the stillness in the room was interrupted by no sounds but the rolling of the thunder without, the quick, convulsive respiration of Goisvintha, and the clinking of the money which the Hun still continued to toss mechanically from hand to hand.

'I shall reap good harvest of gold and silver after to-night's work,' pursued the barbarian, suddenly breaking the silence. 'You have given me money to speak--when the chief returns and hears that I have discovered him, he will give me money to be silent. I shall drink to- morrow with the best men in the army, Hun though I am!'

He returned to his seat as he ceased, and began beating in monotonous measure, with one of his pieces of money on the blade of his sword, some chorus of a favourite drinking song; while Goisvintha, standing pale and breathless near the door of the chamber, looked down on him with fixed, vacant eyes. At length a deep sigh broke from her; her hands involuntarily clenched themselves at her side; her lips moved with a bitter smile; then, without addressing another word to the Hun, she turned, and softly and stealthily quitted the room.

The instant she was gone, a sudden change arose in the barbarian's manner. He started from his seat, a scowl of savage hatred and triumph appeared on his shaggy brows, and he paced to and fro through the chamber like a wild beast in his cage. 'I shall tear him from the pinnacle of his power at last!' he whispered fiercely to himself. 'For what I have told her this night, his kinswoman will hate him--I knew it while she spoke! For his desertion of his post, Alaric may dishonour him, may banish him, may hang him! His fate is at my mercy; I shall rid myself nobly of him and his command! More than all the rest of his nation I loathe this Goth! I will be by when they drag him to the tree, and taunt him with his shame, as he has taunted me with my deformity.' Here he paused to laugh in complacent approval of his project, quickening his steps and hugging himself joyfully in the barbarous exhilaration of his triumph.

His secret meditations had thus occupied him for some time longer, when the sound of a footstep was audible outside the door. He recognised it instantly, and called softly to the person without to approach. At the signal of his voice a man entered--less athletic in build, but in deformity the very counterpart of himself. The following discourse was then immediately held between the two Huns, the new-comer beginning it thus:--

'Have you tracked him to the door?'

'To the very threshold.'

'Then his downfall is assured! I have seen Alaric.'

'We shall trample him under our feet!--this boy, who has been set over us that are his elders, because he is a Goth and we are Huns! But what c f Alaric? How did you gain his ear?'

'The Goths round his tent scoffed at me as a savage, and swore that I was begotten between a demon and a witch. But I remembered the time when these boasters fled from their settlements; when our tribes mounted their black steeds and hunted them like beasts! Aha, their very lips were pale with fear in those days.'

'Speak of Alaric--our time is short,' interrupted the other fiercely.

'I answered not a word to their taunts,' resumed his companion, 'but I called out loudly that I was a Gothic ally, that I brought messages to Alaric, and that I had the privilege of audience like the rest. My voice reached the ears of the king: he looked forth from his tent, and beckoned me in. I saw his hatred of my nation lowering in his eye as we looked on one another, but I spoke with submission and in a soft voice. I told him how his chieftain whom he had set over us secretly deserted his post; I told him how we had seen his favoured warrior for many nights journeying towards the suburbs; how on this night, as on others before, he had stolen from the encampment, and how you had gone forth to track him to his lurking-place.'

'Was the tyrant angered?'

'His cheeks reddened, and his eyes flashed, and his fingers trembled round the hilt of his sword while I spoke! When I ceased he answered me that I lied. He cursed me for an infidel Hun who had slandered a Christian chieftain. He threatened me with hanging! I cried to him to send messengers to our quarters to prove the truth ere he slew me. He commanded a warrior to return hither with me. When we arrived, the most Christian chieftain was nowhere to be beheld--none knew whither he had gone! We turned back again to the tent of the king; his warrior, whom he honoured, spoke the same words to him as the Hun whom he despised. Then the wrath of Alaric rose. "This very night," he cried, "did I with my own lips direct him to await my commands with vigilance at his appointed post! I would visit such disobedience with punishment on my own son! Go, take with you others of your troop--your comrade who has tracked him will guide you to his hiding-place--bring him prisoner into my tent!" Such were his words! Our companions wait us without--lest he should escape let us depart without delay.'

'And if he should resist us,' cried the other, leading the way eagerly towards the door; 'what said the king if he should resist us?'

'Slay him with your own hands.'

Chapter 18

THE FARM-HOUSE

As the night still advanced, so did the storm increase. On the plains in the open country its violence was most apparent. Here no living voices jarred with the dreary music of the elements; no flaming torches opposed the murky darkness or imitated the glaring lightning. The thunder pursued uninterruptedly its tempest symphony, and the fierce wind joined it, swelling into wild harmony when it rushed through the trees, as if in their waving branches it struck the chords of a mighty harp.

In the small chamber of the farm-house sat together Hermanric and Antonina, listening in speechless attention to the increasing tumult of the storm.

The room and its occupants were imperfectly illuminated by the flame of a smouldering wood fire. The little earthenware lamp hung from its usual place in the ceiling, but its oil was exhausted and its light was extinct. An alabaster vase of fruit lay broken by the side of the table, from which it had fallen unnoticed to the floor. No other articles of ornament appeared in the apartment. Hermanric's downcast eyes and melancholy, unchanging expressions betrayed the gloomy abstraction in which he was absorbed. With one hand clasped in his, and the other resting with her head on his shoulder, Antonina listened attentively to the alternate rising and falling of the wind. Her beauty had grown fresher and more woman-like during her sojourn at the farm- house. Cheerfulness and hope seemed to have gained at length all the share in her being assigned to them by nature at her birth. Even at this moment of tempest and darkness there was more of wonder and awe than of agitation and affright in her expression, as she sat hear-kening, with flushed cheek and brightened eye, to the progress of the nocturnal storm.

Thus engrossed by their thoughts, Hermanric and Antonina remained silent in their little retreat, until the reveries of both were suddenly interrupted by the snapping asunder of the bar of wood which secured the door of the room, the stress of which, as it bent under the repeated shocks of the wind, the rotten spar was too weak to sustain any longer. There was something inexpressibly desolate in the flood of rain, wind, and darkness that seemed instantly to pour into the cham-ber through the open door, as it flew back violently on its frail hinges. Antonina changed colour, and shuddered involuntarily, as Hermanric hastily rose and closed the door again, by detaching its rude latch from the sling which held it when not wanted for use. He looked round the room as he did so for some sub-stitute for the broken bar, but nothing that was fit for the purpose immediately met his eye, and he muttered to himself as he returned impatiently to his seat: 'While we are here to watch it the latch is enough; it is new and strong.'

He seemed on the point of again relapsing into his former gloom, when the voice of Antonina arrested his attention, and aroused him for the moment from his thoughts.

'Is it in the power of the tempest to make you, a warrior of a race of heroes, thus sorrowful and sad?' she asked, in accents of gentle reproach. 'Even I, as I look on these walls that are so eloquent of my happiness, and sit by you whose presence makes that happiness, can listen to the raging storm, and feel no heaviness over my heart! What is there to either of us in the tempest that should oppress us with gloom? Does not the thunder come from the same heaven as the sunshine of the summer day? You are so young, so generous, so brave,--you have loved, and pitied, and succoured me,--why should the night language of the sky cast such sorrow and such silence over you?'

'It is not from sorrow that I am silent,' replied Hermanric, with a constrained smile, 'but from weariness with much toil in the camp.'

He stifled a sigh as he spoke. His head returned to its old downcast position. The struggle between his assumed carelessness and his real inquietude was evidently unequal. As she looked fixedly on him, with the vigilant eye of affection, the girl's countenance saddened with his. She nestled closer to his side and resumed the discourse in anxious and entreating tones.

'It is haply the strife between our two nations which has separated us already, and may separate us again, that thus oppresses you,' said she; 'but think, as I do, of the peace that must come, and not of the warfare that now is. Think of the pleasures of our past days, and of the happiness of our present moments,--thus united, thus living, loving, hoping for each other; and, like me, you will doubt not of the future that is in preparation for us both! The season of tranquillity may return with the season of spring. The serene heaven will then be reflected on a serene country and a happy people; and in those days of sunshine and peace, will any hearts among all the glad population be more joyful than ours?'

She paused a moment. Some sudden thought or recollection heightened her colour and caused her to hesitate ere she proceeded. She was about at length to continue, when a peal of thunder, louder than any which had preceded it, burst threateningly over the house and drowned the first accents of her voice. The wind moaned loudly, the rain splashed against the door, the latch rattled long and sharply in its socket. Once more Hermanric rose from his seat, and approaching the fire, placed a fresh log of wood upon the dying embers. His dejection seemed now to communicate itself to Antonina, and as he reseated himself by her side, she did not address him again.

Thoughts, dreary and appalling beyond any that had occupied it before, were rising in the mind of the Goth. His inquietude at the encampment in the suburbs was tranquillity itself compared to the gloom which now oppressed him. All the evaded dues of his nation, his family, and his calling; all the suppressed recollections of the martial occupation he had slighted, and the martial enmities he had disowned, now revived avengingly in his memory. Yet, vivid as these remembrances were, they weakened none of those feelings of passionate devotion to Antonina by which their influence within him had hitherto been overcome. They existed with them--the old recollections with the new emotions--the stern rebukings of the warrior's nature with the anxious forebodings of the lover's heart. And now, his mysterious meeting with Ulpius; Goisvintha's unexpected return to health; the dreary rising and furious progress of the night tempest, began to impress his superstitious mind as a train of unwonted and meaning incidents, destined to mark the fatal return of his kinswoman's influence over his own actions and Antonina's fate.

One by one, his memory revived with laborious minuteness every incident that had attended his different interviews with the Roman girl, from the first night when she had strayed into his tent to the last happy evening that he had spent with her at the deserted farm-house. Then tracing further backwards the course of his existence, he figured to himself his meeting with Goisvintha among the

Italian Alps; his presence at the death of her last child, and his solemn engagement, on hearing her recital of the massacre at Aquileia, to avenge her on the Romans with his own hands. Roused by these opposite pictures of the past, his imagination peopled the future with images of Antonina again endangered, afflicted, and forsaken; with visions of the impatient army, spurred at length into ferocious action, making universal havoc among the people of Rome, and forcing him back for ever into their avenging ranks. No decision for resistance or resignation to flight presented itself to his judgment. Doubt, despair, and apprehension held unimpeded sway over his impressible but inactive faculties. The night itself, as he looked forth on it, was not more dark; the wild thunder, as he listened to it, not more gloomy; the name of Goisvintha, as he thought on it, not more ominous of evil, than the sinister visions that now startled his imagination and oppressed his weary mind.

There was something indescribably simple, touching, and eloquent in the very positions of Hermanric and Antonina as they now sat together--the only members of their respective nations who were united in affection and peace--in the lonely farm-house. Both the girl's hands were clasped over Hermanric's shoulder, and her head rested on them, turned from the door towards the interior of the room, and so displaying her rich, black hair in all its luxuriance. The head of the Goth was still sunk on his breast, as though he were wrapped in a deep sleep, and his hands hung listlessly side by side over the scabbard of his sheathed sword, which lay across his knees. The fire flamed only at intervals, the fresh log that had been placed on it not having been thoroughly kindled as yet. Sometimes the light played on the white folds of Antonina's dress; sometimes over the bright surface of Hermanric's cuirass, which he had removed and laid by his side on the ground; sometimes over his sword, and his hands, as they rested on it; but it was not sufficiently powerful or lasting to illuminate the room, the walls and corners of which it left in almost complete darkness.

The thunder still pealed from without, but the rain and wind had partially lulled. The night hours had moved on more swiftly than our narrative of the events that marked them. It was now midnight.

No sound within the room reached Antonina's ear but the quick rattling of the door-latch, shaken in its socket by the wind. As one by one the moments journeyed slowly onward, it made its harsh music with as monotonous a regularity as though it were moved by their progress, and kept pace with their eternal march. Gradually the girl found herself listening to this sharp, discordant sound, with all the attention she could have bestowed at other times on the ripple of a distant rivulet or the soothing harmony of a lute, when, just as it seemed adapting itself most easily to her senses, it suddenly ceased, and the next instant a gust of wind, like that which had rushed through the open door on the breaking of the rotten bar, waved her hair about her face and fluttered the folds of her light, loose dress. She raised her head and whispered tremulously to Hermanric--

'The door is open again--the latch has given way!'

The Goth started from his reverie and looked up hastily. At that instant the rattling of the latch recommenced as suddenly as it had ceased, and the air of the room recovered its former tranquillity.

'Calm yourself, beloved one,' said Hermanric gently; 'your fancy has misled you--the door is safe.'

He parted back her dishevelled hair caressingly as he spoke. Incapable of doubting the lightest word that fell from his lips, and hearing no suspicious or unwonted sound in the room, she never attempted to justify her suspicions. As she again rested her head on his shoulder, a vague misgiving oppressed her heart, and drew from her an irrepressible sigh; but she gave her apprehensions no expression in words. After listening for a moment more to assure himself of the security of the latch, the Goth resumed insensibly the contemplations from which he had been disturbed; once more his head drooped, and again his hands returned mechanically to their old listless position, side by side, on the scabbard of his sword.

The faint, fickle flames still rose and fell, gleaming here and sinking there, the latch sounded sharply in its socket, the thunder yet uttered its surly peal, but the wind was now subsiding into fainter moans, and the rain began to splash faintly and more faintly against the shutters without. To the watchers in the farm-house nothing was altered to the eye, and little to the ear. Fatal security! The last few minutes had darkly determined their future destinies--in the loved and cherished retreat they were now no longer alone.

They heard no stealthy footsteps pacing round their dwelling, they saw no fierce eyes peering into the interior of the farm-house through a chink in the shutters, they marked no dusky figure passing through the softly and quickly opened door, and gliding into the darkest corner of the room. Yet, now as they sat together, communing in silence with their young, sad hearts, the threatening figure of Goisvintha stood, shrouded in congenial darkness, under their protecting roof and in their beloved chamber, rising still and silent almost at their very sides.

Though the fire of her past fever had raged again through her veins, and though startling visions of the murders at Aquileia had flashed before her mind as the wild lightning before her eyes, she had traced her way through the suburbs and along the high-road, and down the little path to the farm-house gate, without straying, without hesitating. Regardless of the darkness and the storm, she had prowled about the house, had raised the latch, had waited for a loud peal of thunder ere she passed the door, and had stolen shadow-like into the darkest corner of the room, with a patience and a determination that nothing could disturb. And now, when she stood at the goal of her worst wishes, even now, when she looked down upon the two beings by whom she had been thwarted and deceived, her fierce self-possession did not desert her; her lips quivered over her locked teeth, her bosom heaved beneath her drenched garments, but neither sighs nor curses, not even a smile of triumph or a movement of anger escaped her.

She never looked at Antonina; her eyes wandered not for a moment from Hermanric's form. The quickest, faintest gleam of firelight that gleamed over it was followed through its fitful course by her eager glance, rapid and momentary as itself. Soon her attention was fixed wholly upon his hands, as they lay over the scabbard of his sword; and then, slowly and obscurely, a new and fatal resolution sprung up within her. The various emotions pictured in her face became resolved into one sinister expression, and, without removing her eyes from the Goth, she slowly drew from the bosom-folds of her garment a long sharp knife.

The flames alternately trembled into light and subsided into darkness as at first; Hermanric and Antonina yet continued in their old positions, absorbed in their thoughts and in themselves; and still Goisvintha remained unmoved as ever, knife in hand, watchful, steady, silent as before.

But beneath the concealment of her outward tranquillity raged a contention under which her mind darkened and her heart writhed. Twice she returned the knife to its former hiding-place, and twice she drew it forth again; her cheeks grew paler and paler, she pressed her clenched hand convulsively over her bosom, and leant back languidly against the wall behind her. No thought of Antonina had part in this great strife of secret emotions; her wrath had too much of anguish in it to be spent against a stranger and an enemy.

After the lapse of a few moments more, her strength returned--her firmness was aroused. The last traces of grief and despair that had hitherto appeared in her eyes vanished from them in an instant. Rage, vengeance, ferocity, lowered over them as she crept stealthily forward to the very side of the Goth, and, when the next gleam of the fire played upon him, drew the knife fiercely across the back of his hands. The cut was true, strong, and rapid--it divided the tendons from first to last--he was crippled for life.

At that instant the fire touched the very heart of the log that had been laid on it. It crackled gaily; it blazed out brilliantly. The whole room was as brightly illuminated as if a Christmas festival of ancient England had been preparing within its walls!

The warm, cheerful light showed the Goth the figure of his assassin, ere the first cry of anguish had died away on his lips, or the first start of irrepressible horror ceased to vibrate through his frame. The cries of his hapless companion, as the whole scene of vengeance, treachery, and mutilation flashed in one terrible instant before her eyes, seemed not even to reach his ears. Once he looked down upon his helpless hands, when the sword rolled heavily from them to the floor. Then his gaze directed itself immovably upon Goisvintha, as she stood at a little distance from him, with her blood-stained knife, silent as himself.

There was no fury--no defiance--not even the passing distortion of physical suffering in his features, as he now looked on her. Blank, rigid horror--tearless, voiceless, helpless despair, seemed to have petrified the expression of his face into an everlasting form, unyouthful and unhopeful--as if he had been imprisoned from his childhood, and a voice was now taunting him with the pleasures of liberty, from a grating in his dungeon walls. Not even when Antonina, recovering from her first agony of terror, pressed her convulsive kisses on his cold cheek, entreating him to look on her, did he turn his head, or remove his eyes from Goisvintha's form.

At length the deep steady accents of the woman's voice were heard through the desolate silence.

'Traitor in word and thought you may be yet, but traitor in deed you never more shall be!' she began, pointing to his hands with her knife. 'Those hands, that have protected a Roman life, shall never grasp a Roman sword, shall never pollute again by their touch a Gothic weapon! I remembered, as I watched you in the darkness, how the women of my race once punished their recreant warriors when they fled to them from a defeat. So have I punished you! The arm that served not the cause of sister and sister's children--of king and king's nation--shall serve no other! I am half avenged of the murders at Aquileia, now that I am avenged on you! Go, fly with the Roman you have chosen to the city of her people! Your life as a warrior is at an end!'

He made her no answer. There are emotions, the last of a life, which tear back from nature the strongest barriers that custom raises to repress her, which betray the lurking existence of the first rude social feeling of the primeval days of a great nation, in the breasts of their most distant descendants, however widely their acquirements, their prosperities, or their changes may seem to have morally separated them from their ancestors of old. Such were the emotions now awakened in the heart of the Goth. His Christianity, his love, his knowledge of high aims, and his experience of new ideas, sank and deserted him, as though he had never known them. He thought on his mutilated hands, and no other spirit moved within him, but the ancient Gothic spirit of centuries back; the inspiration of his nation's early Northern songs and early Northern achievements--the renown of courage and the supremacy of strength.

Vainly did Antonina, in the midst of the despair that still possessed her, yearn for a word from his lips or a glance from his eyes; vainly did her trembling fingers, tearing the bandages from her robe, stanch the blood on his wounded hands; vainly did her voice call on him to fly and summon help from his companions in the camp! His mind was far away, brooding over the legends of the battle-fields of his ancestors, remembering how, even in the day of victory, they slew themselves if they were crippled in the fray, how they scorned to exist for other interests than the interests of strife, how they mutilated traitors as Goisvintha had mutilated him! Such were the objects that enchained his inward faculties, while his outward senses were still enthralled by the horrible fascination that existed for him in the presence of the assassin by his side. His very consciousness of his existence, though he moved and breathed, seemed to have ceased.

'You thought to deceive me in my sickness, you hoped to profit by my death,' resumed Goisvintha, returning contemptuously her victim's glance. 'You trusted in the night, and the darkness, and the storm; you were secure in your boldness, in your strength, in the secrecy of this lurking-place that you have chosen for your treachery, but your stratagems and your expectations have failed you! At Aquileia I learnt to be wily and watchful as you! I discovered your desertion of the warriors and the camp; I penetrated the paths to your hiding-place; I entered it as softly as I once departed from the dwelling where my children were slain! In my just vengeance I have treated you as treacherously as you would have treated me! Remember your murdered brother; remember the child I put into your arms wounded and received from them dead; remember your broken oaths and forgotten promises, and make to your nation, to your duties, and to me, the atonement--the last and the only one--that in my mercy I have left in your power--the atonement of death.'

Again she paused, and again no reply awaited her. Still the Goth neither moved nor spoke, and still Antonina--kneeling unconsciously upon the sword, now useless to him for ever--continued to stanch the blood on his hands with a mechanical earnestness that seemed to shut out the contemplation of every other object from her eyes. The tears streamed incessantly down her cheeks, but she never turned towards Goisvintha, never suspended her occupation.

Meanwhile, the fire still blazed noisily on the cheerful hearth; but the storm, as if disdaining the office of heightening the human horror of the farm-house scene, was rapidly subsiding. The thunder pealed less frequently and less loudly, the wind fell into intervals of noiseless calm, and occasionally the moonlight streamed, in momentary brightness, through the ragged edges of the fast breaking clouds. The breath of the still morning was already moving upon the firmament of the stormy night.

'Has life its old magic for you yet?' continued Goisvintha, in tones of pitiless reproach. 'Have you forgotten, with the spirit of your people, the end for which your ancestors lived? Is not your sword at your feet? Is not the knife in my hand? Do not the waters of the Tiber, rolling yonder to the sea, offer to you the grave of oblivion that all may seek? Die then! In your last hour be a Goth; even to the Romans you are worthless now! Already your comrades have discovered your desertion; will you wait till you are hung for a rebel? Will you live to implore the mercy of your enemies, or, dishonoured and defenceless, will you endeavour to escape? You are of the blood of my family, but again I say it to you--die!'

His pale lips trembled; he looked round for the first time at Antonina, but his utterance struggled ineffectually, even yet, against unyielding despair. He was still silent.

Goisvintha turned from him disdainfully, and approaching the fire sat down before it, bending her haggard features over the brilliant flames. For a few minutes she remained absorbed in her evil thoughts, but no articulate word escaped her; and when at length she again abruptly broke the silence, it was not to address the Goth or to fix her eyes on him as before.

Still cowering over the fire, apparently as regardless of the presence of the two beings whose happiness she had just crushed for ever as if they had never existed, she began to recite, in solemn, measured, chanting tones, a legend of the darkest and earliest age of Gothic history, keeping time to herself with the knife that she still held in her hand. The malignity in her expression, as she pursued her employment, betrayed the heartless motive that animated it, almost as palpably as the words of the composition she was repeating: thus she now spoke:--

'The tempest-god's pinions o'ershadow the sky, The waves leap to welcome the storm that is nigh, Through the hall of old Odin re-echo the shocks That the fierce ocean hurls at his rampart of rocks, As, alone on the crags that soar up from the sands, With his virgin SIONA the young AGNAR stands; Tears sprinkle their dew on the sad maiden's cheeks, And the voice of the chieftain sinks low while he speaks:--

"Crippled in the fight for ever, Number'd with the worse than slain; Weak, deform'd, disabled!--never Can I join the hosts again!--With the battle that is won AGNAR'S earthly course is run!

"When thy shatter'd frame must yield, If thou seek'st a future field; When thy arm, that sway'd the strife, Fails to shield thy worthless life; When thy hands no more afford Full employment to the sword; Then, preserve--respect thy name; Meet thy death--to live is shame! Such is Odin's mighty will; Such commands I now fulfil!"'

At this point in the legend, she paused and turned suddenly to observe its effect on Hermanric. All its horrible application to himself thrilled through his heart. His head drooped, and a low groan burst from his lips. But even this evidence of the suffering she was inflicting failed to melt the iron malignity of Goisvintha's determination.

'Do you remember the death of Agnar?' she cried. 'When you were a child, I sung it to you ere you slept, and you vowed as you heard it, that when you were a man, if you suffered his wounds you would die his death! He was crippled in a victory, yet he slew himself on the day of his triumph; you are crippled in your treachery, and have forgotten your boy's honour, and will live in the darkness of your shame! Have you lost remembrance of that ancient song? You heard it from me in the morning of your years; listen, and you shall hear it to the end; it is the dirge for your approaching death!'

She continued--

"SIONA, mourn not!--where I go The warriors feel nor pain nor woe; They raise aloft the gleaming steel, Their wounds, though warm, untended heal; Their arrows bellow through the air In showers, as they battle there; In mighty cups their wine is pour'd, Bright virgins throng their midnight board!

"Yet think not that I die unmov'd; I mourn the doom that sets me free, As I think, betroth'd--belov'd, On all the joys I lose in thee! To form my boys to meet the fray, Where'er the Gothic banner streams; To guard thy night, to glad thy day, Made all the bliss of AGNAR'S dreams--Dreams that must now be all forgot, Earth's joys have passed from AGNAR'S lot!

"See, athwart the face of light Float the clouds of sullen Night! Odin's warriors watch for me By the earth-encircling sea! The water's dirges howl my knell; 'Tis time I die--Farewell-Farewell!"

'He rose with a smile to prepare for the spring, He flew from the rock like a bird on the wing; The sea met her prey with a leap and a roar, And the maid stood alone by the wave-riven shore! The winds mutter'd deep, with a woe-boding sound, As she wept o'er the footsteps he'd left on the ground; And the wild vultures shriek'd, for the chieftain who spread Their battle-field banquets was laid with the dead!'

As, with a slow and measured emphasis, Goisvintha pronounced the last lines of the poem she again approached Hermanric. But the eyes of the Goth sought her no longer. She had calmed the emotions that she had hoped to irritate. Of the latter divisions of her legend, those only which were pathetic had arrested the lost chieftain's attention, and the blunted faculties of his heart recovered their old refinement as he listened to them. A solemn composure of love, grief, and pity appeared in the glance of affection that he now directed on the girl's despairing countenance. Years of good thoughts, an existence of tender cares, an eternity of youthful devotion spoke in that rapt, momentary, eloquent gaze, and imprinted on his expression a character ineffably beautiful and calm--a nobleness above the human, and approaching the angelic and divine.

Intuitively Goisvintha followed the direction of his eyes, and looked, like him, on the Roman girl's face. A lowering expression of hatred replaced the scorn that had hitherto distorted her passionate features. Mechanically her hand again half raised the knife, and the accents of her wrathful voice once more disturbed the sacred silence of affection and grief.

'Is it for the girl there that you would still live?' she cried sternly. 'I foreboded it, coward, when I first looked on you! I prepared for it when I wounded you! I made sure that when my anger again threatened this new ruler of your thoughts and mover of your actions, you should have lost the power to divert it from her again! Think you that, because my disdain has delayed it, my vengeance on her is abandoned? Long since I swore to you that she should die, and I will hold to my purpose! I have punished you; I will slay her! Can you shield her from the blow to-night, as you shielded her in your tent? You are weaker before me than a child!'

She ceased abruptly, for at this moment a noise of hurrying footsteps and contending voices became suddenly audible from without. As she heard it, a ghastly paleness chased the flush of anger from her cheeks. With the promptitude of apprehension she snatched the sword of Hermanric from under Antonina, and ran it through the staples intended to hold the rude bar of the door. The next instant the footsteps sounded on the garden path, and the next the door was assailed.

The good sword held firm, but the frail barrier that it sustained yielded at the second shock and fell inwards, shattered, to the floor. Instantly the gap was darkened by human forms, and the firelight glowed over the repulsive countenances of two Huns who headed the intruders, habited in complete armour and furnished with naked swords.

'Yield yourself prisoner by Alaric's command,' cried one of the barbarians, 'or you shall be slain as a deserter where you now stand!'

The Goth had risen to his feet as the door was burst in. The arrival of his pursuers seemed to restore his lost energies, to deliver him at once from an all-powerful thraldom. An expression of triumph and defiance shone over his steady features when he heard the summons of the Hun. For a moment he stooped towards Antonina, as she clung fainting round him. His mouth quivered and his eye glistened as he kissed her cold cheek. In that moment all the hopelessness of his position, all the worthlessness of his marred existence, all the ignominy preparing for him when he returned to the camp, rushed over his mind. In that moment the worst horrors of departure and death, the fiercest rackings of love and despair, assailed but did not overcome him. In that moment he paid his final tribute to the dues of affection, and braced for the last time the fibres of manly dauntlessness and Spartan resolve!

The next instant he tore himself from the girl's arms, the old hero- spirit of his conquering nation possessed every nerve in his frame, his eye brightened again gloriously with its lost warrior-light, his limbs grew firm, his face was calm, he confronted the Huns with a mien of authority and a smile of disdain, and, as he presented to them his defenceless breast, not the faintest tremor was audible in his voice, while he cried in accents of steady command--

'Strike! I yield not!'

The Huns rushed forward with fierce cries, and buried their swords in his body. His warm young blood gushed out upon the floor of the dwelling which had been the love-shrine of the heart that shed it. Without a sigh from his lips or a convulsion on his features, he fell dead at the feet of his enemies; all the valour of his disposition, all the gentleness of his heart, all the vigour of his form, resolved in one humble instant into a senseless and burdensome mass!

Antonina beheld the assassination, but was spared the sight of the death that followed it. She fell insensible by the side of her young warrior--her dress was spotted with his blood, her form was motionless as his own.

'Leave him there to rot! His pride in his superiority will not serve him now--even to a grave!' cried the Hun leader to his companions, as he dried on the garments of the corpse his reeking sword.

'And this woman,' demanded one of his comrades, 'is she to be liberated or secured?'

He pointed as he spoke to Goisvintha. During the brief scene of the assassination, the very exercise of her faculties seemed to have been suspended. She had never stirred a limb or uttered a word.

The Hun recognised her as the woman who had questioned and bribed him at the camp. 'She is the traitor's kinswoman and is absent from the tents without leave,' he answered. 'Take her prisoner to Alaric; she will bear us witness that we have done as he commanded us. As for the girl,' he continued, glancing at the blood on Antonina's dress, and stirring her figure carelessly with his foot, 'she may be dead too, for she neither moves nor speaks, and may be left like her protector to lie graveless where she is. For us, it is time that we depart--the king is impatient of delay.'

As they led her roughly from the house, Goisvintha shuddered, and attempted to pause for a moment when she passed the corpse of the Goth. Death, that can extinguish enmities as well as sunder loves, rose awful and appealing as she looked her last at her murdered brother, and remembered her murdered husband. No tears flowed from her eyes, no groans broke from her bosom; but there was a pang, a last momentary pang of grief and pity at her heart as she murmured while they forced her away--'Aquileia! Aquileia! have I outlived thee for this!'

The troops retired. For a few minutes silence ruled uninterruptedly over the room where the senseless girl still lay by the side of all that was left to her of the object of her first youthful love. But ere long footsteps again house door, and two Goths, who had formed part of the escort allotted to the Hun, approached the young chieftain's corpse. Quickly and silently they raised it in their arms and bore it into the garden. There they scooped a shallow hole with their swords in the fresh, flower-laden turf, and having laid the body there, they hastily covered it, and rapidly departed without returning to the house.

These men had served among the warriors committed to Hermanric's command. By many acts of frank generosity and encouragement, the young chieftain had won their rough attachment. They mourned his fate, but dared not obstruct the sentence, or oppose the act that determined it. At their own risk they had secretly quitted the advancing ranks of their comrades, to use the last privilege and obey the last dictate of human kindness; and they thought not of the lonely girl as they now left her desolate, and hurried away to reassume their appointed stations ere it was too late.

The turf lay caressingly round the young warrior's form; its crushed flowers pressed softly against his cold cheek; the fragrance of the new morning wafted its pure incense gently about his simple grave! Around him flowered the delicate plants that the hand of Antonina had raised to please his eye. Near him stood the dwelling, sacred to the first and last kiss that he had impressed upon her lips; and about him, on all sides, rose the plains and woodlands that had engrossed, with her image, the devotion of all her dearest thoughts. He lay, in his death, in the midst of the magic circle of the best joys of his life! It was a fitter burial-place for the earthly relics of that bright and generous spirit than the pit in the carnage-laden battle-field, or the desolate sepulchres of a northern land!

Chapter 19

THE GUARDIAN RESTORED

Not long is the new-made grave left unwatched to the solemn guardianship of Solitude and Night. More than a few minutes have scarcely elapsed since it was dug, yet already human footsteps press its yielding surface, and a human glance scans attentively its small and homely mound.

But it is not Antonina, whom he loved; it is not Goisvintha, through whose vengeance he was lost, who now looks upon the earth above the young warrior's corpse. It is a stranger, an outcast; a man lost, dishonoured, abandoned--it is the solitary and ruined Ulpius who now gazes with indifferent eyes upon the peaceful garden and the eloquent grave.

In the destinies of woe committed to the keeping of the night, the pagan had been fatally included. The destruction that had gone forth against the body of the young man who lay beneath the earth had overtaken the mind of the old man who stood over his simple grave. The frame of Ulpius, with all its infirmities, was still there, but the soul of ferocious patience and unconquerable daring that had lighted it grandly in its ruin was gone. Over the long anguish of that woeful life the veil of self-oblivion had closed for ever!

He had been dismissed by Alaric, but he had not returned to the city whither he was bidden. Throughout the night he had wandered about the lonely suburbs, striving in secret and horrible suffering for the mastery of his mind. There did the overthrow of all his hopes from the Goths expand rapidly into the overthrow of the whole intellect that had created his aspirations. There had reason burst the bonds that had so long chained, perverted, degraded it! At length, wandering hither and thither, he had dragged the helpless body, possessed no longer by the perilous mind, to the farm-house garden in which he now stood, gazing alternately at the upturned sods of the chieftain's grave and the red gleam of the fire as it glowed from the dreary room through the gap of the shattered door.

His faculties were fatally disordered rather than utterly destroyed. His penetration, his firmness, and his cunning were gone; but a wreck of memory, useless and unmanageable--a certain capacity for momentary observation still remained to him. The shameful miscarriage in the tent of Alaric, which had overthrown his faculties, had passed from him as an event that never happened, but he remembered fragments of his past existence--he still retained a vague consciousness of the ruling purpose of his whole life.

These embryo reflections, disconnected and unsustained, flitted to and fro over his dark mind as luminous exhalations over a marsh--rising and sinking, harmless and delusive, fitful and irregular. What he remembered of the past he remembered carelessly, viewing it with as vacant a curiosity as if it were the visionary spectacle of another man's struggles and misfortunes and hopes, acting under it as under a mysterious influence, neither the end nor the reason of which he cared to discover. For the future, it was to his thoughts a perfect blank; for the present, it was a jarring combination of bodily weariness and mental repose.

He shuddered as he stood shelterless under the open heaven. The cold, that he had defied in the vaults of the rifted wall, pierced in the farm-house garden; his limbs, which had resisted repose on the hard journey from Rome to the camp of the Goths, now trembled so that he was fain to rest them on the ground. For a short time he sat glaring with vacant and affrighted eyes upon the open dwelling before him, as though he longed to enter it but dare not. At length the temptation of the ruddy firelight seemed to vanquish his irresolution; he rose with difficulty, and slowly and hesitatingly entered the house.

He had advanced, thief-like, but a few steps, he had felt but for a moment the welcome warmth of the fire, when the figure of Antonina, still extended insensible upon the floor, caught his eye; he approached it with eager curiosity, and, raising the girl on his arm, looked at her with a long and rigid scrutiny.

For some moments no expression of recognition passed his lips or appeared on his countenance, as, with a mechanical, doting gesture of fondness, he smoothed her dishevelled hair over her forehead. While he was thus engaged, while the remains of the gentleness of his childhood were thus awfully revived in the insanity of his age, a musical string wound round a small piece of gilt wood fell from its concealment in her bosom; he snatched it from the ground--it was the fragment of her broken lute, which had never quitted her since the night when, in her innocent grief, she had wept over it in her maiden bed-chamber.

Small, obscure, insignificant as it was, this little token touched the fibre in the Pagan's shattered mind which the all-eloquent form and presence of its hapless mistress had failed to reach; his memory flew back instantly to the garden on the Pincian Mount, and to his past duties in Numerian's household, but spoke not to him of the calamities he had wreaked since that period on his confiding master. His imagination presented to him at this moment but one image--his servitude in the Christian's abode; and as he now looked on the girl he could regard himself but in one light--as 'the guardian restored'.

'What does she with her music here?' he whispered apprehensively. 'This is not her father's house, and the garden yonder looks not from the summit of the hill!'

As he curiously examined the room, the red spots on the floor suddenly attracted his attention. A panic, a frantic terror seemed instantly to overwhelm him. He rose with a cry of horror, and, still holding the girl on his arm, hurried out into the garden trembling and breathless, as if the weapon of an assassin had scared him from the house.

The shock of her rough removal, the sudden influence of the fresh, cold air, restored Antonina to the consciousness of life at the moment when Ulpius, unable to support her longer, laid her against the little heap of turf which marked the position of the young chieftain's grave. Her eyes opened wildly; their first glance fixed upon the shattered door and the empty room. She rose from the ground, advanced a few steps towards the house, then paused, rigid, breathless, silent, and, turning slowly, faced the upturned turf.

The grave was all-eloquent of its tenant. His cuirass, which the soldiers had thought to bury with the body that it had defended in former days, had been overlooked in the haste of the secret interment, and lay partly imbedded in the broken earth, partly exposed to view--a simple monument over a simple grave! Her tearless, dilated eyes looked down on it as though they would number each blade of grass, each morsel of earth by which it was surrounded! Her hair waved idly about her cheeks, as the light wind fluttered it; but no expression passed over her face, no gestures escaped her limbs. Her mind toiled and quivered, as if crushed by a fiery burden; but her heart was voiceless, and her body was still.

Ulpius had stood unnoticed by her side. At this moment he moved so as to confront her, and she suddenly looked up at him. A momentary expression of bewilderment and suspicion lightened the heavy vacancy of despair which had chased their natural and feminine tenderness from her eyes, but it disappeared rapidly. She turned from the Pagan, knelt down by the grave, and pressed her face and bosom against the little mound of turf beneath her.

No voice comforted her, no arm caressed her, as her mind now began to penetrate the mysteries, to probe the darkest depths of the long night's calamities! Unaided and unsolaced, while the few and waning stars glimmered from their places in the sky, while the sublime stillness of tranquillised Nature stretched around her, she knelt at the altar of death, and raised her soul upward to the great heaven above her, charged with its sacred offering of human grief!

Long did she thus remain; and when at length she arose from the ground, when, approaching the Pagan, she fixed on him her tearless, dreary eyes, he quailed before her glance, as his dull faculties struggled vainly to resume the old, informing power that they had now for ever lost. Nothing but the remembrance aroused by his first sight of the fragment of the lute lived within even yet, as he whispered to her in low, entreating tones--

'Come home--come home! Your father may return before us--come home!'

As the words 'home' and 'father'--those household gods of the heart's earliest existence--struck upon her ears, a change flashed with electric suddenness over the girl's whole aspect. She raised her wan hands to the sky; all her woman's tenderness repossessed itself of her heart; and as she again knelt down over the grave, her sobs rose audibly through the calmed and fragrant air.

With Hermanric's corpse beneath her, with the blood-sprinkled room behind her, with a hostile army and a famine-wasted city beyond her, it was only through that flood of tears, that healing passion of gentle emotions, that she rose superior to the multiplied horrors of her situation at the very moment when her faculties and her life seemed sinking under them alike. Fully, freely, bitterly she wept, on the kindly and parent earth--the patient, friendly ground that once bore the light footsteps of the first of a race not created for death; that now holds in its sheltering arms the loved ones, whom, in mourning, we lay there to sleep; that shall yet be bound to the farthermost of its depths, when the sun-bright presence of returning spirits shines over its renovated frame, and love is resumed in angel perfection at the point where death suspended it in mortal frailness!

'Come home--your father is awaiting you--come home!' repeated the Pagan vacantly, moving slowly away as he spoke.

At the sound of his voice she started up, and clasping his arm with her trembling fingers, to arrest his progress, looked affrightedly into his seared and listless countenance. As she thus gazed on him she appeared for the first time to recognise him. Fear and astonishment mingled in her expression with grief and despair as she sunk at his feet, moaning in tones of piercing entreaty--

'O Ulpius!--if Ulpius you are--have pity on me and take me to my father! My father! my father! In all the lonely world there is nothing left to me but my father!'

'Why do you weep to me about your broken lute?' answered Ulpius, with a dull, unmeaning smile; 'it was not I that destroyed it!'

'They have slain him!' she shrieked distractedly, heedless of the Pagan's reply. 'I saw them draw their swords on him! See, his blood is on me!--me!--Antonina, whom he protected and loved! Look there; that is a grave--his grave--I know it! I have never seen him since; he is down--down there! under the flowers I grew to gather for him! They slew him; and when I knew it not, they have buried him!--or you--you have buried him! You have hidden him under the cold garden earth! He is gone!--Ah, gone, gone--for ever gone!'

And she flung herself again with reckless violence on the grave. After looking steadfastly on her for a moment, Ulpius approached and raised her from the earth.

'Come!' he cried angrily, 'the night grows on--your father waits!'

'The walls of Rome shut me from my father! I shall never see my father nor Hermanric again!' she cried, in tones of bitter anguish, remembering more perfectly all the miseries of her position, and struggling to release herself from the Pagan's grasp.

The walls of Rome! At those words the mind of Ulpius opened to a flow of dark remembrances, and lost the visions that had occupied it until that moment. He laughed triumphantly.

'The walls of Rome bow to my arm!' he cried, in exulting tones; 'I pierced them with my good bar of iron! I wound through them with my bright lantern! Spirits roared on me, and struck me down, and grinned upon me in the thick darkness, but I passed the wall! The thunder pealed around me as I crawled along the winding rifts; but I won my way through them! I came out conquering on the other side! Come, come, come, come! We will return! I know the track, even in the darkness! I can outwatch the sentinels! You shall walk in the pathway that I have broken through the bricks!

The girl's features lost for a moment their expression of grief, and grew rigid with horror, as she glanced at his fiery eyes, and felt the fearful suspicion of his insanity darkening over her mind. She stood powerless, trembling, unresisting, in his grasp, without attempting to delude him into departure or to appease him into delay.

'Why did I make my passage through the wall?' muttered the Pagan in a low, awe-struck voice, suddenly checking himself, as he was about to step forward. 'Why did I tear down the strong brick-work and go forth into the dark suburbs?'

He paused, and for a few moments struggled with his purposeless and disconnected thoughts; but a blank, a darkness, an annihilation overwhelmed Alaric and the Gothic camp, which he vainly endeavoured to disperse. He sighed bitterly to himself--'It is gone!' and still grasping Antonina by the hand, drew her after him to the garden gate.

'Leave me!' she shrieked, as he passed onward into the pathway that led to the high-road. 'Oh, be merciful, and leave me to die where he has died!'

'Peace! or I will rend you limb by limb, as I rent the stones from the wall when I passed through it!' he whispered to her in fierce accents, as she struggled to escape him. 'You shall return with me to Rome! You shall walk in the track that I have made in the rifted brick-work!'

Terror, anguish, exhaustion, overpowered her weak efforts. Her lips moved, partly in prayer and partly in ejaculation; but she spoke in murmurs only, as she mechanically suffered the Pagan to lead her onward by the hand.

They paced on under the waning starlight, over the cold, lonely road, and through the dreary and deserted suburbs,--a fearful and discordant pair! Coldly, obediently, impassively, as if she were walking in a dream, the spirit-broken girl moved by the side of her scarce-human leader. Disjointed exclamation, alternat-

ing horribly between infantine simplicity and fierce wickedness, poured incessantly from the Pagan's lips, but he never addressed himself further to his terror-
stricken companion. So, wending rapidly onward, they gained the Gothic lines;
and here the madman slackened his pace, and paused, beast-like, to glare around
him, as he approached the habitations of men.

Still not opposed by Antonina, whose faculties of observation were petrified by
her terror into perfect inaction, even here, within reach of the doubtful aid of the
enemies of her people, the Pagan crept forward through the loneliest places of the
encampment, and, guided by the mysterious cunning of his miserable race, eluded successfully the observation of the drowsy sentinels. Never bewildered by the
darkness--for the moon had gone down--always led by the animal instinct co-
existent with his disease, he passed over the waste ground between the hostile
encampment and the city, and arrived triumphant at the heap of stones that
marked his entrance to the rifted wall.

For one moment he stopped, and turning towards the girl, pointed proudly to the
dark, low breach he was about to penetrate. Then, drawing her half-fainting form
closer to his side, looking up attentively to the ramparts, and stepping as noiselessly as though turf were beneath his feet, he entered the dusky rift with his helpless charge.

As they disappeared in the recesses of the wall, Night--the stormy, the eventful,
the fatal!--reached its last limit; and the famished sentinel on the fortifications of
the besieged city roused himself from his dreary and absorbing thoughts, for he
saw that the new day was dawning in the east.

Chapter 20

THE BREACH REPASSED

Slowly and mournfully the sentinel at the rifted wall raised his eyes towards the eastern clouds as they brightened before the advancing dawn. Desolate as was the appearance of the dull, misty daybreak, it was yet the most welcome of all the objects surrounding the starving soldier on which he could fix his languid gaze. To look back on the city behind him was to look back on the dreary charnel-house of famine and death; to look down on the waste ground without the walls was to look down on the dead body of the comrade of his watch, who, maddened by the pangs of hunger which he had suffered during the night, had cast himself from the rampart to meet a welcome death on the earth beneath. Famished and despairing, the sentinel crouched on the fortifications which he had now neither strength to pace nor care to defend, yearning for the food that he had no hope to obtain, as he watched the grey daybreak from his solitary post.

While he was thus occupied, the gloomy silence of the scene was suddenly broken by the sound of falling brick-work at the inner base of the wall, followed by faint entreaties for mercy and deliverance, which rose on his ear, strangely mingled with disjointed expression of defiance and exultation from a second voice. He slowly turned his head, and, looking down, saw on the ground beneath a young girl struggling in the grasp of an old man, who was hurrying her onward in the direction of the Pincian Gate.

For one moment the girl's eye met the sentinel's vacant glance, and she renewed, with a last effort of strength, and a greater vehemence of supplication, her cries for help; but the soldier neither moved nor answered. Exhausted as he was, no sight could affect him now but the sight of food. Like the rest of the citizens, he was sunk in a heavy stupor of starvation--selfish, reckless, brutalised. No disasters could depress, no atrocities rouse him. Famine had torn asunder every social tie, had withered every human sympathy among his besieged fellow- citizens, and he was famishing like them.

At the moment when the dawn had first appeared, could he have looked down by some mysterious agency to the interior foundations of the wall, from the rampart on which he kept his weary watch, such a sight must then have presented itself as would have aroused even his sluggish observation to rigid attention and involuntary surprise.

Winding upward and downward among jagged masses of ruined brick-work, now lost amid the shadows of dreary chasms, now prominent over the elevations of rising arches, the dark irregular passages broken by Ulpius in the rotten wall would then have presented themselves to his eyes; not stretching forth in dismal solitude, not peopled only by the reptiles native to the place, but traced in all their mazes by human forms. Then he would have perceived the fierce, resolute Pagan, moving through darkness and obstacles with a sure, solemn progress, drawing after him, like a dog devoted to his will, the young girl whose hapless fate had doomed her to fall into his power. Her half-fainting figure might have been seen, sometimes prostrate on the higher places of the breach, while her fearful guide descended before her into a chasm beyond, and then turned to drag her after him to a darker and a lower depth yet; sometimes bent in supplication, when her lips moved once more with a last despairing entreaty, and her limbs trembled with a final effort to escape from her captor's relentless grasp. While still, through all that opposed him, the same fierce tenacity of purpose would have been invariably visible in every action of Ulpius, constantly confirming him in his mad resolution to make his victim the follower of his progress through the wall, ever guiding him with a strange instinct through every hindrance, and preserving him from every danger in his path, until it brought him forth triumphant, with his prisoner still in his power, again free to tread the desolate streets and mingle with the famine-stricken citizens of Rome.

And now when, after peril and anguish, she once more stood within the city of her home, what hope remained to Antonina of obtaining her last refuge under her father's roof, and deriving her solitary consolation from the effort to regain her father's love? With the termination of his passage through the breach in the wall had ended ever recollection associated with it in the Pagan's shattered memory. A new blank now pervaded his lost faculties, desolate as that which had overwhelmed them in the night when he first stood in the farm-house garden by the young chieftain's grave. He moved onward, unobservant, unthinking, without aim or hope, driven by a mysterious restlessness, forgetting the very presence of Antonina as she followed him, but still mechanically grasping her hand, and dragging her after him he knew not whither.

And she, on her part, made no effort more for deliverance. She had seen the sentinel unmoved by her entreaties, she had seen the walls of her father's house receding from her longing eyes, as Ulpius pitilessly hurried her father and farther from its distant door; and she lost the last faint hope of restoration, the last lingering desire of life, as the sense of her helplessness now weighed heaviest on her mind. Her heart was full of her young warrior, who had been slain, and of her father, from whom she had parted in the hour of his wrath, as she now feebly followed the Pagan's steps, and resigned herself to a speedy exhaustion and death in her utter despair.

They turned from the Pincian Gate and gained the Campus Martius; and here the aspect of the besieged city and the condition of its doomed inhabitants were fully and fearfully disclosed to view. On the surface of the noble area, once thronged with bustling crowds passing to and fro in every direction as their various destinations or caprices might lead them, not twenty moving figures were now discernible. These few, who still retained their strength or the resolution to pace the greatest thoroughfare of Rome, stalked backwards and forwards incessantly, their hollow eyes fixed on vacancy, their wan hands pressed over their mouths; each separate, distrustful, and silent; fierce as imprisoned madmen; restless as spectres disturbed in a place of tombs.

Such were the citizens who still moved over the Campus Martius; and, besetting their path wherever they turned, lay the gloomy numbers of the dying and the dead--the victims already stricken by the pestilence which had now arisen in the infected city, and joined the famine in its work of desolation and death. Around the public fountains, where the water still bubbled up as freshly as in the summertime of prosperity and peace, the poorer population of beleaguered Rome had chiefly congregated to expire. Some still retained strength enough to drink greedily at the margin of the stone basins, across which others lay dead--their heads and shoulders immersed in the water--drowned from lack of strength to draw back after their first draught. Children mounted over the dead bodies of their parents to raise themselves to the fountain's brim; parents stared vacantly at the corpses of their children alternately floating and sinking in the water, into which they had fallen unsuccoured and unmourned.

In other parts of the place, at the open gates of the theatres and hippodromes, in the unguarded porticoes of the palaces and the baths lay the discoloured bodies of those who had died ere they could reach the fountains--of women and children especially--surrounded in frightful contrast by the abandoned furniture of luxury and the discarded inventions of vice--by gilded couches--by inlaid tables--by jewelled cornices--by obscene picture and statues--by brilliantly framed, gaudily tinted manuscripts of licentious songs, still hanging at their accustomed places on the lofty marble walls. Farther on, in the by- streets and the retired courts, where the corpse of the tradesman was stretched on his empty counter; where the soldier of the city guard dropped down overpowered were he reached the limit of his rounds; where the wealthy merchant lay pestilence-stricken upon the last hoards of repulsive food which his gold had procured; the assassin and the robber might be seen--now greedily devouring the offal that lay around them, now falling dead upon the bodies which they had rifled but the moment before.

Over the whole prospect, far and near, wherever it might extend, whatever the horrors by which it might be occupied, was spread a blank, supernatural stillness. Not a sound arose; the living were as silent as the dead; crime, suffering, despair, were all voiceless alike; the trumpet was unheard in the guard-house; the bell never rang from the church; even the thick, misty rain, that now descended from the black and unmoving clouds, and obscured in cold shadows the outlines of distant buildings and the pinnacle tops of mighty palaces, fell noiseless to the ground. The sky had no wind; the earth no echoes--the pervading desolation appalled the eye; the vast stillness weighed dull on the ear--it was a scene as of the last-left city of an exhausted world, decaying noiselessly into primeval chaos.

Through this atmosphere of darkness and death, along these paths of pestilence and famine; unregarding and unregarded, the Pagan and his prisoner passed slowly onward towards the quarter of the city opposite the Pincian Mount. No ray of thought, even yet, brightened the dull faculties of Ulpius; still he walked forward vacantly, and still he was followed wearily by the fast-failing girl.

Sunk in her mingled stupor of bodily weakness and mental despair, she never spoke, never raised her head, never looked forth on the one side or the other. She had now ceased even to feel the strong, cold grasp of the Pagan's hand. Shadowy visions of spheres beyond the world, arrayed in enchanting beauty, and people with happy spirits in their old earthly forms, where a long deathless existence moved smoothly and dreamily onward, without mark of time or taint of woe, were opening before her mind. She lost all memory of afflictions and wrongs, all apprehension of danger from the madman at whose mercy she remained. And thus she still moved feebly onward as the will of Ulpius guided her, with no observation of her present peril, and no anxiety for her impending fate.

They passed the grand circular structure of the Pantheon, entered the long narrow streets leading to the banks of the river, and finally gained the margin of the Tiber--hard by the little island that still rises in the midst of its waters. Here, for the first time, the Pagan paused mechanically in his course, and vacantly directed his dull, dreamy eyes on the prospect before him, where the walls, stretching abruptly outward from their ordinary direction, enclosed the Janiculum Hill, as it rose with its irregular mass of buildings on the opposite bank of the river.

At this sudden change from action to repose, the overtasked energies which had hitherto gifted the limbs of Antonina with an unnatural power of endurance, abruptly relaxed. She sank down helpless and silent; her head drooped towards the hard ground, as towards a welcome pillow, but found no support, for the Pagan's iron grasp of her hand remained unyielding as ever. Infirm though he was, he appeared at this moment to be unconscious that his prisoner was now hanging at his side. Every association connected with her, every recollection of his position with her in her father's house, had vanished from his memory. A darker blindness seemed to have sunk over his bodily perceptions; his eyes rolled slowly to and fro over the prospect before him, but regarded nothing; his panting breaths came thick and fast; his shrunk chest heaved as if some deep, dread agony were pent within it--it was evident that a new crisis in his insanity was at hand.

At this moment one of the bands of marauders--the desperate criminals of famine and plague--who still prowled through the city, appeared in the street. Their trembling hands sought their weapons, and their haggard faces brightened, when they first discerned the Pagan and the girl; but as they approached nearer they saw enough in the figures of the two, at a glance, to destroy their hopes of seizing on them either plunder or food. For an instant they stood by their intended victims, as if debating whether to murder them only for murder's sake, when the appearance of two women, stealthily quitting a house farther on in the street, carrying a basket covered by some tattered garments, attracted their attention. They turned instantly to follow the bearers of the basket, and again Ulpius and Antonina were left alone on the river's bank.

The appearance of the assassins had been powerless, as every other sight or event in the city, in arousing the faculties of Ulpius. He had neither looked on them nor fled from them when they surrounded him; but now when they were gone he slowly turned his head in the direction by which they had departed. His gaze wandered over the wet flagstones of the street, over two corpses stretched on them at a little distance, over the figure of a female slave who lay forsaken near the wall of one of the houses, exerting her last energies to drink from the turbid rain- water which ran down the kennel by her side; and still his eyes remained unregardful of all that they encountered. The next object which by chance attracted his vacant attention was a deserted temple. This solitary building fixed him immediately in contemplation--it was destined to open a new and a warning scene in the dark tragedy of his closing life.

In his course through the city he had passed unheeded many temples far more prominent in situation, far more imposing in structure, than this. It was a building of no remarkable extent or extraordinary beauty. Its narrow porticoes and dark doorway were more fitted to repel than to invite the eye; but it had one attraction, powerful above all glories of architecture and all grandeur of situation to arrest in him those wandering faculties whose sterner and loftier aims were now suspended for ever; it was dedicated to Serapis--to the idol which had been the deity of his first worship, and the inspiration of his last struggled for the restoration of his faith. The image of the god, with the three- headed monster encircled by a serpent, obedient beneath his hand, was carved over the portico.

What flood of emotions rushed into the vacant mind of Ulpius at the instant when he discerned the long-loved, well-known image of the Egyptian god, there was nothing for some moments outwardly visible in him to betray. His moral insensibility appeared but to be deepened as his gaze was now fixed with rigid intensity on the temple portico. Thus he continued to remain motionless, as if what he saw had petrified him where he stood, when the clouds, which had been closing in deeper and deeper blackness as the morning advanced, and which, still charged with electricity, were gathering to revive the storm of the past night, burst abruptly into a loud peal of thunder over his head.

At that warning sound, as if it had been the supernatural signal awaited to arouse him, as if in one brief moment it awakened every recollection of all that he had resolutely attempted during the night of thunder that was past, he started into instant animation. His countenance brightened, his form expanded, he dropped the hand of Antonina, raised his arm aloft towards the wrathful heaven in frantic triumph, then staggering forwards, fell on his knees at the base of the temple steps.

Whatever the remembrances of his passage through the wall at the Pincian Hill, and of the toil and peril succeeding it, which had revived when the thunder first sounded in his ear, they now vanished as rapidly as they had arisen, and left his wandering memory free to revert to the scenes which the image of Serapis was most fitted to recall. Recollections of his boyish enjoyments in the temple at Alexandria, of his youth's enthusiasm, of the triumphs of his early manhood--all disjointed and wayward, yet all bright, glorious, intoxicating--flashed before his shattered mind. Tears, the first that he had shed since his happy youth, flowed quickly down his withered cheeks. He pressed his hot forehead, he beat his parched hand in ecstasy on the cold, wet steps beneath him. He muttered breathless ejaculations, he breathed strange murmurs of endearment, he humbled himself in his rapturous delight beneath the walls of the temple like a dog that has discovered his lost master and fawns affectionately at his feet. Criminal as he was, his joy in his abasement, his glory in his miserable isolation from humanity, was a doom of degradation pitiable to behold.

After an interval his mood changed. He rose to his feet, his trembling limbs strengthened with a youthful vigour as he ascended the temple steps and gained its doorway. He turned for a moment, and looked forth over the street, ere he entered the hallowed domain of his distempered imagination. To him the cloudy sky above was now shining with the radiance of the sun-bright East. The death-laden highways of Rome, as they stretched before him, were beautiful with lofty trees, and populous with happy figures; and along the dark flagstones beneath, where still lay the corpses which he had no eye to see, he beheld already the priests of Serapis with his revered guardian, his beloved Macrinus of former days, at their head, advancing to meet and welcome him in the hall of the Egyptian god. Visions such as these passed gloriously before the Pagan's eyes as he stood triumphant on the steps of the temple, and brightened to him with a noonday light its dusky recesses when, after his brief delay, he turned from the street and disappeared through the doorway of the sacred place.

The rain poured down more thickly than before; the thunder, once aroused, now sounded in deep and frequent peals as Antonina raised herself from the ground and looked around her, in momentary expectation that the dreaded form of Ulpius must meet her eyes. No living creature was visible in the street. The forsaken slave still reclined near the wall of the house where she had first appeared when the Pagan gained the approaches to the temple; but she now lay there dead. No fresh bands of robbers appeared in sight. An uninterrupted solitude prevailed in all directions as far as the eye could reach.

At the moment when Ulpius had relinquished his grasp of her hand, Antonina had sunk to the ground, helpless and resigned, but not exhausted beyond all power of sensation or all capacity for thought. While she lay on the cold pavement of the street, her mind still pursued its visions of a speedy death, and a tranquil life-in-death to succeed it in a future state. But, as minute after minute elapsed, and no harsh voice sounded in her ear, no pitiless hand dragged her from the ground, no ominous footsteps were audible around her, a change passed gradually over her thoughts; the instinct of self-preservation slowly revived within her, and, as she raised herself to look forth on the gloomy prospect, the chances of uninterrupted flight and present safety presented by the solitude of the street, aroused her like a voice of encouragement, like an unexpected promise of help.

Her perception of outer influences returned; she felt the rain that drenched her garments; she shuddered at the thunder sounding over her head; she marked with horror the dead bodies lying before her on the stones. An overpowering desire animated her to fly from the place, to escape from the desolate scene around, even though she should sink exhausted by the effort in the next street. Slowly she arose- -her limbs trembled with a premature infirmity; but she gained her feet. She tottered onward, turning her back on the river, passed bewildered between long rows of deserted houses, and arrived opposite a public garden surrounding a little summer-house, whose deserted portico offered both concealment and shelter. Here, therefore, she took refuge, crouching in the darkest corner of the building, and hiding her face in her hands, as if to shut out all view of the dreary though altered scenes which spread before her eyes.

Woeful thoughts and recollections now moved within her in bewildering confusion. All that she had suffered since Ulpius had dragged her from the farm-house in the suburbs--the night pilgrimage over the plain--the fearful passage through the wall--revived in her memory, mingled with vague ideas, now for the first time aroused, of the plague and famine that were desolating the city; and, with sudden apprehensions that Goisvintha might still be following her, knife in hand, through the lonely streets; while passively prominent over all these varying sources of anguish and dread, the scene of the young chieftain's death lay like a cold weight on her heavy heart. The damp turf of his grave seemed still to press against her breast; his last kiss yet trembled on her lips; she knew, though she dared not look down on them, that the spots of his blood yet stained her garments.

Whether she strove to rise and continue her flight; whether she crouched down again under the portico, resigned for one bitter moment to perish by the knife of Goisvintha--if Goisvintha were near; to fall once more into the hands of Ulpius- -if Ulpius were tracking her to her retreat,--the crushing sense that she was utterly bereaved of her beloved protector--that the friend of her brief days of happiness was lost to her for ever--that Hermanric, who had preserved her from death, had been murdered in his youth and his strength by her side, never deserted her. Since the assassination in the farm-house, she was now for the first time alone; and now for the first time she felt the full severity of her affliction, and knew how dark was the blank which was spread before every aspiration of her future life.

Enduring, almost eternal, as the burden of her desolation seemed now to have become, it was yet to be removed, ere long, by feelings of a tenderer mournfulness and a more resigned woe. The innate and innocent fortitude of disposition, which had made her patient under the rigour of her youthful education, and hopeful under the trials that assailed her on her banishment from her father's house; which had never deserted her until the awful scenes of the past night of assassination and death rose in triumphant horror before her eyes; and which, even then, had been suspended but not destroyed--was now destined to regain its healing influence over her heart. As she still cowered in her lonely refuge, the final hope, the yearning dependence on a restoration to her father's presence and her father's love, that had moved her over the young chieftain's grave, and had prompted her last effort for freedom when Ulpius had dragged her through the passage in the rifted wall, suddenly revived.

Once more she arose, and looked forth on the desolate city and the stormy sky, but now with mild and unshrinking eyes. Her recollections of the past grew tender in their youthful grief; her thoughts for the future became patient, solemn, and serene. Images of her first and her last-left protector, of her old familiar home, of her garden solitude on the Pincian Mount, spread beautiful before her imagination as resting- places to her weary heart. She descended the steps of the summer-house with no apprehension of her enemies, no doubt of her resolution; for she knew the beacon that was now to direct her onward course. The tears gathered full in her eyes as she passed into the garden; but her step never faltered, her features never lost their combined expression of tranquil sorrow and subdued hope. So she once more entered the perilous streets, and murmuring to herself, 'My father! my father!' as if in those simple words lay the hand that was to guide, and the providence that was to preserved her, she began to trace her solitary way in the direction of the Pincian Mount.

It was a spectacle--touching, beautiful, even sublime--to see this young girl, but a few hours freed, by perilous paths and by criminal hands, from scenes which had begun in treachery, only to end in death, now passing, resolute and alone, through the streets of a mighty city, overwhelmed by all that is poignant in human anguish and hideous in human crime. It was a noble evidence of the strong power over the world and the world's perils, with which the simplest affection may arm the frailest being--to behold her thus pursuing her way, superior to every horror of desolation and death that clogged her path, unconsciously discovering in the softly murmured name of 'father', which still fell at intervals from her lips, the pure purpose that sustained her--the steady heroism that ever held her in her doubtful course. The storms of heaven poured over her head--the crimes and sufferings of Rome darkened the paths of her pilgrimage; but she passed firmly onward

through all, like a ministering spirit, journeying along earthly shores in the bright
inviolability of its merciful mission and its holy thoughts--like a ray of light living in the strength of its own beauty, amid the tempest and obscurity of a stranger
sphere.

Once more she entered the Campus Martius. Again she passed the public fountains, still unnaturally devoted to serve as beds for the dying and as sepulchres for
the dead; again she trod the dreary highways, where the stronger among the famished populace yet paced hither and thither in ferocious silence and unsocial separation. No word was addressed, hardly a look was directed to her, as she pursued
her solitary course. She was desolate among the desolate; forsaken among others
abandoned like herself.

The robber, when he passed her by, saw that she was worthless for the interests of
plunder as the poorest of the dying citizens around him. The patrician, loitering
feebly onward to the shelter of his palace halls, avoided her as a new suppliant
among the people for the charity which he had not to bestow, and quickened his
pace as she approached him in the street. Unprotected, yet unmolested, hurrying
from her loneliness and her bitter recollections to the refuge of her father's love,
as she would have hurried when a child from her first apprehension of ill to the
refuge of her father's arms, she gained at length the foot of the Pincian Hill--at
length ascended the streets so often trodden in the tranquil days of old!

The portals and outer buildings of Vetranio's palace, as she passed them, presented a striking and ominous spectacle. Within the lofty steel railings, which protected the building, the famine-wasted slaves of the senator appeared reeling and
tottering beneath full vases of wine which they were feebly endeavouring to carry
into the interior apartments. Gaudy hangings drooped from the balconies, garlands of ivy were wreathed round the statues of the marble front. In the midst of
the besieged city, and in impious mockery of the famine and pestilence which
were wasting it, hut and palace, to its remotest confines, were proceeding in this
devoted dwelling the preparations for a triumphant feast!

Unheedful of the startling prospect presented by Vetranio's abode, her eyes bent
but in one absorbing direction, her steps hurrying faster and faster with each succeeding instant, Antonina approached the home from which she had been exiled
in fear, and to which she was returning in woe. Yet a moment more of strong
exertion, of overpowering anticipation, and she reached the garden gate!

She dashed back the heavy hair matted over her brows by the rain; she glanced
rapidly around her; she beheld the window of her bed-chamber with the old sim-

ple curtain still hanging at its accustomed place; she saw the well-remembered trees, the carefully tended flower-beds, now drooping mournfully beneath the gloomy sky. Her heart swelled within her, her breath seemed suddenly arrested in her bosom, as she trod the garden path and ascended the steps beyond. The door at the top was ajar. With a last effort she thrust it open, and stood once more--unaided and unwelcomed, yet hopeful of consolation, of pardon, of love-- within her first and last sanctuary, the walls of her home!

Chapter 21

FATHER AND CHILD

Forsaken as it appears on an outward view, during the morning of which we now write, the house of Numerian is yet not tenantless. In one of the sleeping apartments, stretched on his couch, with none to watch by its side, lies the master of the little dwelling. We last beheld him on the scene mingled with the famishing congregation in the Basilica of St. John Lateran, still searching for his child amid the confusion of the public distribution of food during the earlier stages of the misfortunes of besieged Rome. Since that time he has toiled and suffered much; and now the day of exhaustion, long deferred, the hours of helpless solitude, constantly dreaded, have at length arrived.

From the first periods of the siege, while all around him in the city moved gloomily onward through darker and darker changes, while famine rapidly merged into pestilence and death, while human hopes and purposes gradually diminished and declined with each succeeding day, he alone remained ever devoted to the same labour, ever animated by the same object--the only one among all his fellow-citizens whom no outward event could influence for good or evil, for hope or fear.

In every street of Rome, at all hours, among all ranks of people, he was still to be seen constantly pursuing the same hopeless search. When the mob burst furiously into the public granaries to seize the last supplies of corn hoarded for the rich, he was ready at the doors watching them as they came out. When rows of houses were deserted by all but the dead, he was beheld within, passing from window to window, as he sought through each room for the treasure that he had lost.

When some few among the populace, in the first days of the pestilence, united in the vain attempt to cast over the lofty walls the corpses that strewed the street, he mingled with them to look on the rigid faces of the dead. In solitary places, where the parent, not yet lost to affection, strove to carry his dying child from the desert roadway to the shelter of a roof; where the wife, still faithful to her duties, received her husband's last breath in silent despair--he was seen gliding by their sides, and for one brief instant looking on them with attentive and mournful eyes. Wherever he went, whatever he beheld, he asked no sympathy and sought no aid. He went his way, a pilgrim on a solitary path, an unregarded expectant for a boon that no others would care to partake.

When the famine first began to be felt in the city, he seemed unconscious of its approach--he made no effort to procure beforehand the provision of a few days' sustenance; if he attended the first public distributions of food, it was only to prosecute his search for his child amid the throng around him. He must have perished with the first feeble victims of starvation, had he not been met, during his solitary wanderings, by some of the members of the congregation whom his piety and eloquence had collected in former days.

By these persons, who entreaties that he would suspend his hopeless search he always answered with the same firm and patient denial, his course was carefully watched and his wants anxiously provided for. Out of every supply of food which they were enabled to collect, his share was invariably carried to his abode. They remembered their teacher in the hour of his dejection, as they had formerly reverenced him in the day of his vigour; they toiled to preserve his life as anxiously as they had laboured to profit by his instructions; they listened as his disciples once, they served him as his children now.

But over these, as over all other offices of human kindness, the famine was destined gradually and surely to prevail. The provision of food garnered up by the congregation ominously lessened with each succeeding day. When the pestilence began darkly to appear, the numbers of those who sought their afflicted teacher at his abode, or followed him through the dreary streets, fatally decreased.

Then, as the nourishment which had supported, and the vigilance which had watched him, thus diminished, so did the hard-tasked energies of the unhappy father fail him faster and faster. Each morning as he arose, his steps were more feeble, his heart grew heavier within him, his wanderings through the city were less and less resolute and prolonged. At length his powers totally deserted him; the last-left members of his congregation, as they approached his abode with the last-left provision of food which they possessed, found him prostrate with exhaustion at his garden gate. They bore him to his couch, placed their charitable offering by his side, and leaving one of their number to protect him from the robber and the assassin, they quitted the house in despair.

For some days the guardian remained faithful to his post, until his sufferings from lack of food overpowered his vigilance. Dreading that, in his extremity, he might be tempted to take from the old man's small store of provision what little remained, he fled from the house, to seek sustenance, however loathsome, in the public streets; and thenceforth Numerian was left defenceless in his solitary abode.

He was first beheld on the scenes which these pages present, a man of austere purpose, of unwearied energy; a valiant reformer, who defied all difficulties that beset him in his progress; a triumphant teacher, leading at his will whoever listened to his words; a father, proudly contemplating the future position which he destined for his child. Far different did he now appear. Lost to his ambition, broken in spirit, helpless in body, separated from his daughter by his own act, he lay on his untended couch in a death-like lethargy. The cold wind blowing through his opened window awakened no sensations in his torpid frame; the cup of water and the small relics of coarse food stood near his hand, but he had no vigilance to discern them. His open eyes looked steadfastly upward, and yet he reposed as one in a deep sleep, or as one already devoted to the tomb; save when, at intervals, his lips moved slowly with a long and painfully drawn breath, or a fever flush tinged his hollow cheek with changing and momentary hues.

While thus in outward aspect appearing to linger between life and death, his faculties yet remained feebly vital within him. Aroused by no external influence, and governed by no mental restraint, they now created before him a strange waking vision, palpable as an actual event.

It seemed to him that he was reposing, not in his own chamber, but in some mysterious world, filled with a twilight atmosphere, inexpressibly soothing and gentle to his aching sight. Through this mild radiance he could trace, at long intervals, shadowy representations of the scenes through which he had passed in search of his lost child. The gloomy streets, the lonely houses abandoned to the unburied dead, which he had explored, alternately appeared and vanished before him in solemn succession; and ever and anon, as one vision disappeared ere another rose, he heard afar off a sound as of gentle, womanly voices, murmuring in solemn accents, 'The search has been made in penitence, in patience, in prayer, and has not been pursued in vain. The lost shall return--the beloved shall yet be restored!'

Thus, as it had begun, the vision long continued. Now the scenes through which he had wandered passed slowly before his eyes, now the soft voices murmured pityingly in his ear. At length the first disappeared, and the last became silent; then ensued a long vacant interval, and then the grey, tranquil light brightened slowly at one spot, out of which he beheld advancing towards him the form of his lost child.

She came to his side, she bent lovingly over him; he saw her eyes, with their old patient, childlike expression, looking sorrowfully down upon him. His heart revived to a sense of unspeakable awe and contrition, to emotions of yearning love and mournful hope; his speech returned; he whispered tremulously, 'Child! child! I repented in bitter woe the wrong that I did to thee; I sought thee, in my loneliness on earth, through the long day and the gloomy night! And now the merciful God has sent thee to pardon me! I loved thee; I wept for thee.'

His voice died within him, for now his outward sensations quickened. He felt warm tears falling on his cheeks; he felt embracing arms clasped round him; he heard tenderly repeated, 'Father! speak to me as you were wont; love me, father, and forgive me, as you loved and forgave me when I was a little child!'

The sound of that well-remembered voice--which had ever spoken kindly and reverently to him; which had last addressed him in tones of despairing supplication; which he had hardly hoped to hear again on earth--penetrated his whole being, like awakening music in the dead silence of night. His eyes lost their vacant expression; he raised himself suddenly on the couch; he saw that what had begun as a vision had ended as a reality; that his dream had proved the immediate fore- runner of its own fulfilment; that his daughter in her bodily presence was indeed restored; and his head drooped forward, and he trembled and wept upon her bosom, in the overpowering fulness of his gratitude and delight.

For some moments Antonina, calming with the resolute heroism of affection her own thronging emotions of awe and affright, endeavoured to soothe and support her fast-failing parent. Her horror almost overwhelmed her, as she thought that now, when, through grief and peril, she was at last restored to him, he might expire in her arms; but even yet her resolution did not fail her. The last hope of her brief and bitter life was now the hope of reviving her father, and she clung to it with the tenacity of despair.

She calmed her voice while she spoke to him; she entreated him to remember that his daughter had returned to watch over him, to be his obedient pupil as in days of old. Vain effort! Even while the words passed her lips, his arms, which had been pressed over her, relaxed; his head grew heavier on her bosom. In the despair of the moment, she tore herself from him, and looked round to seek the help that none were near to afford. The cup of water, the last provision of food, attracted her eye. With quick instinct she caught them up. Hope, success, salvation, lay in those miserable relics. She pressed the food into his mouth; she moistened his parched lips, his dry brow, with the water. During one moment of horrible suspense she saw him still insensible; then the vital functions revived; his eyes opened again and fixed famine-struck on the wretched nourishment before him. He devoured it ravenously; he drained the cup of water to its last drop; he sank back again on the couch. But now the torpid blood moved once more in his veins; his heart beat less and less feebly: he was saved. She saw it as she bent over him-- saved by the lost child in the hour of her return! It was a sensation of ecstatic triumph and gratitude which no woeful remembrances had power to embitter in its bright, sudden birth. She knelt down by the side of the couch, almost crushed by her own emotions. Over the grave of the young warrior she had raised her heart to Heaven in agony and grief, and now by her father's side she poured forth her whole soul to her Creator in trembling ejaculations of thankfulness and hope.

Thus--the one slowly recovering whatever of life and vigour yet continued in his weakened frame, the other still filled with her all- absorbing emotions of gratitude--the father and daughter long remained. And now, as morning waned towards noon, the storm began to subside. Gradually and solemnly the vast thunder-clouds rolled asunder, and the bright blue heaven beyond appeared through their fantastic rifts. The lessening rain-drops fell light and silvery to the earth, and breeze and sunshine were wafted at fitful intervals over the plague-tainted atmosphere of Rome. As yet, subdued by the shadows of the floating clouds, the dawning sunbeams glittered softly through the windows of Numerian's chamber. They played, warm and reviving, over his worn features, like messengers of resurrection and hope from their native heaven. Life seemed to expand within him under their fresh and gentle ministering. Once more he raised himself, and turned towards his child; and now his heart throbbed with a healthful joy, and his arms closed round her, not in the helplessness of infirmity, but in the welcome of love.

His words, when he spoke to her, fell at first almost inarticulately from his lips-- they were mingled together in confused phrases of tenderness, contrition, thanksgiving. All the native enthusiasm of his disposition, all the latent love for his child, which had for years been suppressed by his austerity, or diverted by his ambition, now at last burst forth.

Trembling and silent in his arms, Antonina vainly endeavoured to return his caresses and to answer his words of welcome. Now for the first time she knew how deep was her father's affection for her; she felt how foreign to his real nature had been his assumed severity in their intercourse of former days; and in the quick flow of new feelings and old recollections produced by the delighting surprise of the discovery, she found herself speechless. She could only listen eagerly, breathlessly, while he spoke. His words, faltering and confused though they were, were words of endearment which she had never heard from him before; they were words which no mother had ever pronounced beside her infant bed, and they sank divinely consoling over her heart, as messages of pardon from an angel's lips.

Gradually Numerian's voice grew calmer. He raised his daughter in his arms, and bent wistfully on her face his attentive and pitying eyes. 'Returned, returned!' he murmured, while he gazed on her, 'never again to depart! Returned, beautiful and patient, kinder and more tender than ever! Love me and pardon me, Antonina. I sought for you in bitter loneliness and despair. Think not of me as what I was, but as what I am! There were days when you were an infant, when I had no thought but how to cherish and delight you, and now those days have come again. You shall read no gloomy task-books; you shall never be separated from me more; you shall play sweet music on the lute; you shall be all garlanded with flowers which I will provide for you! We will find friends and glad companions; we will bring happiness with us wherever we are seen. God's blessing goes forth from children like you--it has fallen upon me--it has raised me from the dead! My Antonina shall teach me to worship, as I once taught her. She shall pray for me in the morning, and pray for me at night; and when she thinks not of it, when she sleeps, I shall come softly to her bedside, and wait and watch over her, so that when she opens her eyes they shall open on me--they are the eyes of my child who has been restored to me--there is nothing on earth that can speak to me like them of happiness and peace!'

He paused for a moment, and looked rapturously on her face as it was turned towards him. His features partially saddened while he gazed, and taking her long hair, still wet and dishevelled from the rain, in his hands, he pressed it over his lips, over his face, over his neck. Then, when he saw that she was endeavouring to speak, when he beheld the tears that were now filling her eyes, he drew her closer to him, and hurriedly continued in lower tones--

'Hush! hush! No more grief, no more tears! Tell me not whither you have wandered--speak not of what you have suffered; for would not every word be a reproach to me? And you have come to pardon and not to reproach! Let not the recollection that it was I who cast you off be forced on me from your lips; let us remember only that we are restored to each other; let us think that God has accepted my penitence and forgiven me my sin, in suffering my child to return! Or, if we must speak of the days of separation that are past, speak to me of the days that found you tranquil and secure; rejoice me by telling me that it was not all danger and woe in the bitter destiny which my guilty anger prepared for my own child! Say to me that you met protectors as well as enemies in the hour of your flight--that all were not harsh to you as I was--that those of whom you asked shelter and safety looked on your face as on a petition for charity and kindness from friends whom they loved! Tell me only of your protectors, Antonina, for in that there will be consolation; and you have come to console!'

As he waited for her reply he felt her tremble on his bosom, he saw the shudder that ran over her frame. The despair in her voice, thought she only pronounced in answer to him the simple words, 'There was one'--and then ceased, unable to proceed--penetrated coldly to his heart.

'Is he not at hand?' he hurriedly resumed. 'Why is he not here? Let us seek him without delay. I must humble myself before him in my gratitude. I must show him that I was worthy that my Antonina should be restored.'

'He is dead!' she gasped, sinking down in the arms that embraced her, as the recollections of the past night again crowded in all their horror on her memory. 'They murdered him by my side. O father! father! he loved me; he would have reverenced and protected you!'

'May the merciful God receive him among the blessed angels, and honour him among the holy martyrs!' cried the father, raising his tearful eyes in supplication. 'May his spirit, if it can still be observant of the things of earth, know that his name shall be written on my heart with the name of my child; that I will think on him as on a beloved companion, and mourn for him as a son that has been taken from me!'

He ceased, and looked down on Antonina, whose features were still hidden from him. Each felt that a new bond of mutual affection had been created between them by what each had spoken; but both now remained silent.

During this interval the thoughts of Numerian wandered from the reflections which had hitherto occupied him. The few mournful words which his daughter had spoken had been sufficient to banish its fulness of joy from his heart, and to turn him from the happy contemplation of the present to the dark recollections of the past. Vague doubts and fears now mingled with his gratitude and hope, and involuntarily his thoughts reverted to what he would fain have forgotten for ever--to the morning when he had driven Antonina from her home.

Baseless apprehensions of the return of the treacherous Pagan and his profligate employer, with the return of their victim--despairing convictions of his own help-lessness and infirmity rose startlingly in his mind. His eyes wandered vacantly round the room, his hands closed trembling over his daughter's form; then, sud-denly releasing her, he arose as one panic-stricken, and exclaiming, 'The doors must be secured--Ulpius may be near--the senator may return!' endeavoured to cross the room. But his strength was unequal to the effort; he leaned back for support against the wall, and breathlessly repeating, 'Secure the doors--Ulpius, Ulpius!' he motioned to Antonina to descend.

She trembled as she obeyed him. Remembering her passage through the breach in the wall, and her fearful journey through the streets of Rome, she more than shared her father's apprehensions as she descended the stairs.

The door remained half open, as she had left it when she entered the house. Ere she hurriedly closed and barred it, she cast a momentary glance on the street beyond. The gaunt figures of the slaves still moved wearily to and fro, amid the mockery of festal preparation in Vetranio's palace; and here and there a few ghast-ly figures lay on the ground contemplating them in languid amazement. Over all other parts of the street the deadly tranquillity of plague and famine still pre-vailed.

Hurriedly ascending the steps, Antonina hastened to assure her father that she had obeyed his commands, and that they were now secure from all intrusion from without. But, during her brief absence, a new and more ominous prospect of calamity had presented itself before the old man's mind.

As she entered the room, she saw that he had returned to his couch, and that he was holding before him the little wooden bowl which had contained his last sup-ply of food, and which was now empty. He addressed not a word to her when he heard her enter; his features were rigid with horror and despair as he looked down on the empty bowl; he muttered vacantly, 'It was the last provision that remained, and it was I that exhausted it! The beasts of the forest carry food to their young, and I have taken the last morsel from my child!'

In an instant the utter desolateness of their situation--forgotten in the first joy of their meeting--forced itself with appalling vividness upon Antonina's mind. She endeavoured to speak of comfort and hope to her father; but the fearful realities of the famine in the city now rose palpably before her, and suspended the vain words of solace on her lips. In the midst of still populous Rome, within sight of those surrounding plains where the creative sun ripened hour by hour the vegetation of the teeming earth, where field and granary displayed profusely their abundant stores, the father and daughter now looked on each other, as helpless to replace their exhausted provision of food as if they had been abandoned on the raft of the shipwrecked in an unexplored sea, or banished to a lonely island whose inland products were withered by infected winds, and around whose arid shores ran such destroying waters as seethe over the 'Cities of the Plain'.

The silence which had long prevailed in the room, the bitter reflections which still held the despairing father and the patient daughter speechless alike, were at length interrupted by a hollow and melancholy voice from the street, pronouncing, in the form of a public notice, these words:--

'I, Publius Dalmatius, messenger of the Roman Senate, proclaim, that in order to clear the streets from the dead, three thousand sestertii will be given by the Prefect for every ten bodies that are cast over the walls. This is the true decree of the Senate.'

The voice ceased; but no sound of applause, no murmur of popular tumult was heard in answer. Then, after an interval, it was once more faintly audible as the messenger passed on and repeated the decree in another street; and then the silence again sank down over all things more awfully pervading than before.

Every word of the proclamation, when repeated in the distance as when spoken under his window, had clearly reached Numerian's ears. His mind, already sinking in despair, was riveted on what he had heard from the woe-boding voice of the herald, with a fascination as absorbing as that which rivets the eye of the traveller, already giddy on the summit of a precipice, upon the spectacle of the yawning gulfs beneath. When all sound of the proclamation had finally died away, the unhappy father dropped the empty bowl which he had hitherto mechanically continued to hold before him, and glancing affrightedly at his daughter, groaned to himself: 'The corpses are to be cast over the walls--the dead are to be flung forth to the winds of heaven--there is no help for us in the city. O God, God!-- she may die!--her body may be cast away like the rest, and I may live to see it!'

He rose suddenly from the couch; his reason seemed for a moment to be shaken as he tottered to the window, crying, 'Food! food!--I will give my house and all it contains for a morsel of food. I have nothing to support my own child--she will starve before me by tomorrow if I have no food! I am a citizen of Rome--I demand help from the Senate! Food! food!'

In tones declining lower and lower he continued to cry thus from the window, but no voice answered him either in sympathy or derision. Of all the people--now increased in numbers--collected in the street before Vetranio's palace, no one turned even to look on him. For days and days past, such fruitless appeals as his had been heard, and heard unconcernedly, at every hour and in every street of Rome--now ringing through the heavy air in the shrieks of delirium; now faintly audible in the last faltering murmurs of exhaustion and despair.

Thus vainly entreating help and pity from a populace who had ceased to give the one or to feel the other, Numerian might long have remained; but now his daughter approached his side, and drawing him gently towards his couch, said in tender and solemn accents: 'Remember, father, that God sent the ravens to feed Elijah, and replenished the widow's cruse! He will not desert us, for He has restored us to each other, and has sent me hither not to perish in the famine, but to watch over you!'

'God has deserted the city and all that it contains!' he answered distractedly. 'The angel of destruction has gone forth into our streets, and death walks in his shadow! On this day, when hope and happiness seemed opening before us both; our little household has been doomed! The young and the old, the weary and the watchful, they strew the streets alike--the famine has mastered them all--the famine will master us--there is no help, no escape! I, who would have died patiently for my daughter's safety, must now die despairing, leaving her friendless in the wide, dreary, perilous world; in the dismal city of anguish, of horror, of death--where the enemy threatens without, and hunger and pestilence waste within! O Antonina! you have returned to me but for a little time; the day of our second separation draws near!'

For a few moments his head drooped, and his sobs choked his utterance; then he once more rose painfully to his feet. Heedless of Antonina's entreaties, he again endeavoured to cross the room, only again to find his feeble powers unequal to sustain him. As he fell back panting upon a seat, his eyes assumed a wild, unnatural expression--despair of mind and weakness of body had together partially unhinged his faculties. When his daughter affrightedly approached to soothe and succour him, he impatiently waved her back; and began to speak in a dull, hoarse, monotonous voice, pressing his hand firmly over his brow, and directing his eyes backwards and forwards incessantly, on object after object, in every part of the room.

'Listen, child, listen!' he hastily began. 'I tell you there is no food in the house, and no food in Rome!--we are besieged--they have taken from us our granaries in the suburbs, and our fields on the plains--there is a great famine in the city--those who still eat, eat strange food which men sicken at when it is named. I would seek even this, but I have no strength to go forth into the byways and force it from others at the point of the sword! I am old and feeble, and heart-broken--I shall die first, and leave fatherless my good, kind daughter, whom I sought for so long, and whom I loved as my only child!'

He paused for an instant, not to listen to the words of encouragement and hope which Antonina mechanically addressed to him while he spoke, but to collect his wandering thoughts, to rally his failing strength. His voice acquired a quicker tone, and his features presented a sudden energy and earnestness of expression, as if some new project had flashed across his mind, when, after an interval, he continued thus:--

'But though my child shall be bereaved of me, though I shall die in the hour when I most longed to live for her, I must not leave her helpless; I will send her among my congregation who have deserted me, but who will repent when they hear that I am dead, and will receive Antonina among them for my sake! Listen to this-- listen, listen! You must tell them to remember all that I once revealed to them of my brother, from whom I parted in my boyhood--my brother, whom I have never seen since. He may yet be alive, he may be found--they must search for him; for to you he would be father to the fatherless, and guardian to the unguarded--he may now be in Rome, he may be rich and powerful--he may have food to spare, and shelter that is good against all enemies and strangers! Attend, child, to my words: in these latter days I have thought of him much; I have seen him in dreams as I saw him for the last time in my father's house; he was happier and more beloved than I was, and in envy and hatred I quitted my parents and part- ed from him. You have heard nothing of this; but you must hear it now, that when I am dead you may know you have a protector to seek! So I received in anger my brother's farewell, and fled from my home--(those days were well remembered by me once, but all things grow dull on my memory now). Long years of turmoil and change passed on, and I never met him; and men of many nations were my companions, but he was not among them; then much affliction fell upon me, and I repented and learnt the fear of God, and went back to my father's house. Since that, years have passed--I know not how many. I could have told them when I spoke of my former life to him--to my friend, when we stood near St. Peter's, ere the city was besieged, looking on the sunset, and speaking of the early days of our companionship; but now my very remembrance fails me; the famine that threatens us with separation and death casts darkness over my thoughts; yet hear me, hear me patiently--for your sake I must continue!'

'Not now, father--not now! At another time, on a happier day!' murmured Antonina, in tremulous, entreating tones.

'My home, when I arrived to look on it, was gone,' pursued the old man sadly, neither heeding nor hearing her. 'Other houses were built where my father's house had stood; no man could tell me of my parents and my brother; then I returned, and my former companions grew hateful in my eyes; I left them, and they followed me with persecution and scorn.--Listen, listen!--I set forth secretly in the night, with you, to escape them, and to make perfect my reformation where they should not be near to hinder it; and we travelled onward many days until we came to Rome, and I made my abode there. But I feared that my companions whom I abhorred might discover and persecute me again, and in the new city of my dwelling I called myself by another name than the name that I bore; thus I knew that all trace of me would be lost, and that I should be kept secure from men whom I thought on only as enemies now. Go, child! go quickly!--bring your tablets and write down the names that I shall tell you; for so you will discover your protector when I am gone! Say not to him that you are the child of Numerian-- he knows not the name; say that you are the daughter of Cleander, his brother, who died longing to be restored to him. Write--write carefully, Cleander!--that was the name my father gave to me; that was the name I bore until I fled from my evil companions and changed it, dreading their pursuit! Cleander! write and remember, Cleander! I have seen in visions that my brother shall be discovered: he will not be discovered to me, but he will be discovered to you! Your tablets-- your tablets!--write his name with mine--it is--'

He stopped abruptly. His mental powers, fluctuating between torpor and ani- mation--shaken, but not overpowered by the trials which had assailed them--sud- denly rallied, and resuming somewhat of their accustomed balance, became awak- ened to a sense of their own aberration. His vague revelations of his past life (which the reader will recognise as resembling his communications on the same subject to the fugitive land- owner, previously related) now appeared before him in all their incongruity and uselessness. His countenance fell--he sighed bitterly to himself: 'My reason begins to desert me!--my judgment, which should guide my child--my resolution, which should uphold her, both fail me! How should my brother, since childhood lost to me, be found by her? Against the famine that threatens us I offer but vain words! Already her strength declines; her face, that I loved to look on grows wan before my eyes! God have mercy upon us!--God have mercy upon us!'

He returned feebly to his couch; his head declined on his bosom; sometimes a low groan burst from his lips, but he spoke no more.

Deep as was the prostration under which he had now fallen, it was yet less painful to Antonina to behold it than to listen to the incoherent revelations which had fallen from his lips but the moment before, and which, in her astonishment and affright, she had dreaded might be the awful indications of the overthrow of her father's reason. As she again placed herself by his side, she trembled to feel that her own weariness was fast overpowering her; but she still struggled with her rising despair--still strove to think only of capacity for endurance and chances of relief.

The silence in the room was deep and dismal while they now sat together. The faint breezes, at long intervals, drowsily rose and fell as they floated through the open window; the fitful sunbeams alternately appeared and vanished as the clouds rolled upward in airy succession over the face of heaven. Time moved sternly in its destined progress, and Nature varied tranquilly through its appointed limits of change, and still no hopes, no saving projects, nothing but dark recollections and woeful anticipations occupied Antonina's mind; when, just as her weary head was drooping towards the ground, just as sensation and fortitude and grief itself seemed declining into a dreamless and deadly sleep, a last thought, void of discernible connection or cause, rose suddenly within her--animating, awakening, inspiring. She started up. 'The garden, father--the garden!' she cried breathlessly. 'Remember the food that grows in our garden below! Be comforted, we have provision left yet--God has not deserted us!'

He raised his face while she spoke; his features assumed a deeper mournfulness and hopelessness of expression; he looked upon her in ominous silence, and laid his trembling fingers on her arm to detain her, when she hurriedly attempted to quit the room.

'Do not forbid me to depart,' she anxiously pleaded. 'To me every corner in the garden is known; for it was my possession in our happier days--our last hopes rest in the garden, and I must search through it without delay! Bear with me,' she added, in low and melancholy tones--'bear with m e, dear father, in all that I would now do! I have suffered, since we parted, a bitter affliction, which clings dark and heavy to all my thoughts--there is no consolation for me but the privilege of caring for your welfare--my only hope of comfort is in the employment of aiding you!'

The old man's hand had pressed heavier on her arm while she addressed him; but when she ceased it dropped from her, and he bent his head in speechless submission to her entreaty.

For one moment she lingered, looking on him silent as himself; the next, she left the apartment with hasty and uncertain steps.

On reaching the garden, she unconsciously took the path leading to the bank where she had once loved to play secretly upon her lute and to look on the distant mountains reposing in the warm atmosphere which summer evenings shed over their blue expanse. How eloquent was this little plot of ground of the quiet events now for ever gone by!--of the joys, the hopes, the happy occupations, which rise with the day that chronicles them, and pass like that day, never to return the same!--which the memory alone can preserve as they were, and the heart can never resume but in a changed form, divested of the presence of the companion of the incident of the departed moment, which formed the charm of the past and makes the imperfection of the present.

Tender and thronging were the remembrances which the surrounding prospect called up, as the sad mistress of the garden looked again on her little domain! She saw the bank where she could never more sit to sing with a renewal of the same feelings which had once inspired her music; she saw the drooping flowers that she could never restore with the same childlike enjoyment of the task which had animated her in former hours! Young though she still was, the emotions of the youthful days that were gone could never be revived as they had once existed! As waters they had welled up, and as waters they had flowed forth, never to return to their source! Thoughts of these former years--of the young warrior who lay cold beneath the heavy earth--of the desponding father who mourned hopeless in the room above--gathered thick at her heart as she turned from her flower-beds-- not, as in other days, to pour forth her happiness to the music of her lute, but to search laboriously for the sustenance of life.

At first, as she stooped over those places in the garden where she knew that fruits and vegetables had been planted by her own hand, her tears blinded her. She hastily dashed them away, and looked eagerly around.

Alas! others had reaped the field from which she had hoped abundance! In the early days of the famine Numerian's congregation had entered the garden, and gathered for him whatever it contained; its choicest and its homeliest products were alike exhausted; withered leaves lay on the barren earth, and naked branches waved over them in the air. She wandered from path to path, searching amid the briars and thistles, which already cast an aspect of ruin over the deserted place; she explored its most hidden corners with the painful perseverance of despair; but the same barrenness spread around her wherever she turned. On this once fertile spot, which she had entered with such joyful faith in its resources, there remained but a few poor decayed roots, dropped and forgotten amid tangled weeds and faded flowers.

She saw that they were barely sufficient for one scanty meal as she collected them and returned slowly to the house. No words escaped her, no tears flowed over her cheeks when she reascended the steps--hope, fear, thought, sensation itself had been stunned within her from the first moment when she had discovered that, in the garden as in the house, the inexorable famine had anticipated the last chances of relief.

She entered the room, and, still holding the withered roots, advanced mechanically to her father's side. During her absence his mental and bodily faculties had both yielded to wearied nature--he lay in a deep, heavy sleep.

Her mind experienced a faint relief when she saw that the fatal necessity of confessing the futility of the hopes she had herself awakened was spared her for a while. She knelt down by Numerian, and gently smoothed the hair over his brow; then she drew the curtain across the window, for she feared even that the breeze blowing through it might arouse him.

A strange, secret satisfaction at the idea of devoting to her father every moment of the time and every particle of the strength that might yet be reserved for her; a ready resignation to death in dying for him--overspread her heart, and took the place of all other aspirations and all other thoughts.

She now moved to and fro through the room with a cautious tranquillity which nothing could startle; she prepared her decayed roots for food with a patient attention which nothing could divert. Lost, through the aggravated miseries of her position, to recent grief and present apprehension, she could still instinctively perform the simple offices of the woman and the daughter, as she might have performed them amid a peaceful nation and a prosperous home. Thus do the first-born affections outlast the exhaustion of all the stormy emotions, all the aspiring thoughts of after years, which may occupy, but which cannot absorb, the spirit within us; thus does their friendly and familiar voice, when the clamour of contending passions has died away in its own fury, speak again, serene and sustaining as in the early time, when the mind moved secure within the limits of its native simplicity, and the heart yet lay happy in the pure tranquillity of its first repose!

The last scanty measure of food was soon prepared; it was bitter and unpalatable when she tasted it--life could barely be preserved, even in the most vigorous, by provision so wretched; but she set it aside as carefully as if it had been the most precious luxury of the most abundant feast.

Nothing had changed during the interval of her solitary employment--her father yet slept; the gloomy silence yet prevailed in the street. She placed herself at the window, and partially drew aside the curtain to let the warm breezes from without blow over her cold brow. The same ineffable resignation, the same unnatural quietude, which had sunk down over her faculties since she had entered the room, overspread them still. Surrounding objects failed to impress her attention; recollections and forebodings stagnated in her mind. A marble composure prevailed over her features. Sometimes her eyes wandered mechanically from the morsels of food by her side to her sleeping father, as her one vacant idea of watching for his service, till the feeble pulses of life had throbbed their last, alternately revived and declined; but no other evidences of bodily existence or mental activity appeared in her. As she now sat in the half-darkened room, by the couch on which her father reposed--her features pale, calm, and rigid, her form enveloped in cold white drapery--there were moments when she looked like one of the penitential devotees of the primitive Church, appointed to watch in the house of mourning, and surprised in her saintly vigil by the advent of Death.

Time flowed on--the monotonous hours of the day waned again towards night; and plague and famine told their lapse in the fated highways of Rome. For father and child the sand in the glass was fast running out, and neither marked it as it diminished. The sleeper still reposed, and the guardian by his side still watched; but now her weary gaze was directed on the street, unconsciously attracted by the sound of voices which at length rose from it at intervals, and by the light of the torches and lamps which appeared in the great palace of the senator Vetranio, as the sun gradually declined in the horizon, and the fiery clouds around were quenched in the vapours of the advancing night. Steadily she looked upon the sight beneath and before her; but even yet her limbs never moved; no expression relieved the blank, solemn peacefulness of her features.

Meanwhile, the soft, brief twilight glimmered over the earth, and showed the cold moon, poised solitary in the starless heaven; then, the stealthy darkness arose at her pale signal, and closed slowly round the City of Death!

Chapter 22

THE BANQUET OF FAMINE

Of all prophecies, none are, perhaps, so frequently erroneous as those on which we are most apt to venture in endeavouring to foretell the effect of outward events on the characters of men. In no form of our anticipations are we more frequently baffled than in such attempts to estimate beforehand the influence of circumstance over conduct, not only in others, but also even in ourselves. Let the event but happen, and men, whom we view by the light of our previous observation of them, act under it as the living contradictions of their own characters. The friend of our daily social intercourse, in the progress of life, and the favourite hero of our historic studies, in the progress of the page, astonish, exceed, or disappoint our expectations alike. We find it as vain to foresee a cause as to fix a limit for the arbitrary inconsistencies in the dispositions of mankind.

But, though to speculate upon the future conduct of others under impending circumstances be but too often to expose the fallacy of our wisest anticipations, to contemplate the nature of that conduct after it has been displayed is a useful subject of curiosity, and may perhaps be made a fruitful source of instruction. Similar events which succeed each other at different periods are relieved from monotony, and derive new importance from the ever-varying effects which they produce on the human character. Thus, in the great occurrence which forms the foundation of our narrative, we may find little in the siege of Rome, looking at it as a mere event, to distinguish it remarkably from any former siege of the city-- the same desire for glory and vengeance, wealth and dominion, which brought Alaric to her walls, brought other invaders before him. But if we observed the effect of the Gothic descent upon Italy on the inhabitants of her capital, we shall find ample matter for novel contemplation and unbounded surprise.

We shall perceive, as an astonishing instance of the inconsistencies of the human character, the spectacle of a whole people resolutely defying an overwhelming foreign invasion at their very doors, just at the period when they had fallen most irremediably from the highest position of national glory to the lowest depths of national degradation; resisting an all-powerful enemy with inflexible obstinacy, for the honour of the Roman name, which they had basely dishonoured or carelessly forgotten for ages past. We shall behold men who have hitherto laughed at the very name of patriotism, now starving resolutely in their country's cause; who stopped at no villainy to obtain wealth, now hesitating to employ their ill-gotten gains in the purchase of the most important of all gratifications--their own security and peace. Instances of the unimaginable effect produced by the event of the siege of Rome on the characters of her inhabitants might be drawn from all classes, from the lowest to the highest, from patrician to plebeian; but to produce them here would be to admit too long an interruption in the progress of the present narrative. If we are to enter at all into detail on such a subject, it must be only in a case clearly connected with the actual requirements of our story; and such a case may be found, at this juncture, in the conduct of the senator Vetranio, under the influence of the worst calamities attending the blockade of Rome by the Goths.

Who, it may be asked, knowing the previous character of this man, his frivolity of disposition, his voluptuous anxiety for unremitting enjoyment and ease, his horror of the slightest approaches of affliction or pain, would have imagined him capable of rejecting in disdain all the minor chances of present security and future prosperity which his unbounded power and wealth might have procured for him, even in a famine-stricken city, and rising suddenly to the sublime of criminal desperation, in the resolution to abandon life as worthless the moment it had ceased to run in the easy current of all former years? Yet to this determination had he now arrived; and, still more extraordinary, in this determination had he found others, of his own patrician order, to join him.

The reader will remember his wild announcement of his intended orgie to the Prefect Pompeianus during the earlier periods of the siege; that announcement was now to be fulfilled. Vetranio had bidden his guests to the Banquet of Famine. A chosen number of the senators of the great city were to vindicate their daring by dying the revellers that they had lived; by resigning in contempt all prospect of starving, like the common herd, on a lessening daily pittance of loathsome food; by making their triumphant exit from a fettered and ungrateful life, drowned in floods of wine, and lighted by the fires of the wealthiest palace of Rome!

It had been intended to keep this frantic determination a profound secret, to let the mighty catastrophe burst upon the remaining inhabitants of the city like a prodigy from heaven; but the slaves intrusted with the organisation of the suicide banquet had been bribed to their tasks with wine, and in the carelessness of intoxication had revealed to others whatever they heard within the palace walls. The news passed from mouth to mouth. There was enough in the prospect of beholding the burning palace and the drunken suicide of its desperate guests to animate even the stagnant curiosity of a famishing mob.

On the appointed evening the people dragged their weary limbs from all quarters of the city towards the Pincian Hill. Many of them died on the way; many lost their resolution to proceed to the end of their journey, and took shelter sullenly in the empty houses on the road; many found opportunities for plunder and crime as they proceeded, which tempted them from their destination; but many persevered in their purpose--the living dragging the dying along with them, the desperate driving the cowardly before them in malignant sport, until they gained the palace gates. It was by their voices, as they reached her ear from the street, that the fast-sinking faculties of Antonina had been startled, though not revived; and there, on the broad pavement, lay these citizens of a fallen city--a congregation of pestilence and crime--a starving and an awful band!

The moon, brightened by the increasing darkness, now clearly illuminated the street, and revealed, in a narrow space, a various and impressive scene.

One side of the roadway in which stood Vetranio's palace was occupied, along each extremity, as far as the eye could reach at night, by the groves and outbuildings attached to the senator's mansion. The palace grounds, at the higher and farther end of the street--looking from the Pincian Gate--crossed it by a wide archway, and then stretched backward, until they joined the trees of the little garden of Numerian's abode. In a line with this house, but separated from it by a short space, stood a long row of buildings, let out floor by floor to separate occupants, and towering to an unwieldy altitude; for in ancient Rome, as in modern London, in consequence of the high price of land in an over-populated city, builders could only secure space in a dwelling by adding inconveniently to its height. Beyond these habitations rose the trees surrounding another patrician abode; and beyond that the houses took a sudden turn, and nothing more was visible in a straight line but the dusky, indefinite objects of the distant view.

The whole appearance of the street before Vetranio's mansion, had it been unoccupied by the repulsive groups now formed in it, would have been eminently beautiful at the hours of which we now write. The nobly symmetrical frontage of the palace itself, with its graceful succession of long porticoes and colossal statues, contrasted by the picturesquely irregular appearance of the opposite dwelling of Numerian and the lofty houses by its side; the soft, indistinct masses of foliage running parallel along the upper ends of the street, terminated and connected by the archway garden across the road, on which was planted a group of tall pine-trees, rising in gigantic relief against the transparent sky; the brilliant light streaming across the pavement from Vetranio's gaily- curtained windows, immediately opposed by the tranquil moonlight which lit the more distant view--formed altogether a prospect in which the natural and the artificial were mingled together in the most exquisite proportions--a prospect whose ineffable poetry and beauty might, on any other night, have charmed the most careless eye and exalted the most frivolous mind. But now, overspread as it was by groups of people gaunt with famine and hideous with disease; startled as it was, at gloomy intervals, by contending cries of supplication, defiance, and despair--its brightest beauties of Nature and Art appeared but to shine with an aspect of bitter mockery around the human misery which their splendour disclosed.

Upwards of a hundred people--mostly of the lowest orders--were congregated before the senator's devoted dwelling. Some few among them passed slowly to and fro in the street, their figures gliding shadowy and solemn through the light around them; but the greater number lay on the pavement before the wall of Numerian's dwelling and the doorways of the lofty houses by its side. Illuminated by the full glare of the light from the palace windows, these groups, huddled together in the distorted attitudes of suffering and despair, assumed a fearful and unearthly appearance. Their shrivelled faces, their tattered clothing, their wan forms, here prostrate, there half-raised, were bathed in a steady red glow. High above them, at the windows of the tall houses, now tenanted in every floor by the dead, appeared a few figures (the mercenary guardians of the dying within) bending forward to look out upon the palace opposite--their haggard faces showing pale in the clear moonlight. Sometimes their voices were heard calling in mockery to the mass of people below to break down the strong steel gates of the palace, and tear the full wine-cup from its master's lips. Sometimes those beneath replied with execrations, which rose wildly mingled with the wailing of women and children, the moans of the plague-stricken, and the supplications of the famished to the slaves passing backwards and forwards behind the palace railings for charity and help.

In the intervals, when the tumult of weak voices was partially lulled, there was heard a dull, regular, beating sound, produced by those who had found dry bones on their road to the palace, and were pounding them on the pavement, in sheltered places, for food. The wind, which had been refreshing during the day, had changed at sunset, and now swept up slowly over the street in hot, faint gusts, plague-laden, from the East. Particles of the ragged clothing on some prostrate forms lying most exposed in its course waved slowly to and fro, as it passed, like banners planted by Death on the yielding defences of the citadel of Life. It wound through the open windows of the palace, hot and mephitic, as if tainted with the breath of the foul and furious words which it bore onward into the banqueting-hall of the senator's reckless guests. Driven over such scenes as now spread beneath it, it derived from them a portentous significance; it seemed to blow like an atmosphere exuded from the furnace-depths of centre earth, breathing sinister warnings of some deadly convulsion in the whole fabric of Nature over the thronged and dismal street.

Such was the prospect before the palace, and such the spectators assembled in ferocious anxiety to behold the destruction of the senator's abode. Meanwhile, within the walls of the building, the beginning of the fatal orgie was at hand.

It had been covenanted by the slaves (who, during the calamities in the besieged city, had relaxed in their accustomed implicit obedience to their master with perfect impunity), that, as soon as the last labours of preparation were completed, they should be free to consult their own safety by quitting the devoted palace. Already some of the weakest and most timid of their numbers might be seen passing out hastily into the gardens by the back gates, like engineers who had fired a train, and were escaping ere the explosion burst forth. Those among the menials who still remained in the palace were for the greater part occupied in drinking from the vases of wine which had been placed before them, to preserved to the last moment their failing strength.

The mockery of festivity had been extended even to their dresses--green liveries girt with cherry-coloured girdles arrayed their wasted forms. They drank in utter silence. Not the slightest appearance of revelry or intoxication prevailed among their ranks. Confusedly huddled together, as if for mutual protection, they ever and anon cast quick glances of suspicion and apprehension upon some six or eight of the superior attendants of the palace, who walked backwards and forwards at the outer extremity of the hall occupied by their comrades, and occasionally advancing along the straight passages before them to the front gates of the building, appeared to be exchanging furtive signals with some of the people in the street. Reports had been vaguely spread of a secret conspiracy between some of the principal of the slaves and certain chosen ruffians of the populace, to murder all the inmates of the palace, seize on its treasures, and, opening the city gates to the Goths, escape with their booty during the confusion of the pillage of Rome.

Nothing had as yet been positively discovered; but the few attendants who kept ominously apart from the rest were unanimously suspected by their fellows, who now watched them over their wine-cups with anxious eyes. Different as was the scene among the slaves still left in the palace from the scene among the people dispersed in the street, the one was nevertheless in its own degree as gloomily suggestive of some great impending calamity as the other.

The grand banqueting-hall of the palace, prepared though it now was for festivity, wore a changed and melancholy aspect.

The massive tables still ran down the whole length of the noble room, surrounded by luxurious couches, as in former days, but not a vestige of food appeared upon their glittering surfaces. Rich vases, flasks, and drinking-cups, all filled with wine, alone occupied the festal board. Above, hanging low from the ceiling, burnt ten large lamps, corresponding to the number of guests assembled, as the only procurable representatives of the hundreds of revellers who had feasted at Vetranio's expense during the brilliant nights that were now passed for ever. At the lower end of the room, beyond the grand door of entrance, hung a thick black curtain, apparently intended to conceal mysteriously some object behind it. Before the curtain burnt a small lamp of yellow glass, raised upon a high gilt pole, and around and beneath it, heaped against the side walls, and over part of the table, lay a various and confused mass of rich objects, all of a nature more or less inflammable, and all besprinkled with scented oils. Hundreds of yards of gorgeously variegated hangings, rolls upon rolls of manuscripts, gaudy dresses of all colours, toys, utensils, innumerable articles of furniture formed in rare and beautifully inlaid woods, were carelessly flung together against the walls of the apartment, and rose high towards its ceiling.

On every part of the tables not occupied by the vases of wine were laid gold and jewelled ornaments which dazzled the eye by their brilliancy; while, in extraordinary contrast to the magnificence thus profusely displayed, there appeared in one of the upper corners of the hall an old wooden stand covered by a coarse cloth, on which were placed one or two common earthenware bowls, containing what my be termed a 'mash' of boiled bran and salted horseflesh. Any repulsive odour which might have arisen from this strange compound was overpowered by the various perfumes sprinkled about the room, which, mingling with the hot breezes wafted through the windows from the street, produced an atmosphere as oppressive and debilitating, in spite of its artificial allurements to the sense of smell, as the air of a dungeon or the vapours of a marsh.

Remarkable as was the change in the present appearance of the banqueting-hall, it was but the feeble reflection of the alteration for the worse in the aspect of the host and his guests. Vetranio reclined at the head of the table, dressed in a scarlet mantle. An embroidered towel with purple tassels and fringes, connected with rings of gold, fell over his breast, and silver and ivory bracelets were clasped round his arms. But of the former man the habiliments were all that remained. His head was bent forward, as if with the weakness of age; his emaciated arms seemed barely able to support the weight of the ornaments which glittered on them; his eyes had contracted a wild, unsettled expression; and a deadly paleness overspread the once plump and jovial cheeks which so many mistresses had kissed in mercenary rapture in other days. Both in countenance and manner the elegant voluptuary of our former acquaintance at the Court of Ravenna was entirely and fatally changed. Of the other eight patricians who lay on the couches around their altered host--some wild and reckless, some gloomy and imbecile--all had suffered in the ordeal of the siege, the famine, and the pestilence, like him.

Such were the member of the assemblage, represented from the ceiling by nine of the burning lamps. The tenth and last lamp indicated the presence of one more guest who reclined a little apart from the rest.

This man was hump-backed; his gaunt, bony features were repulsively disproportioned to his puny frame, which looked doubly contemptible, enveloped as it was in an ample tawdry robe. Sprung from the lowest ranks of the populace, he had gradually forced himself into the favour of his superiors by his skill in coarse mimicry, and his readiness in ministering to the worst vices of all who would employ him. Having lost the greater part of his patrons during the siege, finding himself abandoned to starvation on all sides, he had now, as a last resource, obtained permission to participate in the Banquet of Famine, to enliven it by a final exhibition of his buffoonery, and to die with his masters, as he had lived with them--the slave, the parasite, and the imitator of the lowest of their vices and the worst of their crimes.

At the commencement of the orgie, little was audible beyond the clash of the wine-cups, the low occasional whispering of the revellers, and the confused voices of the people without, floating through the window from the street. The desperate compact of the guests, now that its execution had actually begun, awed them at first in spite of themselves. At length, when there was a lull of all sounds--when a temporary calm prevailed over the noises outside--when the wine-cups were emptied, and left for a moment ere they were filled again--Vetranio feebly rose, and, announcing with a mocking smile that he was about to speak a funeral oration over his friends and himself, pointed to the wall immediately behind him as to an object fitted to awaken the astonishment or the hilarity of his moody guests.

Against the upper part of the wall were fixed various small statues in bronze and marble, all representing the owner of the palace, and all hung with golden plates. Beneath these appeared the rent-roll of his estates, written in various colours on white vellum, and beneath that, scratched on the marble in faint irregular characters, was no less an object than his own epitaph, composed by himself. It may be translated thus:--

Stop, Spectator!

If thou has reverently cultivated the pleasures of the taste, pause amid these illustrious ruins of what was once a palace, and peruse with respect on this stone the epitaph of VETRANIO, a senator. He was the first man who invented a successful nightingale sauce; his bold and creative genius added much, and would have added more, to THE ART OF COOKERY--but, alas for the interests of science! he lived in the days when the Gothic barbarians besieged THE IMPERIAL CITY; famine left him no matter for gustatory experiment; and pestilence deprived him of cooks to enlighten! Opposed at all points by the force of adverse circumstances, finding his life of no further use to the culinary interests of Rome, he called his chosen friends together to assist him, conscientiously drank up every drop of wine remaining in his cellars, lit the funeral pile of himself and his guests, in the banqueting-hall of his own palace, and died, as he had lived, the patriotic CATO of his country's gastronomy!

'Behold!' cried Vetranio, pointing triumphantly to the epitaph--'behold in every line of those eloquent letters at once the seal of my resolute adherence to the engagement that unites us here, and the foundation of my just claim to the reverence of posterity on the most useful of the arts which I exercised for the benefit of my species! Read, friends, brethren, fellow-martyrs of glory, and, as you read, rejoice with me over the hour of our departure from the desecrated arena, no longer worthy the celebration of the Games of Life! Yet, ere the feast proceeds, hear me while I speak--I make my last oration as the arbiter of our funeral sports, as the host of the Banquet of Famine!

'Who would sink ignobly beneath the slow superiority of starvation, or perish under the quickly glancing steel of the barbarian conqueror's sword, when such a death as ours is offered to the choice?--when wine flows bright, to drown sensation in oblivion, and a palace and its treasures furnish alike the scene of the revel and the radiant funeral pile? The mighty philosophers of India--the inspired

Gymnosophists--died as we shall die! Calanus before Alexander, Zamarus in the presence of Augustus, lit the fires that consumed them! Let us follow their glorious example! No worms will prey upon our bodies, no hired mourners will howl discordant at our funerals! Purified in the radiance of primeval fire, we shall vanish triumphant from enemies and friends--a marvel to the earth, a vision of glory to the gods themselves!

'Is it a day more or a day less of life that is now of importance to us? No; it is only towards the easiest and the noblest death that our aspirations can turn! Among our number there is now not one whom the care of existence can further occupy!

'Here, at my right hand, reclines my estimable comrade of a thousand former feasts, Furius Balburius Placidus, who, when we sailed on the Lucrine Lake, was wont to complain of intolerable hardship if a fly settled on the gilded folds of his umbrella; who languished for a land of Cimmerian darkness if a sunbeam penetrated the silken awnings of his garden-terrace; and who now wrangles for a mouthful of horseflesh with the meanest of his slaves, and would exchange the richest of his country villas for a basket of dirty bread! O Furius Balburius Placidus, of what further use is life to thee?

'There, at my left, I discern the changed though still expressive countenance of the resolute Thascius, he who chastised a slave with a hundred lashes if his warm water was not brought immediately at his command; he whose serene contempt for every member of the human species by himself once ranked him among the greatest of human philosophers; even he now wanders through his palace unserved, and fawns upon the plebeian who will sell him a measure of wretched bran! Oh, admired friend, oh, rightly reasoning Thascius, say, is there anything in Rome which should delay thee on thy journey to the Elysian Fields?

'Farther onward at the table, drinking largely while I speak, I behold, O Marcus Moecius Moemmius, thy once plump and jovial form!--thou, in former days accustomed to rejoice in the length of thy name, because it enabled thy friends to drink the more in drinking a cup to each letter of it, tell me what banqueting-hall is now open to thee but this?--and thus desolate in the city of thy social triumphs, what should disincline thee to make of our festal solemnity thy last revel on earth?

'Thou, too, facetious hunchback, prince of parasites, unscrupulous Reburrus, where, but at this banquet of famine, will thy buffoonery now procure for thee a draught of reviving wine? Thy masters have abandoned thee to thy native dunghill! No more shalt thou wheedle for them when they borrow, or bully for them when they pay! No more charges of poisoning or magic shalt thou forge to imprison their troublesome creditors! Oh, officious sycophant, thy occupations are no more! Drink while thou canst, and then resign thy carcass to congenial mire!

'And you, my five remaining friends, whom--little desirous of further delay--I will collectively address, think on the days when the suspicion of an infectious malady in any one of your companions was sufficient to separate you from the dearest of them; when the slaves who came to you from their palaces underwent long ceremonies of ablution before they approached your presence; and remembering this, reflect that most, perhaps all of us, now meet here plague-tainted already; and then say, of what advantage is it to languish for a life which is yours no longer?

'No, my friends, my brethren of the banquet; feeling that when life is worthless it is folly to live, you cannot shrink from the lofty resolution by which we are bound, you cannot pause on our joyful journey of departure from the scenes of earth--I wrong you even by a doubt! Let me now, rather, ask your attention for a worthier subject--the enumeration of the festal ceremonies by which the progress of the banquet will be marked. That task concluded, that last ceremony of my last welcome to you these halls duly performed, I join you once more in your final homage to the deity of our social lives--the God of Wine!

'It is not unknown to you--learned as you are in the jovial antiquities of the table--that it was, among some of the ancients, a custom for a master-spirit of philosophy to preside--the teacher as well as the guest--at their feasts. This usage it has been my care to revive, and, as this four meeting is unparalleled in its heroic design, so it was my ambition to bid to it one unparalleled, either as a teacher or a guest. Fired by an original idea, unobserved of my slaves, aided only by my singing-boy, the faithful Glyco, I have succeeded in placing behind that black curtain such an associate of our revels as you have never feasted with before, whose appearance at the fitting moment must strike you irresistibly with astonishment, and whose discourse--not of human wisdom only--will be inspired by the midnight secrets of the tomb. By my side, on this parchment, lies the formulary of questions to be addressed by Reburrus, when the curtain is withdrawn, to the Oracle of the Mysteries of other Spheres.

'Before you, behold in those vases all that remains of my once well- stocked cellars, and all that is provided for the palates of my guests! We sit at the Banquet of Famine, and no coarser sustenance than inspiring wine finds admittance at the Bacchanalian board. Yet, should any among us, in his last moments, be feeble enough to pollute his lips with nourishment alone worthy of the vermin of the earth, let him seek the wretched and scanty table, type of the wretched and scanty food that covers it, placed yonder in obscurity behind me. There will he find (in all barely sufficient for one man's poorest meal) the last morsels of the vilest nourishment left in the palace. For me, my resolution is fixed--it is only the generous wine-cup that shall now approach my lips!

'Above me are the ten lamps, answering to the number of my friends here assembled. One after another, as the wine overpowers us, those burning images of life will be extinguished in succession by the guests who remain proof against our draughts; and the last of these, lighting this torch at the last lamp, will consummate the banquet, and celebrate its glorious close, by firing the funeral pile of my treasures heaped yonder against my palace walls! If my powers fail me before yours, swear to me that whoever among you is able to lift the cup to his lips after it has dropped from the hands of the rest, will fire the pile! Swear it by your lost mistresses, your lost friends, your lost treasures!--by your own lives, devoted to the pleasures of wine and the purification of fire!'

As, with flashing eyes and flushed countenance, Vetranio sank back on his couch, his companions, inflamed with the wine they had already drunk, arose cup in hand, and turned towards him. Their voices, discordantly mingled, pronounced the oath together; then, as they resumed their former positions, their eyes all turned towards the black curtain in ardent expectation.

They had observed the sinister and sarcastic expression of Vetranio's eye as he spoke of his concealed guest; they knew that the hunchback Reburrus possessed, among his other powers of buffoonery, the art of ventriloquism; and they suspected the presence of some hideous or grotesque image of a heathen god or demon in the hidden recess, which the jugglery of the parasite was to gift with the capacity of speech. Blasphemous comments upon life, death, and immortality were eagerly awaited. The general impatience for the withdrawal of the curtain was perceived by Vetranio, who, waving his hand for silence, authoritatively exclaimed--

'The hour has not yet arrived. More draughts must be drunk, more libations poured out, ere the mystery of the curtain is revealed! Ho, Glyco!' he continued, turning towards the singing-boy, who had silently entered the room, 'the moment is yours! Tune your lyre, and recite my last ode, which I have addressed to you! Let the charms of Poetry preside over the feast of Death!'

The boy advanced, trembling; his once ruddy face was colourless and haggard; his eyes were fixed with a look of rigid terror on the black curtain; his features palpably expressed the presence within him of some secret and overwhelming recollection which had crushed all his other faculties and perceptions. Steadily, almost guiltily, averting his face from his master's countenance, he stood by Vetranio's couch, a frail and fallen being, a mournful spectacle of perverted docility and degraded youth.

Still true, however, to the duties of his vocation, he ran his thin, trembling fingers over the lyre, and mechanically preluded the commencement of the ode. But during the silence of attention which now prevailed, the confused noises from the people in the street penetrated more distinctly into the banqueting-room; and at this moment, high above them all--hoarse, raving, terrible, rose the voice of one man.

'Tell me not,' it cried, 'of perfumes wafted from the palace!--foul vapours flow from it!--see, they sink, suffocating over me!--they bathe sky and earth, and men who move around us, in fierce, green light!'

Then other voices of men and women, shrill and savage, broke forth in interruption together:--'Peace, Davus! you awake the dead about you!' 'Hide in the darkness; you are plague-struck; your skin is shrivelled; your gums are toothless!' 'When the palace is fired you shall be flung into the flames to purify your rotten carcass!'

'Sing!' cried Vetranio furiously, observing the shudders that ran over the boy's frame and held him speechless. 'Strike the lyre, as Timotheus struck it before Alexander! Drown in melody the barking of the curs who wait for our offal in the street!'

Feebly and interruptedly the terrified boy began; the wild continuous noises of the moaning voices from without sounding their awful accompaniment to the infidel philosophy of his song as he breathed it forth in faint and faltering accents. It ran thus:--

TO GLYCO

Ah, Glyco! why in flow'rs array'd? Those festive wreaths less quickly fade Than briefly-blooming joy! Those high-prized friends who share your mirth Are counterfeits of brittle earth, False coin'd in Death's alloy!

The bliss your notes could once inspire, When lightly o'er the god-like lyre Your nimble fingers pass'd, Shall spring the same from others' skill--When you're forgot, the music still The player shall outlast!

The sun-touch'd cloud that mounts the sky, That brightly glows to warm the eye, Then fades we know not where, Is image of the little breath Of life--and then, the doom of Death That you and I must share!

Helpless to make or mar our birth, We blindly grope the ways of earth, And live our paltry hour; Sure, that when life has ceased to please, To die at will, in Stoic ease, Is yielded to our pow'r!

Who, timely wise, would meanly wait The dull delay of tardy Fate, When Life's delights are shorn? No! When its outer gloss has flown, Let's fling the tarnish'd bauble down As lightly as 'twas worn.

'A health to Glyco! A deep draught to a singer from heaven come down upon earth!' cried the guests, seizing their wine-cups, as the ode was concluded, and draining them to the last drop. But their drunken applause fell noiseless upon the ear to which it was addressed. The boy's voice, as he sang the final stanza of the ode, had suddenly changed to a shrill, almost an unearthly tone, then suddenly sank again as he breathed forth the last few notes; and now as his dissolute audience turned towards him with approving glances, they saw him standing before them cold, rigid, and voiceless. The next instant his fixed features were suddenly distorted, his whole frame collapsed as if torn by an internal spasm--he fell back heavily to the floor. Those around approached him with unsteady feet, and raised him in their arms. His soul had burst the bonds of vice in which others had entangled it; the voice of Death had whispered to the slave of the great despot, Crime-'Be free!' 'We have heard the note of the swan singing its own funeral hymn!' said the patrician Placidus, looking in maudlin pity from the corpse of the boy to the face of Vetranio, which presented for the moment an involuntary expression of grief and remorse.

'Our miracle of beauty and boy-god of melody has departed before us to the Elysian fields!' muttered the hunchback Reburrus, in harsh, sarcastic accents.

Then, during the short silence that ensued, the voices from the street, joined on this occasion to a noise of approaching footsteps on the pavement, became again distinctly audible in the banqueting-hall. 'News! news!' cried these fresh auxiliaries of the horde already assembled before the palace. 'Keep together, you who still care for your lives! Solitary citizens have been lured by strange men into desolate streets, and never seen again! Jars of newly salted flesh, which there were no beasts left in the city to supply, have been found in a butcher's shop! Keep together! Keep together!'

'No cannibals among the mob shall pollute the body of my poor boy!' cried Vetranio, rousing himself from his short lethargy of grief. 'Ho! Thascius! Marcus! you who can yet stand! let us bear him to the funeral pile! He has died first--his ashes shall be first consumed!'

The two patricians arose as the senator spoke, and aided him in carrying the body to the lower end of the room, where it was laid across the table, beneath the black curtain, and between the heaps of drapery and furniture piled up against each of the walls. Then, as his guests reeled back to their places, Vetranio, remaining by the side of the corpse, and seizing in his unsteady hands a small vase of wine, exclaimed in tones of fierce exultation: 'The hour has come--the Banquet of Famine has ended--the Banquet of Death has begun! A health to the guest behind the curtain! Fill--drink--behold!'

He drank deeply from the vase as he ceased, and drew aside the black drapery above him. A cry of terror and astonishment burst from the intoxicated guests as they beheld in the recess now disclosed to view the corpse of an aged woman, clothed in white, and propped up on a high, black throne, with the face turned towards them, and the arms (artificially supported) stretched out as if in denunciation over the banqueting-table. The lamp of yellow glass, which burnt high above the body, threw over it a lurid and flickering light; the eyes were open, the jaw had fallen, the long grey tresses drooped heavily on either side of the white hollow cheeks.

'Behold!' cried Vetranio, pointing to the corpse--'Behold my secret guest! Who so fit as the dead to preside at the Banquet of Death? Compelling the aid of Glyco, shrouded by congenial night, seizing on the first corpse exposed before me in the street, I have set up there, unsuspected by all, the proper idol of our worship, and philosopher at our feast! Another health to the queen of the fatal revels--to the teacher of the mysteries of worlds unseen--rescued from rotting unburied, to perish in the consecrated flames with the senators of Rome! A health!--a health to the mighty mother, ere she begin the mystic revelations! Fill--drink!'

Fired by their host's example, recovered from their momentary awe, already inflamed by the mad recklessness of debauchery, the guests started from their couches, and with Bacchanalian shouts answered Vetranio's challenge. The scene at this moment approached the supernatural. The wild disorder of the richly laden tables; the wine flowing over the floor from overthrown vases; the great lamps burning bright and steady over the confusion beneath; the fierce gestures, the disordered countenances of the revellers, as they waved their jewelled cups over their heads in frantic triumph; and then the gloomy and terrific prospect at the lower end of the hall--the black curtain, the light burning solitary on its high pole, the dead boy lying across the festal table, the living master standing by his side, and, like an evil spirit, pointing upward in mockery to the white-robed corpse of the woman, as it towered above all in its unnatural position, with its skinny arms stretched forth, with its ghastly features appearing to move as the faint and flickering light played over them,--produced together such a combination of scarce-earthly objects as might be painted, but cannot be described. It was an embodiment of a sorcerer's vision--an apocalypse of sin triumphing over the world's last relics of mortality in the vaults of death.

'To your task, Reburrus!' cried Vetranio, when the tumult was lulled; 'to your questions without delay! Behold the teacher with whom you are to hold commune! Peruse carefully the parchment in your hand; question, and question loudly--you speak to the apathetic dead!'

For some time before the disclosure of the corpse, the hunchback had been seated apart at the end of the banqueting-hall opposite the black- curtained recess, conning over the manuscript containing the list of questions and answers which formed the impious dialogue he was to hold, by the aid of his powers of ventriloquism, with the violated dead. When the curtain was withdrawn he had looked up for a moment, and had greeted the appearance of the sight behind it with a laugh of brutal derision, returning immediately to the study of his blasphemous formulary which had been confided to his care. At the moment when Vetranio's commands were addressed to him he arose, reeled down the apartment towards the corpse, and, opening the dialogue as he approached it, began in loud jeering tones: 'Speak, miserable relic of decrepit mortality!'

He paused as he uttered the last word, and gaining a point of view from which the light of the lamp fell full upon the solemn and stony features of the corpse, looked up defiantly at it. In an instant a frightful change passed over him, the manuscript dropped from his hand, his deformed frame shrank and tottered, a shrill cry of recognition burst from his lips, more like the yell of a wild beast than the voice of a man.

The next moment, when the guests started up to question or deride him, he turned slowly and faced them. Desperate and drunken as they were, his look awed them into utter silence. His face was deathlike in hue, as the face of the corpse above him--thick drops of perspiration trickled down it like rain--his dry glaring eyes wandered fiercely over the startled countenances before him, and, as he extended towards them his clenched hands, he muttered in a deep gasping whisper: 'Who has done this? MY MOTHER! MY MOTHER!'

As these few words--of awful import though of simple form--fell upon the ears of those whom he addressed, such of them as were not already sunk in insensibility looked round on each other almost sobered for the moment, and all speechless alike. Not even the clash of the wine-cups was now heard at the banqueting-table--nothing was audible but the sound, still fitfully rising and falling, of the voices of terror, ribaldry, and anguish from the street; and the hoarse convulsive accents of the hunchback, still uttering at intervals his fearful identification of the dead body above him: 'MY MOTHER! MY MOTHER!'

At length Vetranio, who was the first to recover himself, addressed the terrified and degraded wretch before him, in tones which, in spite of himself, betrayed, as he began, an unwonted tremulousness and restraint. 'What, Reburrus!' he cried, 'are you already drunken to insanity, that you call the first dead body which by chance I encountered in the street, and by chance brought hither, your mother? Was it to talk of your mother, whom dead or alive we neither know nor care for, that you were admitted here? Son of obscurity and inheritor of rags, what are your plebeian parents to us!' he continued, refilling his cup, and lashing himself into assumed anger as he spoke. 'To your dialogue without delay, or you shall be flung from the windows to mingle with your rabble-equals in the street!'

Neither by word nor look did the hunchback answer the senator's menaces. For him, the voice of the living was stifled in the presence of the dead. The retribution that had gone forth against him had struck his moral, as a thunderbolt might have stricken his physical being. His soul strove in agony within him, as he thought on the awful fatality which had set the dead mother in judgment on the degraded son--which had directed the hand of the senator unwittingly to select the corpse of the outraged parent as the object for the infidel buffoonery of the reckless child, at the very close of his impious career. His past life rose before him, for the first time, like a foul vision, like a nightmare of horror, impurity, and crime. He staggered up the room, groping his way along the wall, as if the darkness of midnight had closed round his eyes, and crouched down by the open window. Beneath him rose the evil and ominous voices from the street; around him spread the pitiless array of his masters; before him appeared the denouncing vision of the corpse.

He would have remained but a short time unmolested in his place of refuge, but for an event which now diverted from him the attention of Vetranio and his guests. Drinking furiously to drown all recollection of the catastrophe they had just witnessed, three of the revellers had already suffered the worst consequences of an excess, which their weakened frames were ill-fitted to bear. One after another, at short intervals, they fell back senseless on their couches; and one after another, as they succumbed, the three lamps burning nearest to them were extinguished. The same speedy termination to the debauch seemed to be in reserve for the rest of their companions, with the exception of Vetranio and the two patricians who reclined at his right hand and his left. These three still preserved the appearance of self-possession, but an ominous change had already overspread their countenances. The expression of wild joviality, of fierce recklessness, had departed from their wild features; they silently watched each other with vigilant and suspicious eyes; each in turn, as he filled his wine-cup, significantly handled the torch with which the last drinker was to fire the funeral pile. As the numbers of their rivals decreased, and the flame of lamp after lamp was extinguished, the fatal contest for a suicide supremacy assumed a present and powerful interest, in which all other purposes and objects were forgotten. The corpse at the foot of the banqueting-table, and the wretch cowering in his misery at the window, were now alike unheeded. In the bewildered and brutalised minds of the guests, one sensation alone remained--the intensity of expectation which precedes the result of a deadly strife.

But ere long--awakening the attention which might otherwise never have been aroused--the voice of the hunchback was heard, as the spirit of repentance now moved within him, uttering, in wild, moaning tones, a strange confession of degradation and sin--addressed to none; proceeding, independent of consciousness or will, from the depths of his stricken soul. He half raised himself, and fixed his sunken eyes upon the dead body, as these words dropped from his lips: 'It was the last time that I beheld her alive, when she approached me--lonely, and feeble, and poor--in the street, beseeching me to return to her in the days of her old age and her solitude, and to remember how she had loved me in my childhood for my very deformity, how she had watched me throughout the highways of Rome, that none should oppress or deride me! The tears ran down her cheeks, she knelt to me on the hard pavement, and I, who had deserted her for her poverty, to make myself a slave in palaces among the accursed rich, flung down money to her as to a beggar who wearied me, and passed on! She died desolate; her body lay unburied, and I knew it not! The son who had abandoned the mother never saw her more, until she rose before him there--avenging, horrible, lifeless--a sight of death never to leave him! Woe, woe to the accursed in his deformity, and the accursed of his mother's corpse!'

He paused, and fell back again to the ground, grovelling and speechless. The tyrannic Thascius, regarding him with a scowl of drunken wrath, seized an empty vase, and poising it in his unsteady hand, prepared to hurl it at the hunchback's prostrate form, when again a single cry--a woman's--rising above the increasing uproar in the street, rang shrill and startling through the banqueting-hall. The patrician suspended his purpose as he heard it, mechanically listening with the half-stupid, half-cunning attention of intoxication. 'Help! help!' shrieked the voice beneath the palace windows--'he follows me still--he attacked my dead child in my arms! As I flung myself down upon it on the ground, I saw him watching his opportunity to drag it by the limbs from under me--famine and madness were in his eyes--I drove him back--I fled--he follows me still!--save us, save us!'

At this instant her voice was suddenly stifled in the sound of fierce cries and rushing footsteps, followed by an appalling noise of heavy blows, directed at several points, against the steel railings before the palace doors. Between the blows, which fell slowly and together at regular intervals, the infuriated wretches, whose last exertions of strength were strained to the utmost to deal them, could be heard shouting breathlessly to each other: 'Strike harder, strike harder! the back gates are guarded against us by our comrades admitted to the pillage of the palace instead of us. You who would share the booty, strike firm! the stones are at your feet, the gates of entrance yield before you.'

Meanwhile a confused sound of trampling footsteps and contending voices became audible from the lower apartments of the palace. Doors were violently shut and opened--shouts and execrations echoed and re-echoed along the lofty stone passages leading from the slaves' waiting-rooms to the grand staircase; treachery betrayed itself as openly within the building as violence still proclaimed itself in the assault on the gates outside. The chief slaves had not been suspected by their fellows without a cause; the bands of pillage and murder had been organised in the house of debauchery and death; the chosen adherents from the street had been secretly admitted through the garden gates, and had barred and guarded them against further intrusion--another doom than the doom they had impiously prepared for themselves was approaching the devoted senators, at the hands of the slaves whom they had oppressed, and the plebeians whom they had despised.

At the first sound of the assault without and the first intimation of the treachery within, Vetranio, Thascius, and Marcus started from their couches; the remainder of the guests, incapable either of thought or action, lay, in stupid insensibility, awaiting their fate. These three men alone comprehended the peril that threatened them, and, maddened with drink, defied, in their ferocious desperation, the death that was in store for them. 'Hark! they approach, the rabble revolted from our rule,' cried Vetranio scornfully, 'to take the lives that we despise and the treasures that we have resigned! The hour has come; I go to fire the pile that involves in one common destruction our assassins and ourselves!'

'Hold!' exclaimed Thascius, snatching the torch from his hand; 'the entrance must first be defended, or, ere the flames are kindled, the slaves will be here! Whatever is movable--couches, tables, corpses--let us hurl them all against the door!'

As he spoke he rushed towards the black-curtained recess, to set the example to his companions by seizing the corpse of the woman; but he had not passed more than half the length of the apartment, when the hunchback, who had followed him unheeded, sprang upon him from behind, and, with a shrill cry, fastening his fingers on his throat, hurled him torn and senseless to the floor. 'Who touches the body that is mine?' shrieked the deformed wretch, rising from his victim, and threatening with his blood-stained hands Vetranio and Marcus, as they stood bewildered, and uncertain for the moment whether first to avenge their comrade or to barricade the door--'The son shall rescue the mother! I go to bury her! Atonement! Atonement!'

He leaped upon the table as he spoke, tore asunder with resistless strength the cords which fastened the corpse to the throne, seized it in his arms, and the next instant gained the door. Uttering fierce, inarticulate cries, partly of anguish and partly of defiance, he threw it open, and stepped forward to descend, when he was met at the head of the stairs by the band of assassins hurrying up, with drawn swords and blazing torches, to their work of pillage and death. He stood before them--his deformed limbs set as firmly on the ground as if he were preparing to descend the stairs at one leap--with the corpse raised high on his breast; its unearthly features were turned towards them, its bare arms were still stretched forth as they had been extended over the banqueting-table, its grey hair streamed back and mingled with his own: under the fitful illumination of the torches, which played red and wild over him and his fearful burden, the dead and the living looked joined to each other in one monstrous form.

Huddled together, motionless, on the stairs, their shouts of vengeance and fury frozen on their lips, the assassins stood for one moment, staring mechanically, with fixed, spell-bound eyes, upon the hideous bulwark opposing their advance on the victims whom they had expected so easily to surprise. The next instant a superstitious panic seized them; as the hunchback suddenly moved towards them to descend, the corpse seemed to their terror-stricken eyes to be on the eve of bursting its way through their ranks. Ignorant of its introduction into the palace, imagining it, in the revival of their slavish fears, to be the spectral offspring of the magic incantations of the senators above, they turned with one accord and fled down the stairs. The sound of their cries of fear grew fainter and fainter in the direction of the garden as they hurried through the secret gates at the back of the building. Then the heavy, regular tamp of the hunchback's footsteps, as he paced the solitary corridors after them, bearing his burden of death, became audible in awful distinctness; then that sound also died away and was lost, and nothing more was heard in the banqueting-room save the sharp clang of the blows still dealt against the steel railings from the street.

But now these grew rare and more rare in their recurrence; the strong metal resisted triumphantly the utmost efforts of the exhausted rabble who assailed it. As the minutes moved on, the blows grew rapidly fainter and fewer; soon they diminished to three, struck at long intervals; soon to one, followed by deep execrations of despair; and, after that, a great silence sank down over the palace and the street, where such strife and confusion had startled the night-echoes but a few moments before.

In the banqueting-hall this rapid succession of events--the marvels of a few minutes--passed before Vetranio and Marcus as visions beheld by their eyes, but neither contained nor comprehended by their minds. Stolid in their obstinate recklessness, stupefied by the spectacle of the startling perils--menacing yet harmless, terrifying though transitory--which surrounded them, neither of the senators moved a muscle or uttered a word, from the period when Thascius had fallen beneath the hunchback's attack, to the period when the last blow against the palace railings, and the last sound of voices from the street, had ceased in silence. Then the wild current of drunken exultation, suspended within them during this brief interval, flowed once more, doubly fierce, in its old course. Insensible, the moment after they had passed away, to the warning and terrific scenes they had beheld, each now looked round on the other with a glance of triumphant levity. 'Hark!' cried Vetranio, 'the mob without, feeble and cowardly to the last, abandon their puny efforts to force my palace gates! Behold our banqueting-tables still sacred from the intrusion of the revolted menials, driven before my guest from the dead, like a flock of sheep before a single dog! Say, O Marcus! did I not well to set the corpse at the foot of our banqueting-table? What marvels has it not effected, borne before us by the frantic Reburrus, as a banner of the hosts of death, against the cowardly slaves whose fit inheritance is oppression, and whose sole sensation is fear! See, we are free to continue and conclude the banquet as we had designed! The gods themselves have interfered to raise us in security above our fellow-mortals, whom we despise! Another health, in gratitude to our departed guest, the instrument of our deliverance, under the auspices of omnipotent Jove!'

As Vetranio spoke, Marcus alone, out of all the revellers, answered his challenge. These two--the last-remaining combatants of the strife--having drained their cups to the health proposed, passed slowly down each side of the room, looking contemptuously on their prostrate companions, and extinguishing every lamp but the two which burnt over their own couches. Then returning to the upper end of the tables, they resumed their places, not to leave them again until the fatal rivalry was finally decided, and the moment of firing the pile had actually arrived.

The torch lay between them; the last vases of wine stood at their sides. Not a word escaped the lips of either, to break the deep stillness prevailing over the palace. Each fixed his eyes on the other, in stern and searching scrutiny, and cup for cup, drank in slow and regular alternation. The debauch, which had hitherto presented a spectacle of brutal degradation and violence, now that it was restricted to two men only--each equally unimpressed by the scenes of horror he had beheld, each vying with the other for the attainment of the supreme of depravity--assumed an appearance of hardly human iniquity; it became a contest for a satanic superiority of sin.

For some time little alteration appeared in the countenances of either of the suicide-rivals; but they had now drunk to that final point of excess at which wine either acts as its own antidote, or overwhelms in fatal suffocation the pulses of life. The crisis in the strife was approaching for both, and the first to experience it was Marcus. Vetranio, as he watched him, observed a dark purple flush overspreading his face, hitherto pale, almost colourless. His eyes suddenly dilated; he panted for breath. The vase of wine, when he strove with a last effort to fill his cup from it, rolled from his hand to the floor. The stare of death was in his face as he half-raised himself and for one instant looked steadily on his companion; the moment after, without word or groan, he dropped backward over his couch.

The contest of the night was decided! The host of the banquet and the master of the palace had been reserved to end the one and to fire the other!

A smile of malignant triumph parted Vetranio's lips as he now arose and extinguished the last lamp burning besides his own. That done, he grasped the torch. His eyes, as he raised it, wandered dreamily over the array of his treasures, and the forms of his dead or insensible fellow-patricians around him, to be consumed by his act in annihilating fire. The sensation of his solemn night-solitude in his fated palace began to work in vivid and varying impressions on his mind, which was partially recovering some portion of its wonted acuteness, under the bodily reaction now produced in him by the very extravagance of the night's excess. His memory began to retrace confusedly the scenes with which the dwelling that he was about to destroy had been connected at distant or at recent periods. At one moment the pomp of former banquets, the jovial congregation of guests since departed or dead, revived before him; at another, he seemed to be acting over again his secret departure from his dwelling on the night before his last feast, his stealthy return with the corpse that he had dragged from the street, his toil in setting it up in mockery behind the black curtain, and inventing the dialogue to be spoken before it by the hunchback. Now his thoughts reverted to the minutest circumstances of the confusion and dismay among the members of his household when the first extremities of the famine began to be felt in the city; and now, without visible connection or cause, they turned suddenly to the morning when he had hurried through the most solitary paths in his grounds to meet the betrayer Ulpius at Numerian's garden gate. Once more the image of Antonina--so often present to his imagination since the original was lost to his eyes--grew palpable before him. He thought of her, as listening at his knees to the sound of his lute; as awakening, bewildered and terrified, in his arms; as flying distractedly before her father's wrath; as now too surely lying dead, in her beauty and her innocence, amid the thousand victims of the famine and the plague.

These and other reflections, while they crowded in whirlwind rapidity on his mind, wrought no alteration in the deadly purpose which they suspended. His delay in lighting the torch was the unconscious delay of the suicide, secure in his resolution ere he lifts the poison to his lips--when life rises before him as a thing that is past, and he stands for one tremendous moment in the dark gap between the present and the future--no more the pilgrim of Time--not yet the inheritor of Eternity!

So, in the dimly lighted hall, surrounded by the victims whom he had hurried before him to their doom, stood the lonely master of the great palace; and so spoke within him the mysterious voices of his last earthly thoughts. Gradually they sank and ceased, and stillness and vacancy closed like dark veils over his mind. Starting like one awakened from a trance he once more felt the torch in his hand, and once more the expression of fierce desperation appeared in his eyes as he lit it steadily at the lamp above him.

The dew was falling pure to the polluted earth; the light breezes sang their low daybreak anthem among the leaves to the Power that bade them forth; night had expired, and morning was already born of it, as Vetranio, with the burning torch in his hand, advanced towards the funeral pile.

He had already passed the greater part of the length of the room, when a faint sound of footsteps ascending a private staircase which led to the palace gardens, and communicated with the lower end of the banqueting- hall by a small door of inlaid ivory, suddenly attracted his attention. He hesitated in his deadly purpose, listening to the slow, regular approaching sound, which, feeble though it was, struck mysteriously impressive upon his ear in the dreary silence of all things around him. Holding the torch high above his head, as the footsteps came nearer, he fixed his eyes in intense expectation upon the door. It opened, and the figure of a young girl clothed in white stood before him. One moment he looked upon her with startled eyes; the next the torch dropped from his hand, and smouldered unheeded on the marble floor. It was Antonina!

Her face was overspread with a strange transparent paleness; her once soft, round cheeks had lost their girlish beauty of form; her expression, ineffably mournful, hopeless, and subdued, threw a simple, spiritual solemnity over her whole aspect. She was changed, awfully changed to the profligate senator from the being of his former admiration; but still there remained in her despairing eyes enough of the old look of gentleness and patience, surviving through all anguish and dread, to connect her, even as she was now, with what she had been. She stood in the chamber of debauchery and suicide between the funeral pile and the desperate man who was vowed to fire it, a feeble, helpless creature, yet powerful in the influence of her presence, at such a moment and in such a form, as a saving and reproving spirit, armed with the omnipotence of Heaven to mould the purposes of man.

Awed and astounded, as if he beheld an apparition from the tomb, Vetranio looked upon this young girl--whom he had loved with the least selfish passion that ever inspired him; whom he had lamented as long since lost and dead with the sincerest grief he had ever felt; whom he now saw standing before him at the very moment ere he doomed himself to death, altered, desolate, supplicating-- with emotions which held him speechless in wonder, and even in dread. While he still gazed upon her in silence, he heard her speaking to him in low, melancholy, imploring accents, which fell upon his ear, after the voices of terror and desperation that had risen around him throughout the night, like tones never addressed to it before.

'Numerian, my father, is sinking under the famine,' she began; 'if no help is given to him, he may die even before sunrise! You are rich and powerful; I have come to you, having nothing now but his life to live for, to beg sustenance for him!' She paused, overpowered for the moment, and bent her eyes wistfully on the senator's face. Then seeing that he vainly endeavoured to answer her, her head drooped upon her breast, and her voice sank lower as she continued:--

'I have striven for patience under much sorrow and pain through the long night that is past; my eyes were heavy and my spirit was faint; I could have rendered up my soul willingly in my loneliness and feebleness to God who gave it, but that it was my duty to struggle for my life and my father's, now that I was restored to him after I had lost all beside! I could not think, or move, or weep, as, looking forth upon your palace, I watched and waited through the hours of darkness. But, as morning dawned, the heaviness at my heart was lightened; I remembered that the palace I saw before me was yours; and, though the gates were closed, I knew that I could reach it through your garden that joins to my father's land. I had none in Rome to ask mercy of but you; so I set forth hastily, ere my weakness should overpower me, remembering that I had inherited much misery at your hands, but hoping that you might pity me for what I had suffered when you saw me again. I came wearily through the garden; it was long before I found my way hither; will you send me back as helpless as I came? You first taught me to dis-obey my father in giving me the lute; will you refuse to aid me in succouring him now? He is all that I have left in the world! Have mercy upon him!--have mercy upon me!'

Again she looked up in Vetranio's face. His trembling lips moved, but still no sound came from them. The expression of confusion and awe yet prevailed over his features as he pointed slowly towards the upper end of the banqueting-table. To her this simple action was eloquent beyond all power of speech; she turned her feeble steps instantly in the direction he had indicated.

He watched her, by the light of the single lamp that still burnt, passing--strong in the shielding inspiration of her good purpose--amid the bodies of his suicide com-panions without pausing on her way. Having gained the upper end of the room, she took from the table a flask of wine, and from the wooden stand behind it the bowl of offal disdained by the guests at the fatal banquet, returning immediately to the spot where Vetranio still stood. Here she stopped for a moment, as if about to speak once more; but her emotions overpowered her. From the sources which despair and suffering had dried up, the long-prisoned tears once more flowed forth at the bidding of gratitude and hope. She looked upon the senator, silent as himself, and her expression at that instant was destined to remain on his memo-ry while memory survived. Then, with faltering and hasty steps, she departed by the way she had come; and in the great palace, which his evil supremacy over the wills of others had made a hideous charnel-house, he was once more left alone.

He made no effort to follow or detain her as she left him. The torch still smoul-dered beside him on the floor, but he never stooped to take it up; he dropped down on a vacant couch, stupefied by what he had beheld. That which no entreaties, no threats, no fierce violence of opposition could have effected in him, the appearance of Antonina had produced--it had forced him to pause at the very moment of the execution of his deadly design.

He remembered how, from the very first day when he had seen her, she had mysteriously influenced the whole progress of his life; how his ardour to possess her had altered his occupations, and even interrupted his amusements; how all his energy and all his wealth had been baffled in the attempt to discover her when she fled from her father's house; how the first feeling of remorse that he had ever known had been awakened within him by his knowledge of the share he had had in producing her unhappy fate.   Recalling all this; reflecting that, had she approached him at an earlier period, she would have been driven back affrighted by the drunken clamour of his companions; and had she arrived at a later, would have found his palace in flames; thinking at the same time of her sudden presence in the banqueting-hall when he had believed her to be dead, when her appearance at the moment before he fired the pile was most irresistible in its supernatural influence over his actions--that vague feeling of superstitious dread which exists intuitively in all men's minds, which had never before been aroused in his, thrilled through him.   His eyes were fixed on the door by which she had departed, as if he expected her to return.   Her destiny seemed to be portentously mingled with his own; his life seemed to move, his death to wait at her bidding.   There was no repentance, no moral purification in the emotions which now suspended his bodily faculties in inaction; he was struck for the time with a mental paralysis.

The restless moments moved onward and onward, and still he delayed the consummation of the ruin which the night's debauch had begun.   Slowly the tender daylight grew and brightened in its beauty, warmed the cold prostrate bodies in the silent hall, and dimmed the faint glow of the wasting lamp; no black mist of smoke, no red glare of devouring fire arose to quench its fair lustre; no roar of flames interrupted the murmuring morning tranquillity of nature, or startled from their heavy repose the exhausted outcasts stretched upon the pavement of the street. Still the noble palace stood unshaken on its firm foundations; still the adornments of its porticoes and its statues glittered as of old in the rays of the rising sun; and still the hand of the master who had sworn to destroy it, as he had sworn to destroy himself, hung idly near the torch which lay already extinguished in harmless ashes at his feet.

Chapter 23

THE LAST EFFORTS OF THE BESIEGED

We return to the street before the palace. The calamities of the siege had fallen fiercely on those who lay there during the night. From the turbulent and ferocious mob of a few hours since, not even the sound of a voice was now heard. Some, surprised in a paroxysm of hunger by exhaustion and insensibility, lay with their hands half forced into their mouths, as if in their ravenous madness they had endeavoured to prey upon their own flesh. Others now and then wearily opened their languid eyes upon the street, no longer regardful, in the present extremity of their sufferings, of the building whose destruction they had assembled to behold, but watching for a fancied realisation of the visions of richly spread tables and speedy relief called up before them, as if in mockery, by the delirium of starvation and disease.

The sun had as yet but slightly risen above the horizon, when the attention of the few among the populace who still preserved some perception of outward events was suddenly attracted by the appearance of an irregular procession--composed partly of citizens and partly of officers of the Senate, and headed by two men-- which slowly approached from the end of the street leading into the interior of the city. This assembly of persons stopped opposite Vetranio's palace; and then such members of the mob who watched them as were not yet entirely abandoned by hope, heard the inspiring news that the procession they beheld was a procession of peace, and that the two men who headed it were the Spaniard, Basilius, a governor of a province, and Johannes, the chief of the Imperial notaries--appointed ambassadors to conclude a treaty with the Goths.

As this intelligence reached them, men who had before appeared incapable of the slightest movement now rose painfully, yet resolutely, to their feet, and crowded round the two ambassadors as round two angels descended to deliver them from bondage and death. Meanwhile, some officers of the Senate, finding the front gates of the palace closed against them, proceeded to the garden entrance at the back of the building, to obtain admission to its owner. The absence of Vetranio and his friends from the deliberations of the government had been attributed to their disgust at the obstinate and unavailing resistance offered to the Goths. Now, therefore, when submission had been resolved upon, it had been thought both expedient and easy to recall them peremptorily to their duties. In addition to this motive for seeking the interior of the palace, the servants of the Senate had another errand to perform there. The widely rumoured determination of Vetranio and his associates to destroy themselves by fire, in the frenzy of a last debauch--disbelieved or disregarded while the more imminent perils of the city were under consideration--became a source of some apprehension and anxiety to the acting members of the Roman council, now that their minds were freed from part of the responsibility which had weighed on them, by their resolution to treat for peace.

Accordingly, the persons now sent into the palace were charged with the duty of frustrating its destruction, if such an act had been really contemplated, as well as the duty of recalling its inmates to their appointed places in the Senate-house. How far they were enabled, at the time of their entrance into the banqueting-hall, to accomplish their double mission, the reader is well able to calculate. They found Vetranio still in the place which he had occupied since Antonina had quitted him. Startled by their approach from the stupor which had hitherto weighed on his faculties, the desperation of his purpose returned; he made an effort to tear from its place the lamp which still feebly burned, and to fire the pile in defiance of all opposition. But his strength, already taxed to the utmost, failed him. Uttering impotent threats of resistance and revenge, he fell, swooning and helpless, into the arms of the officers of the Senate who held him back. One of them was immediately dismissed, while his companions remained in the palace, to communicate with the leaders of the assembly outside. His report concluded, the two ambassadors moved slowly onward, separating themselves from the procession which had accompanied them, and followed only by a few chosen attendants--a mournful and a degraded embassy, sent forth by the people who had once imposed their dominion, their customs, and even their language, on the Eastern and Western worlds, to bargain with the barbarians whom their fathers had enslaved for the purchase of a disgraceful peace.

On the departure of the ambassadors, all the spectators still capable of the effort repaired to the Forum to await their return, and were joined there by members of the populace from other parts of the city. It was known that the first intimation of the result of the embassy would be given from this place; and in the eagerness of their anxiety to hear it, in the painful intensity of their final hopes of deliverance, even death itself seemed for a while to be arrested in its fatal progress through the ranks of the besieged.

In silence and apprehension they counted the tardy moments of delay, and watched with sickening gaze the shadows lessening and lessening, as the sun gradually rose in the heavens to the meridian point.

At length, after an absence that appeared of endless duration, the two ambassadors re-entered Rome. Neither of them spoke as they hurriedly passed through the ranks of the people; but their looks of terror and despair were all-eloquent to every beholder--their mission had failed.

For some time no member of the government appeared to have resolution enough to come forward and harangue the people on the subject of the unsuccessful embassy. After a long interval, however, the Prefect Pompeianus himself, urged partly by the selfish entreaties of his friends, and partly by the childish love of display which still adhered to him through all his present anxieties and apprehensions, stepped into one of the lower balconies of the Senate-house to address the citizens beneath him.

The chief magistrate of Rome was no longer the pompous and portly personage whose intrusion on Vetranio's privacy during the commencement of the siege has been described previously. The little superfluous flesh still remaining on his face hung about it like an ill-fitting garment; his tones had become lachrymose; the oratorical gestures, with which he was wont to embellish profusely his former speeches, were all abandoned; nothing remained of the original man but the bombast of his language and the impudent complacency of his self-applause, which now appeared in contemptible contrast to his crestfallen demeanour and his disheartening narrative of degradation and defeat.

'Men of Rome, let each of you exercise in his own person the heroic virtues of a Regulus or a Cato!' the prefect began. 'A treaty with the barbarians is out of our power. It is the scourge of the empire, Alaric himself, who commands the invading forces! Vain were the dignified remonstrances of the grave Basilius, futile was the persuasive rhetoric of the astute Johannes, addressed to the slaughtering and vainglorious Goth! On their admission to his presence, the ambassadors, anxious to awe him into a capitulation, enlarged, with sagacious and commendable patriotism, on the expertness of the Romans in the use of arms, their readiness for war, and their vast numbers within the city walls. I blush to repeat the barbarian's reply. Laughing immoderately, he answered, "The thicker the grass, the easier it is to cut!"

'Still undismayed, the ambassadors, changing their tactics, talked indulgently of their willingness to purchase a peace. At this proposal, his insolence burst beyond all bounds of barbarous arrogance. "I will not relinquish the siege," he cried, "until I have delivered to me all the gold and silver in the city, all the household goods in it, and all the slaves from the northern countries." "What then, O King, will you leave us?" asked our amazed ambassadors. "YOUR LIVES!" answered the implacable Goth. Hearing this, even the resolute Basilius and the wise Johannes despaired. They asked time to communicate with the Senate, and left the camp of the enemy without further delay. Such was the end of the embassy; such the arrogant ferocity of the barbarian foe!'

Here the Prefect paused, from sheer weakness and want of breath. His oration, however, was not concluded. He had disheartened the people by his narrative of what had occurred to the ambassadors; he now proceeded to console them by his relation of what had occurred to himself, when, after an interval, he thus resumed:--

'But even yet, O citizens of Rome, it is not time to despair! There is another chance of deliverance still left to us, and that chance has been discovered by me. It was my lot, during the absence of the ambassadors, to meet with certain men of Tuscany, who had entered Rome a few days before the beginning of the siege, and who spoke of a project for relieving the city which they would communicate to the Prefect alone. Ever anxious for the public welfare, daring all treachery from strangers for advantage of my office, I accorded to these men a secret interview. They told me of a startling and miraculous event. The town of Neveia, lying, as you well know, in the direct road of the barbarians when they marched upon Rome, was protected from their pillaging bands by a tempest of thunder and lightning terrible to behold. This tempest arose not, as you may suppose, from an accidental convulsion of the elements, but was launched over the heads of the invaders by the express interference of the tutelary deities of the town, invocated by the inhabitants, who returned in their danger to the practice of their ancient manner of worship. So said the men of Tuscany; and such pious resources as those employed by the people of Neveia did they recommend to the people of Rome! For my part, I acknowledge to you that I have faith in their project. The antiquity of our former worship is still venerable in my eyes. The prayers of the priests of our new religion have wrought no miraculous interference in our behalf: let us therefore imitate the example of the inhabitants of Neveia, and by the force of our invocations hurl the thunders of Jupiter on the barbarian camp! Let us trust for deliverance to the potent interposition of the gods whom our fathers worshipped--those gods who now, perhaps, avenge themselves for our desertion of their temples by our present calamities. I go without delay to propose to the Bishop Innocentius and to the Senate, the public performance of solemn cere- monies of sacrifice at the Capitol! I leave you in the joyful assurance that the gods, appeased by our returning fidelity to our altars, will not refuse the super- natural protection which they accorded to the people of a provincial town to the citizens of Rome!'

No sounds either of applause or disapprobation followed the Prefect's notable proposal for delivering the city from the besiegers by the public apostasy of the besieged. As he disappeared from their eyes, the audience turned away speechless. An universal despair now overpowered in them even the last energies of discord and crime; they resigned themselves to their doom with the gloomy indifference of beings in whom all mortal sensations, all human passions, good or evil, were extinguished. The Prefect departed on his ill-omened expedition to propose the practice of Paganism to the bishop of a Christian church; but no profitable effort for relief was even suggested, either by the government or the people.

And so this day drew in its turn towards a close--more mournful and more disas- trous, more fraught with peril, misery, and gloom, than the days that had pre- ceded it.

The next morning dawned, but no preparations for the ceremonies of the ancient worship appeared at the Capitol. The Senate and the bishop hesitated to incur the responsibility of authorising a public restoration of Paganism; the citizens, hopeless of succour, heavenly or earthly, remained unheedful as the dead of all that passed around them.

There was one man in Rome who might have succeeded in rousing their languid energies to apostasy; but where and how employed was he?

Now, when the opportunity for which he had laboured resolutely, though in vain, through a long existence of suffering, degradation, and crime, had gratuitously presented itself more tempting and more favourable than even he in his wildest visions of success had ever dared to hope--where was Ulpius? Hidden from men's eyes, like a foul reptile, in his lurking-place in the deserted temple--now raving round his idols in the fury of madness, now prostrate before them in idiot adoration--weaker for the interests of his worship, at the crisis of its fate, than the weakest child crawling famished through the streets--the victim of his own evil machinations at the very moment when they might have led him to triumph--the object of that worst earthly retribution, by which the wicked are at once thwarted, doomed, and punished, here as hereafter, through the agency of their own sins.

Three more days passed. The Senate, their numbers fast diminishing in the pestilence, occupied the time in vain deliberations or in moody silence. Each morning the weary guards looked forth from the ramparts, with the fruitless hope of discerning the long-promised legions from Ravenna on their way to Rome; and each morning devastation and death gained ground afresh among the hapless besieged.

At length, on the fourth day, the Senate abandoned all hope of further resistance and determined on submission, whatever might be the result. it was resolved that another embassy, composed of the whole acting Senate, and followed by a considerable train, should proceed to Alaric; that one more effort should be made to induce him to abate his ruinous demands on the conquered; and that if this failed, the gates should be thrown open, and the city and the people abandoned to his mercy in despair.

As soon as the procession of this last Roman embassy was formed in the Forum, its numbers were almost immediately swelled, in spite of opposition, by those among the mass of the people who were still able to move their languid and diseased bodies, and who, in the extremity of their misery, had determined at all hazards to take advantage of the opening of the gates, and fly from the city of pestilence in which they were immured, careless whether they perished on the swords of the Goths or languished unaided on the open plains. All power of enforcing order had long since been lost; the few soldiers gathered about the senators made one abortive effort to drive the people back, and then resigned any further resistance to their will.

Feebly and silently the spirit-broken assembly now moved along the great highways, so often trodden, to the roar of martial music and the shouts of applauding multitudes, by the triumphal processions of victorious Rome; and from every street, as it passed on, the wasted forms of the people stole out like spectres to join it.

Among these, as the embassy approached the Pincian Gate, were two, hurrying forth to herd with their fellow-sufferers, on whose fortunes in the fallen city our more particular attention has been fixed. To explain their presence on the scene (if such an explanation be required) it is necessary to digress for a moment from the progress of events during the last days of the siege to the morning when Antonina departed from Vetranio's palace to return with her succour of food and wine to her father's house.

The reader is already acquainted, from her own short and simple narrative, with the history of the closing hours of her mournful night vigil by the side of her sinking parent, and with the motives which prompted her to seek the palace of the senator, and entreat assistance in despair from one whom she only remembered as the profligate destroyer of her tranquility under her father's roof. It is now, therefore, most fitting to follow her on her way back through the palace gardens. No living creature but herself trod the grassy paths, along which she hastened with faltering steps--those paths which she dimly remembered to have first explored when in former days she ventured forth to follow the distant sounds of Vetranio's lute.

In spite of her vague, heavy sensations of solitude and grief, this recollection remained painfully present to her mind, unaccountably mingled with the dark and dreary apprehension which filled her heart as she hurried onward, until she once more entered her father's dwelling; and then, as she again approached his couch, every other feeling became absorbed in a faint, overpowering fear, lest, after all her perseverance and success in her errand of filial devotion, she might have returned too late.

The old man still lived--his weary eyes opened gladly on her, when she aroused him to partake of the treasured gifts from the senator's banqueting table. The wretched food which the suicide-guests had disdained, and the simple flask of wine which they would have carelessly quaffed at one draught, were viewed both by parent and child as the saving and invigorating sustenance of many days. After having consumed as much as they dared of their precarious supply, the remainder was carefully husbanded. It was the last sign and promise of life to which they looked--the humble yet precious store in which alone they beheld the earnest of their security, for a few days longer, from the pangs of famine and the separation of death.

And now, with their small provision of food and wine set like a beacon of safety before their sight, a deep, dream-like serenity--the sleep of the oppressed and wearied faculties--arose over their minds. Under its mysterious and tranquilising influence, all impressions of the gloom and misery in the city, of the fatal evidences around them of the duration of the siege, faded away before their perceptions as dim retiring objects, which the eye loses in vacancy.

Gradually, as the day of the first unsuccessful embassy declined, their thoughts began to flow back gently to the world of bygone events which had crumbled into oblivion beneath the march of time. Her first recollections of her earliest child-hood revived in Antonina's memory, and then mingled strangely with tearful remembrances of the last words and looks of the young warrior who had expired by her side, and with calm, solemn thoughts that the beloved spirit, emancipated from the sphere of shadows, might now be hovering near the quiet garden-grave where her bitterest tears of loneliness and affliction had been shed, or moving around her--an invisible and blessed presence--as she sat at her father's feet and mourned their earthly separation!

In the emotions thus awakened, there was nothing of bitterness or agony--they calmed and purified the heart through which they moved. She could now speak to the old man, for the first time, of her days of absence from him, of the brief joys and long sorrows of her hours of exile, without failing in her melancholy tale. Sometimes her father listened to her in sorrowful and speechless attention; or spoke, when she paused, of consolation and hope, as she had heard him speak among his congregation while he was yet strong in his resolution to sacrifice all things for the reformation of the Church. Sometimes resigning himself to the influence of his thoughts, as they glided back to the times that were gone, he again revealed to her the changing events of his past life--not as before, with unsteady accents and wandering eyes; but now with a calmness of voice and a coherence of language which forbade her to doubt the strange and startling narrative that she heard.

Once more he spoke of the image of his lost brother (as he had parted from him in his boyhood) still present to his mind; of the country that he had quitted in after years; of the name that he had changed--from Cleander to Numerian--to foil his former associates, if they still pursued him; and of the ardent desire to behold again the companion of his first home, which now, when his daughter was restored to him, when no other earthly aspiration but this was unsatisfied, remained at the close of his life, the last longing wish of his heart.

Such was the communion in which father and daughter passed the hours of their short reprieve from the judgment of famine pronounced against the city of their sojourn; so did they live, as it were, in a quiet interval of existence, in a tranquil pause between the toil that is over and the toil that is to come in the hard labour of life.

But the term to these short days of repose after long suffering and grief was fast approaching. The little hoard of provision diminished as rapidly as the stores that had been anxiously collected before it; and, on the morning of the second embassy to Alaric, the flask of wine and the bowl of food were both emptied. The brief dream of security was over and gone; the terrible realities of the struggle for life had begun again!

Where or to whom could they now turn for help? The siege still continued; the food just exhausted was the last food that had been left on the senator's table; to seek the palace again would be to risk refusal, perhaps insult, as the result of a second entreaty for aid, where all power of conferring it might now but too surely be lost. Such were the thoughts of Antonina as she returned the empty bowl to its former place; but she gave them no expression in words.

She saw, with horror, that the same expression of despair, almost of frenzy, which had distorted her father's features on the day of her restoration to him, now marked them again. Once more he tottered towards the window, murmuring in his bitter despondency against the delusive security and hope which had held him idle for the interests of his child during the few days that were past. But, as he now looked out on the beleaguered city, he saw the populace hastening along the gloomy street beneath, as rapidly as their wearied limbs would carry them, to join the embassy. He heard them encouraging each other to proceed, to seize the last chance of escaping through the open gates from the horrors of famine and plague; and caught the infection of the recklessness and despair which had seized his fellow-sufferers from one end of Rome to the other.

Turning instantly, he grasped his daughter's hand and drew her from the room, commanding her to come forth with him and join the citizens in their flight, ere it was too late. Startled by his words and actions, she vainly endeavoured, as she obeyed, to impress her father with the dread of the Goths which her own bitter experience taught her to feel, now that her only protector among them lay cold in the grave. With Numerian, as with the rest of the people, all apprehension, all doubt, all exercise of reason, was overpowered by the one eager idea of escaping from the fatal precincts of Rome.

So they mingled with the throng, herding affrightedly together in the rear of the embassy, and followed in their ranks as best they might.

The sun shone down brightly from the pure blue sky; the wind bore into the city the sharp threatening notes of the trumpets from the Gothic camp, as the Pincian Gate was opened to the ambassadors and their train. With one accord the crowd instantly endeavoured to force their way out after them in a mass; but they now moved in a narrow space, and were opposed by a large reinforcement of the city guard. After a short struggle they were overpowered, and the gates were closed. Some few of the strongest and the foremost of their numbers succeeded in following the ambassadors; the greater part, however, remained on the inner side of the gate, pressing closely up to it in their impatience and despair, like prisoners awaiting their deliverance, or preparing to force their escape.

Among these, feeblest amid the most feeble, were Numerian and Antonina, hemmed in by the surrounding crowd, and shut out either from flight from the city or a return to home.

Chapter 24

THE GRAVE AND THE CAMP

While the second and last embassy from the Senate proceeds towards the tent of the Gothic king, while the streets of Rome are deserted by all but the dead, and the living populace crowd together in speechless expectation behind the barrier of the Pincian Gate, an opportunity is at length afforded of turning our attention towards a scene from which it has been long removed. Let us now revisit the farm-house in the suburbs, and look once more on the quiet garden and on Hermanric's grave.

The tranquility of the bright warm day is purest around the retired path leading to the little dwelling. Here the fragrance of wild flowers rises pleasantly from the waving grass; the lulling, monotonous hum of insect life pervades the light, steady air; the sunbeams, intercepted here and there by the clustering trees, fall in irregular patches of brightness on the shady ground; and, saving the birds which occasionally pass overhead, singing in their flight, no living creature appears on the quiet scene, until, gaining the wicket-gate which leads into the farm- house garden, we look forth upon the prospect within.

There, following the small circular footpath which her own persevering steps have day by day already traced, appears the form of a solitary woman, pacing slowly about the mound of grassy earth which marks the grave of the young Goth.

For some time she proceeds on her circumscribed round with as much undeviating, mechanical regularity, as if beyond that narrow space rose a barrier which caged her from ever setting foot on the earth beyond. At length she pauses in her course when it brings her nearest to the wicket, advances a few steps towards it, then recedes, and recommences her monotonous progress, and then again break-ing off on her round, finally succeeds in withdrawing herself from the confines of the grave, passes through the gate, and following the path to the high-road, slow-ly proceeds towards the eastern limits of the Gothic camp. The fixed, ghastly, unfeminine expression on her features marks her as the same woman whom we last beheld as the assassin at the farm-house, but beyond this she is hardly recog-nisable again. Her formerly powerful and upright frame is bent and lean; her hair waves in wild, white locks about her shrivelled face; all the rude majesty of her form has departed; there is nothing to show that it is still Goisvintha haunting the scene of her crime but the savage expression debasing her countenance and betraying the evil heart within, unsubdued as ever in its yearning for destruction and revenge.

Since the period when we last beheld her, removed in the custody of the Huns from the dead body of her kinsman, the farm-house had been the constant scene of her pilgrimage from the camp, the chosen refuge where she brooded in solitude over her fierce desires. Scorning to punish a woman whom he regarded as insane for an absence from the tents of the Goths which was of no moment wither to the army or to himself, Alaric had impatiently dismissed her from his presence when she was brought before him. The soldiers who had returned to bury the body of their chieftain in the garden of the farm-house, found means to inform her secret-ly of the charitable act which they had performed at their own peril, but beyond this no further intercourse was held with her by any of her former associates.

All her actions favoured their hasty belief that her faculties were disordered, and others shunned her as she shunned them. Her daily allowance of food was left for her to seek at a certain place in the camp, as it might have been left for an ani-mal too savage to be cherished by the hand of man. At certain periods she returned secretly from her wanderings to take it. Her shelter for the night was not the shelter of her people before the walls of Rome; her thoughts were not their thoughts. Widowed, childless, friendless, the assassin of her last kinsman, she moved apart in her own secret world of bereavement, desolation, and crime.

Yet there was no madness, no remorse for her share in accomplishing the fate of Hermanric, in the dark and solitary existence which she now led. From the moment when the young warrior had expiated with his death his disregard of the enmities of his nation and the wrongs of his kindred, she thought of him only as of one more victim whose dishonour and ruin she must live to requite on the Romans with Roman blood, and matured her schemes of revenge with a stern resolution which time, and solitude, and bodily infirmity were all powerless to disturb.

She would pace for hours and hours together, in the still night and in the broad noonday, round and round the warrior's grave, nursing her vengeful thoughts within her, until a ferocious anticipation of triumph quickened her steps and brightened her watchful eyes. Then she would enter the farm-house, and, drawing the knife from its place of concealment in her garments, would pass its point slowly backwards and forwards over the hearth on which she had mutilated Hermanric with her own hand, and from which he had advanced, without a tremor, to meet the sword-points of the Huns. Sometimes, when darkness had gathered over the earth, she would stand--a boding and menacing apparition-- upon the grave itself, and chaunt, moaning to the moaning wind, fragments of obscure Northern legends, whose hideous burden was ever of anguish and crime, of torture in prison vaults, and death by the annihilating sword--mingling with them the gloomy story of the massacre at Aquileia, and her fierce vows of vengeance against the households of Rome. The forager, on his late return past the farm-house to the camp, heard the harsh, droning accents of her voice, and quickened his onward step. The venturesome peasant from the country beyond, approaching under cover of the night to look from afar on the Gothic camp, beheld her form, shadowy and threatening, as he neared the garden, and fled affrighted from the place. Neither stranger nor friend intruded on her dread solitude. The foul presence of cruelty and crime violated undisturbed the scenes once sacred to the interests of tenderness and love, once hallowed by the sojourn of youth and beauty!

But now the farm-house garden is left solitary, the haunting spirit of evil has departed from the grave, the footsteps of Goisvintha have traced to their close the same paths from the suburbs over which the young Goth once eagerly hastened on his night journey of love; and already the walls of Rome rise--dark, near, and hateful--before her eyes. Along these now useless bulwarks of the fallen city she wanders, as she has often wandered before, watching anxiously for the first opening of the long-closed gates. Let us follow her on her way.

Her attention was now fixed only on the broad ramparts, while she passed slowly along the Gothic tents towards the encampment at the Pincian Gate. Arrived there, she was aroused for the first time from her apathy by an unwonted stir and confusion prevailing around her. She looked towards the tent of Alaric, and beheld before it the wasted and crouching forms of the followers of the embassy awaiting their sentence from the captain of the Northern hosts. In a few moments she gathered enough from the words of the Goths congregated about this part of the camp to assure her that it was the Pincian Gate which had given egress to the Roman suppliants, and which would therefore, in all probability, be the entrance again thrown open to admit their return to the city. Remembering this, she began to calculate the numbers of the conquered enemy grouped together before the king's tent, and then mentally added to them those who might be present at the interview proceeding within--mechanically withdrawing herself, while thus occupied, nearer and nearer to the waste ground before the city walls.

Gradually she turned her face towards Rome: she was realising a daring purpose, a fatal resolution, long cherished during the days and nights of her solitary wanderings. 'The ranks of the embassy,' she muttered, in a deep, thoughtful tone, 'are thickly filled. Where there are many there must be confusion and haste; they march together, and know not their own numbers; they mark not one more or one less among them.'

She stopped. Strange and dark changes of colour and expression passed over her ghastly features. She drew from her bosom the bloody helmet- crest of her husband, which had never quitted her since the day of his death; her face grew livid under an awful expression of rage, ferocity, and despair, as she gazed on it. Suddenly she looked up at the city--fierce and defiant, as if the great walls before her were mortal enemies against whom she stood at bay in the death-struggle.

'The widowed and the childless shall drink of thy blood!' she cried, stretching out her skinny hand towards Rome, 'though the armies of her nation barter their wrongs with thy people for bags of silver and gold! I have pondered on it in my solitude, and dreamed of it in my dreams! I have sworn that I would enter Rome, and avenge my slaughtered kindred, alone among thousands! Now, now, I will hold to my oath! Thou blood- stained city of the coward and the traitor, the enemy of the defenceless, and the murderer of the weak! thou who didst send forth to Aquileia the slayers of my husband and the assassins of my children, I wait no longer before thy walls! This day will I mingle, daring all things, with thy returning citizens and penetrate, amid Romans, the gates of Rome! Through the day will I lurk, cunning and watchful, in thy solitary haunts, to steal forth on thee at nights, a secret minister of death! I will watch for thy young and thy weak once in unguarded places; I will prey, alone in the thick darkness, upon thy unprotected lives; I will destroy thy children, as their fathers destroyed at Aquileia the children of the Goths! Thy rabble will discover me and arise against me; they will tear me in pieces and trample my mangled body on the pavement of the streets; but it will be after I have seen the blood that I have sworn to shed flowing under my knife! My vengeance will be complete, and torments and death will be to me as guests that I welcome, and as deliverers whom I await!'

Again she paused--the wild triumph of the fanatic on the burning pile was flashing in her face--suddenly her eyes fell once more upon the stained helmet-crest; then her expression changed again to despair, and her voice grew low and moaning, when she thus resumed:--

'I am weary of my life; when the vengeance is done I shall be delivered from this prison of the earth--in the world of shadows I shall see my husband, and my little ones will gather round my knees again. The living have no part in me; I yearn towards the spirits who wander in the halls of the dead.'

For a few minutes more she continued to fix her tearless eyes on the helmet-crest. But soon the influence of the evil spirit revived in all its strength; she raised her head suddenly, remained for an instant absorbed in deep thought, then began to retrace her steps rapidly in the direction by which she had come.

Sometimes she whispered softly, 'I must be doing ere the time fail me: my face must be hidden and my garments changed. Yonder, among the houses, I must search, and search quickly!' Sometimes she reiterated her denunciations of vengeance, her ejaculations of triumph in her frantic project. At the recapitulation of these the remembrance of Antonina was aroused; and then a bloodthirsty superstition darkened her thoughts, and threw a vague and dreamy character over her speech.

When she spoke now, it was to murmur to herself that the victim who had twice escaped her might yet be alive; that the supernatural influences which had often guided the old Goths, on the day of retribution, might still guide her; might still direct the stroke of her destroying weapon--the last stroke ere she was discovered and slain--straight to the girl's heart.

Thoughts such as these--wandering and obscure--arose in close, quick succession within her; but whether she gave them expression in word and action, or whether she suppressed them in silence, she never wavered or halted in her rapid progress. Her energies were braced to all emergencies, and her strong will suffered them not for an instant to relax.

She gained a retired street in the deserted suburbs, and looking round to see that she was unobserved, entered on of the houses abandoned by its inhabitants on the approach of the besiegers. Passing quickly through the outer halls, she stopped at length in one of the sleeping apartments; and here she found, among other possessions left behind in the flight, the store of wearing apparel belonging to the owner of the room.

From this she selected a Roman robe, upper mantle, and sandals--the most common in colour and texture that she could find--and folding them up into the smallest compass, hid them under her own garments. Then, avoiding all those whom she met on her way, she returned in the direction of the king's tent; but when she approached it, branched off stealthily towards Rome, until she reached a ruined building half-way between the city and the camp. In this concealment she clothed herself in her disguise, drawing the mantle closely round her head and face; and from this point--calm, vigilant, determined, her hand on the knife beneath her robe, her lips muttering the names of her murdered husband and children--she watched the high-road to the Pincian Gate.

There for a short time let us leave her, and enter the tent of Alaric, while the Senate yet plead before the Arbiter of the Empire for mercy and peace.

At the moment of which we write, the embassy had already exhausted its powers of intercession, apparently without moving the leader of the Goths from his first pitiless resolution of fixing the ransom of Rome at the price of every possession of value which the city contained. There was a momentary silence now in the great tent. At one extremity of it, congregated in a close and irregular group, stood the wearied and broken-spirited members of the Senate, supported by such of their attendants as had been permitted to follow them; at the other appeared the stately forms of Alaric and the warriors who surrounded him as his council of war. The vacant space in the middle of the tent was strewn with martial weapons, separating the representatives of the two nations one from the other; and thus accidentally, yet palpably, typifying the fierce hostility which had sundered in years past, and was still to sunder for years to come, the people of the North and the people of the South.

The Gothic king stood a little in advance of his warriors, leaning on his huge, heavy sword. His steady eye wandered from man to man among the broken-spirited senators, contemplating, with cold and cruel penetration, all that suffering and despair had altered for the worse in their outward appearance. Their soiled robes, their wan cheeks, their trembling limbs were each marked in turn by the cool, sarcastic examination of the conqueror's gaze. Debased and humiliated as they were, there were some among the ambassadors who felt the insult thus silently and deliberately inflicted on them the more keenly for their very helplessness. They moved uneasily in their places, and whispered among each other in low and bitter accents.

At length one of their number raised his downcast eyes and broke the silence. The old Roman spirit, which long years of voluntary frivolity and degradation had not yet entirely depraved, flushed his pale, wasted face as he spoke thus:--

'We have entreated, we have offered, we have promised--men can do no more! Deserted by our Emperor and crushed by pestilence and famine, nothing is now left to us but to perish in unavailing resistance beneath the walls of Rome! It was in the power of Alaric to win everlasting renown by moderation to the unfortunate of an illustrious nation; but he has preferred to attempt the spoiling of a glorious city and the subjugation of a suffering people! Yet let him remember, though destruction may sate his vengeance, and pillage enrich his hoards, the day of retribution will yet come. There are still soldiers in the empire, and heroes who will lead them confidently to battle, though the bodies of their countrymen lie slaughtered around them in the streets of pillaged Rome!'

A momentary expression of wrath and indignation appeared on Alaric's features as he listened to this bold speech; but it was almost immediately replaced by a scornful smile of derision.

'What! ye have still soldiers before whom the barbarian must tremble for his conquests!' he cried. 'Where are they? Are they on their march, or in ambush, or hiding behind strong walls, or have they lost their way on the road to the Gothic camp? Ha! here is one of them!' he exclaimed, advancing towards an enfeebled and disarmed guard of the Senate, who quailed beneath his fierce glance. 'Fight, man!' he loudly continued; 'fight while there is yet time, for imperial Rome! Thy sword is gone--take mine, and be a hero again!'

With a rough laugh, echoed by the warriors behind him, he flung his ponderous weapon as he spoke towards the wretched object of his sarcasm. The hilt struck heavily against the man's breast; he staggered and fell helpless to the ground. The laugh was redoubled among the Goths; but now their leader did not join in it. His eye glowed in triumphant scorn as he pointed to the prostrate Roman, exclaiming--

'So does the South fall beneath the sword of the North! So shall the empire bow before the rule of the Goth! Say, as ye look on these Romans before us, are we not avenged of our wrongs? They die not fighting on our swords; they live to entreat our pity, as children that are in terror of the whip!'

He paused. His massive and noble countenance gradually assumed a thoughtful expression. The ambassadors moved forward a few steps--perhaps to make a final entreaty, perhaps to depart in despair; but he signed with his hand in command to them to be silent and remain where they stood. The marauder's thirst for present plunder, and the conqueror's lofty ambition of future glory, now stirred in strong conflict within him. He walked to the opening of the tent, and thrusting aside its curtain of skins, looked out upon Rome in silence. The dazzling majesty of the temples and palaces of the mighty city, as they towered before him, gleaming in the rays of the unclouded sunlight, fixed him long in contemplation. Gradually, dreams of a future dominion amid those unrivalled structures, which now waited but his word to be pillaged and destroyed, filled his aspiring soul, and saved the city from his wrath. He turned again toward the shrinking ambassadors--in a voice and look superior to them as a being of a higher sphere--and spoke thus:--

'When the Gothic conqueror reigns in Italy, the palaces of her rulers shall be found standing for the places of his sojourn. I will ordain a lower ransom; I will spare Rome.'

A murmur arose among the warriors behind him. The rapine and destruction which they had eagerly anticipated was denied them for the first time by their chief. As their muttered remonstrances caught his ear, Alaric instantly and sternly fixed his eyes upon them; and, repeating in accents of deliberate command, 'I will ordain a lower ransom; I will spare Rome,' steadily scanned the countenances of his ferocious followers.

Not a word of dissent fell from their lips; not a gesture of impatience appeared in their ranks; they preserved perfect silence as the king again advanced towards the ambassadors and continued--

'I fix the ransom of the city at five thousand pounds of gold; at thirty thousand pounds of silver.'

Here he suddenly ceased, as if pondering further on the terms he should exact. The hearts of the Senate, lightened for a moment by Alaric's unexpected announcement that he would moderate his demands, sank within them again as they thought on the tribute required of them, and remembered their exhausted treasury. But it was no time now to remonstrate or to delay; and they answered with one accord, ignorant though they were of the means of performing their promise, 'The ransom shall be paid.'

The king looked at them when they spoke, as if in astonishment that men whom he had deprived of all freedom of choice ventured still to assert it by intimating their acceptance of terms which they dared not decline. The mocking spirit revived within him while he thus gazed on the helpless and humiliated embassy; and he laughed once more as he resumed, partly addressing himself to the silent array of the warriors behind him--

'The gold and silver are but the first dues of the tribute; my army shall be rewarded with more than the wealth of the enemy. You men of Rome have laughed at our rough bearskins and our heavy armour, you shall clothe us with your robes of festivity! I will add to the gold and silver of your ransom, four thousand garments of silk, and three thousand pieces of scarlet cloth. My barbarians shall be barbarians no longer! I will make patricians, epicures, Romans of them!'

The members of the ill-fated embassy looked up as he paused, in mute appeal to the mercy of the triumphant conqueror; but they were not yet to be released from the crushing infliction of his rapacity and scorn.

'Hold!' he cried, 'I will have more--more still! You are a nation of feasters;--we will rival you in your banquets when we have stripped you of your banqueting robes! To the gold, the silver, the silk, and the cloth, I will add yet more--three thousand pounds weight of pepper, your precious merchandise, bought from far countries with your lavish wealth!--see that you bring it hither, with the rest of the ransom, to the last grain! The flesh of our beasts shall be seasoned for us like the flesh of yours!'

He turned abruptly from the senators as he pronounced the last words, and began to speak in jesting tones and in the Gothic language to the council of warriors around him. Some of the ambassadors bowed their heads in silent resignation; others, with the utter thoughtlessness of men bewildered by all that they had seen and heard during the interview that was now close, unhappily revived the recollection of the broken treaties of former days, by mechanically inquiring, in the terms of past formularies, what security the besiegers would require for the payment of their demands.

'Security!' cried Alaric fiercely, instantly relapsing as they spoke into his sterner mood. 'Behold yonder the future security of the Goths for the faith of Rome!' and flinging aside the curtain of the tent, he pointed proudly to the long lines of his camp, stretching round all that was visible of the walls of the fallen city.

The ambassadors remembered the massacre of the hostages of Aquileia, and the evasion of the payment of tribute-money promised in former days, and were silent as they looked through the opening of the tent.

'Remember the conditions of the ransom,' pursued Alaric in warning tones, 'remember my security that the ransom shall be quickly paid! So shall you live for a brief space in security, and feast and be merry again while your territories yet remain to you. Go! I have spoken--it is enough!'

He withdrew abruptly from the senators, and the curtain of the tent fell behind them as they passed out. The ordeal of the judgment was over; the final sentence had been pronounced; the time had already arrived to go forth and obey it.

The news that terms of peace had been at last settled filled the Romans who were waiting before the tent with emotions of delight, equally unalloyed by reflections on the past or forebodings for the future. Barred from their reckless project of flying to the open country by the Goths surrounding them in the camp, shut out from retreating to Rome by the gates through which they had rashly forced their way, exposed in their helplessness to the brutal jeers of the enemy while they waited in a long agony of suspense for the close of the perilous interview between Alaric and the Senate, they had undergone every extremity of suffering, and had yielded unanimously to despair when the intelligence of the concluded treaty sounded like a promise of salvation in their ears.

None of the apprehensions aroused in the minds of their superiors by the vastness of the exacted tribute now mingled with the unreflecting ecstasy of their joy at the prospect of the removal of the blockade. They arose to return to the city from which they had fled in dismay, with cries of impatience and delight. They fawned like dogs upon the ambassadors, and even upon the ferocious Goths. On their departure from Rome they had mechanically preserved some regularity in their progress, but now they hurried onward without distinction of place or discipline of march--senators, guards, plebeians, all were huddled together in the disorderly equality of a mob.

Not one of them, in their new-born security, marked the ruined building on the high-road; not one of them observed the closely-robed figure that stole out from it to join them in their rear; and then, with stealthy footstep and shrouded face, soon mingled in the thickest of their ranks. The attention of the ambassadors was still engrossed by their forebodings of failure in collecting the ransom; the eyes of the people were fixed only on the Pincian Gate; their ears were open to no sounds but their own ejaculations of delight. Not one disguised stranger only, but many, might now have joined them in their tumultuous progress, alike unquestioned and unobserved.

So they hastily re-entered the city, where thousands of heavy eyes were strained to look on them, and thousands of attentive ears drank in their joyful news from the Gothic camp. Then were heard in all directions the sounds of hysterical weeping and idiotic laughter, the low groans of the weak who died victims of their sudden transport, and the confused outbursts of the strong who had survived all extremities, and at last beheld their deliverance in view.

Still silent and serious, the ambassadors now slowly penetrated the throng on their way back to the Forum; and as they proceeded the crowd gradually dispersed on either side of them. Enemies, friends, and strangers, all whom the ruthless famine had hitherto separated in interests and sympathies, were now united together as one family, by the expectation of speedy relief.

But there was one among the assembly that was now separating who stood alone in her unrevealed emotions, amid the rejoicing thousands around her. The women and children in the throng, as, preoccupied by their own feeling, they unheedfully passed her by, saw not the eager, ferocious attention in her eyes, as she watched them steadily till they were out of sight. Within their gates the stranger and the enemy waited for the treacherous darkness of night, and waited unobserved. Where she had first stood when the thick crowd hemmed her in, there she still continued to stand after they slowly moved past her and space grew free.

Yet beneath this outward calm and silence lurked the wildest passions that ever raged against the weak restraint of human will; even the firm self-possession of Goisvintha was shaken when she found herself within the walls of Rome.

No glance of suspicion had been cast upon her; not one of the crowd had approached to thrust her back when she passed through the gates with the heedless citizens around her. Shielded from detection, as much by the careless security of her enemies as by the stratagem of her disguise, she stood on the pavement of Rome, as she had vowed to stand, afar from the armies of her people--alone as an avenger of blood!

It was no dream; no fleeting, deceitful vision. The knife was under her hand; the streets stretched before her; the living beings who thronged them were Romans; the hours of the day were already on the wane; the approach of her vengeance was as sure as the approach of darkness that was to let it loose. A wild exultation quickened in her the pulses of life, while she thought on the dread projects of secret assassination and revenge which now opposed her, a solitary woman, in deadly enmity against the defenceless population of a whole city.

As her eyes travelled slowly from side to side over the moving throng; as she thought on the time that might still elapse ere the discovery and death--the martyrdom in the cause of blood--which she expected and defied, would overtake her, her hands trembled beneath her robe, and she reiterated in whispers to herself: 'Husband, children, brother--there are five deaths to avenge! Remember Aquileia! Remember Aquileia!'

Suddenly, as she looked from group to group among the departing people, her eyes became arrested by one object; she instantly stepped forwards, then abruptly restrained herself and moved back where the crowd was still thick, gazing fixedly ever in the same direction. She saw the victim twice snatched from her hands--at the camp and in the farm- house--a third time offered to her grasp in the streets of Rome.

The chance of vengeance last expected was the chance that had first arrived. A vague, oppressing sensation of awe mingled with the triumph at her heart--a supernatural guidance seemed to be directing her with fell rapidity, through every mortal obstacle, to the climax of her revenge!

She screened herself behind the people; she watched the girl from the most distant point; but concealment was now vain--their eyes had met. The robe had slipped aside when she suddenly stepped forward, and in that moment Antonina had seen her.

Numerian, moving slowly with his daughter through the crowd, felt her hand tighten round his, and saw her features stiffen into sudden rigidity; but the change was only for an instant. Ere he could speak, she caught him by the arm, and drew him forward with convulsive energy. Then, in accents hardly articulate, low, breathless, unlike her wonted voice, he heard he exclaim, as she struggled on with him, 'She is there--there behind us! to kill me, as she killed him! Home! home!'

Exhausted already, through long weakness and natural infirmity, by the rough contact of the crowd, bewildered by Antonina's looks and actions, and by the startling intimation of unknown peril, conveyed to him in her broken exclamations of affright, Numerian's first impulse, as he hurried onward by her side, led him to entreat protection and help from the surrounding populace. But even could he have pointed out to them the object of his dread amid that motley throng of all nations, the appeal he now made would have remained unanswered.

Of all the results of the frightful severity of privation suffered by the besieged, none were more common than those mental aberrations which produced visions of danger, enemies, and death, so palpable as to make the persons beholding them implore assistance against the hideous creation of their own delirium. Accordingly, most of those to whom the entreaties of Numerian were addressed passed without noticing them. Some few carelessly bid him remember that there were no enemies now; that the days of peace were approaching; and that a meal of good food, which he might soon expect to enjoy, was the only help for a famished man. No one, in that period of horror and suffering, which was now draw-ing to a close, saw anything extraordinary in the confusion of the father and the terror of the child. So they pursued their feeble flight unprotected, and the foot-steps of Goisvintha followed them as they went.

They had already commenced the ascent of the Pincian Hill, when Antonina stopped abruptly, and turned to look behind her. Many people yet thronged the street below; but her eyes penetrated among them, sharpened by peril, and instantly discerned the ample robe and the tall form, still at the same distance from them, and pausing as they had paused. For one moment, the girl's eyes fixed in the wild, helpless stare of terror on her father's face; but the next, that myste-rious instinct of preservation, which is co-existent with the instinct of fear--which gifts the weakest animal with cunning to improve its flight, and takes the place of reason, reflection, and resolve, when all are banished from the mind--warned her against the fatal error of permitting the pursuer to track her to her home.

'Not there! not there!' she gasped faintly as Numerian endeavoured to lead her up the ascent. 'She will see us as we enter the doors!--through the streets! Oh, father, if you would save me! we may lose her in the streets!--the guards, the people are there! Back! back!'

Numerian trembled as he marked the terror in her looks and gestures; but it was vain to question or oppose her. Nothing short of force could restrain her,--no commands or entreaties could draw from her more than the same breathless excla-mation: 'Onward, father; onward, if you would save me!' She was insensible to every sensation but fear, incapable of any other exertion than flight.

Turning and winding, hurrying forward ever at the same rapid pace, they passed unconsciously along the intricate streets that led to the river side; and still the avenger tracked the victim, constant as the shadow to the substance; steady, vigi-lant, unwearied, as a bloodhound on a hot scent.

And now, even the sound of the father's voice ceased to be audible in the daugh-ter's ears; she no longer felt the pressure of his hand, no longer perceived his very presence at her side. At length, frail and shrinking, she again paused, and looked back. The street they had reached was very tranquil and desolate: two slaves were walking at its further extremity. While they were in sight, no living creature appeared in the roadway behind; but as soon as they had passed away, a shadow stole slowly forward over the pavement of a portico in the distance, and the next moment Goisvintha appeared in the street.

The sun glared down fiercely over her dark figure as she stopped and for an instant looked stealthily around her. She moved to advance, and Antonina saw no more. Again she turned to renew her hopeless flight; and again her father--perceiving only as the mysterious cause of her dread a solitary woman, who, though she followed, attempted not to arrest, or even to address them--prepared to accompany her to the last, in despair of all other chances of securing her safety.

More and more completely did her terror now enchain her faculties, as she still unconsciously traced her rapid way through the streets that led to the Tiber. It was not Numerian, not Rome, not daylight in a great city, that was before her eyes: it was the storm, the assassination, the night at the farm-house, that she now lived through over again.

Still the quick flight and the ceaseless pursuit were continued, as if neither were ever to have an end; but the close of the scene was, nevertheless, already at hand. During the interval of the passage through the streets, Numerian's mind had gradually recovered from its first astonishment and alarm; at length he perceived the necessity of instant and decisive action, while there was yet time to save Antonina from sinking under the excess of her own fears. Though a vague, awful foreboding of disaster and death filled his heart, his resolution to penetrate at once, at all hazards, the dark mystery of impending danger indicated by his daughter's words and actions, did not fail him; for it was aroused by the only motive powerful enough to revive all that suffering and infirmity had not yet destroyed of the energy of his former days--the preservation of his child. There was something of the old firmness and vigour of the intrepid reformer of the Church, in his dim eyes, as he now stopped, and enclosing Antonina in his arms, arrested her instantly in her flight.

She struggled to escape; but it was faintly, and only for a moment. Her strength and consciousness were beginning to abandon her. She never attempted to look back; she felt in her heart that Goisvintha was still behind, and dared not to verify the frightful conviction with her eyes. Her lips moved; but they expressed an altered and a vain petition: 'Hermanric! O Hermanric!' was all they murmured now.

They had arrived at the long street that ran by the banks of the Tiber. The people had either retired to their homes or repaired to the Forum to be informed of the period when the ransom would be paid. No one but Goisvintha was in sight as Numerian looked around him; and she, after having carefully viewed the empty street, was advancing towards them at a quickened pace.

For an instant the father looked on her steadily as she approached, and in that instant his determination was formed. A flight of steps at his feet led to the narrow doorway of a small temple, the nearest building to him.

Ignorant whether Goisvintha might not be secretly supported by companions in her ceaseless pursuit, he resolved to secure this place for Antonina, as a temporary refuge at least; while standing before it, he should oblige the woman to declare her purpose, if she followed them even there. In a moment he had begun the ascent of the steps, with the exhausted girl by his side. Arrived at the summit, he guided her before him into the doorway, and stopped on the threshold to look round again. Goisvintha was nowhere to be seen.

Not duped by the woman's sudden disappearance into the belief that she had departed from the street--persisting in his resolution to lead his daughter to a place of repose, where she might most immediately feel herself secure, and might therefore most readily recover her self- possession, Numerian drew Antonina with him into the temple. He lingered there for a moment, ere he departed to watch the street from the portico outside.

The light in the building was dim,--it was admitted only from a small aperture in the roof, and through the narrow doorway, where it was intercepted by the overhanging bulk of the outer portico. A crooked pile of dark heavy-looking substances on the floor, rose high towards the ceiling in the obscure interior. Irregular in form, flung together one over the other in strange disorder, for the most part dusky in hue, yet here and there gleaming at points with a metallic brightness, these objects presented a mysterious, indefinite, and startling appearance. It was impossible, on a first view of their confused arrangement, to discover what they were, or to guess for what purpose they could have been pile together on the floor of a deserted temple. From the moment when they had first attracted Numerian's observation, his attention was fixed on them, and as he looked a faint thrill of suspicion--vague, inexplicable, without apparent cause or object--struck chill to his heart.

He had moved a step forward to examine the hidden space at the back of the pile, when his further advance was instantly stopped by the appearance of a man who walked forth from it dressed in the floating, purple-edged robe and white fillet of the Pagan priests. Before either father or daughter could speak, even before they could move to depart, he stepped up to them, and, placing his hand on the shoulder of each, confronted them in silence.

At the moment when the stranger approached, Numerian raised his hand to thrust him back, and, in so doing, fixed his eyes on the man's countenance, as a ray of light from the doorway floated over it. Instantly his arm remained outstretched and rigid, then it dropped to his side, and the expression of horror on the face of the child became reflected, as it were, on the face of the parent. Neither moved under the hand of the dweller in the temple when he laid it heavily on each, and both stood before him speechless as himself.

Chapter 25

THE TEMPLE AND THE CHURCH

It was Ulpius. The Pagan was changed in bearing and countenance as well as in apparel. He stood more firm and upright; a dull, tawny hue overspread his face; his eyes, so sunken and lustreless in other days, were now distended and bright with the glare of insanity. It seemed as if his bodily powers had renewed their vigour, while his mental faculties had declined towards their ruin.

No human eye had ever beheld by what foul and secret means he had survived through the famine, on what unnatural sustenance he had satisfied the cravings of inexorable hunger; but there, in his gloomy shelter, the madman and the outcast had lived and moved, and suddenly and strangely strengthened, after the people of the city had exhausted all their united responses, lavished in vain all their united wealth, and drooped and died by thousands around him!

His grasp still lay heavy on the father and daughter, and still both confronted him--silent, as if death-struck by his gaze; motionless, as if frozen at his touch. His presence was exerting over them a fatal fascination. The power of action, suspended in Antonina as she entered their ill-chosen refuge, was now arrested in Numerian also; but with him no thought of the enemy in the street had any part, at this moment, in the resistless influence which held him helpless before the enemy in the temple.

It was a feeling of deeper awe and darker horror. For now, as he looked upon the hideous features of Ulpius, as he saw the forbidden robe of priesthood in which

the Pagan was arrayed, he beheld not only the traitor who had successfully plotted against the prosperity of his household, but the madman as well,--the moral
leper of the whole human family--the living Body and the dead Soul--the disinherited of that Divine Light of Life which it is the awful privilege of mortal man
to share with the angels of God.

He still clasped Antonina to his side, but it was unconsciously. To all outward
appearance he was helpless as his helpless child, when Ulpius slowly removed his
grasp from their shoulders, separated them, and locking the hand of each in his
cold, bony fingers, began to speak.

His voice was deep and solemn, but his accents, in their hard, unvarying tone,
seemed to express no human emotion. His eyes, far from brightening as he spoke,
relapsed into a dull, vacant insensibility. The connection between the action of
speech and the accompanying and explaining action of look which is observable
in all men, seemed lost in him. It was fearful to behold the death-like face, and
to listen at the same moment to the living voice.

'Lo! the votaries come to the temple!' murmured the Pagan. 'The good servants
of the mighty worship gather at the voice of the priest! In the far provinces, where
the enemies of the gods approach to profane the sacred groves, behold the scattered people congregating by night to journey to the shrine of Serapis! Adoring
thousands kneel beneath the lofty porticoes, while within, in the secret hall where
the light is dim, where the air quivers round the breathing deities on their
pedestals of gold, the high priest Ulpius reads the destinies of the future, that are
unrolled before his eyes like a book!'

As he ceased, and, still holding the hands of his captives, looked on them fixedly
as ever, his eyes brightened and dilated again; but they expressed not the slightest
recognition either of father or daughter. The delirium of his imagination had
transported him to the temple at Alexandria; the days were revived when his glory
had risen to its culminating point, when the Christians trembled before him as
their fiercest enemy, and the Pagans surrounded him as their last hope. The victims of his former and forgotten treachery were but as two among the throng of
votaries allured by the fame of his eloquence, by the triumphant notoriety of his
power to protect the adherents of the ancient creed.

But it was not always thus that his madness declared itself: there were moments
when it rose to appalling frenzy. Then he imagined himself to be again hurling
the Christian assailants from the topmost walls of the besieged temple, in that
past time when the image of Serapis was doomed by the Bishop of Alexandria to

be destroyed. His yells of fury, his frantic execrations of defiance were heard afar, in the solemn silence of pestilence-stricken Rome. Those who, during the most fatal days of the Gothic blockade, dropped famished on the pavement before the little temple, as they endeavoured to pass it on their onward way, presented a dread reality of death, to embody the madman's visions of battle and slaughter. As these victims of famine lay expiring in the street, they heard above them his raving voice cursing them for Christians, triumphing over them as defeated enemies destroyed by his hand, exhorting his imaginary adherents to fling the slain above on the dead below, until the bodies of the besiegers of the temple were piled, as barriers against their living comrades, round its walls. Sometimes his frenzy gloried in the fancied revival of the foul and sanguinary ceremonies of Pagan superstition. Then he bared his arms, and shouted aloud for the sacrifice; he committed dark and nameless atrocities--for now again the dead and the dying lay before him, to give substance to the shadow of his evil thoughts; and Plague and Hunger were as creatures of his will, and slew the victim for the altar ready to his hands.

At other times, when the raving fit had passed away, and he lay panting in the darkest corner of the interior of the temple, his insanity assumed another and a mournful form. His voice grew low and moaning; the wreck of his memory--wandering and uncontrollable--floated back, far back, on the dark waters of the past; and his tongue uttered fragments of words and phrases that he had murmured at his father's knees--farewell, childish wishes that he had breathed in his mother's ear--innocent, anxious questions which he had addressed to Macrinus, the high priest, when he first entered the service of the gods at Alexandria. His boyish reveries--the gentleness of speech and poetry of thought of his first youthful days, were now, by the unsearchable and arbitrary influences of his disease, revived in his broken words, renewed in his desolate old age of madness and crime, breathed out in unconscious mockery by his lips, while the foam still gathered about them, and the last flashes of frenzy yet lightened in his eyes.

This unnatural calmness of language and vividness of memory, this treacherous appearance of thoughtful, melancholy self-possession, would often continue through long periods, uninterrupted; but, sooner or later, the sudden change came; the deceitful chain of thought snapped asunder in an instant; the word was left half uttered; the wearied limbs started convulsively into renewed action; and as the dream of violence returned and the dream of peace vanished, the madman rioted afresh in his fury; and journeyed as his visions led him, round and round his temple sanctuary, and hither and thither, when the night was dark and death was busiest in Rome, among the expiring in deserted houses, and the lifeless in the silent streets.

But there were other later events in his existence that never revived within him. The old familiar image of the idol Serapis, which had drawn him into the temple when he re-entered Rome, absorbed in itself and in its associated remembrances all that remained active of his paralysed faculties. His betrayal of his trust in the house of Numerian, his passage through the rifted wall, his crushing repulse in the tent of Alaric, never for a moment occupied his wandering thoughts. The clouds that hung over his mind might open to him parting glimpses of the toils and triumphs of his early career; but they descended in impenetrable darkness on all the after-days of his dreary life.

Such was the being to whose will, by a mysterious fatality, the father and child were now submitted; such the existence--solitary, hopeless, loathsome--of their stern and wily betrayer of other days!

Since he had ceased speaking, the cold, death-like grasp of his hand had gradually strengthened, and he had begun to look slowly and inquiringly round him from side to side. Had this change marked the approaching return of his raving paroxysm, the lives of Numerian and Antonina would have been sacrificed the next moment; but all that it now denoted was the quickening of the lofty and obscure ideas of celebrity and success, of priestly honour and influence, of the splendour and glory of the gods, which had prompted his last words.

He moved suddenly, and drew the victims of his dangerous caprice a few steps farther into the interior of the temple; then led them close up to the lofty pile of objects which had first attracted Numerian's eyes on entering the building. 'Kneel and adore!' cried the madman fiercely, replacing his hands on their shoulders and pressing them to the ground--'You stand before the gods, in the presence of their high priest!'

The girl's head sank forward, and she hid her face in her hands; but her father looked up tremblingly at the pile. His eyes had insensibly become more accustomed to the dim light of the temple, and he now saw more distinctly the objects composing the mass that rose above him.

Hundreds of images of the gods, in gold, silver, and wood--many in the latter material being larger than life; canopies, vestments, furniture, utensils, all of ancient Pagan form, were heaped together, without order or arrangement, on the floor, to a height of full fifteen feet.

There was something at once hideous and grotesque in the appearance of the pile. The monstrous figures of the idols, with their rude carved draperies and symbolic weapons, lay in every wild variety of position, and presented every startling eccentricity of line, more especially towards the higher portions of the mass, where they had evidently been flung up from the ground by the hand that had raised the structure.

The draperies mixed among the images and the furniture were here coiled serpent-like around them, and there hung down towards the ground, waving slow and solemn in the breezes that wound through the temple doorway. The smaller objects of gold and silver, scattered irregularly over the mass, shone out from it like gleaming eyes; while the pile itself, seen in such a place under a dusky light, looked like some vast, misshapen monster--the gloomy embodiment of the bloodiest superstitions of Paganism, the growth of damp airs and teeming ruin, of shadow and darkness, of accursed and infected solitude!

Even in its position, as well as in the objects of which it was composed, the pile wore an ominous and startling aspect; its crooked outline, expanding towards the top, was bent over fearfully in the direction of the doorway; it seemed as if a single hand might sway it in its uncertain balance, and hurl it instantly in one solid mass to the floor.

Many toilsome hours had passed away, long secret labour had been expended in the erection of this weird and tottering structure; but it was all the work of one hand. Night after night had the Pagan entered the deserted temples in the surrounding streets, and pillaged them of their contents to enrich his favoured shrine: the removal of the idols from their appointed places, which would have been sacrilege in any meaner man, was in his eyes the dread privilege of the high priest alone.

He had borne heavy burdens, and torn asunder strong fastenings, and journeyed and journeyed again for hours together over the same gloomy streets, without loitering in his task; he had raised treasures and images one above another; he had strengthened the base and heightened the summit of this precious and sacred heap; he had repaired and rebuilt, whenever it crumbled and fell, this new Babel that he longed to rear to the Olympus of the temple roof, with a resolute patience and perseverance that no failure or fatigue could overcome.

It was the dearest purpose of his dreamy superstition to surround himself with innumerable deities, as well as to assemble innumerable worshippers; to make the sacred place of his habitation a mighty Pantheon, as well as a point of juncture for the scattered congregations of the Pagan world. This was the ambition in which his madness expanded to the fiercest fanaticism; and as he now stood erect with his captives beneath him, his glaring eyes looked awe-struck when he fixed them on his idols; he uplifted his arms in solemn, ecstatic triumph, and in low tones poured forth his invocations, wild, intermingled, and fragmentary, as the barbarous altar which his solitary exertions had reared.

Whatever was the effect on Numerian of his savage and confused ejaculations, they were unnoticed, even unheard, by Antonina; for now, while the madman's voice softened to an undertone, and while she hid all surrounding objects from her eyes, her senses were awakened to sounds in the temple which she had never remarked before.

The rapid current of the Tiber washed the foundation walls of one side of the building, within which the clear, lulling bubble of the water was audible with singular distinctness. But besides this another and a shriller sound caught the ear. On the summit of the temple roof still remained several rows of little gilt bells, originally placed there, partly with the intention of ornamenting this portion of the outer structure, partly in order that the noise they produced, when agitated by the wind, might scare birds from settling in their flight on the consecrated edifice. The sounds produced by these bells were silvery and high pitched; now, when the breeze was strong, they rang together merrily and continuously; now, when it fell, their notes were faint, separate, and irregular, almost plaintive in their pure metallic softness. But, however their tone might vary under the capricious influences of the wind, it seemed always wonderfully mingled within the temple with the low, eternal bubbling of the river, which filled up the slightest pauses in the pleasant chiming of the bells, and ever preserved its gentle and monotonous harmony just audible beneath them.

There was something in this quaint, unwonted combination of sounds, as they were heard in the vaulted interior of the little building, strangely simple, attractive, and spiritual; the longer they were listened to, the more completely did the mind lose the recollection of their real origin, and gradually shape out of them wilder and wilder fancies, until the bells as they rang their small peal seemed like happy voices of a heavenly stream, borne lightly onward on its airy bubbles, and ever rejoicing over the gliding current that murmured to them as it ran.

Spite of the peril of her position, and of the terror which still fixed her speechless and crouching on the ground, the effect on Antonina of the strange mingled music of the running water and the bells was powerful enough, when she first heard it, to suspend all her other emotions in a momentary wonder and doubt.

She withdrew her hands from her face, and glanced round mechanically to the doorway, as if she imagined that the sounds proceeded from the street.

When she looked, the declining sun, gliding between two of the outer pillars which surrounded the temple, covered with a bright glow the smooth pavement before the entrance. A swarm of insects flew drowsily round and round in the warm mellow light; their faint monotonous humming deepened, rather than interrupted, the perfect silence prevailing over all things without.

But a change was soon destined to appear in the repose of the quiet, vacant scene; hardly a minute had elapsed while Antonina still looked on it before she saw stealing over the sunny pavement a dark shadow, the same shadow that she had last beheld when she stopped in her flight to look behind her in the empty street. At first it slowly grew and lengthened, then it remained stationary, then it receded and vanished as gradually as it had advanced, and then the girl heard, or fancied that she heard, a faint sound of footsteps, retiring along the lateral colonnades towards the river side of the building.

A low cry of horror burst from her lips as she sank back towards her father; but it was unheeded. The voice of Ulpius had resumed in the interval its hollow loudness of tone; he had raised Numerian from the ground; his strong, cold grasp, which seemed to penetrate to the old man's heart, which held him motionless and helpless as if by a fatal spell, was on his arm.

'Hear it! hear it!' cried the Pagan, waving his disengaged hand as if he were addressing a vast concourse of people--'I advance this man to be one of the servants of the high priest! He has travelled from a far country to the sacred shrine; he is docile and obedient before the altar of the gods; the lost is cast for his future life; his dwelling shall be in the temple to the day of his death! He shall minister before me in white robes, and swing the smoking censer, and slay the sacrifice at my feet!'

He stopped. A dark and sinister expression appeared in his eyes as the word 'sacrifice' passed his lips; he muttered doubtingly to himself--'The sacrifice!--is it yet the hour of the sacrifice?'--and looked round towards the doorway.

The sun still shone gaily on the outer pavement; the insects still circled slowly in the mellow light; no shadow was now visible; no distant footsteps were heard; there was nothing audible but the happy music of the bubbling water, and the chiming, silvery bells.

For a few moments the madman looked out anxiously towards the street, without uttering a word or moving a muscle. The raving fit was nearly possessing him again, as the thought of the sacrifice flashed over his darkened mind; but once more its approach was delayed.

He slowly turned his head in the direction of the interior of the temple. 'The sun is still bright in the outer courts,' he murmured in an undertone, 'the hour of the sacrifice is not yet! Come!' he continued in a louder voice, shaking Numerian by the arm. 'It is time that the servant of the temple should behold the place of the sacrifice, and sharpen the knife for the victim before sunset! Arouse thee, bond-man, and follow me!'

As yet, Numerian had neither spoken, nor attempted to escape. The preceding events, though some space has been occupied in describing them, passed in so short a period of time, that he had not hitherto recovered from the first over-whelming shock of the meeting with Ulpius. But now, awed though he still was, he felt that the moment of the struggle for freedom had arrived.

'Leave me, and let us depart!--there can be no fellowship between us again!' he exclaimed with the reckless courage of despair, taking the hand of Antonina, and striving to free himself from the madman's grasp. But the effort was vain; Ulpius tightened his hold and laughed in triumph. 'What! the servant of the temple is in terror of the high priest, and shrinks from walking in the place of the sacrifice!' he cried. 'Fear not, bondman! The mighty one, who rules over life and death, and time and futurity, deals kindly with the servant of his choice! Onward! onward! to the place of darkness and doom, where I alone am omnipotent, and all others are creatures who tremble and obey! To thy lesson, learner! by sunset the victim must be crowned!'

He looked round on Numerian for an instant, as he prepared to drag him for-ward, and their eyes met. In the fierce command of his action, and the savage exultation of his glance, the father saw repeated in a wilder form the very attitude and expression which he had beheld in the Pagan on the morning of the loss of his child. All the circumstances of that miserable hour--the vacant bed-chamber--the banished daughter--the triumph of the betrayer--the anguish of the betrayed--rushed over his mind, and rose up before it vivid as a pictured scene before his eyes.

He struggled no more; the powers of resistance in mind and body were crushed alike. He made an effort to remove Antonina from his side, as if, in forgetfulness of the hidden enemy without, he designed to urge her flight through the open door, while the madman's attention was yet distracted from her. But, beyond this last exertion of the strong instinct of paternal love, every other active emotion seemed dead within him.

Vainly had he striven to disentangle the child from the fate that might be in store for the parent. To her the dread of the dark shadow on the pavement was superior to all other apprehensions. She now clung more closely to her father, and tightened her clasp round his hand. So, when the Pagan advanced into the interior of the temple, it was not Numerian alone who followed him to the place of sacrifice, but Antonina as well.

They moved to the back of the pile of idols. Behind it appeared a high partition of gilt and inlaid wood reaching to the ceiling, and separating the outer from the inner part of the temple. A low archway passage, protected by carved gates similar to those at the front of the building, had been formed in the partition, and through this Ulpius and his prisoners now passed into the recess beyond.

This apartment was considerably smaller than the first hall of the temple which they had just left. The ceiling and the floor both sloped downwards together, and here the rippling of the waters of the Tiber was more distinctly audible to them than in the outer division of the building. At the moment when they entered it the place was very dark; the pile of idols intercepted even the little light that could have been admitted through its narrow entrance; but the dense obscurity was soon dissipated. Dragging Numerian after him to the left side of the recess, Ulpius drew back a sort of wooden shutter, and a vivid ray of sunlight immediately streamed in through a small circular opening pierced in this part of the temple.

Then there became apparent, at the lower end of the apartment, a vast yawning cavity in the wall, high enough to admit a man without stooping, but running downwards almost perpendicularly to some lower region which it was impossible to see, for no light shot upwards from this precipitous artificial abyss, in the darkness of which the eye was lost after it had penetrated to the distance of a few feet only from the opening. At the base of the confined space thus visible appeared the commencement of a flight of steps, evidently leading far downwards into the cavity. On the abruptly sloping walls, which bounded it on all sides, were painted, in the brilliant hues of ancient fresco, representations of the deities of the mythology--all in the attitude of descending into the vault, and all followed by figures of nymphs bearing wreaths of flowers, beautiful birds, and other similar adjuncts of the votive ceremonies of Paganism. The repulsive contrast between the bright colours and graceful forms presented by the frescoes, and the perilous and gloomy appearance of the cavity which they decorated, increased remarkably the startling significance in the character of the whole structure. Its past evil uses seemed ineradicably written over every part of it, as past crime and torment remain ineradicably written on the human face; the mind imbibed from it terrifying ideas of deadly treachery, of secret atrocities, of frightful refinements of torture, which no uninitiated eye had ever beheld, and no human resolution had ever been powerful enough to resist.

But the impressions thus received were not produced only by what was seen in and around this strange vault, but by what was heard there besides. The wind penetrated the cavity at some distance, and through some opening that could not be beheld, and was apparently intercepted in its passage, for it whistled upwards towards the entrance in shrill, winding notes, sometimes producing another and nearer sound, resembling the clashing of many small metallic substances violently shaken together. The noise of the wind, as well as the bubbling of the current of the Tiber, seemed to proceed from a greater distance than appeared compatible with the narrow extent of the back part of the temple, and the proximity of the river to its low foundation walls.

It was evident that the vault only reached its outlet after it had wound backwards, underneath the building, in some strange complication of passages or labyrinth of artificial caverns, which might have been built long since as dungeons for the living, or as sepulchres for the dead.

'The place of the sacrifice--aha! the place of the sacrifice!' cried the Pagan exultingly, as he drew Numerian to the entrance of the cavity, and solemnly pointed into the darkness beneath.

The father gazed steadily into the chasm, never turning now to look on Antonina, never moving to renew the struggle for freedom. Earthly loves and earthly hopes began to fade away from his heart--he was praying. The solemn words of Christian supplication fell in low, murmuring sounds from his lips, in the place of idolatry and bloodshed, and mingled with the incoherent ejaculations of the madman who kept him captive, and who now bent his glaring eyes on the darkness of the vault, half forgetful, in the gloomy fascination which it exercised even over him, of the prisoners whom he held at its mouth.

The single ray of light, admitted from the circular aperture of the wall, fell wild and fantastic over the widely-differing figures of the three, as they stood so strangely united together before the abyss that opened beneath them. The shadows were above and the shadows were around; there was no light in the ill-omened place but the one vivid ray that streamed over the gaunt figure of Ulpius, as he still pointed into the darkness; over the rigid features of Numerian, praying in the bitterness of expected death; and over the frail youthful form of Antonina as she nestled trembling at her father's side. It was an unearthly and a solemn scene!

Meanwhile the shadow which the girl had observed on the pavement before the doorway of the temple now appeared there again, but not to retire as before; for, the instant after, Goisvintha stealthily entered the outer apartment of the building left vacant by its first occupants. She passed softly around the pile of idols, looked into the inner recess of the temple, and saw the three figures standing together in the ray of light, gloomy and motionless, before the mouth of the cavity. Her first glance fixed on the Pagan, whom she instinctively doubted and dreaded, whose purpose in keeping captive the father and daughter she could not divine; her next was directed on Antonina.

The girl's position was a guarded one; still holding her father's hand, she was partly protected by his body; and stood unconsciously beneath the arm of Ulpius, as it was raised while he grasped Numerian's shoulder. Marking this, and remembering that Antonina had twice escaped her already, Goisvintha hesitated for a moment, and then, with cautious step and lowering brow, began to retire again towards the doorway of the building. 'Not yet--not yet the time!' she muttered, as she resumed her former lurking-place; 'they stand where the light is over them--the girl is watched and shielded--the two men are still on either side of her! Not yet the moment of the blow; the stroke of the knife must be sure and safe! Sure, for this time she must die by my hand! Safe, for I have other vengeance to wreak besides the vengeance on her! I, who have been patient and cunning since the night when I escaped from Aquileia, will be patient and cunning still! If she passes the door, I slay her as she goes out; if she remains in the temple--'

At the last word, Goisvintha paused and gazed upward; the setting sun threw its fiery glow over her haggard face; her eye brightened fiercely in the full light as she looked. 'The darkness is at hand!' she continued; 'the night will be thick and black in the dim halls of the temple; I shall see her when she shall not see me!--the darkness is coming; the vengeance is sure!'

She closed her lips, and with fatal perseverance continued to watch and wait, as she had resolutely watched and waited already. The Roman and the Goth; the opposite in sex, nation, and fate; the madman who dreamed of the sanguinary superstitions of Paganism before the temple altar, and the assassin who brooded over the chances of bloodshed beneath the temple portico, were now united in a mysterious identity of expectation, uncommunicated and unsuspected by either--the hour when the sun vanished from the heaven was the hour of the sacrifice for both!

****

There is now a momentary pause in the progress of events. Occurrences to be hereafter related render it necessary to take advantage of this interval to inform the reader of the real nature and use of the vault in the temple wall, the external appearance of which we have already described.

The marking peculiarity in the construction of the Pagan religion may be most aptly compared to the marking peculiarity in the construction of the pagan temples. Both were designed to attract the general eye by the outward effect only, which was in both the false delusive reflection of the inward substance.

In the temple, the people, as they worshipped beneath the long colonnades, or beheld the lofty porticoes from the street, were left to imagine the corresponding majesty and symmetry of the interior of the structure, and were not admitted to discover how grievously it disappointed the brilliant expectations which the exterior was so well calculated to inspire; how little the dark, narrow halls of the idols, the secret vaults and gloomy recesses within, fulfilled the promise of the long flights of steps, the broad extent of pavement, the massive sun-brightened pillars without. So in the religion, the votary was allured by the splendour of processions; by the pomp of auguries; by the poetry of the superstition which peopled his native woods with the sportive Dryads, and the fountains from which he drank with their guardian Naiads; which gave to mountain and lake, to sun and moon and stars, to all things around and above him, their fantastic allegory, or their gracious legend of beauty and love: but beyond this, his first acquaintance with his worship was not permitted to extend, here his initiation concluded. He was kept in ignorance of the dark and dangerous depths which lurked beneath this smooth and attractive surface; he was left to imagine that what was displayed was but the prelude to the future discovery of what was hidden of beauty in the rites of Paganism; he was not admitted to behold the wretched impostures, the loathsome orgies, the hideous incantations, the bloody human sacrifices perpetrated in secret, which made the foul, real substance of the fair exterior form. His first sight of the temple was not less successful in deceiving his eye than his first impression of the religion in deluding his mind.

With these hidden and guilty mysteries of the Pagan worship, the vault before which Ulpius now stood with his captives was intimately connected.

The human sacrifices offered among the Romans were of two kinds; those publicly and those privately performed. The first were of annual recurrence in the early years of the Republic; were prohibited at a later date; were revived by Augustus, who sacrificed his prisoners of war at the altar of Julius Caesar; and were afterwards--though occasionally renewed for particular purposes under some subsequent reigns--wholly abandoned as part of the ceremonies of Paganism during the later periods of the empire.

The sacrifices perpetrated in private were much longer practised. They were connected with the most secret mysteries of the mythology; were concealed from the supervision of government; and lasted probably until the general extinction of heathen superstition in Italy and the provinces.

Many and various were the receptacles constructed for the private immolation of human victims in different parts of the empire--in its crowded cities as well as in its solitary woods--and among all, one of the most remarkable and the longest preserved was the great cavity pierced in the wall of the temple which Ulpius had chosen for his solitary lurking-place in Rome.

It was not merely as a place of concealment for the act of immolation, and for the corpse of the victim, that the vault had been built. A sanguinary artifice had complicated the manner of its construction, by placing in the cavity itself the instrument of the sacrifice; by making it, as it were, not merely the receptacle, but the devourer also of its human prey. At the bottom of the flight of steps leading down into it (the top of which, as we have already observed, was alone visible from the entrance in the temple recess) was fixed the image of a dragon formed in brass.

The body of the monster, protruding opposite the steps almost at a right angle from the wall, was moved in all directions by steel springs, which communicated with one of the lower stairs, and also with a sword placed in the throat of the image to represent the dragon's tongue. The walls around the steps narrowed so as barely to admit the passage of the human body when they approached the dragon. At the slightest pressure on the stair with which the spring communicated, the body of the monster bent forward, and the sword instantly protruded from its throat, at such a height from the steps as ensure that it should transfix in a vital part the person who descended. The corpse, then dropping by its own weight off the sword, fell through a tunnelled opening beneath the dragon, running downward in an opposite direction to that taken by the steps above, and was deposited on an iron grating washed by the waters of the Tiber, which ran under the arched foundations of the temple. The grating was approached by a secret subterranean passage leading from the front of the building, by which the sacrificing priests were enabled to reach the dead body, to fasten weights to it, and opening the grating, to drop it into the river, never to be beheld again by mortal eyes.

In the days when this engine of destruction was permitted to serve the purpose for which the horrible ingenuity of its inventors had constructed it, its principal victims were young girls. Crowned with flowers, and clad in white garments, they were lured into immolating themselves by being furnished with rich offerings, and told that the sole object of their fatal expedition down the steps of the vault was to realise the pictures adorning its walls (which we have described a few pages back), by presenting their gifts at the shrine of the idol below.

At the period of which we write, the dragon had for many years--since the first prohibitions of Paganism--ceased to be fed with its wonted prey. The scales forming its body grew gradually corroded and loosened by the damp; and when moved by the wind which penetrated to them from beneath, whistling up in its tortuous course through the tunnel that ran in one direction below, and the vault of the steps that ascended in another above, produced the clashing sound which has been mentioned as audible at intervals from the mouth of the cavity. But the springs which moved the deadly apparatus of the whole machine being placed within it, under cover, continued to resist the slow progress of time and of neglect, and still remained as completely fitted as ever to execute the fatal purpose for which they had been designed.

The ultimate destiny of the dragon of brass was the destiny of the religion whose bloodiest superstitions it embodied: it fell beneath the resistless advance of Christianity. Shortly after the date of our narrative, the interior of the building beneath which it was placed having suffered from an accident, which will be related farther on, the exterior was dismantled, in order that its pillars might furnish materials for a church. The vault in the wall was explored by a monk who had been present at the destruction of other Pagan temples, and who volunteered to discover its contents. With a torch in one hand, and an iron bar in the other, he descended into the cavity, sounding the walls and the steps before him as he proceeded. For the first and the last time the sword protruded harmless from the monster's throat when the monk pressed the fatal stair, before stepping on it, with his iron bar. The same day the machine was destroyed and cast into the Tiber, where its victims had been thrown before it in former years.

*****

Some minutes have elapsed since we left the father and daughter standing by the Pagan's side before the mouth of the vault; and as yet there appears no change in the several positions of the three. But already, while Ulpius still looks down steadfastly into the cavity at his feet, his voice, as he continues to speak, grows louder, and his words become more distinct. Fearful recollections associated with the place are beginning to stir his weary memory, to lift the darkness of oblivion from his idle thoughts.

'They go down, far down there!' he abruptly exclaimed, pointing into the black depths of the vault, 'and never arise again to the light of the upper earth! The great Destroyer is watchful in his solitude beneath, and looks through the darkness for their approach! Hark! the hissing of his breath is like to the clash of weapons in a deadly strife!'

At this moment the wind moved the loose scales of the dragon. During an instant Ulpius remained silent, listening to the noise they produced. For the first time an expression of dread appeared on his face. His memory was obscurely reviving the incidents of his discovery of the deadly machinery in the vault when he first made his sojourn in the temple, when--filled with the confused remembrance of the mysterious rites and incantations, the secret sacrifices which he had witnessed and performed at Alexandria--he had found and followed the subterranean passage which led to the iron grating beneath the dragon. As the wind lulled again, and the clashing of the metal ceased with it, he began to give these recollections expression in words, uttering them in slow, solemn accents to himself.

'I have seen the Destroyer; the Invisible has revealed himself to me!' he murmured. 'I stood on the iron bars; the restless waters toiled and struggled beneath my feet as I looked up into the place of darkness. A voice called to me, "Get light, and behold me from above! Get light! get light!" Sun, and moon, and stars gave no light there! but lamps burnt in the city, in the houses of the dead, when I walked by them in the night-time; and the lamp gave light when sun, and moon, and stars gave none! From the top steps I looked down, and saw the Powerful One in his golden brightness; and approached not, but watched and listened in fear. The voice again!--the voice was heard again!--"Sacrifice to me in secret, as thy brethren sacrifice! Give me the living where the living are, and the dead where the dead!" The air came up cold, and the voice ceased, and the lamp was like sun, and moon, and stars--it gave no light in the place of darkness!'

While he spoke, the loose metal again clashed in the vault, for the wind was strengthening as the evening advanced. 'Hark! the signal to prepare the sacrifice!' cried the Pagan, turning abruptly to Numerian. 'Listen, bondman! the living and the dead are within our reach. The breath of the Invisible strikes them in the street and in the house; they stagger in the highways, and drop at the temple steps. When the hour comes we shall go forth and find them. Under my hand they go down into the cavern beneath. Whether they are hurled dead, or whether they go down living, they fall through to the iron bars, where the water leaps and rejoices to receive them! It is mine to sacrifice them above, and thine to wait for them below, to lift the bars and give them to the river to be swallowed up! The dead drop down first, the living that are slain by the Destroyer follow after!'

Here he paused suddenly. Now, for the first time, his eye rested on Antonina, whose very existence he seemed hitherto to have forgotten. A revolting smile of mingled cunning and satisfaction instantly changed the whole character of his countenance as he gazed on her and then looked round significantly to the vault. 'Here is one,' he whispered to Numerian, taking her by the arm. 'Keep her captive--the hour is near!'

Numerian had hitherto stood unheedful while he spoke; but when he touched Antonina the bare action was enough to arouse the father to resistance--hopeless though it was--once more. He shook off the grasp of Ulpius from the girl's arm, and drew back with her--breathless, vigilant, desperate--to the side-wall behind him.

The madman laughed in proud approval. 'My bondman obeys me and seizes the captive!' he cried. 'He remembers that the hour is near and loosens not his hold! Come,' he continued, 'come out into the hall beyond!--it is time that we watch for more victims for the sacrifice till the sun goes down. The Destroyer is mighty and must be obeyed!'

He walked to the entrance leading into the first apartment of the temple, and then waited to be followed by Numerian, who, now for the first time separated from Ulpius, remained stationary in the position he had last occupied, and looked eagerly around him. No chance of escape presented itself; the mouth of the vault on one side, and the passage through the partition on the other, were the only outlets to the place. There was no hope but to follow the Pagan into the great hall of the temple, to keep carefully at a distance from him, and to watch the opportunity of flight through the doorway. The street, so desolate when last beheld, might now afford more evidence that it was inhabited. Citizens, guards might be passing by, and might be summoned into the temple--help might be at hand.

As he moved forward with Antonina, such thoughts passed rapidly through the father's mind, unaccompanied at the moment by the recollection of the stranger who had followed them from the Pincian Gate, or of the apathy of the famished populace in aiding each other in any emergency. Seeing that he was followed as he had commanded, Ulpius passed on before them to the pile of idols; but a strange and sudden alteration appeared in his gait. He had hitherto walked with the step of a man--young, strong, and resolute of purpose; now he dragged one limb after the other as slowly and painfully as if he had received a mortal hurt. He tottered with more than the infirmity of his age, his head dropped upon his breast, and he moaned and murmured inarticulately in low, long-drawn cries.

He had advanced to the side of the pile, half-way towards the doorway of the temple, when Numerian, who had watched with searching eyes the abrupt change in his demeanour, forgetting the dissimulation which might still be all-important, abandoned himself to his first impulse, and hurriedly pressing forward with Antonina, attempted to pass the Pagan and escape. But at the moment Ulpius stopped in his slow progress, reeled, threw out his hands convulsively, and seizing Numerian by the arm, staggered back with him against the side-wall of the temple. The fingers of the tortured wretch closed as if they were never to be unlocked again--closed as if with the clutch of death, with the last frantic grasp of a drowning man.

For days and nights past he had toiled incessantly under the relentless tyranny of his frenzy, building up higher and higher his altar of idols, and pouring forth his invocations before his gods in the place of the sacrifice; and now, at the moment when he was most triumphant in his ferocious activity of purpose, when his fancied bondman and his fancied victim were most helpless at his command--now, when his strained faculties were strung to their highest pitch, the long-deferred paroxysm had seized him, which was the precursor of his repose, of the only repose granted by his awful fate--a change (the mournful change already described) in the form of his insanity. For at those rare periods when he slept, his sleep was not unconsciousness, not rest: it was a trance of hideous dreams--his tongue spoke, his limbs moved, when he slumbered as when he woke. It was only when his visions of the pride, the power, the fierce conflicts, and daring resolutions of his maturer years gave place to his dim, quiet, waking dreams of his boyish days, that his wasted faculties reposed, and his body rested with them in the motionless languor of perfect fatigue. Then, if words were still uttered by his lips, they were as murmurs of an infant--happy sleep; for the innocent phrases of his childhood which they then revived, seemed for a time to bring with them the innocent tranquillity of his childhood as well.

'Go! go!--fly while you are yet free!' cried Numerian, dropping the hand of Antonina, and pointing to the door. But for the second time the girl refused to move forward a step. No horror, no peril in the temple could banish for an instant her remembrance of the night at the farm-house in the suburbs. She kept her head turned towards the vacant entrance, fixed her eyes on it in the unintermitting watchfulness of terror, and whispered affrightedly, 'Goisvintha! Goisvintha!' when her father spoke.

The clasp of the Pagan's fingers remained fixed and deathlike as at first; he leaned back against the wall, as still as if life and action had for ever departed from him. The paroxysm had passed away; his face, distorted but the moment before, was now in repose, but it was a repose that was awful to look on. Tears rolled slowly from his half-closed eyes over his seamed and wrinkled cheeks--tears which were not the impressive expression of mental anguish (for a vacant and unchanging smile was on his lips), but the mere mechanical outburst of the physical weakness that the past crisis of agony had left behind it. Not the slightest appearance of thought or observation was perceptible in his features: his face was the face of an idiot.

Numerian, who had looked on him for an instant, shuddered and averted his eyes, recoiling from the sight before him. But a more overpowering trial of his resolution was approaching, which he could not avoid. Ere long the voice of Ulpius grew audible once more; but now its tones were weak, piteous, almost childish, and the words they uttered were quiet words of love and gentleness, which dropping from such lips, and pronounced in such a place, were fearful to hear. The temple and all that was in it vanished from his sight as from his memory. Swayed by the dread and supernatural influences of his disease, the madman passed back in an instant over the dark valley of life's evil pilgrimage to the long-quitted precincts of his boyish home. While in bodily presence he stood in the place of his last crimes, the outcast of reason and humanity, in mental consciousness he lay in his mother's arms, as he had lain there ere yet he had departed to the temple at Alexandria; and his heart communed with her heart, and his eyes looked on her as they had looked before his father's fatal ambition had separated for ever parent and child!

'Mother!--come back, mother!' he whispered. 'I was not asleep: I saw you when you came in, and sat by my bedside, and wept over me when you kissed me! Come back, and sit by me still! I am going away, far away, and may never hear your voice again! How happy we should be, mother, if I stayed with you always! But it is my father's will that I should go to the temple in another country, and live there to be a priest; and his will must be obeyed. I may never return; but we shall not forget one another! I shall remember your words when we used to talk together happily, and you shall still remember mine!'

Hardly had the first sentence been uttered by Ulpius when Antonina felt her father's whole frame suddenly tremble at her side. She turned her eyes from the doorway, on which they had hitherto been fixed, and looked on him. The Pagan's hand had fallen from his arm: he was free to depart, to fly as he had longed to fly but a few minutes before, and yet he never stirred. His daughter touched him, spoke to him, but he neither moved nor answered. It was not merely the shock of the abrupt transition in the language of Ulpius from the ravings of crime to the murmurs of love--it was not merely astonishment at hearing from him, in his madness, revelations of his early life which had never passed his lips during his days of treacherous servitude in the house on the Pincian Hill, that thus filled Numerian's inmost soul with awe, and struck his limbs motionless. There was more in all that he heard than this. The words seemed as words that had doomed him at once and for ever. His eyes, directed full on the face of the madman, were dilated with horror, and his deep, gasping, convulsive breathings mingled heavily, during the moment of silence that ensued, with the chiming of the bells above and the bubbling of the water below--the lulling music of the temple, playing its happy evening hymn at the pleasant close of day.

'We shall remember, mother!--we shall remember!' continued the Pagan softly, 'and be happy in our remembrances! My brother, who loves me not, will love you when I am gone! You will walk in my little garden, and think on me as you look at the flowers that we have planted and watered together in the evening hours, when the sky was glorious to behold, and the earth was all quiet around us! Listen, mother, and kiss me! When I go to the far country, I will make a garden there like my garden here, and plant the same flowers that we have planted here, and in the evening I will go out and give them water at the hour when you go out to give my flowers water at home; and so, though we see each other no more, it will yet be as if we laboured together in the garden as we labour now!'

The girl still fixed her eager gaze on her father. His eyes presented the same rigid expression of horror; but he was now wiping off with his own hand, mechanically, as if he knew it not, the foam which the paroxysms had left round the madman's lips, and, amid the groans that burst from him, she could hear such words as, 'Lord God!--mercy, Lord God! Thou, who hast thus restored him to me--thus, worse than dead!--mercy! mercy!'

The light on the pavement beneath the portico of the temple was fading visibly--the sun had gone down.

For the third time the madman spoke, but his tones were losing their softness; they were complaining, plaintive, unutterably mournful; his dreams of the past were already changing. 'Farewell, brother--farewell for years and years!' he cried. 'You have not given me the love that I gave you. The fault was not mine that our

father loved me the best, and chose me to be sent to the temple to be a priest at
the altar of the gods! The fault was not mine that I partook not in your favoured
sports, and joined not the companions whom you sought; it was our father's will
that I should not live as you lived, and I obeyed it! You have spoken to me in
anger, and turned from me in disdain; but farewell again, Cleander--farewell in
forgiveness and in love!'

He might have spoken more, but his voice was drowned in one long shriek of
agony which burst from Numerian's lips, and echoed discordantly through the
hall of the temple, and he sank down with his face to the ground at the Pagan's
feet. The dark and terrible destiny was fulfilled. The enthusiast for the right and
the fanatic for the wrong; the man who had toiled to reform the Church, and the
man who had toiled to restore the Temple; the master who had received and trusted the servant in his home, and the servant who in that home had betrayed the
master's trust--the two characters, separated hitherto in the sublime disunion of
good and bad, now struck together in tremendous contact, as brethren who had
drawn their life from one source, who as children had been sheltered under the
same roof!

Not in the hours when the good Christian succoured the then forsaken Pagan,
wandering homeless in Rome, was the secret disclosed; no chance word of it was
uttered when the deceiver told the feigned relation of his life to the benefactor
whom he was plotting to deceive, or when, on the first morning of the siege, the
machinations of the servant triumphed over the confidence of the master: it was
reserved to be revealed in the words of delirium, at the closing years of madness,
when he who discovered it was unconscious of all that he spoke, and his eyes were
blinded to the true nature of all that he saw; when earthly voices that might once
have called him back to repentance, to recognition, and to love, were become to
him as sounds that have no meaning; when, by a ruthless and startling fatality, it
was on the brother who had wrought for the true faith that the whole crushing
weight of the terrible disclosure fell, unpartaken by the brother who had wrought
for the false! But the judgments pronounced in Time go forth from the tribunal
of that Eternity to which the mysteries of life tend, and in which they shall be
revealed--neither waiting on human seasons nor abiding by human justice, but
speaking to the soul in the language of immortality, which is heard in the world
that is now, and interpreted in the world that is to come.

Lost, for an instant, even the recollection that Goisvintha might still be watching
her opportunity from without, calling despairingly on her father, and vainly striving to raise him from the ground, Antonina remembered not, in the overwhelming trial of the moment, the revelations of Numerian's past life that had been dis-

closed to her in the days when the famine was at its worst in Rome. The name of 'Cleander', which she had then heard her father pronounce, as the name that he had abandoned when he separated himself from the companions of his sinful choice, passed unheeded by her when the Pagan unconsciously uttered it. She saw the whole scene but as a fresh menace of danger, as a new vision of terror, more ominous of ill than all that had preceded it.

Thick as was the darkness in which the lulling and involuntary memories of the past had enveloped the perceptions of Ulpius, the father's piercing cry of anguish seemed to have penetrated it with a sudden ray of light. The madman's half-closed eyes opened instantly and fixed, dreamily at first, on the altar of idols. He waved his hands to and fro before him, as if her were parting back the folds of a heavy veil that obscured his sight; but his wayward thoughts did not resume as yet their old bias towards ferocity and crime. When he spoke again, his speech was still inspired by the visions of his early life--but now of his early life in the temple at Alexandria. His expressions were more abrupt, more disjointed than before; yet they continued to display the same evidence of the mysterious, instinctive vivid-ness of recollection, which was the result of the sudden change in the nature of his insanity. His language wandered (still as if the words came from him unde-signedly and unconsciously) over the events of his boyish introduction to the serv-ice of the gods, and, though confusing them in order, still preserved them in sub-stance, as they have been already related in the history of his 'apprenticeship to the temple'.

Now he was in imagination looking down once more from the summit of the Temple of Serapis on the glittering expanse of the Nile and the wide country around it; and now he was walking proudly through the streets of Alexandria by the side of his uncle, Macrinus, the high priest. Now he was wandering at night, in curiosity and awe, through the gloomy vaults and subterranean corridors of the sacred place; and now he was listening, well pleased, to the kindly greeting, the inspiring praises of Macrinus during their first interview. But at this point, and while dwelling on this occasion, his memory became darkened again; it vainly endeavoured to retrace the circumstances attending the crowning evidence of the high priest's interest in his pupil, and anxiety to identify him completely with his new protector and his new duties, which had been displayed when he conferred on the trembling boy the future distinction of one of his own names.

And here, let it be remembered, as a chief link in the mysterious chain of fatali-ties which had united to keep the brothers apart as brethren after they had met as men, that both had, from widely different causes, abandoned in after-life the names which they bore in their father's house; that while one, by his own act and

for his own purpose, transformed himself from Cleander, the associate of the careless and the criminal, to Numerian, the preacher of the Gospel and reformer of
the Church, the other had (to quote the words of the fourth chapter), 'become
from the boy Emilius the student Ulpius,' by the express and encouraging command of his master, Macrinus, the high priest.

While the Pagan still fruitlessly endeavoured to revive the events connected with
the change in his designation on his arrival in Alexandria, and, chafing under the
burden of oblivion that weighed upon his thoughts, attempted for the first time
to move from the wall against which he had hitherto leaned; while Antonina still
strove in vain to recall her father to the recollection of the terrible exigencies of
the moment as he crouched prostrate at the madman's feet--the doorway of the
temple was darkened once more by the figure of Goisvintha. She stood on the
threshold, a gloomy and indistinct form in the fading light, looking intently into
the deeply shadowed interior of the building. As she marked the altered positions
of the father and daughter, she uttered a suppressed ejaculation of triumph; but,
while the sound passed her lips, she heard, or thought she heard, a noise in the
street behind. Even now her vigilance and cunning, her deadly, calculating resolution to await in immovable patience the fitting time for striking the blow deliberately and with impunity, did not fail her. Turning instantly, she walked to the
top step of the temple, and stood there for a few moments, watchfully surveying
the open space before her.

But in those few moments the scene in the building changed once more. The
madman, while he still wavered between relapsing into the raving fit and contin-
uing under the influence of the tranquil mood in which he had been premature-
ly disturbed, caught sight of Goisvintha when her approach suddenly shadowed
the entrance to the temple. Her presence, momentary though it was, was for him
the presence of a figure that had not appeared before; that had stood in a strange
position between the shade within and the faint light without; it was a new object,
presented to his eyes while they were straining to recover such imperfect faculties
of observation as had been their wont, and it ascendancy over him was instantaneous and all-powerful.

He started, bewildered like a deep sleeper suddenly awoke; violent shudderings
ran for a moment over his frame; then it strengthened again with its former
unnatural strength; the demon raged within him in renewed fury as he tore his
robe which Numerian held as he lay at his feet from the feeble grasp that confined
it, and, striding up to the pile of idols, stretched out his hands in solemn depre-
cation. 'The high priest has slept before the altar of the gods!' he cried loudly,
'but they have been patient with their well-beloved; their thunder has not struck

him for his crime! Now the servant returns to his service--the rites of Serapis begin!'

Numerian still remained prostrate, spirit-broken; he slowly clasped his hands together on the floor, and his voice was now to be heard, still supplicating in low and stifled accents, as if in unceasing prayer lay his last hope of preserving his own reason. 'God! Thou art the God of Mercy; be merciful to him!' he murmured. 'Thou acceptest of repentance; grant repentance to him! If at any time I have served Thee without blame, let the service be counted to him; let the vials of Thy wrath be poured out on me!'

'Hark! the trumpet blows for the sacrifice!' interrupted the raving voice of the Pagan, as he turned from the altar, and extended his arms in frenzied inspiration. 'The roar of music and the voice of exultation soar upward from the highest mountain-tops! The incense smokes, and in and out, and round and round, the dancers whirl about the pillars of the temple! The ox for the sacrifice is without spot; his horns are gilt; the crown and fillet adorn his head. The priest stands before him naked from the waist upwards; he heaves the libation out of the cup; the blood flows over the altar! Up! up! tear forth with reeking hands the heart while it is yet warm, futurity is before you in the quivering entrails, look on them and read! read!'

While he spoke, Goisvintha had entered the temple. The street was still desolate; no help was at hand.

Not advancing at once, she concealed herself near the door behind a projection in the pile of idols, watching from it until Ulpius, in the progress of his frenzy, should turn away from Antonina, whom he stood fronting at this instant. But she had not entered unperceived; Antonina had seen her again. And now the bitterness of death, when the young die unprotected in their youth, came over the girl, and she cried in a low wailing voice, as she knelt by Numerian's side: 'I must die, father, I must die, as Hermanric died! Look up at me, and speak to me before I die!'

Her father was still praying; he heard nothing, for his heart was bleeding in atonement at the shrine of his boyish home, and his soul still communed with its Maker. The voice that followed hers was the voice of Ulpius.

'Oh, beautiful are the gardens round the sacred altars, and lofty the trees that embower the glittering shrines!' he exclaimed, rapt and ecstatic in his new visions. 'Lo, the morning breaks, and the spirits of light are welcomed by a sacrifice! The sun goes down behind the mountain, and the beams of evening tremble on the victim beneath the knife of the adoring priest! The moon and stars shine high in the firmament, and the Genii of Nights are saluted in the still hours with blood!'

As he paused, the lament of Antonina was continued in lower and lower tones: 'I must die, father, I must die!' And with it murmured the supplicating accents of Numerian: 'God of Mercy! deliver the helpless and forgive the afflicted! Lord of Judgment! deal gently with Thy servants who have sinned!' While, mingling with both in discordant combination, the strange music of the temple still poured on its lulling sound--the rippling of the running waters and the airy chiming of the bells!

'Worship!--emperors, armies, nations, glorify and worship me!' shouted the madman, in thunder-tones of triumph and command, as his eye for the first time encountered the figure of Numerian prostrate at his feet. 'Worship the demi-god who moves with the deities through spheres unknown to man! I have heard the moans of the unburied who wander on the shores of the Lake of the Dead--worship! I have looked on the river whose black current roars and howls in its course through the caves of everlasting night--worship! I have seen the furies lashed by serpents on their wrinkled necks, and followed them as they hurled their torches over the pining ghosts! I have stood unmoved in the hurricane-tumult of hell--worship! worship! worship!'

He turned round again towards the altar of idols, calling upon his gods to proclaim his deification, and at the moment when he moved, Goisvintha sprang forward. Antonina was kneeling with her face turned from the door, as the assassin seized her by her long hair and drove the knife into her neck. The moaning accents of the girl, bewailing her approaching fate, closed in one faint groan; she stretched out her arms, and fell forward over her father's body.

In the ferocious triumph of the moment, Goisvintha raised her arm to repeat the stroke; but at that instant the madman looked round. 'The sacrifice--the sacrifice!' he shouted, leaping at one spring like a wild beast at her throat. She struck ineffectually at him with the knife, as he fastened his long nails in her flesh and hurled her backwards to the floor. Then he yelled and gibbered in frantic exultation, set his foot on her breast, and spat on her as she lay beneath him.

The contact of the girl's body when she fell--the short but terrible tumult of the attack that passed almost over him--the shrill, deafening cries of the madman, awoke Numerian from his trance of despairing remembrance, aroused him in his agony of supplicating prayer. He looked up.

The scene that met his eyes was one of those scenes which crush every faculty but the faculty of mechanical action--before which, thought vanishes from men's minds, utterance is suspended on their lips, expression is paralysed on their faces. The coldness of the tomb seemed breathed over Numerian's aspect by the contemplation of the terrible catastrophe: his eyes were glassy and vacant, his lips parted and rigid; even the remembrance of the discovery of his brother seemed lost to him as he stooped over his daughter and bound a fragment of her robe round her neck. The mute, soulless, ghastly stillness of death looked settled on his features, as, unconscious now of weakness or age, he rose with her in his arms, stood motionless for one moment before the doorway, and looked slowly round on Ulpius; then he moved forward with heavy regular steps. The Pagan's foot was still on Goisvintha's breast as the father passed him; his gaze was still fixed on her; but his cries of triumph were calmed; he laughed and muttered incoherently to himself.

The moon was rising, soft, faint, and tranquil, over the quiet street as Numerian descended the temple steps with his daughter in his arms, and, after an instant's pause of bewilderment and doubt, instinctively pursued his slow, funereal course along the deserted roadway in the direction of home. Soon, as he advanced, he beheld in the moonlight, down the long vista of the street at its termination, a little assemblage of people walking towards him with calm and regular progress. As they came nearer, he saw that one of them held an open book, that another carried a crucifix, and that others followed these two with clasped hands and drooping heads. And then, after an interval, the fresh breezes that blew towards him bore onward these words, slowly and reverently pronounced:--

'Know, therefore, that God exacteth of thee less than thine iniquity deserveth.

'Canst thou, by searching, find out God? Canst thou find out the Almighty to perfection?'

Then the breeze fell, the words grew indistinct, but the procession still moved forward. As it came nearer and nearer, the voice of the reader was again plainly heard:--

'If iniquity be in thy hand, put it far away, and let not wickedness dwell in thy tabernacles.

'For then shalt thou lift up thy face without spot; yea, thou shalt be steadfast, and shalt not fear;

'Because thou shalt forget thy misery, and remember it as waters that pass away:

And thine age shall be clearer than the noonday; thou shalt shine forth, thou shalt be as the morning.'

The reader stopped and closed the book; for now Numerian had met the members of the little procession, and they looked on him standing voiceless before them in the clear moonlight, with his daughter's head drooping over his shoulder as he carried her in his arms.

There were some among those who gathered round him whose features he would have recognised at another time as the features of the surviving adherents of his former congregation. The assembly he had met was composed of the few sincere Christians in Rome, who had collected, on the promulgation of the news that Alaric had ratified terms of peace, to make a pilgrimage through the city, in the hopeless endeavour, by reading from the Bible and passing exhortation, to awaken the reckless populace to a feeling of contrition for their sins, and of devout gratitude for their approaching deliverance from the horrors of the siege.

But now, when Numerian confronted them, neither by word nor look did he express the slightest recognition of any who surrounded him. To all the questions addressed to him, he replied by hurried gestures that none could comprehend. To all the promises of help and protection heaped upon him in the first outbreak of the grief and pity of his adherents of other days, he answered but by the same dull, vacant glance. It was only when they relieved him of his burden, and gently prepared to carry the senseless girl among them back to her father's house, that he spoke; and then, in faint entreating tones, he besought them to let him hold her hand as they went, so that he might be the first to feel her pulse beat--if it yet moved.

They turned back by the way they had come--a sorrowful and slow-moving procession! As they passed on, the reader again opened the Sacred Book; and then these words rose through the soothing and heavenly tranquillity of the first hours of night:--

'Behold, happy is the man whom God correcteth: therefore despise not thou the chastening of the Almighty:

'For he maketh sore, and bindeth up: he woundeth, and his hands make whole.'

Chapter 26

RETRIBUTION

As, in the progress of Life, each man pursues his course with the passions, good and evil, set, as it were, on either side of him; and viewing their results in the actions of his fellow-men, finds his attention, while still attracted by the spectacle of what is noble and virtuous, suddenly challenged by the opposite display of what is mean and criminal--so, in the progress of this narrative, which aims to be the reflection of Life, the reader who has journeyed with us thus far, and who may now be inclined to follow the little procession of Christian devotees, to walk by the side of the afflicted father, and to hold with him the hand of his ill-fated child, is yet, in obedience to the conditions of the story, required to turn back for awhile to the contemplation of its darker passages of guilt and terror--he must enter the temple again; but he will enter it for the last time.

The scene before the altar of idols was fast proceeding to its fatal climax.

The Pagan's frenzy had exhausted itself in its own fury--his insanity was assuming a quieter and a more dangerous form; his eye grew cunning and suspicious; a stealthy deliberation and watchfulness appeared in all his actions. He now slowly lifted his foot from Goisvintha's breast, and raised his hands at the same time to strike her back if she should attempt to escape. Seeing that she lay senseless from her fall, he left her; retired to one of the corners of the temple, took from it a rope that lay there, and returning, bound her arms behind her at the hands and wrists. The rope cut deep through the skin--the pain restored her to her senses; she suffered the sharp agony in her own body, in the same place where she had inflicted it on the young chieftain at the farm- house beyond the suburbs.

The minute after, she felt herself dragged along the ground, farther into the interior of the building. The madman drew her up to the iron gates of the passage through the partition, and fastening the end of the rope to them, left her there. This part of the temple was enveloped in total darkness--her assailant addressed not a word to her--she could not obtain even a glimpse of his form, but she could hear him still laughing to himself in hoarse, monotonous tones, that sounded now near, and now distant again.

She abandoned herself as lost--prematurely devoted to the torment and death that she had anticipated; but, as yet, her masculine resolution and energy did not decline. The very intensity of the anguish she suffered from the bindings at her wrists, producing a fierce bodily effort to resist it, strengthened her iron-strung nerves. She neither cried for help nor appealed to the Pagan for pity. The gloomy fatalism which she had inherited from her savage ancestors sustained her in a suicide-pride.

Ere long the laughter of Ulpius, while he moved slowly hither and thither in the darkness of the temple, was overpowered by the sound of her voice--deep, groaning, but yet steady--as she uttered her last words--words poured forth like the wild dirges, the fierce death-songs of the old Goths when they died deserted on the bloody battle-field, or were cast bound into deep dungeons, a prey to the viper and the asp. Thus she spoke:-- 'I swore to be avenged! while I went forth from Aquileia with the child that was killed and the child that was wounded; while I climbed the high wall in the night-time, and heard the tumult of the beating waves near the bank where I buried the dead; while I wandered in the darkness over the naked heath and through the lonely forest; while I climbed the pathless sides of the mountains, and made my refuge in the cavern by the waters of the dark lake.

'I swore to be avenged! while the warriors approached me on their march, and the roaring of the trumpets and the clash of the armour sounded in my ears; while I greeted my kinsman, Hermanric, a mighty chieftain, at the king's side, among the invading hosts; while I looked on my last child, dead like the rest, and knew that he was buried afar from the land of his people, and from the others that the Romans had slain before him.

'I swore to be avenged! while the army encamped before Rome, and I stood with Hermanric, looking on the great walls in the misty evening; while the daughter of the Roman was a prisoner in our tent, and I eyed her as she lay on my knees; while for her sake my kinsman turned traitor, and withheld my hand from the blow;

while I passed unseen into the lonely farm-house to deal judgment on him with my knife; while I saw him die the death of a deserter at my feet, and knew that it was a Roman who had lured him from his people, and blinded him to the righteousness of revenge.

'I swore to be avenged! while I walked round the grave of the chieftain who was the last of my race; while I stood alone out of the army of my people in the city of the slayers of my babes; while I tracked the footsteps of the Roman who had twice escaped me, as she fled through the street; while I watched and was patient among the pillars of the temple, and waited till the sun went down, and the victim was unshielded for the moment to strike.

'I swore to be avenged! and my oath has been fulfilled--the knife that still bleeds drops with her blood; the chief vengeance has been wreaked! The rest that were to be slain remain for others, and not for me! For now I go to my husband and my children; now the hour is near at hand when I shall herd with their spirits in the Twilight World of Shadows, and make my long-abiding place with them in the Valley of Eternal Repose! The Destinies have willed it--it is enough!'

Her voice trembled and grew faint as she pronounced the last words. The anguish of the fastenings at her wrists was at last overpowering her senses--conquering, in spite of all resistance, her stubborn endurance. For a little while yet she spoke at intervals, but her speech was fragmentary and incoherent. At one moment she still gloried in her revenge, at another she exulted in the fancied contemplation of the girl's body still lying before her, and her hands writhed beneath their bonds in the effort to repossess themselves of the knife and strike again. But soon all sounds ceased to proceed from her lips, save the loud, thick, irregular breathings, which showed that she was yet conscious and yet lived.

Meanwhile the madman had passed into the inner recess of the temple, and had drawn the shutter over the opening in the wall, through which light had been admitted into the place when Numerian and Antonina first entered it. Even the black chasm formed by the mouth of the vault of the dragon now disappeared, with all other objects, in the thick darkness. But no obscurity could confuse the senses of Ulpius in the temple, whose every corner he visited in his restless wanderings by night and by day alike. Led as if by a mysterious penetration of sight, he traced his way unerringly to the entrance of the vault, knelt down before it, and placing his hands on the first of the steps by which it was descended, listened, breathless and attentive, to the sounds that rose from the abyss--listened, rapt and unmoving, a formidable and unearthly figure--like a magician waiting for a voice from the oracles of Hell--like a spirit of Night looking down into the mid-caverns

of the earth, and watching the mysteries of subterranean creation, the giant pulses of Action and Heat, which are the life-springs of the rolling world.

The fitful wind whistled up, wild and plaintive; the river chafed and bubbled
through the iron grating below; the loose scales of the dragon clashed as the night
breezes reached them: and these sounds were still to him as the language of his
gods, which filled him with a fearful rapture, and inspired him, in the terrible
degradation of his being, as with a new soul. He listened and listened yet.
Fragments of wild fancies--the vain yearnings of the disinherited mind to recover
its divine birthright of boundless thought--now thrilled through him, and held
him still and speechless where he knelt.

But at length, through the gloomy silence of the recess, he heard the voice of
Goisvintha raised once more, and in hoarse, wild tones calling aloud for light and
help. The agony of pain and suspense, the awful sense of darkness and stillness,
of solitary bondage and slow torment, had at last effected that which no open
peril, no common menace of violent death could have produced. She yielded to
fear and despair--sank prostrate under a paralysing, superstitious dread. The misery that she had inflicted on others recoiled in retribution on herself, as she now
shuddered under the consciousness of the first emotions of helpless terror that she
had ever felt.

Ulpius instantly rose from the vault, and advanced straight through the darkness
to the gates of the partition; but he passed his prisoner without stopping for an
instant, and hastening into the outer apartment of the temple, began to grope
over the floor for the knife which the woman had dropped when he bound her.
He was laughing to himself once more, for the evil spirit was prompting him to
a new project, tempting him to a pitiless refinement of cruelty and deceit.

He found the knife, and returning with it to Goisvintha, cut the rope that confined her wrists. Then she became silent when the first sharpness of her suffering
was assuaged; he whispered softly in her ear, 'Follow me, and escape!'

Bewildered and daunted by the darkness and mystery around her, she vainly
strained her eyes to look through the obscurity as Ulpius drew her on into the
recess. He placed her at the mouth of the vault, and here she strove to speak; but
low, inarticulate sounds alone proceeded from her powerless utterance. Still there
was no light; still the burning, gnawing agony at her wrists (relieved but for an
instant when the rope was cut) continued and increased; and still she felt the presence of the unseen being at her side, whom no darkness could blind, and who
bound and loosed at his arbitrary will.

By nature fierce, resolute, and vindictive under injury, she was a terrible evidence of the debasing power of crime, as she now stood, enfeebled by the weight of her own avenging guilt, upraised to crush her in the hour of her pride; by the agency of Darkness, whose perils the innocent and the weak have been known to brave; by Suspense, whose agony they have resisted; by Pain, whose infliction they have endured in patience.

'Go down, far down the steep steps, and escape!' whispered the madman, in soft, beguiling tones. 'The darkness above leads to the light below! Go down, far down!'

He quitted his hold of her as he spoke. She hesitated, shuddered, and drew back; but again she was urged forward, and again she heard the whisper, 'The darkness above leads to the light below! Go down, far down!'

Despair gave the firmness to proceed, and dread the hope to escape. Her wounded arms trembled as she now stretched them out and felt for the walls of the vault on either side of her. The horror of death in utter darkness, from unseen hands, and the last longing aspiration to behold the light of heaven once more, were at their strongest within her as she began slowly and cautiously to tread the fatal stairs.

While she descended, the Pagan dropped into his former attitude at the month of the vault, and listened breathlessly. Minutes seemed to elapse between each step as she went lower and lower down. Suddenly he heard her pause, as if panic-stricken in the darkness, and her voice ascended to him, groaning, 'Light! light! oh, where is the light!' He rose up, and stretched out his hands to hurl her back if she should attempt to return; but she descended again. Twice he heard her heavy footfall on the steps--then there was an interval of deep silence--then a sharp, grinding clash of metal echoed piercingly through the vault, followed by the noise of a dull, heavy fall, faintly audible far beneath--and then the old familiar sounds of the place were heard again, and were not interrupted more. The sacrifice to the Dragon was achieved!

*****

The madman stood on the steps of the sacred building, and looked out on the street shining before him in the bright Italian moonlight. No remembrance of Numerian and Antonina, and of the earlier events in the temple, remained within him. He was pondering imperfectly, in vague pride and triumph, over the sacrifice that he had offered up at the shrine of the Dragon of brass. Thus secretly exulting, he now remained inactive. Absorbed in his wandering meditations, he delayed to trace the subterranean passages leading to the iron grating where the corpse of Goisvintha lay washed by the waters, as they struggled onward through the bars, and waiting but his hand to be cast into the river, where all past sacrifices had been engulphed before it.

His tall solitary figure was lit by the moonlight streaming through the pillars of the portico; his loose robes waved slowly about him in the wind, as he stood firm and erect before the door of the temple: he looked more like the spectral genius of departed Paganism than a living man. But, lifeless though he seemed, his quick eye was still on the watch, still directed by the restless suspicion of insanity. Minute after minute quietly elapsed, and as yet nothing was presented to his rapid observation but the desolate roadway, and the high, gloomy houses that bounded it on either side. It was soon, however, destined to be attracted by objects which startled the repose of the tranquil street with the tumult of action and life.

He was still gazing earnestly on the narrow view before him, vaguely imagining to himself, the while, Goisvintha's fatal descent into the vault, and thinking triumphantly of her dead body that now lay on the grating beneath it, when a red glare of torchlight, thrown wildly on the moon-brightened pavement, whose purity it seemed to stain, caught his eye.

The light appeared at the end of the street leading from the more central portion of the city, and ere long displayed clearly a body of forty or fifty people advancing towards the temple. The Pagan looked eagerly on them as they came nearer and nearer. The assembly was composed of priests, soldiers, and citizens--the priests bearing torches, the soldiers carrying hammers, crowbars, and other similar tools, or bending under the weight of large chests secured with iron fastenings, close to which the populace walked, as if guarding them with jealous care. This strange procession was preceded by two men, who were considerably in advance of it--a priest and soldier. An expression of impatience and exultation appeared on their pale, famine-wasted countenances, as they approached the temple with rapid steps.

Ulpius never moved from his position, but fixed his piercing eyes on them as they advanced. Not vainly did he now stand, watchful and menacing, before the entrance of his gloomy shrine. He had seen the first degradations heaped on fallen Paganism, and he was now to see the last. He had immolated all his affections and all his hopes, all his faculties of body and mind, his happiness in boyhood, his enthusiasm in youth, his courage in manhood, his reason in old age, at the altar of his gods; and now they were to exact from him, in their defence, lonely criminal, maddened, as he already was in their cause, more than all this! The decree had gone forth from the Senate which devoted to legalised pillage the treasures in the temples of Rome.

Rulers of a people impoverished by former exactions, and comptrollers only of an exhausted treasury, the government of the city had searched vainly among all ordinary resources for the means of paying the heavy ransom exacted by Alaric as the price of peace. The one chance of meeting the emergency that remained was to strip the Pagan temples of the mass of jewelled ornaments and utensils, the costly robes, the idols of gold and silver which they were known to contain, and which, under that mysterious hereditary influence of superstition, whose power it is the longest labour of truth to destroy, had remained untouched and respected, alike by the people and the senate, after the worship that they represented had been interdicted by the laws, and abandoned by the nation.

This last expedient for freeing Rome from the blockade was adopted almost as soon as imagined. The impatience of the starved populace for the immediate collection of the ransom allowed the government little time for the tedious preliminaries of deliberation. The soldiers were provided at once with the necessary implements for the task imposed on them; certain chosen members of the senate and the people followed them, to see that they honestly gathered in the public spoil; and the priests of the Christian churches volunteered to hallow the expedition by their presence, and led the way with their torches into every secret apartment of the temples where treasure might be contained. At the close of the day, immediately after it had been authorised, this strange search for the ransom was hurriedly commenced. Already much had been collected; votive offerings of price had been snatched from the altars, where they had so long hung undisturbed; hidden treasure-chests of sacred utensils had been discovered and broken open; idols had been stripped of their precious ornaments and torn from their massive pedestals; and now the procession of gold-seekers, proceeding along the banks of the Tiber, had come in sight of the little temple of Serapis, and were hastening forward to empty it, in its turn, of every valuable that it contained.

The priest and the soldier, calling to their companions behind to hurry on, had now arrived opposite the temple steps, and saw confronting them in the pale moonlight, from the eminence on which he stood, the weird and solitary figure of Ulpius--the apparition of a Pagan in the gorgeous robes of his priesthood, bidden back from the tombs to stay the hand of the spoiler before the shrine of his gods.

The soldier dropped his weapon to the ground, and, trembling in every limb, refused to proceed. But the priest, a tall, stern, emaciated man, went on defence-less and undaunted. He signed himself solemnly with the cross as he slowly ascended the steps; fixed his unflinching eyes on the madman, who glared back on him in return; and called aloud in a harsh, steady voice: 'Man or demon! in the name of Christ, whom thou deniest, stand back!'

For an instant, as the priest approached him, the Pagan averted his eyes and looked on the concourse of people and the armed soldiers rapidly advancing. His fingers closed round the hilt of Goisvintha's knife, which he had hitherto held loosely in his hand, as he exclaimed in low, concentrated tones, 'Aha! the siege--the siege of Serapis!' The priest, now standing on the same step with him, stretched out his arm to thrust him back, and at that moment received the stroke of the knife. He staggered, lifted his hand again to sign his forehead with the cross, and, as he raised it, rolled back dead on the pavement of the street.

The soldier, standing motionless with superstitious terror a few feet from the corpse, called to his companions for help. Hurling his bloody weapon at them in defiance, as they ran in confusion to the base of the temple steps, Ulpius entered the building, and locked and chained the gates.

Then the assembled people thronging round the corpse of the priest, heard the madman shouting in his frenzy, as if to a great body of adherents round him, to pour down the molten lead and the scorching sand; to hurl back every scaling lad-der planted against the walls; to massacre each prisoner who was seized mounting the ramparts to the assault; and as they looked up to the building from the street, they saw at intervals, through the bars of the closed gates, the figure of Ulpius passing swift and shadowy, his arms extended, his long grey hair and white robes streaming behind him, as he rushed round and round the temple reiterating his wild Pagan war-cries as he went. The enfeebled, superstitious populace trembled while they gazed--a spectre driven on a whirlwind would not have been more ter-rible to their eyes.

But the priest among the crowd, roused to fury by the murder of one of their own body, revived the courage of those around them. Even the shouts of Ulpius were now overpowered by the sound of their voices, raised to the highest pitch, prom-ising heavenly and earthly rewards--salvation, money, absolution, promotion--to all who would follow them up the steps and burst their way into the temple. Animated by the words of the priests, and growing gradually confident in their own numbers, the boldest in the throng seized a piece of timber lying by the river side, and using it as a battering-ram, assailed the gate. But they were weakened with famine; they could gain little impetus, from the necessity of ascending the temple steps to the attack; the iron quivered as they struck it, but hinge and lock remained firm alike. They were preparing to renew the attempt, when a tremendous shock--a crash as if the whole heavy roof of the building had fallen in--drove them back in terror to the street.

Recalled by the sight of the armed men, the priests and the attendant crowd of people who were advancing to invade his sanctuary, to the days when he had defended the great Temple of Serapis at Alexandria, against enemies similar in appearance, though far superior in numbers; persuaded in the revival of these, the most sanguinary visions of his insanity, that he was still resisting the Christian fanatics, supported by his adherents in his sacred fortress of former years, the Pagan displayed none of his accustomed cunning and care in moving through the darkness around him. He hurried hither and thither, encouraging his imaginary followers, and glorying in his dreams of slaughter and success, forgetful in his frenzy of all that the temple contained.

As he pursued his wild course round and round the altar of idols, his robe became entangled, and was torn by the projecting substances at one corner of it. The whole overhanging mass tottered at the moment, but did not yet fall. A few of the smaller idols, however, at the outside dropped to the ground, and with them an image of Serapis, which they happened partially to support--a heavy monstrous figure, carved life- size in wood, and studded with gold, silver, and precious stones--fell at the Pagan's feet. But this was all--the outer materials of the perilous structure had been detached only at one point; the pile itself still remained in its place.

The madman seized the image of Serapis in his arms, and passed blindly onward with it through the passage in the partition into the recess beyond. At that instant the shock of the first attack on the gates resounded through the building. Shouting, as he heard it, 'A sally! a sally! men of the Temple, the gods and the high priest lead you on!' and still holding the idol before him, he rushed straight forward to the entrance, and struck in violent collision against the backward part of the pile.

The ill-balanced, top-heavy mass of images and furniture of many temples swayed, parted, and fell over against the gates and the wall on either side of them. Maimed and bleeding, struck down by the lower part of the pile, as it was forced back against the partition when the upper part fell, the fury of Ulpius was but increased by the crashing ruin around him. He struggled up again into an erect position; mounted on the top of the fallen mass--now spread out at the sides over the floor of the building, but confined at one end by the partition, and at the other by the opposite wall and the gates--and still clasping the image of Serapis in his arms, called louder and louder to 'the men of the Temple' to mount with him the highest ramparts and pour down on the besiegers the molten lead!

The priests were again the first men to approach the gates of the building after the shock that had been heard within it. The struggle for the possession of the temple had assumed to them the character of a holy warfare against heathenism and magic--a sacred conflict to be sustained by the Church, for the sake of her servant who had fallen a martyr at the outset of the strife. Strong in their fanatical boldness, they advanced with one accord close to the gates. Some of the smaller images of the fallen pile had been forced through the bars, behind which appeared the great idols, the broken masses of furniture, the long robes and costly hangings, all locked together in every wild variety of position--a chaos of distorted objects heaped up by an earthquake! Above and further inward, the lower part of the Pagan's robe was faintly discernible through the upper interstices in the gate, as he stood, commanding, on the summit of his prostrate altar, with his idol in his arms.

The priests felt an instant conviction of certain triumph when they discerned the cause of the shock that had been heard within the temple. One of their number snatched up a small image that had fallen through to the pavement where he stood, and holding it before the people below, exclaimed exultingly--

'Children of the Church! the mystery is revealed! Idols more precious than this lie by hundreds on the floor of the temple! It is no demon, but a man, one man, who still defies us within!--a robber who would defraud the Romans of the ransom of their lives!--the pillage of many temples is around him. Remember now, that the nearer we came to this place the fewer were the spoils of idolatry that we gathered in; the treasure which is yours, the treasure which is to free you from the famine, has been seized by the assassin of our holy brother; it is there scattered at his feet! To the gates! To the gates again! Absolution for all their sins to the men who burst in the gates!'

Again the mass of timber was taken up; again the gates were assailed; and again they stood firm--they were now strengthened, barricaded by the fallen pile. It seemed hopeless to attempt to break them down without a reinforcement of men, without employing against them the heaviest missiles, the strongest engines of war.

The people gave vent to a cry of fury as they heard from the temple the hollow laughter of the madman triumphing in their defeat. The words of the priest, in allaying their superstitious fears, had aroused the deadly passions that superstition brings forth. A few among the throng hurried to the nearest guard-house for assistance, but the greater part pressed closely round the temple--some pouring forth impotent execrations against the robber of the public spoil, some joining the priests in calling on him to yield. But the clamour lasted not long; it was suddenly and strangely stilled by the voice of one man in the crowd, calling loudly to the rest to fire the temple!

The words were hardly spoken ere they were repeated triumphantly on all sides. 'Fire the temple!' cried the people ferociously. 'Burn it over the robber's head! A furnace--a furnace! to melt down the gold and silver ready to our hands! Fire the temple! Fire the temple!'

Those who were most active among the crowd (which was now greatly increased by stragglers from all parts of the city) entered the houses behind them, and returned in a few minutes with every inflammable substance that they could collect in their hands. A heap of fuel, two or three feet in height, was raised against the gates immediately, and soldiers and people pressed forward with torches to light it. But the priest who had before spoken waved them back. 'Wait!' he cried; 'the fate of his body is with the people, but the fate of his soul is with the Church!'

Then, turning to the temple, he called solemnly and sternly to the madman, 'Thy hour is come! repent, confess, and save thy soul!'

'Slay on! slay on!' answered the raving voice from within. 'Slay, till not a Christian is left! Victory! Serapis! See, they drop from our walls!--they writhe bleeding on the earth beneath us! There is no worship but the worship of the gods! Slay! Slay on!'

'Light!' cried the priest. 'His damnation be on his own head! Anathema! Maranatha! Let him die accursed!'

The dry fuel was fired at once at all points--it was an anticipation of an 'Auto da Fe', a burning of a heretic, in the fifth century! As the flames rose, the people fell back and watched their rapid progress. The priests, standing before them in a line, stretched out their hands in denunciation against the temple, and repeated together the awful excommunication service of the Roman Church.

*****

The fire at the gates had communicated with the idols inside. It was no longer on his prostrate altar, but on his funeral pile that Ulpius now stood; and the image that he clasped was the stake to which he was bound. A red glare, dull at first, was now brightening and brightening below him; flames, quick and noiseless, rose and fell, and rose again, at different points, illuminating the interior of the temple with fitful and changing light. The grim, swarthy forms of the idols seemed to sway and writhe like living things in torment, as fire and smoke alternately displayed and concealed them. A deadly stillness now overspread the face and form of the Pagan, as he looked down steadfastly on the deities of his worship engendering his destruction beneath him. His cheek--the cheek which had rested in boyhood on his mother's bosom--was pressed against the gilded breast of the god Serapis, his taskmaster in life--his pillow in death!

'I rise! I rise to the world of light, with my deities whom I have served!' he murmured; 'the brightness of their presence is like a flaming fire; the smoke of their breath pours forth around me like the smoke of incense! I minister in the Temples of the Clouds; and the glory of eternal sunlight shines round me while I adore! I rise! I rise!'

The smoke whirled in black volumes over his head; the fierce voice of the fast-spreading fire roared on him; the flames leapt up at his feet--his robes kindled, burst into radiant light, as the pile yawned and opened under him.

*****

Time had passed. The strife between the Temple and the Church was ended. The priests and the people had formed a wider circle round the devoted building; all that was inflammable in it had been burnt; smoke and flame now burst only at intervals through the gates, and gradually both ceased to appear. Then the crowd approached nearer to the temple, and felt the heat of the furnace they had kindled, as they looked in.

The iron gates were red hot--from the great mass behind (still glowing bright in some places, and heaving and quivering with its own heat) a thin, transparent vapour rose slowly to the stone roof of the building, now blackened with smoke. The priests looked eagerly for the corpse of the Pagan; they saw two dark, charred objects closely united together, lying in a chasm of ashes near the gate, at a spot where the fire had already exhausted itself, but it was impossible to discern which was the man and which was the idol.

The necessity of providing means for entering the temple had not been forgotten while the flames were raging. Proper implements for forcing open the gates were now at hand, and already the mob began to dip their buckets in the Tiber, and pour water wherever any traces of the fire remained. Soon all obstacles were removed; the soldiers crowded into the building with spades in their hands, trampled on the black, watery mire of cinders which covered what had once been the altar of idols, and throwing out into the street the refuse ashes and the stone images which had remained unconsumed, dug in what was left, as in a new mine, for the gold and silver which the fire could not destroy.

The Pagan had lived with his idols, had perished with his idols!--and now where they were cast away, there he was cast away with them. The soldiers, as they dug into fragments the black ruins of his altar, mingled him in fragments with it! The people, as they cast the refuse thrown out to them into the river, cast what remained of him with what remained of his gods! And when the temple was deserted, when the citizens had borne off all the treasure they could collect, when nothing but a few heaps of dust was left of all that had been burnt, the night-wind blew away before it the ashes of Ulpius with the ashes of the deities that Ulpius had served!

Chapter 27

THE VIGIL OF HOPE

A new prospect now opens before us. The rough paths through which we have hitherto threaded our way grow smoother as we approach their close. Rome, so long dark and gloomy to our view, brightens at length like a landscape when the rain is past and the first rays of returning sunlight stream through the parting clouds. Some days have elapsed, and in those days the temples have yielded all their wealth; the conquered Romans have bribed the triumphant barbarians to mercy; the ransom of the fallen city has been paid.

The Gothic army is still encamped round the walls, but the gates are opened, markets for food are established in the suburbs, boats appear on the river and waggons on the highroads, laden with provisions, and proceeding towards Rome. All the hidden treasure kept back by the citizens is now bartered for food; the merchants who hold the market reap a rich harvest of spoil, but the hungry are filled, the weak are revived, every one is content.

It is the end of the second day since the free sale of provisions and the liberty of egress from the city have been permitted by the Goths. The gates are closed for the night, and the people are quietly returning, laden with their supplies of food, to their homes. Their eyes no longer encounter the terrible traces of the march of pestilence and famine through every street; the corpses have been removed, and the sick are watched and sheltered. Rome is cleansed from her pollutions, and the virtues of household life begin to revive wherever they once existed. Death has thinned every family, but the survivors again assemble together in the social hall.

Even the veriest criminals, the lowest outcasts of the population, are united harm-lessly for a while in the general participation of the first benefits of peace.

To follow the citizens to their homes; to trace in their thoughts, words, and action the effect on them of their deliverance from the horrors of the blockade; to con-template in the people of a whole city, now recovering as it were from a deep swoon, the varying forms of the first reviving symptoms in all classes, in good and bad, rich and poor--would afford matter enough in itself for a romance of search-ing human interest, for a drama of the passions, moving absorbingly through strange, intricate, and contrasted scenes. But another employment than this now claims our care. It is to an individual, and not to a divided source of interest, that our attention turns; we relinquish all observations on the general mass of the pop-ulace to revert to Numerian and Antonina alone--to penetrate once more into the little dwelling on the Pincian Hill.

The apartment where the father and daughter had suffered the pangs of famine together during the period of the blockade, presented an appearance far different from that which it had displayed on the occasion when they had last occupied it. The formerly bare walls were now covered with rich, thick hangings; and the sim-ple couch and scanty table of other days had been exchanged for whatever was most luxurious and complete in the household furniture of the age. At one end of the room three women, attended by a little girl, were engaged in preparing some dishes of fruit and vegetables; at the other, two men were occupied in low, earnest conversation, occasionally looking round anxiously to a couch placed against the third side of the apartment, on which Antonina lay extended, while Numerian watched by her in silence. The point of Goisvintha's knife had struck deep, but, as yet, the fatal purpose of the assassination had failed.

The girl's eyes were closed; her lips were parted in the languor of suffering; one of her hands lay listless on her father's knee. A slight expression of pain, melan-choly in its very slightness, appeared on her pale face, and occasionally a long-drawn, quivering breath escaped her--nature's last touching utterance of its own feebleness! The old man, as he sat by her side, fixed on her a wistful, inquiring glance. Sometimes he raised his hand, and gently and mechanically moved to and fro the long locks of her hair, as they spread over the head of the couch; but he never turned to communicate with the other persons in the room--he sat as if he saw nothing save his daughter's figure stretched before him, and heard nothing save the faint, fluttering sound of her breathing, close at his ear.

It was now dark, and one lamp hanging from the ceiling threw a soft equal light over the room. The different persons occupying it presented but little evidence of health and strength in their countenances, to contrast them in appearance with the wounded girl; all had undergone the wasting visitation of the famine, and all were pale and languid, like her. A strange, indescribable harmony prevailed over the scene. Even the calmness of absorbing expectation and trembling hope, expressed in the demeanour of Numerian, seemed reflected in the actions of those around him, in the quietness with which the women pursued their employment, in the lower and lower whispers in which the men continued their conversation. There was something pervading the air of the whole apartment that conveyed a sense of the solemn, unworldly stillness which we attach to the abstract idea of religion.

Of the two men cautiously talking together, one was the patrician, Vetranio; the other, a celebrated physician of Rome.

Both the countenance and manner of the senator gave melancholy proof that the orgie at his palace had altered him for the rest of his life. He looked what he was, a man changed for ever in constitution and character. A fixed expression of anxiety and gloom appeared in his eyes; his emaciated face was occasionally distorted by a nervous, involuntary contraction of the muscles; it was evident that the paralysing effect of the debauch which had destroyed his companions would remain with him to the end of his existence. No remnant of his careless self-possession, his easy, patrician affability, appeared in his manner, as he now listened to his companion's conversation; years seemed to have been added to his life since he had headed the table at 'The Banquet of Famine'.

'Yes,' said the physician, a cold, calm man, who spoke much, but pronounced all his words with emphatic deliberation,--'Yes, as I have already told you, the wound in itself was not mortal. If the blade of the knife had entered near the centre of the neck, she must have died when she was struck. But it passed outwards and backwards; the large vessels escaped, and no vital part has been touched.'

'And yet you persist in declaring that you doubt her recovery!' exclaimed Vetranio, in low, mournful tones.

'I do,' pursued the physician. 'She must have been exhausted in mind and body when she received the blow--I have watched her carefully; I know it! There is nothing of the natural health and strength of youth to oppose the effects of the wound. I have seen the old die from injuries that the young recover, because life in them was losing its powers of resistance; she is in the position of the old!'

'They have died before me, and she will die before me! I shall lose all--all!' sighed Vetranio bitterly to himself.

'The resources of our art are exhausted,' continued the other; 'nothing remains but to watch carefully and wait patiently. The chances of life or death will be decided in a few hours; they are equally balanced now.'

'I shall lose all!--all!' repeated the senator mournfully, as if he heeded not the last words.

'If she dies,' said the physician, speaking in warmer tones, for he was struck with pity, in spite of himself, at the spectacle of Vetranio's utter dejection, 'if she dies, you can at least remember that all that could be done to secure her life has been done by you. Her father, helpless in his lethargy and his age, was fitted only to sit and watch her, as he has sat and watched her day after day; but you have spared nothing, forgotten nothing. Whatever I have asked for, that you have provided; the hangings round the room, and the couch that she lies on, are yours; the first fresh supplies of nourishment from the newly-opened markets were brought here from you; I told you that she was thinking incessantly of what she had suffered, that it was necessary to preserve her against her own recollections, that the presence of women about her might do good, that a child appearing sometimes in the room might soothe her fancy, might make her look at what was passing, instead of thinking of what had passed--you found them, and sent them! I have seen parents less anxious for their children, lovers for their mistresses, than you for this girl.'

'My destiny is with her,' interrupted Vetranio, looking round superstitiously to the frail form on the couch. 'I know nothing of the mysteries that the Christians call their "Faith", but I believe now in the soul; I believe that one soul contains the fate of another, and that her soul contains the fate of mine!'

The physician shook his head derisively. His calling had determined his philosophy--he was as ardent a materialist as Epicurus himself.

'Listen,' said Vetranio; 'since I first saw her, a change came over my whole being; it was as if her life was mingled with mine! I had no influence over her, save an influence for ill: I loved her, and she was driven defenceless from her home! I sent my slaves to search Rome night and day; I exerted all my power, I lavished my wealth to discover her; and, for the first time in this one effort, I failed in what I had undertaken. I felt that through me she was lost--dead! Days passed on; life weighed weary on me; the famine came. You know in what way I determined that my career should close; the rumour of the Banquet of Famine reached you as it reached others!'

'It did,' replied the physician. 'And I see before me in your face,' he added, after a momentary pause, 'the havoc which that ill-omened banquet has worked. My friend, be advised!--abandon for ever the turmoil of your Roman palace, and breathe in tranquillity the air of a country home. The strength you once had is gone never to return--if you would yet live, husband what is still left.'

'Hear me,' pursued Vetranio, in low, gloomy tones. 'I stood alone in my doomed palace; the friends whom I had tempted to their destruction lay lifeless around me; the torch was in my hand that was to light our funeral pile, to set us free from the loathsome world! I approached triumphantly to kindle the annihilating flames, when she stood before me--she, whom I had sought as lost and mourned as dead! A strong hand seemed to wrench the torch from me; it dropped to the ground! She departed again; but I was powerless to take it up; her look was still before me; her face, her figure, she herself, appeared ever watching between the torch and me!'

'Lower!--speak lower!' interrupted the physician, looking on the senator's agitated features with unconcealed astonishment and pity. 'You retard your own recovery,--you disturb the girl's repose by discourse such as this.'

'The officers of the senate,' continued Vetranio, sadly resuming his gentler tones, 'when they entered the palace, found me still standing on the place where we had met! Days passed on again; I stood looking out upon the street, and thought of my companions whom I had lured to their death, and of my oath to partake their fate, which I had never fulfilled. I would have driven my dagger to my heart; but her face was yet before me, my hands were bound! In that hour I saw her for the second time; saw her carried past me--wounded, assassinated! She had saved me once; she had saved me twice! I knew that now the chance was offered me, after having wrought her ill, to work her good; after failing to discover her when she was lost, to succeed in saving her when she was dying; after having survived the deaths of my friends at my own table, to survive to see life restored under my influence, as well as destroyed! These were my thoughts; these are my thoughts still--thoughts felt only since I saw her! Do you know now why I believe that her soul contains the fate of mine? Do you see me, weakened, shattered, old before my time; my friends lost, my fresh feelings of youth gone for ever; and can you not now comprehend that her life is my life?--that if she dies, the one good purpose of my existence is blighted?--that I lose all I have henceforth to live for?--all, all!'

As he pronounced the concluding words, the girl's eyes half unclosed, and turned languidly towards her father. She made an effort to lift her hand caressingly from his knee to his neck; but her strength was unequal even to this slight action. The hand was raised only a few inches ere it sank back again to its old position; a tear rolled slowly over her cheek as she closed her eyes again, but she never spoke.

'See,' said the physician, pointing to her, 'the current of life is at its lowest ebb! If it flows again, it must flow to-night.'

Vetranio made no answer; he dropped down on the seat near him, and covered his face with his robe.

The physician, beholding the senator's situation, and reflecting on the strange hurriedly-uttered confession which had just been addressed to him, began to doubt whether the scenes through which his patron had lately passed had not affected his brain. Philosopher though he was, the man of science had never observed the outward symptoms of the first working of good and pure influences in elevating a degraded mind; he had never watched the denoting signs of speech and action which mark the progress of mental revolution while the old nature is changing for the new; such objects of contemplation existed not for him. He gently touched Vetranio on the shoulder. 'Rise,' said he, 'and let us depart. Those are around her who can watch her best. Nothing remains for us but to wait and hope. With the earliest morning we will return.'

He delivered a few farewell directions to one of the women in attendance, and then, accompanied by the senator, who, without speaking again, mechanically rose to follow him, quitted the room. After this, the silence was only interrupted by the sound of an occasional whisper, and of quick, light footsteps passing backwards and forwards. Then the cooling, reviving draughts which had been prepared for the night were poured ready into the cups; and the women approached Numerian, as if to address him, but he waved his hand impatiently when he saw them; and then they too, in their turn, departed, to wait in an adjoining apartment until they should be summoned again.

Nothing changed in the manner of the father when he was left alone in the chamber of sickness, which the lapse of a few hours might convert into the chamber of death. He sat watching Antonina, and touching the outspread locks of her hair from time to time, as had been his wont. It was a fair, starry night; the fresh air of the soft winter climate of the South blew gently over the earth, the great city was sinking fast into tranquillity, calling voices were sometimes heard faintly from the principal streets, and the distant noises of martial music sounded cheerily from the Gothic camp as the sentinels were posted along the line of watch; but soon these noises ceased, and the stillness of Rome was as the stillness round the couch of the wounded girl.

Day after day, and night after night, since the assassination in the temple, Numerian had kept the same place by his daughter's side. Each hour as it passed found him still absorbed in his long vigil of hope; his life seemed suspended in its onward course by the one influence that now enthralled it. At the brief intervals when his bodily weariness overpowered him on his melancholy watch, it was observed by those around him that, even in his short dreaming clumbers, his face remained ever turned in the same direction, towards the head of the couch, as if drawn thither by some irresistible attraction, by some powerful ascendancy, felt even amid the deepest repose of sensation, the heaviest fatigue of the overlaboured mind, and worn, sinking heart. He held no communication, save by signs, with the friends about him; he seemed neither to hope, to doubt, nor to despair with them; all his faculties were strung up to vibrate at one point only, and were dull and unimpressible in every other direction.

But twice had he been heard to speak more than the fewest, simplest words. The first time, when Antonina uttered the name of Goisvintha, on the recovery of her senses after her wound, he answered eagerly by reiterated declarations that there was nothing henceforth to fear; for he had seen the assassin dead under the Pagan's foot on leaving the temple. The second time, when mention was incautiously made before him of rumours circulated through Rome of the burning of an unknown Pagan priest, hidden in the temple of Serapis, with vast treasures around him, the old man was seen to start and shudder, and heard to pray for the soul that was now waiting before the dread judgment-seat; to murmur about a vain restoration and a discovery made too late; to mourn over horror that thickened round him, over hope fruitlessly awakened, and bereavement more terrible than mortal had ever suffered before; to entreat that the child, the last left of all, might be spared--with many words more, which ran on themes like these, and which were counted by all who listened to them but as the wanderings of a mind whose higher powers were fatally prostrated by feebleness and grief.

One long hour of the night had already passed away since parent and child had been left together, and neither word nor movement had been audible in the melancholy room. But, as the second hour began, the girl's eyes unclosed again, and she moved painfully on the couch. Accustomed to interpret the significance of her slightest actions, Numerian rose and brought her one of the reviving draughts that had been left ready for use. After she had drunk, when her eyes met her father's fixed on her in mute and mournful inquiry, her lips closed, and formed themselves into an expression which he remembered they had always assumed when, as a little child, she used silently to hold up her face to him to be kissed. The miserable contrast between what she was now and what she had been them, was beyond the passive endurance, the patient resignation of the spirit-broken old man; the empty cup dropped from his hands, he knelt down by the side of the couch and groaned aloud.

'O father! father!' cried the weak, plaintive voice above him. 'I am dying! Let us remember that our time to be together here grows shorter and shorter, and let us pass it as happily as we can!'

He raised his head, and looked up at her, vacant and wistful, forlorn already, as if the death-parting was over.

'I have tried to live humbly and gratefully,' she sighed faintly. 'I have longed to do more good on the earth than I have done! Yet you will forgive me now, father, as you have always forgiven me! You have been patient with me all my life; more patient than I have ever deserved! But I had no mother to teach me to love you as I ought, to teach me what I know now, when my death is near, and time and opportunity are mine no longer!'

'Hush! hush!' whispered the old man affrightedly; 'you will live! God is good, and knows that we have suffered enough. The curse of the last separation is not pronounced against us! Live, live!'

'Father,' said the girl tenderly, 'we have that within us which not death itself can separate. In another world I shall still think of you when you think of me! I shall see you even when I am no more here, when you long to see me! When you got out alone, and sit under the trees on the garden bank where I used to sit; when you look forth on the far plains and mountains that I used to look on; when you read at night in the Bible that we have read in together, and remember Antonina as you lie down sorrowful to rest; then I shall see you! then you will feel that I am looking on you! You will be calm and consoled, even by the side of my grave; for you will think, not of the body that is beneath, but of the spirit that is waiting for you, as I have often waited for you here when you were away, and I knew that the approach of the evening would bring you home again!'

'Hush! you will live!--you will live!' repeated Numerian in the same low, vacant tones. The strength that still upheld him was in those few simple words; they were the food of a hope that was born in agony and cradled in despair.

'Oh, if I might live!' said the girl softly, 'if I might live but for a few days yet, how much I have to live for!' She endeavoured to bend her head towards her father as she spoke; for the words were beginning to fall faintly and more faintly from her lips--exhaustion was mastering her once again. She dwelt for a moment now on the name of Hermanric, on the grave in the farm-house garden; then reverted again to her father. The last feeble sounds she uttered were addressed to him; and their burden was still of consolation and of love.

Soon the old man, as he stooped over her, saw her eyes close again--those innocent, gentle eyes which even yet preserved their old expression while the face grew wan and pale around them--and darkness and night sank down over his soul while he looked. 'She sleeps,' he murmured in a voice of awe, as he resumed his watching position by the side of the couch. 'They call death a sleep; but on her face there is no death!'

The night grew on. The women who were in attendance entered the room about midnight, wondering that their assistance had not yet been required. They beheld the solemn, unruffled composure on the girl's wasted face; the rapt attention of Numerian, as he ever preserved the same attitude by her side; and went out again softly without uttering a word, even in a whisper. There was something dread and impressive in the very appearance of this room, where Death, that destroys, was in mortal conflict with Youth and Beauty, that adorn, while the eyes of one old man watched in loneliness the awful progress of the strife.

Morning came, and still there was no change. Once, when the lamp that lit the room was fading out as the dawn appeared, Numerian had risen and looked close on his daughter's face--he thought at that moment that her features moved; but he saw that the flickering of the dying light on them had deceived him; the same stillness was over her. He placed his ear close to her lips for an instant, and then resumed his place, not stirring from it again. The slow current of his blood seemed to have come to a pause--he was waiting as a man waits with his head on the block ere the axe descends--as a mother waits to hear that the breath of life has entered her new-born child.

The sun rose bright in a cloudless sky. As the fresh, sharp air of the early dawn warmed under its spreading rays, the women entered the apartment again, and partly drew aside the curtain and shutter from the window. The beams of the new light fell fair and glorifying on the girl's face; the faint, calm breeze ruffled the lighter locks of her hair. Once this would have awakened her; but it did not disturb her now.

Soon after the voice of the child who sojourned with the women in the house was heard beneath, in the hall, through the half-opened door of the room. The little creature was slowly ascending the stairs, singing her faltering morning song to herself. She was preceded on her approach by a tame dove, bought at the provision market outside the walls, but preserved for the child as a pet and plaything by its mother. The bird fluttered, cooing, into the room, perched upon the head of the couch, and began dressing its feathers there. The women had caught the infection of the old man's enthralling suspense; and moved not to bid the child retire, or to take away the dove from its place--they watched like him. But the soft, lulling notes of the bird were powerless over the girl's ear, as the light sunbeam over her face--still she never woke.

The child entered, and pausing in her song, climbed on to the side of the couch. She held out one little hand for the dove to perch upon, placed the other lightly on Antonina's shoulder, and pressed her fresh, rosy lips to girl's faded cheek. 'I and my bird have come to make Antonina well this morning,' she said gravely.

The still, heavily-closed eyelids moved!--they quivered, opened, closed, then opened again. The eyes had a faint, dreaming, unconscious look; but Antonina lived! Antonina was awakened at last to another day on earth!

Her father's rigid, straining gaze still remained fixed upon her as at first, but on his countenance there was a blank, an absence of all appearance of sensation and life. The women, as they looked on Antonina and looked on him, began to weep; the child resumed very softly its morning song, now addressing it to the wounded girl and now to the dove.

At this moment Vetranio and the physician appeared on the scene. The latter advanced to the couch, removed the child from it, and examined Antonina intently. At length, partly addressing Numerian, partly speaking to himself, he said: 'She has slept long, deeply, without moving, almost without breathing--a sleep like death to all who looked on it.'

The old man spoke not in reply, but the women answered eagerly in the affirmative.

'She is saved,' pursued the physician, leisurely quitting the side of the couch and smiling on Vetranio; 'be careful of her for days and days to come.'

'Saved! saved!' echoed the child joyfully, setting the dove free in the room, and running to Numerian to climb on his knees. The father glanced down when the clear young voice sounded in his ear. The springs of joy, so long dried up in his heart, welled forth again as he saw the little hands raised towards him entreatingly; his grey head drooped--he wept.

At a sign from the physician the child was led from the room. The silence of deep and solemn emotion was preserved by all who remained; nothing was heard but the suppressed sobs of the old man, and the faint, retiring notes of the infant voice still singing its morning song. And now one word, joyfully reiterated again and again, made all the burden of the music--

'SAVED! SAVED!'

THE CONCLUSION

'UBI THESAURUS IBI COR.'

Shortly after the opening of the provision markets outside the gates of Rome, the Goths broke up their camp before the city and retired to winter quarters in Tuscany. The negotiations which ensued between Alaric and the Court and Government at Ravenna, were conducted with cunning moderation by the conqueror, and with infatuated audacity by the conquered, and ultimately terminated in a resumption of hostilities. Rome was besiege and second and a third time by 'the barbarians'. On the latter occasion the city was sacked, its palaces were burnt, its treasures were seized; the monuments of the Christian religion were alone respected.

But it is no longer with the Goths that our narrative is concerned; the connection with them which it has hitherto maintained closes with the end of the first siege of Rome. We can claim the reader's attention for historical events no more--the march of our little pageant, arrayed for his pleasure, is over. If, however, he has felt, and still retains, some interest in Antonina, he will not refuse to follow us, and look on her again ere we part.

More than a month had passed since the besieging army had retired to their winter quarters, when several of the citizens of Rome assembled themselves on the plains beyond the walls, to enjoy one of those rustic festivals of ancient times, which are still celebrated, under different usages, but with the same spirit, by the Italians of modern days.

The place was a level plot of ground beyond the Pincian Gate, backed by a thick grove of pine trees, and looking towards the north over the smooth extent of the country round Rome. The persons congregated were mostly of the lower class. Their amusements were dancing, music, games of strength and games of chance;

and, above all, to people who had lately suffered the extremities of famine, abundant eating and drinking--long, serious, ecstatic enjoyment of the powers of mastication and the faculties of taste.

Among the assembly were some individuals whose dress and manner raised them, outwardly at least, above the general mass. These persons walked backwards and forwards together on different parts of the ground as observers, not as partakers in the sports. One of their number, however, in whatever direction he turned, preserved an isolated position. He held an open letter in his hand, which he looked at from time to time, and appeared to be wholly absorbed in his own thoughts. This man we may advantageously particularise on his own account, as well as on account of the peculiarity of his accidental situation; for he was the favoured minister of Vetranio's former pleasures--'the industrious Carrio'.

The freedman (who was last introduced to the reader in Chapter XIV., as exhibiting to Vetranio the store of offal which he had collected during the famine for the consumption of the palace) had contrived of late greatly to increase his master's confidence in him. On the organisation of the Banquet of Famine, he had discreetly refrained from testifying the smallest desire to save himself from the catastrophe in which the senator and his friends had determined to involve themselves. Securing himself in a place of safety, he awaited the end of the orgie; and when he found that its unexpected termination left his master still living to employ him, appeared again as a faithful servant, ready to resume his customary occupation with undiminished zeal.

After the dispersion of his household during the famine, and amid the general confusion of the social system in Rome, on the raising of the blockade, Vetranio found no one near him that he could trust but Carrio--and he trusted him. Nor was the confidence misplaced: the man was selfish and sordid enough; but these very qualities ensured his fidelity to his master as long as that master retained the power to punish and the capacity to reward.

The letter which Carrio held in his hand was addressed to him at a villa--from which he had just returned--belonging to Vetranio, on the shores of the Bay of Naples, and was written by the senator from Rome. The introductory portions of this communication seemed to interest the freedman but little: they contained praised of his diligence in preparing the country-house for the immediate habitation of its owner, and expressed his master's anxiety to quit Rome as speedily as possible, for the sake of living in perfect tranquillity, and breathing the reviving air of the sea, as the physicians had counselled. It was the latter part of the letter that Carrio perused and re-perused, and then meditated over with unwonted attention and labour of mind. It ran thus:--

'I have now to repose in you a trust, which you will execute with perfect fidelity as you value my favour or respect the wealth from which you may obtain your reward. When you left Rome you left the daughter of Numerian lying in danger of death: she has since revived. Questions that I have addressed to her during her recovery have informed me of much in her history that I knew not before; and have induced me to purchase, for reasons of my own, a farm-house and its lands, beyond the suburbs. (The extent of the place and its situation are written on the vellum that is within this.) The husbandman who cultivated the property had survived the famine, and will continue to cultivate it for me. But it is my desire that the garden, and all that it contains, shall remain entirely at the disposal of Numerian and his daughter, who may often repair to it; and who must henceforth be regarded there as occupying my place and having my authority. You will divide your time between overlooking the few slaves whom I leave at the palace in my absence, and the husbandman and his labourers whom I have installed at the farm; and you will answer to me for the due performance of your own duties and the duties of those under you--being assured that by well filling this office you will serve your own interests in these, and in all things besides.'

The letter concluded by directing the freedman to return to Rome on a certain day, and to go to the farm-house at an appointed hour, there to meet his master, who had further directions to give him, and who would visit the newly acquired property before he proceeded on his journey to Naples.

Nothing could exceed the perplexity of Carrio as he read the passage in his patron's letter which we have quoted above. Remembering the incidents attending Vetranio's early connection with Antonina and her father, the mere circumstances of a farm having been purchased to flatter what was doubtless some accidental caprice on the part of the girl, would have little perplexed him. But that this act should be followed by the senator's immediate separation of himself from the society of Numerian's daughter; that she was to gain nothing after all from these lands which had evidently been bought at her instigation, but the authority over a little strip of garden; and yet, the inviolability of this valueless privilege should be insisted on in such serious terms, and with such an imperative tone of command as the senator had never been known to use before--these were inconsistencies which all Carrio's ingenuity failed to reconcile. The man had been born and reared in vice; vice had fed him, clothed him, freed him, given him character, reputation, power in his own small way--he lived in it as in the atmosphere that he breathed; to show him an action, referable only to a principle of pure integrity, was to set him a problem which it was hopeless to solve. And yet it is impossible, in one point of view, to pronounce him utterly worthless. Ignorant of all distinctions between good and bad, he thought wrong from sheer inability to see right.

However his instructions might perplex him, he followed them now--and continued in after days to follow them--to the letter. If to serve one's own interests be an art, of that art Carrio deserved to be head professor. He arrived at the farm-house, not only punctually, but before the appointed time, and calling the honest husbandman and the labourers about him, explained to them every particular of the authority that his patron had vested in him, with a flowing and peremptory solemnity of speech which equally puzzled and impressed his simple audience. He found Numerian and Antonina in the garden when he entered it. The girl had been carried there daily in a litter since her recovery, and her father had followed. They were never separated now; the old man, when his first absorbing anxiety for her was calmed, remembered again more distinctly the terrible disclosure in the temple, and the yet more terrible catastrophe that followed it, and he sought constant refuge from the horror of the recollection in the presence of his child.

The freedman, during his interview with the father and daughter, observed, for once, an involuntary and unfeigned respect; but he spoke briefly, and left them together again almost immediately. Humble and helpless as they were, they awed him; they looked, thought, and spoke like beings of another nature than his; they were connected, he knew not how, with the mystery of the grave in the garden. He would have been self-possessed in the presence of the Emperor himself, but he was uneasy in theirs. So he retired to the more congenial scene of the public festival which was in the immediate neighbourhood of the farm-house, to await the hour of his patron's arrival, and to perplex himself afresh by a re-perusal of Vetranio's letter.

The time was now near at hand when it was necessary for the freedman to return to his appointed post. He carefully rolled up his note of instructions, stood for a few minutes vacantly regarding the amusements which had hitherto engaged so little of his attention, and then, turning, he proceeded through the pine-grove on his way back. We will follow him.

On leaving the grove, a footpath conducted over some fields to the farm- house. Arrived here, Carrio hesitated for a moment; then moved slowly onward to await his master's approach in the lane that led to the highroad. At this point we will part company with him, to enter the garden by the wicket-gate.

The trees, the flower-beds, and the patches of grass, all remained in their former positions--nothing had been added or taken away since the melancholy days that were past; but a change was visible in Hermanric's grave. The turf above it had been renewed, and a border of small evergreen shrubs was planted over the track which Goisvintha's footsteps had traced. A white marble cross was raised at one end of the mound; the short Latin inscription on it signified--'PRAY FOR THE DEAD'.

The sunlight was shining calmly over the grave, and over Numerian and Antonina as they sat by it. Sometimes when the mirth grew louder at the rustic festival, it reached them in faint, subdued notes; sometimes they heard the voices of the labourers in the neighbouring fields talking to each other at their work; but, besides these, no other sounds were loud enough to be distinguished. There was still and expression of the melancholy and feebleness that grief and suffering leave behind them on the countenances of the father and daughter; but resignation and peace appeared there as well--resignation that was perfected by the hard teaching of woe, and peach that was purer for being imparted from the one to the other, like the strong and deathless love from which it grew.

There was something now in the look and attitude of the girl, as she sat thinking of the young warrior who had died in her defence and for her love, and training the shrubs to grow closer round the grave, which, changed though she was, recalled in a different form the old poetry and tranquillity of her existence when we first saw her singing to the music of her lute in the garden on the Pincian Hill. No thoughts of horror and despair were suggested to her as she now looked on the farm-house scene. Hers was not the grief which shrinks selfishly from all that revives the remembrance of the dead: to her, their influence over the memory was a grateful and a guardian influence that gave a better purpose to the holiest life, and a nobler nature to the purest thoughts.

Thus they were sitting by the grave, sad yet content; footsore already on the pilgrimage of life, yet patient to journey farther if they might--when an unusual tumult, a noise of rolling wheels, mingled with a confused sound of voices, was heard in the lane behind them. They looked round, and saw that Vetranio was approaching them alone through the wicket-gate.

He came forward slowly; the stealthy poison instilled by the Banquet of Famine palpably displayed its presence within him as the clear sunlight fell on his pale, wasted face. He smiled kindly as he addressed Antonina; but the bodily pain and mental agitation which that smile was intended to conceal, betrayed themselves in his troubled voice as he spoke.

'This is our last meeting for years--it may be our last meeting for life,' he said; 'I linger at the outset of my journey, but to behold you as guardian of the one spot of ground that is most precious to you on earth--as mistress, indeed, of the little that I give you here!' He paused a moment and pointed to the grave, then continued: 'All the atonement that I owe to you, you can never know--I can never tell!--think only that I bear away with me a companion in the solitude to which I go in the remembrance of you. Be calm, good, happy still, for my sake, and while you forgive the senator of former days, forget not the friend who now parts from you in some sickness and sorrow, but also in much patience and hope! Farewell!'

His hand trembled as he held it out; a flush overspread the girl's cheek while she murmured a few inarticulate words of gratitude, and, bending over it, pressed it to her lips. Vetranio's heart beat quick; the action revived an emotion that he dared not cherish; but he looked at the wan, downcast face before him, at the grave that rose mournful by his side, and quelled it again. Yet an instant he lingered to exchange a farewell with the old man, then turned quickly, passed through the gate, and they saw him no more.

Antonina's tears fell fast on the grass beneath as she resumed her place. When she raised her head again, and saw that her father was looking at her, she nestled close to him and laid one of her arms round his neck: the other gradually dropped to her side, until her hand reached the topmost leaves of the shrubs that grew round the grave.

*****

Shall we longer delay in the farm-house garden? No! For us, as for Vetranio, it is now time to depart! While peace still watches round the walls of Rome; while the hearts of the father and daughter still repose together in security, after the trials that have wrung them, let us quit the scene! Here, at last, the narrative that we have followed over a dark and stormy track reposes on a tranquil field; and here let us cease to pursue it!

So the traveller who traces the course of a river wanders through the day among the rocks and precipices that lead onward from its troubled source; and, when the evening is at hand, pauses and rests where the banks are grassy and the stream is smooth.

Printed in the United Kingdom
by Lightning Source UK Ltd.
1242